Deveraux is the author of forty-two *New York Times* bestsellers, including *Moonlight Masquerade* and *A Knight in Shining Armor*. She was honoured with a *Romantic Times* Pioneer Award in 2013 for her distinguished career. To date, there are more than sixty million copies of her books in print worldwide.

To find out more about Jude, visit her website: www.jude-deveraux.com, follow her on Twitter @judedeveraux1, or connect with her on Facebook: www.facebook.com/JudeDeveraux.

Praise for Jude Deveraux and her spellbinding Nantucket Brides:

'Jude Deveraux's Nantucket Brides series will sweep you away. A beautiful island, a sexy man, and plenty of secrets – this is a wonderful writer at her best' Susan Mallery, *New York Times* bestselling author

'A novel about star-crossed love, life, death and reincarnation . . . a romantic story of love so deep it survives centuries' *Kirkus Reviews*

'A new Jude Deveraux novel means a very late night turning the pages straight through to the delicious end' Susan Elizabeth Phillips, *New York Times* bestselling author

'*True Love*, with its star-crossed lovers and twisty plot, evokes everything that makes Nantucket so special – the history, the atmosphere, the secrets, and the magic' Susan Wiggs, *New York Times* bestselling author

'Deveraux is at her spellbinding romantic best' *Booklist*

JUDE DEVERAUX

For All Time

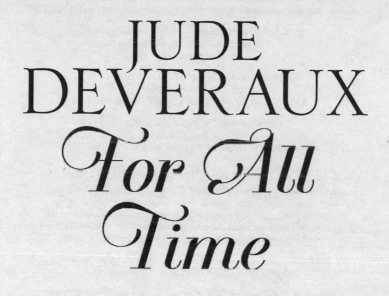

headline
ETERNAL

Published by arrangement with Ballantine Books,
an imprint of The Random House Publishing Group,
a division of Random House LLC.

First published in Great Britain in 2014
by HEADLINE ETERNAL
An imprint of HEADLINE PUBLISHING GROUP

First published in paperback in 2015
by HEADLINE ETERNAL
An imprint of HEADLINE PUBLISHING GROUP

1

Cataloguing in Publication Data is available from the British Library

ISBN 978 1 4722 1140 8

Offset in Sabon by Avon DataSet Ltd, Bidford-on-Avon, Warwickshire

Printed and bound by CPI Group (UK) Ltd, Croydon, CR0 4YY

Headline's policy is to use papers that are natural, renewable and recyclable products and made from wood grown in well-managed forests and other controlled sources. The logging and manufacturing processes are expected to conform to the environmental regulations of the country of origin.

HEADLINE PUBLISHING GROUP
An Hachette UK Company
338 Euston Road
London NW1 3BH

www.headlineeternal.com
www.headline.co.uk
www.hachette.co.uk

Titlepage photograph: © Karen Batten

For All Time

By Jude Deveraux

Nantucket Brides
True Love
For All Time
Ever After

Chapter One

Nantucket

 $\mathcal{G}$ raydon Montgomery couldn't take his eyes off the young woman. The bride and his cousin Jared, the groom, were standing at the front of the little chapel, the pastor between them, and Graydon kept looking across them at her. She had on a blue bridesmaid dress, was holding a bouquet of flowers, and her attention was fully on the ceremony.

While she was pretty, she wasn't conventionally so. She wasn't the type of woman who'd make people do double takes. With her oval face, eyes the color of bluebells, and flawless skin, she looked like a girl you'd see in the newspaper as having attended a debutante ball. She'd be able to wear pearls and long gloves without looking like she'd rather be in jeans.

Earlier, when the four wedding attendants had been waiting outside, there'd been a lot of commotion inside the little chapel. At the last minute, some kind of mix-up had caused a great deal of chaos. In normal circumstances, Graydon would have made an effort to find out what was happening, but not today. Today he was distracted by her.

Sounds of angry shouts and furniture crashing to the floor had come from inside the chapel. The two bridesmaids and the other groomsman went to the door to see what was going on, but Graydon stood where he was. He wasn't even curious. All he could do was gaze at the back of the young woman. She had long blonde hair that curled down her back, and a nice figure. Not flashy, but trim and subdued.

Through all the turmoil, Graydon had stood back from them. He was only vaguely aware of the surroundings, of the big tent that was set up for dinner and dancing, of the moonlight on the wooded area around them, even of the brightly lit chapel where the wedding was to be. He seemed only able to think about what the young woman had said to him just minutes before.

When Graydon had been asked to escort a bridesmaid down the aisle, he'd thought it would be an easy, enjoyable task. After all, he was certainly used to red carpets and ceremonies of all kinds.

But when he was introduced to the young woman, he'd been shocked by what she said—and he still hadn't recovered.

When the noise inside the chapel finally calmed down and they prepared to go inside, Graydon moved to stand beside her and crooked his arm for her to take. When she put her hand on his arm, he smiled warmly at her, slipped his hand over hers, and clasped it gently.

Without a word, she snatched her hand away, took two steps back, and glared at him. There was no mistaking her meaning: He was to make no overtures of any kind toward her. And that seemed to include even friendliness.

Graydon didn't think he'd ever before been at a loss for words, but in the face of her anger, every language he knew seemed to disappear from his mind. All he could do was stand there and blink. Finally, he managed to nod his agreement. No touching, no smiles, no anything outside what was necessary to get the job done.

As they walked down the aisle together, she kept her distance from him. Her hand was on his arm, but her body was two feet away from his. Graydon held his head high, doing his best to swallow his pride. Never before had a woman found him . . . well, repulsive. Truthfully, no woman had ever before tried to get away from him.

He wasn't naive—he knew well that a lot of the fawning and flirting directed his way was because of what he'd come to think of as the "unfortunate circumstances of my birth," but still . . . That she didn't want anything to do with him wounded his ego.

When they got to the front of the chapel, she seemed relieved to get away from him. She went to the left, and Graydon went to the other side to wait for the bride to come down the aisle with her father.

Throughout the ceremony Graydon couldn't help peering around the bride and groom to look at her. What was her name? Toby, wasn't it? Surely that was a nickname, and he wondered what her birth name was.

As the ceremony neared the end, Graydon felt that old familiar pull, what people called the "twin bond," and he knew his brother was there. He glanced to his left, through the crowd of people packed into the chapel. Family was in chairs but the back was full of guests standing and watching. It took Graydon only seconds to find his brother in the very back, purposely hidden behind other people. Rory wasn't dressed properly for a wedding, but then his leather jacket and casual slacks fit in with the American style. At least his brother didn't have on jeans.

Rory nodded toward the blonde bridesmaid in question. He'd never seen his brother stare at a woman before and he was curious as to why.

As was sometimes the case with identical twins, he and his brother often communicated without words. But there was no way Graydon could tell his brother the one and only thought in his mind: She can tell you and me apart.

Frowning, Rory let Graydon know that he didn't understand. He slanted his head to one side and Graydon nodded. They had just arranged to meet outside as soon as possible.

That done, Graydon gave his attention back to the young woman. In a moment they'd again walk down the aisle, and he looked forward to it.

Chapter Two

After the ceremony, Toby left the chapel and was on her way to the big tent to check on the wedding guests there. Even though she wasn't a professional planner, she had done most of the work to put this wedding together. A lot of the ideas had come from her friend Alix, the bride, but it had been Toby who put in endless hours and lost sleep to pull it off. For the last several weeks, whenever there was a problem, the solution had been "Ask Toby." That she'd been able to solve most of those problems made her feel good. Right now all she wanted to do was see that everyone was happy and do her best to enjoy the celebration.

"Miss Wyndam, I don't mean to take your time, but I'd like to apologize," a man's voice said from behind her. She knew who he was, as his voice was quite distinctive: deep and smooth.

Too smooth. Too slick. Too cultured. Too much like all the men her mother had tried to force on her.

Toby hesitated before turning to look at him. Last night she and her roommate, Lexie, had taken the bride out for drinks. Toward the back of the restaurant had been a man with a girl on his lap and two more laughing at whatever he'd said. When he saw Toby and her friends enter, he set aside the girl on his lap, got up, and went to their table. He was smiling in a way that seemed to say he expected the young women to stop what they were doing and give their attention to him. He was handsome enough, but there was something—maybe his presumption or her feeling that he was a bit shallow—that made Toby instantly dislike him. She had picked up her bag and left, and the other two women had followed her.

Earlier this evening, the groomsman who was asking for her forgiveness had tried to make Toby and Lexie believe that he had been the man in the bar last night. But she knew he wasn't. And whatever his reasons for doing this, she didn't like liars.

Turning, she looked up at him. He looked like his distant cousin Jared Kingsley, who was Toby's friend and landlord, only this man was younger and, well, cleaner. He stood as straight and as inflexible as a marble statue. There wasn't a hair on his head out of place, a speck of lint on him, or even a crease in his tuxedo. He was so perfectly shaved and laundered that he didn't look real.

"An apology isn't necessary," she said as she stepped past him. "Now if you'll excuse me, I have guests to attend to."

"How did you know?" he asked.

Toby really did have a lot to do for the wedding, but she heard the appeal in his voice. "How did I know what?"

"That it was my brother and not me in the bar last night."

Her impulse was to laugh. Surely he was joking. To her, the two of them looked nothing alike. She got herself under control and as she looked back at him, she even managed a bit of a smile. After all, he was Jared's cousin. "He looks like a pirate, while you look like a . . . a . . . lawyer." Turning, she started back to the big tent.

"So you do think we're identical," he said from behind her.

Toby stopped walking. Flattery got nowhere with her, but a man who could make her laugh got her attention.

She turned back to him. They were in the wooded area around the two tents and the chapel, with the only light coming from inside. It made the area around them almost golden. "All right," she said, looking up at him. "What's your apology?"

"The pirate version or the one from the lawyer?"

It looked like he wasn't serious after all. She didn't smile. "Excuse me, but I have work to do." She again turned away.

"My brother gets into trouble and I cover for him," he said. "It keeps our father from anger that I fear would be injurious to his health."

She knew when she heard the truth, so she looked at him. Toby knew a lot about parental problems.

"Usually . . ." he said. "No, actually, we always get away with it. You're the first one outside the family to recognize our exchange. I really do apologize. When your friend thought I was the one she had seen last night in the bar, it was just less complicated to act as though she was right. Until then, I didn't even know my brother was here on the island."

When he finished, he just stood there and looked at her with an unreadable expression on his face. He had a strong jaw and a straight nose. His eyes were a deep, dark blue, with heavy black brows over them. His mouth had a curve to it, as though he was about to break into a smile, but at the same time there was something intense about him that made her think there was a depth that he hid from others.

"Maybe I jumped to conclusions," she said and gave him a

small smile. "Why don't you go inside and get some food? And thank you for coming to Nantucket to escort me down the aisle."

"It was my pleasure."

He was staring at her in a way that she'd never seen before, as though he didn't understand who—or what—she was. It was beginning to make her uncomfortable.

"All right, then," she said. "I'll leave you to . . . uh, find your brother." Again, she turned away from him.

"Do you know anywhere I can stay?"

She turned back, frowning. "I thought everyone had been given a place for the night." She and Lexie had worked frantically to get every guest a bed. This man had flown in from Maine for the sole purpose of being a groomsman. Had she and Lexie forgotten to take care of where he was to stay? "I'm sorry for the oversight," she said, "but I'm sure we can find you a bed somewhere."

"I apologize for not being clear," he said. "I have accommodations for tonight, but I want to stay on Nantucket for a week. Perhaps I could rent a place?"

In other circumstances she would have said that what he was asking was nearly impossible. The summer weather on Nantucket was divine, as though it had been made up in a fairy tale. Warm but not hot; cool but not cold; sunshine but not blistering; constant breezes that refreshed. The paradise of perfect weather drew about sixty thousand tourists in the summer, and everything needed to be booked in advance.

But this man was related to the Kingsley family and they owned several houses on the island. "I'll ask Jared," she said. "He's often in New York, so maybe you could stay in his house. Or the guesthouse, but then . . ." She trailed off.

He gave a bit of a smile. "Were you about to say that my aunt is staying there and she seems to have formed an . . . an attachment to the bride's father?"

Toby smiled. "Yes, she has. Is she the reason you want to stay?"

"I want a holiday," he said. "At home I rarely have time off, but I thought perhaps now I'd be able to manage it."

Toby glanced at the tent. Inside, as far as she could see, everything seemed to be fine. The caterers were very experienced and they were keeping the buffet table laden. The band had arrived and soon the floor would be cleared for dancing. Right now everyone seemed to be happy, eating, drinking, and laughing.

She looked back at the man. What was his name? She'd been introduced to so many people in the last twenty-four hours that she couldn't remember all of them. "Where are you from? Your accent—" She stopped because it didn't seem polite to say that he had a slight, almost undetectable accent.

But he smiled. "My English tutor will feel that he's failed, as will my American relatives. I'm from Lanconia, but my grandfather is from Warbrooke, Maine. When I was growing up, I spent time there every summer."

"You and your brother?"

"Yes," he said. "I was with my brother, Rory, and a hundred or so other relatives. It was always an exciting time, the happiest of my life, really. What about you? Are you a Nantucket native?"

"Oh, no. Not at all. Lexie—she's my roommate—would say that I haven't been blessed with that honor. She's descended from the proprietors, the first English people who lived on the island. My ancestors came over on the *Mayflower,* but Lexie says that since they didn't land on Nantucket, they're just poor, sad dissidents."

"Not the blessed ones," he said, and his smile made his face soften. "My ancestors were tribes of bearskin-clad warriors who loved to fight each other. What would your roommate think of them?"

"She'd feel very sorry for you," Toby said, and they smiled at each other. For a moment they were silent. "I better go see that everyone has what they need. You should go in and get something to eat."

"What about you? Have you eaten?"

Toby sighed. "Not since early this morning. There's been too much to do. Some of the flowers fell down, the plane was late with supplies, one of the band members wasn't feeling well, and then of course there was the whole secrecy thing, and . . . Sorry. More than you wanted to know. I need to go." But she didn't move.

"So you did all of this? You were in charge of it?"

"More or less. The bride made a lot of the decisions, and Lexie helped with the work, but she has a lot of other responsibilities and . . ." Toby shrugged.

"Let me guess. She's not as detail-oriented as you are, so she left everything up to you."

"Oh, yes!" Toby said. "I love Lexie, but when it got to be too many things to do, she ran away."

"What's that American expression about been and done?"

"Been there, done that?" Toby asked. "Is that the one?"

"Yes. When we were kids, whenever there was work to do, my brother would hide under a table that had a big cloth over it. I think my father knew where he was, but back then Rory's antics amused him. What about you?"

"Your brother's antics did not amuse me."

"No, I meant—" Graydon broke off and for the first time he laughed, showing his perfectly even, white teeth.

Toby relaxed her shoulders, and as she looked back at the tent, she wished she didn't have to deal with everyone.

"I guess you have to go inside," he said.

"Yes, I do. I'm not sure how it happened but I became a wedding planner."

"My guess is that it was because they knew you'd do the perfect job that you did."

"Are you saying that I was used?" Her tone was teasing.

"Completely." His eyes were laughing, sparkling in the lights from the tent. "Who knows you so well?"

"That would be Jared. Your cousin."

"Separated by generations," he said, "but, alas, my blood relative. I think I should make it up to you."

Toby lost her smile and took a step back. Moonlight always seemed to do something to men. In the next second he'd probably be reaching for her. "I'd better—"

"How about if I go inside and get you something to eat?"

"What?"

"I don't know much about event planning, but from what I've seen, if you were to go in there, you'd be surrounded by people asking you questions such as—"

"Where's the ketchup? I've already been asked that twice."

"My thoughts exactly," he said. "If you stand over there, out of sight, I can go inside, get food and beverages, and bring them out here. You'll get to eat before you have to return."

"I shouldn't," Toby said but there wasn't any conviction in her voice. She'd hoped to sneak away once everyone started dancing, but by then the food might be gone. "You think I might have a few scallops?"

"I'll get half a dozen hot off the grill. What else do you want?"

Toby suddenly realized how hungry she was, and as she looked at him, he smiled. "I shall get a mix of everything. Do you like champagne?"

"Love it."

"Chocolate?"

"Especially if it's around strawberries," she said.

"I'll do my best. Wish me luck."

"I wish you a cornucopia full of luck," she said.

"I'll try to live up to that." He slipped away into the darkness and for a moment she lost sight of him, but then she saw him at the end of the buffet line. There weren't many people there, as most were sitting at the tables. Toby expected him to pick up a plate and start to fill it, but he did an odd thing. He spoke quietly to one of the staff, a pretty female. She nodded, disappeared for a moment, then returned with a tray.

Turning, he looked at Toby, just her face visible at the doorway of the tent, and raised his eyebrows in question. She nodded. Yes, the tray was fine.

She watched as the man followed the waitress down the line and pointed out foods to be put on the tray that she, not he, carried. He spoke to a young man behind the long table, who turned away to the grill that had been set up. He said something to another waiter, who went to the bar and returned with a bottle of champagne and two flutes. By the time he was a quarter of the way down the line, Jared's cousin had three people hurrying to do his bidding. "How extraordinary," Toby said out loud.

"There you are!" Lexie said as she came to stand next to Toby. "Why are you out here? And what is extraordinary?"

Toby didn't look at Lexie but put her arm out to motion her to get out of the light. "Sssh. I'm hiding."

"So am I." Lexie moved behind Toby and peered around the doorway. "Who are you hiding from? For me, it's Nelson and Plymouth."

Toby shook her head when the waitress held up some white bread with tongs, then nodded at a whole-wheat roll.

Lexie followed Toby's line of vision. "Isn't that the guy we saw in the bar? The one you were so nasty to but who walked you down the aisle anyway? You stood so far away from him you were practically off-island."

"It wasn't quite that bad," Toby said. "But then, there are two of them."

"So you snubbed both of them?"

Toby nodded at some coleslaw the waitress held up. "What's his name? I can't remember it."

"Which one? The guy in the bar or the one you walked down the aisle with?"

"This one, the aisle one," Toby said. "What's up with you? You sound like you're angry."

Lexie stepped away from the tent opening. "Four people told me that Nelson bought an engagement ring."

"For you?"

"You're not funny," Lexie said.

Toby gave her last nod at the food, then stepped away to look at her friend. "You knew this was going to happen. You've been dating the guy for years, so of course he's going to ask you to marry him. Do you think he's going to do it tonight?"

"Probably. Which is why I've been avoiding him. And it doesn't help that Plymouth is here. I've been hiding from him too."

Roger Plymouth was Lexie's boss and it was Toby's opinion that he thought of Lexie as a great deal more than just his personal assistant. Even though they'd been roommates for over two years, Toby had only recently met Lexie's boss. She'd heard not even one good thing about him, so she was shocked when she saw him. Roger Plymouth was tall, muscular, and drop-dead gorgeous. He was so beautiful that people often just stood and stared at him. But Lexie swore she was immune to his external assets and that he was the biggest pest on earth. "Did you ever think that your hesitation about Nelson has to do with your attraction to Roger Plymouth?"

"Since there is no attraction, how could I think that?" Lexie asked. "The man is nothing but a great nuisance."

"Sure he is," Toby said as she glanced around the side of the tent, wondering when the man was going to show up with the food.

Lexie was watching her. "He went off into the bushes with someone."

"Who?" Toby asked.

"The man you're so fascinated with. His name is . . . Grayson. No, it's Graydon Montgomery. What made you stop sneering at him?"

"I've never sneered at anyone in my life!"

"Ha!" Lexie said. "I've seen you turn men into whimpering idiots with that how-dare-you-even-think-of-touching-me look of yours. I wish I could do that! I'd give it to Plymouth and watch him crawl."

"He'd crawl along behind you," Toby said. "So who is Graydon talking to?"

"I didn't see, and they went into the bushes. It's not a female, if that's what's worrying you. When he gets here I'll leave. Tell me what to do about Nelson and his ring."

"You should say yes or no to him," Toby said. "Let him know one way or the other. Do you love him?"

"Sure I do, but he doesn't make my heart skip a beat. But maybe that's good. We'd get married, move into the house he inherited, and have two kids. It's all great. I couldn't ask for anything more in my life."

Toby glanced around the side of the tent but saw no one. "But you would like an adventure," she said to her friend. "And maybe an adventurous man."

Lexie ignored the last part of that statement. "I was thinking that maybe you and I could go on a cruise together. I got my passport and . . ." She didn't finish, as she was looking at Toby. "So what's with you and this guy Graydon? I take it you forgave him for lying about saying he was his brother. And by the way, how did you know they weren't the same?"

"Because pirates and lawyers are not alike," Toby said, smiling.

"What does that mean?"

"Nothing. It's just a joke." She looked at Lexie. "I hope you know that you're going to have to face your problem head-on. Nelson is a very nice man and if you marry him you can keep your job with Roger Plymouth and you'd never have to leave your beloved island."

"I know," Lexie said. "I guess the sane and sensible thing would be to say yes to Nelson and let you plan our wedding. Think I could wear black?"

"Lexie," Toby said firmly, "if you feel that way, you shouldn't even think about saying yes to Nelson."

"I'm sure you're right. It's just that tonight I don't want to decide my entire future. Oh, no!"

"What is it?"

"I think I saw Plymouth. I still can't believe you invited him here. Where's he staying, since his house is filled with guests? Or has he jumped into bed with one or two of them?"

Besides Roger's beauty, he was also very rich and owned a multimillion-dollar house on the water. Since the original plan was that he would be away at the time of the wedding, he'd agreed to allow his six-bedroom house to be used for guests. But because of the last-minute changes in the wedding, Toby had called him and asked if he would walk Lexie down the aisle.

It had been interesting to see the way the man looked at Lexie, as though she were the most beautiful, desirable woman on earth.

"I don't know where Roger is staying," Toby said as she looked around the tent again. "You certainly are interested in his whereabouts."

"So I can avoid him," Lexie said quickly. "You like this guy Graydon, don't you?"

"I don't know," Toby said. "I just met him, but he seems nice enough. He wants to stay on Nantucket for a week, so I said I'd help him find a place. Maybe he could stay in Kingsley House since Jared will probably be in New York."

"Why did he ask you about housing? Why not one of his own relatives? I'm a cousin too, and then there's his aunt Jilly. And besides that, why didn't he plan this trip beforehand?"

"He was only asked to be a groomsman three days ago," Toby said. "I think he likes Nantucket. Maybe he wants to see the island. It does happen." Many people came to visit and ended up staying for years.

"You do know, don't you, that he stared at you through the whole ceremony?"

Toby was glad for the darkness to cover the way the blood rushed to her face. "I did see him look at me a few times, yes."

"Look at you?! Ha! That man hardly blinked. So now he wants to stay on Nantucket for a while and he's asked you to help him find a place. How very interesting."

"You know," Toby said calmly, "I do believe I just saw Nelson heading this way. Is that a ring box he's holding open? I think I saw the flash of a diamond."

Lexie moved farther into the darkness. "You haven't heard the end of this," she said before she disappeared.

"I'm sure I haven't," Toby muttered, but then Lexie's question of should she or shouldn't she marry Nelson had been going on for a long time. Ever since she'd met Roger Plymouth, Toby thought he was the problem, not Nelson. When Toby was alone, she looked around the tent, but there was no sign of Graydon. With a sigh, she started to go inside. It looked like he wasn't going to return, so it was time to go back to work.

"May I escort you to a table?"

Toby stopped walking and couldn't help the smile that nearly cracked her face. When she turned to look at Graydon, she was more subdued. He was holding out his arm to her and she took it.

"I beg you to forgive my tardiness, but I was waysided by my brother."

"Is that the same as waylaid?"

"If it means I was dragged into the bushes and lectured, yes, that's the correct term. Tell me, Miss Wyndam, do you have siblings?"

"No, I don't. It was just me."

"Then someday maybe I can tell you what you've had the pleasure of missing."

"I would love to hear it," Toby said, smiling up at him as she held on to his arm.

Earlier, Graydon had walked out of the big tent behind three people carrying food and furniture. It had taken more time than he would have liked to arrange a private dinner, but he'd done it. It seemed that a second, much smaller tent had been set up and Graydon had commandeered it. A table, chairs, candles, were all to be put inside, then he and Miss Wyndam would—

"What the hell are you doing?"

His brother's voice and the Lanconian language took the smile off Graydon's face. His plan had been to try to win over the young lady before he had to ask his brother to make what he wanted to do possible. "I'm having dinner," Graydon said. "With a young woman. I'll talk to you later."

His brother's dismissal was so unusual that for a moment Rory couldn't speak. It was only when his brother turned away that he recovered himself. "Unless you want a third dinner guest, we'll talk now."

Graydon halted, gritted his teeth for a moment, then turned

back. He waited while the catering people went past him to the little tent, then he stepped into the wooded area with his brother. "Let's make this quick. She's waiting for me."

Rory couldn't seem to take the astonishment off his face. "You picked up a girl? You?! I assume she's the girl you were making a fool of yourself over at the ceremony. She's pretty but not exactly something to set a man on fire. I could set you up with—"

Rory stepped back just in time to miss his brother's fist slamming into his face. If they hadn't spent a lot of time training together, Rory would be flat on his back now.

"By the wrath of Naos, but that was close!" Rory said, and stood there staring, wide-eyed.

Graydon adjusted his cuffs. "I guess I should apologize for that but my apology quota is filled for tonight. Is there something you wanted to say to me?"

Never before had anything come between the brothers. But tonight Graydon—the calm one—had almost struck Rory—the hot-tempered one—in anger.

Rory lost his attitude. "You . . . what? Fell in love with this girl? At first sight?" He was astonished.

"No," Graydon said. "Not at all." He looked at his brother in the dim light. "She can tell us apart."

Rory blinked for a moment. "How do you know?"

"She knew it wasn't me in the bar. What were you thinking when you confronted her?"

"I didn't. At least not her specifically. It was three very pretty girls and I said hello. The one you like turned her little nose up at me and walked out. I haven't been put down like that in . . . well, ever, actually. Do you think you and I are getting old?"

"I think she didn't want to be accosted by a stranger."

Rory gave a little smile. "So you figured out another way to pick her up?" He nodded toward the small tent. "Champagne and chocolate-covered strawberries? That should do it. These

American girls—" Again Rory stepped back when his brother looked ready to punch him.

"All right," Rory said, "no more jokes. How do you know she can tell us apart?"

"The other bridesmaid, the dark-haired one, said they saw me at the bar. I didn't think about it, but I said I was there. The blonde—she's called Toby—got quite angry at me for lying."

"But you got her to forgive you?"

"I hope so. Look, I have to go, but I want you to do something for me."

"Find out about her?"

"No!" Graydon said. "I'll do that on my own. I want to stay here," he said softly. He looked back at his brother. "In fact, I am going to stay here on Nantucket for an entire week."

Rory was trying to cover his shock. For all that they were identical twins, they were very different personalities. His brother was the responsible one, the one who put duty before . . . well, before life. Rory was a man of impulse, a man who didn't believe in duty in any form.

"How can you get away with being gone that long?" Rory asked. "You can't even escape for twenty-four hours without consequences. Our father will send soldiers to find you, and your disappearance will be on the news. The entire planet will start looking for you in the hope of a reward."

"No, they won't," Graydon said as he looked hard at his brother. "No one will look for me because you are going to take my place."

Rory laughed at that. "We may fool outsiders but our family will know."

"Who? Our parents? I rarely see them. Will our Montgomery-Taggert relatives tell? Their loyalty to each other is of legendary proportions. Do you think the press will be astute enough to figure it out?"

"What about Danna?" Rory asked.

Graydon put his hands in his pockets, an unusual gesture for him, more like something Rory would do—and the casual stance shocked his twin. "She, least of all, will know which of us is the crown prince. I see her less often than I do our parents. Rory?" He looked at his brother. "You are going to do this for me."

Between them were years of unspoken words. Graydon had covered for Rory hundreds of times. Since they were children, Graydon had often taken the blame for things that Rory did. When they were younger, it had been a game. Rory did the naughty deeds and Graydon took the blame. He used to say, "Being you makes me seem less . . ." "Less like the Perfect Prince?" Rory had finished for him. "Yes," Graydon had said, smiling.

But as they grew up, people around them—and there were a lot of retainers—figured it out. By the time the boys were twelve, it was known that if something good was done, Graydon did it. Bad behavior was Rory's territory.

Rory was staring at his brother—who seemed to have turned into someone he didn't know. "All this is because of some girl who says she can tell you from me?" Rory didn't realize it, but he was beginning to stand taller, straighter. Just the thought of pretending to be his brother for an extended time was doing something to him.

"She has no idea there's any significance to what she saw," Graydon said.

"But she said she can tell the crown prince from the landless one?"

"She doesn't know," Graydon said.

"Doesn't know that you'll someday be the king of a country? Doesn't know that you're to marry a Lanconian duke's daughter? Does she even know that she turned down the UYB in favor of a future king? What does she know?"

Graydon kept his hands in his pockets. "She doesn't know any of it. Not a word."

"The legend about whoever can tell the Montgomery-Taggert twins apart?"

"No, of course not. Rory," Graydon said firmly, "I want to see if . . ."

"If what?" Rory asked, anger in his voice. "You want to see if you can make her fall in love with you because of some stupid legend? By Jura, but that's cruel! You can't do that! There's no future for you two. You know you can't marry her. And even Danna, as sweet as she is, wouldn't put up with a cute blonde mistress."

"I'm not in love with this girl and I don't plan to be." Graydon took a breath. "I just want what you've had since we were twelve years old. I want some time of freedom. Think of it as an extended bachelor party." He was nose to nose with his brother. "You are going to be me for a whole week. Do you understand me?"

"Sure," Rory said as he took a step back. He'd never seen his brother so fierce and angry. He could almost imagine the warriors their family was descended from. "I'll stay in the palace and live a life of ease. Get waited on day and night. I'll have champagne for breakfast."

Graydon stepped away. "That's how your life is now, but while I'm here you'll take over my duties at home. I can postpone the important meetings but you'll have to attend to charity matters, make a few presentations, and go to at least one ribbon cutting. Wherever you're needed, you'll be there. Now, I'm going to have dinner with a lovely young lady and—"

"Tell her," Rory said. "Promise me that you will tell her who you are and why you have to return home and leave her behind."

Graydon didn't turn around, but he nodded once, then went back toward the tent.

It was Rory's turn to put his hands in his pockets, and he fell back against a tree. His brother had just knocked the air out of him. His request that Rory exchange places with him wasn't that unusual, as they'd been doing that all their lives. Graydon usually took over for Rory, and they'd done it as recently as a month ago when Graydon wanted an evening off from his duties. It always entertained Rory to see his straitlaced brother trying to be him. Graydon wasn't one to drive a car at two hundred miles an hour or race a boat across choppy waters. "But it isn't just me, it's a whole kingdom I'm risking," Graydon had said when Rory laughed at his brother's seeming timidity. Graydon's words had taken away the laughter. What he was saying was that Rory was expendable; Graydon was not. "UYB," Rory had muttered. It was a term he'd come up with when they were kids. "Useless Younger Brother"—eventually abbreviated to UYB.

Rory's self-worth was further trampled when Graydon began to win over the girls. The last time this had happened, Rory had coaxed Graydon into having dinner with a girl he'd been dating for months. He wanted to go to a party given by his ex and he didn't want to have to deal with his current girl's jealousy.

It was never easy for Graydon to get away from his bodyguards, but that night he'd managed it, and the exchange went off perfectly. Except that afterward, Rory's girlfriend wanted him to be the way he was on the night of the exchange. "You were sooooo romantic," she kept saying. "Remind me again what I did," Rory said. She sighed in a dreamy way. "You played the lute, sang to me, and fed me those tiny grapes. You—" Rory cut her off and never again asked his brother to take his place on a date. He and the girl broke up soon afterward. "You've just changed," she said when they parted. "There was one night when you made me feel like I was the center of the world, then it was back to . . . to being you."

Later, Rory asked Graydon what he thought of the girl. "Very pretty but not a brain in her head. Want me to get Mother to find someone for you?"

Graydon was referring to Danna, who'd been chosen for the future king's wife. Danna was tall and beautiful, sublimely educated, and the daughter of a Lanconian duke. She could ride a horse with perfect form, play the piano at concert level, host a formal dinner for two hundred with ease. As for her personality, she loved charity work, never forgot anyone's name, and was always gracious and considerate. She never put a foot wrong or lost her temper with anyone.

All in all, Danna was utterly and completely perfect, and she was to marry Graydon and become the next Queen of Lanconia.

The only problem was that Graydon didn't love Danna. He liked her well enough, but there was only friendship between them. But at thirty-one years old, Graydon knew it was time that he marry and produce an heir to the throne. As always, he took his duties very, very seriously. He wasn't his brother; he couldn't marry only for love. No, Graydon had to find a woman who could do all the things required of her as a princess and later as a queen. Hours of standing, smiling endlessly, being deeply involved in charity work, et cetera. The woman had to be as dedicated as Graydon was, and in this modern age that was nearly impossible to find.

Rory looked across the moonlit landscape. He could hear the band inside the tent beginning to make sounds of rock 'n' roll. Could his brother even dance to that? Graydon was more of a waltz man than a down and dirty rocker.

The truth was that Rory knew his brother could handle the change quite easily. He'd have a few problems but nothing could stop him for long.

The true problem was going to be Rory's. He knew he could put his shoulders back and carry himself like his brother. Unbending, inflexible, he could put on that I-will-be-king look that Graydon had perfected.

No, the problem was that Rory had a secret so deeply hidden that even his brother didn't know it. Rory was totally and absolutely in love with the woman his brother was going to marry.

He moved away from the tree and stood up straight. Maybe it was selfish of him, but he was going to do whatever he could to make this exchange happen. A few days with Danna were better than none at all. And the first thing Rory was going to do was see if he could clear a path for Graydon by getting rid of the roommate. Rory had been told that she worked for Roger Plymouth, a man he'd met several times. Maybe they could work out something.

Chapter Three

As soon as Toby saw the inside of the little tent, she knew what the man was after. The question was why she had ever doubted his intention.

She stood there looking at the table with a cloth that went to the floor, lit candles, chairs that were draped in misty blue fabric, and she thought, Scene for Seduction. As she stepped back, she glared up at this man she had begun to think was such a nice person. "No, thanks," she said, her voice as cool as the scene was warm. She started back toward the big tent where she'd be surrounded by people—not seducers.

When she was about twenty feet away, she heard him say, "Now what did I do wrong?" She took another couple of steps and meant to go on, but she stopped and turned to look at him. He was still standing by the tent and there was an expression of absolute bewilderment on his face.

She walked back to him. "What have you heard about me?"

Graydon blinked at her a few times. He'd assumed that she'd walked away because someone had told her that Graydon was a prince and she wanted nothing to do with him. When women outside his country found out that he was royalty, they went either of two ways. They ran away, or their eyes lit up and they started asking how many crowns he owned. It looked like this young woman was a runner.

But if so, why was she asking what he knew about her? "I don't know much about you at all," he said, his voice conveying his consternation. "Your name is Toby. You are a friend of the bride and the other bridesmaid. I'm afraid I don't know much more than that. Should I have asked someone about you?"

Toby was beginning to be the one who was confused. "If you know nothing about me, then why all this?" She motioned to the tent. The flap was still open, with candlelight wafting over them.

"Oh," Graydon said, seeming to at last understand. "You're thinking like an American."

"How else could I think?"

"Miss Wyndam, again I apologize. I have no ulterior motive with this dinner than to sit at a table and eat in peace, perhaps with some intelligent conversation. I would have asked my brother to join me, but you are prettier than he is, and you haven't eaten, so . . . ." He shrugged. "I must tell you that I have now apologized to you more than I have collectively in the entirety of my life."

Toby couldn't help but smile at the last part of his little speech. "Do we Americans often confuse you?"

"Endlessly," he said. "You wouldn't possibly reconsider and join me for dinner, would you? My brother is not happy with me at the moment and he wouldn't be good company."

"All right," Toby said, and stepped inside the tent. She was beginning to feel that from their first meeting she'd been too harsh with this man.

He held her chair out for her, then took his. "May I?" he asked as he picked up a large spoon and fork and motioned to serve her. "What should I know about you that would cause you to refuse to dine with a man?"

"Nothing," she said quickly, but he kept looking at her and waiting. While he looked somewhat like Jared, whose skin was always tan from spending time on his boat, she had an idea that this man's skin was naturally darker. "Some of the boys on the island—and I do mean boys—have started trying to . . . to see who can, well, I guess you could say, win me."

"I see." He put scallops on her plate. "What is that American phrase? To 'lure you astray'?"

She smiled at the old-fashioned term. "Yes, that's what they've tried to do." She helped herself to salad.

"But none of the young men appeals to you?"

Toby didn't like where this conversation was going, as she certainly didn't want to discuss her personal life. "You said your brother isn't happy with you right now. Why not?"

"We had an argument about you."

"Me? How could that be?" Her voice rose in alarm. "I don't know either of you well enough to cause you two to argue."

"I misspoke. Sorry again. My brother thinks I must tell you about myself. That not to do so is cruel."

Frowning, Toby looked at him through the candlelight. "I think you should tell me what this is about." She had visions of his having a prison record, that he was just out of rehab or under investigation by Interpol.

"My American grandfather married the woman who inherited the throne of Lanconia, so that makes me and my younger brother princes."

"Oh." It took Toby a moment to recover her equanimity. "Did your grandfather do a good job?"

"Yes, he did," Graydon said. "He took my old country into the twentieth century. Thanks to him, we are now self-supporting. We're still old-fashioned enough that we draw tourists but that helps the economy. When my father reached forty, my grandparents turned the throne over to him and my mother. My parents have done a wonderful job, but with fewer Americanizations."

"So you're to be a king. Is there anything else I should know about you?"

"Later this year there will be a ceremony in which my engagement to Lady Danna Hexonbath will be announced."

Toby took her time eating a scallop while she thought about what he'd told her. "So you want a bit of a vacation here on Nantucket before you take on the responsibility of a wife and even of a country?"

"That's exactly right," he said. "Rory is going to be me."

"What does that mean?"

"My brother is going to impersonate me so I can have this week off." When Toby looked skeptical, he continued. "You seem able to tell us apart, but no one else can. Well, my grandparents can, but then, Rory and I spent most of our childhoods with them. My parents were busy running the country."

Toby saw a tiny flash race through his eyes. She thought, He was hurt by his parents' neglect of him. But she wasn't going to say that out loud. "Do you love her?" Toby asked.

When her words seemed to jolt Graydon, Toby knew that she'd made a mistake. The warmth in his eyes disappeared and his spine straightened. "Of course," he said.

He's lying, Toby thought. Or else he's hiding the truth. He either loves her very much and he wants that kept private, or he doesn't love her at all—and he doesn't want that known. Surely, she thought, he wouldn't be in some arranged marriage. Not in the twenty-first century! But then, she'd seen a documentary on

TV that said arranged marriages were still common in most of the world.

"All right," Toby said, "I'll see if I can find you a place to stay." As she looked at him, her mind was racing with ideas. "However . . ." She paused. "I don't think we should tell anyone what your, ah, job is. The family will know, but we shouldn't tell outsiders."

"Especially since I'm here in hiding," he said in agreement.

"Do you have people with you? To help you do things?"

"To serve me food, to drive me places, that sort of thing?" She hesitated, but then nodded.

"Thanks to my cousins in Maine, I'm a fully functioning person. I can even put on my shirt and tie my own shoes."

"I didn't mean any disrespect," Toby said and glanced toward the entrance of the tent. Maybe it was time for her to go.

"I do have to be honest," he said. "There are things I don't know how to do."

"Such as?"

"Buy food. I've been to a grocery before, in Maine, but I didn't pay for it. Rory uses a credit card so maybe I can borrow it. I know how to drive a car but at home they stop traffic whenever I'm on the main road, so . . ." He shrugged, leaving the rest to her imagination.

Toby was blinking at him. She had a vision of him sitting in Jared's huge house and slowly starving to death. Or maybe he'd die in a car crash because he didn't know what to do at a stop sign. Nantucket had no red lights but it did have a few rotaries that the tourists went through at full speed—and blew their horns if anyone got in their way. They could be dangerous!

"Maybe Jared can . . ." she began, but trailed off. Jared was going to be off-island at his architectural firm, and she and Lexie had full-time jobs. It was summer and everyone was busy. "I think you need to stay with someone."

"Are you saying that I need a caretaker?" He was smiling, teasing.

"Everyone needs companionship. I do think you should stay in town so you can walk to restaurants. Victoria spent a lot of time here over the years, but she's never kept a car here."

"Who is Victoria?"

"Red hair, green suit?"

"Oh, yes," Graydon said. "I remember her well."

"All men do." Victoria was tall and beautiful, and had an exaggerated hourglass shape. That she was the same age as Toby's mother didn't diminish Victoria's sex appeal. Men still watched her walk across the room.

"Where does she stay when she's here?"

"Kingsley House," Toby said.

"Perfect," Graydon said, smiling. "This Victoria would be my roommate?"

"I thought you were about to get engaged."

"I like beauty around me, whether it's a Van Dyck painting or a beautiful woman in a suit so tight I could see the lace underneath."

The way he said that, with such an air of innocence, made her laugh. "I don't think Dr. Huntley would like that, and he seems to have laid claim to Victoria. She may move to his house, but it's awfully small. I'll find you something. Lexie will know where."

He held out the plate of chocolate-covered strawberries. "I don't mean to be presumptuous, but where do you live?"

"Just down the lane from Kingsley House. And speaking of presumptions, if you're about to be engaged, why are you asking about me?"

"I'm not trying to lure you into anything. It's just that I've never met someone outside my family who could tell Rory and me apart. People who have known us all our lives can't tell one from the other. That you can makes me feel a bond with you.

Besides, you and Aunt Jilly are the only people I know here, and I don't think I'll be asking her for help."

Toby nodded. His aunt and Ken, the father of Toby's friend Alix, had recently become a couple. They made it obvious that they didn't need or want anyone else. It really did seem that this man knew very few people on the island, and for all that he wouldn't be here very long, it could be lonely. "I'll ask around," she said, but even as she thought it, she couldn't imagine where he could stay and be comfortable. A hotel? Who would he talk to? Maybe she could find him a place with one of the Kingsleys. But who would fit with this man with his perfect table manners? And who would resist telling that they had a prince living with them? Then what would happen? The people on the island would probably protect him—they were used to high-ranking visitors—but what if the off-islanders heard he was here? He might as well put himself in a glass cage.

"You're looking at me very hard," Graydon said. "I can assure you that I'm a flesh and blood human being."

"It's not a matter of how you see yourself but how others see you."

"How perceptive you are."

"I wish Jared's aunt Addy were still alive. She'd take you into her house and under her wing and protect you. And give you lots of rum to drink."

Graydon laughed. "That sounds perfect, but I can assure you that I need no protection. Maybe from a stray bullet now and then, but not many."

His tone was joking, but Toby didn't laugh. She'd heard too many stories of assassination attempts on royalty. "Do you have a bodyguard?"

"I do at home, and I left one in Maine, but I'm here by myself."

"But what if someone recognizes you?"

"Miss Wyndam, one of the best things about being a prince

of a small, obscure country is that no one in the outside world recognizes me. I am not—thank heaven—a member of the British royal family. Their every movement is recorded and talked about and criticized, but outside our own borders we Lanconians are not that interesting." He didn't add that in his own country everything he did was in the headlines.

Toby, who wouldn't have missed a second of Prince William's wedding, suddenly had a vision of it from the other side. Where was the privacy, the romance, of such a wedding for the couple? "Will your wedding be a gala?"

"Oh, yes," Graydon said. "We have a huge old cathedral and it will be packed with people. The entire country will have a three-day holiday."

"You said an 'engagement ceremony.' What will that be like?"

He held the plate for her to take the last strawberry. "It'll be the first of many celebrations over the year."

"And they will all involve you?"

"Yes," Graydon said and bent his head for a moment. "Once the engagement is announced, I'm fair game. I will go to each of the six provinces and participate in days, weeks even, of games and feasts, and I'll laugh at all the bawdy jokes that they can come up with."

"What about your bride?"

"Traditionally, she's considered a maiden, so she doesn't usually attend. She stays at home, but then Danna has her horses and she must prepare her trousseau."

"It doesn't seem fair that she gets to enjoy herself while you have to run around, does it?"

Graydon laughed. "I think it's the other way around. Some would say I have the better bargain—I get to party and she doesn't."

"Then there's the wedding, and after that . . . ?"

"After that Danna and I will take on a lot of my parents' duties. My mother doesn't like to travel, so Danna and I will visit the United States and any other country where we hope to persuade people to buy what we produce or sell us what we need."

"You are actually a businessman," she said.

"I like to think of it that way, but I have to wear a lot of different uniforms and smile constantly."

As Toby ate the last strawberry, she leaned back in the chair. "This really is your last moment of peace, isn't it?"

"Yes," he said, smiling at her understanding. "I would like to have a week of no schedule, with no one telling me where I have to be when." He paused. "Now I must ask. Why are the men on this island working so hard to win you? I can see your beauty, but is there anything else?"

"Just that I won't go out with them," she said. "It's male machismo, that they feel they must win what they can't have. When—?"

She was cut off because Lexie threw back the tent flap and looked at Toby. "Sorry to interrupt, but people are getting worried about you. They won't cut the cake without you there, and if another kid asks me when they're going to get cake I might throw them on top of the thing—except that they'd like that too much. Brats! Do you know where the keys to Jared's truck are? And Plymouth wants me to leave tomorrow morning to go to the south of France to chaperone his sister." Lexie looked at Graydon. "Oh, hi. You and I are cousins." She looked back at Toby and waited for an answer.

Toby took a breath. "I'll be there in ten minutes. Give the kids the cupcakes stored in the blue cooler at the back corner of the tent. The truck keys are over the visor. You want to leave tomorrow?"

"Yeah," Lexie said. "Tomorrow." She held up her naked left hand. "Now I have a reason to postpone everything." As she turned away, she looked back at Graydon. "Toby is great, isn't she?"

"I do believe she is," Graydon said.

Smiling, Lexie left the tent.

The instant Toby stood up, so did Graydon. "It looks like I'm needed," she said.

"Who is Plymouth?"

"Lexie's boss, and I fully believe there's more to them than just work."

Graydon's eyes were intent. "What does he do?"

"For a living? Nothing that I know of. Family money. I think he plays all the time. A lot of people who come here are like that." She glanced at the table. "I'll send someone to clear this away."

"I can arrange that," Graydon said.

Toby remembered how he'd easily commandeered three of the waitstaff to put everything out for him. At the time she'd not understood how he'd done it, but a prince would be able to do that. "Should I curtsy?" she asked, trying to keep a straight face.

"Yes, please do," he said. "I love it when women bend before me."

"Hold your breath." She was laughing as she left the tent.

For a while, Graydon stood there looking after her. He liked that she was perceptive and wasn't intimidated by his . . . as she said, his "job." Never before had he felt so quickly at ease with a person.

Abruptly, he came out of his reverie. He remembered her roommate saying she wanted to leave the country tomorrow, and she was going with a rich man who did nothing. That fit the description of every friend his brother had—and Graydon knew, without a doubt in the world, that his brother was behind this trip. It seemed that Rory—yet again—thought that his brother couldn't handle his own life.

Graydon took his phone out of his pocket and texted his brother, NOW!

Chapter Four

Toby went back into the big tent, into the noise of the band and the many guests, but all she could think of was the man she'd had dinner with. A prince! And somehow, she'd been given full charge of him.

She looked up at the swags of ribbons and flowers that hung around the top of the big white tent. She and Alix and Lexie had spent hours consulting to come up with the design, but it was Toby who had done the actual work. She'd wired every little bouquet together, trying to make it seem as though someone had skipped through a field and gathered wildflowers.

Turning full circle, she looked at each one. For the last weeks, her whole life had revolved around this wedding. She couldn't help envisioning the great extravaganza that Prince Graydon's wedding would be. If she helped him now, would she get an invitation?

No, no, she told herself, she couldn't think like that. She must help him without thought of anything for herself.

As she looked around the room at the crowded dance floor, she tried to see if everyone was having a good time. In one corner was a large round table packed with older kids. They were silent, not participating in anything. Each one was tapping out messages on his or her phone. Earlier, Toby had stopped by and asked who they were writing to. It turned out that they were texting one another. Shaking her head, not understanding why they didn't just talk, she left them. They certainly seemed to be enjoying themselves.

The bride, in her beautiful dress from the 1950s—found in a Kingsley attic—was dancing with a little boy named Tyler. They were holding hands and the boy was smiling angelically. As Toby watched, Jared walked up to the two of them and asked to join in, but Tyler's face instantly went from happy to ferocious. He glared up at Jared and said "No!" loud enough to be heard over the band.

When Toby laughed, Jared put his arm around her waist and pulled her onto the floor. "Laughing at me, are you?" He had to put his head close to her ear to be heard, but then, abruptly, the fast, loud song ended and a slow one began. "Thank God," he mumbled and pulled Toby closer to him for the dance.

As he twirled her about on the dance floor, Jared couldn't help remembering how they'd met. A few summers ago he'd designed a guest wing for the house Toby's parents owned on Nantucket and stayed in every summer. Toby's dad, Barrett, flew in and out every weekend, but her mother, Lavidia, stayed on the island.

Once a week Jared stopped by the site to check on the construction—and every time he went he had to listen to Mrs. Wyndam berate her pretty daughter, Toby, who had recently graduated from an exclusive all-girls college. One day Mrs. Wyndam had been loudly telling Toby that she wasn't standing up straight enough, that her clothes were a disgrace, and that she was never going to get a husband if she didn't start paying attention to how she looked.

"I guess I better go save my daughter," Barrett had said with a sigh and he'd plodded off to the patio.

All that summer Jared had heard the incessant complaints of Mrs. Wyndam—all of them directed toward her daughter. As for young Toby, she didn't seem to be affected by anything her mother said. She stood in silence, keeping her eyes down, never challenging her mother. Jared had the impression the girl was immune to the woman's harangues. Toby spent her days in the kitchen baking treats she carried out to the construction crew, or she was in the garden tending to the flowers.

It was in September, just before the Wyndams were to leave the island, that Jared saw Toby kneeling at one of the flower beds. She was crying.

He didn't have to ask what was wrong, as he'd just heard her mother telling Barrett that Toby was "impossible," that she wouldn't go out with the son of some man who owned a yacht. Jared knew both father and son and he wouldn't have let any female relative of his alone with either of them.

Jared put his roll of plans down and sat on the edge of a chaise longue. "What are you going to do to fix this?" There was no need for a preamble of explanation; they both knew what the problem was.

"What can I do?" Toby said, her voice angry, and it was the first time he'd seen any emotion in her. "I have no training for an actual job. I know that if I ran away my father would support me, but what kind of freedom is that?"

"Your garden is nice and I've seen how you create those big flower arrangements."

"Great! I can put flowers together so they look quite pretty. Who's going to pay for that?" She looked at him. "A florist?" she whispered.

"That would be my guess, and I happen to know one who could use some help for the winter. If you want to stay on Nantucket, that is."

"Stay? Alone in this big house? So far from town?"

"Do you clean up the kitchen after you use it? I'm asking because my cousin Lexie lives near Kingsley House and she's looking for a new roommate. Her last one could only fry things and she never cleaned up after herself."

For the first time Toby's eyes had hope in them. "I scour, disinfect, and put lemon juice on the counters to make them smell good."

Jared wrote on the back of one of his business cards. "This is my private cell number. If you think there's any possibility that you'd take the house, let me know. But I can only hold off Lexie about twenty-four hours before she rents it to somebody else."

For a moment, Jared hesitated. Was he making a wrong decision? He didn't really know this girl and she seemed almost delicate. He'd seen her quietly and serenely take whatever her mother dished out. Lexie was a strong character, and Jared wasn't sure Toby could stand up to her. And what if she was one of those girls who went wild the moment she was out from under her parents' rule? Jared looked her up and down, trying to figure out what would happen.

At his look, Toby straightened her back. "Mr. Kingsley, do you have an alternative reason for this offer?"

At first he didn't know what she meant, but her eyes let him know her meaning. Jared was used to women liking him, saying yes to him, but not this girl. She was putting him in his place flatly and without question. In that moment Jared saw how someone as fragile-looking as Toby could stand up to her mother. As he looked at her, he knew that if he'd ever had a little sister, she was it. She brought out something protective in him. "I only want to help, and you and Lexie will do fine."

He glanced up to see her mother at the window, frowning, probably thinking that Jared was too close to Toby. He stood up. "If you want to do this, I'll see that you get a job."

He wanted to say but didn't, If I have to hire you myself. "I'll come back tomorrow at eleven and you can tell me your decision."

"I think I'll probably be waiting with my bags packed."

"I'll be sure to bring my truck." Smiling, he walked away. The next morning she moved in with Lexie and he'd been looking after the two young women ever since.

"How does it feel to be a married man?" Toby asked him.

"Perfect. Where have you been tonight?" he asked as he twirled Toby about the dance floor. "I was going to search for you, but Lex threatened my life if I did. So what's up?"

"Do you know that the man who walked me down the aisle is a prince?"

"Isn't that name already taken?"

At first she didn't know what he meant, then she understood and laughed. "No, he's a real live honest-to-gosh prince who will someday be a king."

Jared lowered her in a dip. "Since he and I are related, does that make me a duke? Or maybe I'm a prince too."

"Prince of Fishes," Toby said as he pulled her up. "He wants to stay on the island for a week and he needs some peace and privacy."

"So nobody is to know he's here? Won't the flags on his line of cars give him away?"

"Jared! This is for real. Stop making jokes."

He led her in a circle. "I've never heard you talk about a man like this. So what were you two doing when nobody could find you?" Jared's protective instincts were coming to the fore.

"Eating dinner," she said. "When Prince Graydon goes back to his own country, his engagement to a young Lanconian woman is going to be announced. A year later they'll be married."

"American girls aren't good enough for him? Or is he planning to sow some wild oats here on Nantucket before he returns home?" His tone told her what he thought of that idea.

Toby tried to pull away from him, but Jared held her fast. "Okay, I'll quit. What do you need?"

"Your cousin"—she emphasized the connection—"needs a place to stay while he's here. And it would be better if he had a roommate, someone to help him out."

"You mean like cut up his meat for him? Help him get his clothes on in the morning?"

"I don't know what he can and can't do. Is it possible for him to stay at Kingsley House?"

"That place is full to the brim for the next week. We had to put relatives in there, and Lexie's boss took a bedroom. What about your house?"

"We only have two bedrooms, and besides, I don't think that would be appropriate."

Jared gave her a serious look. "Did this guy make any unwelcome advances at you?"

"No, not at all."

It was the end of the dance and the band was leaving to take a break. Jared stopped and looked at her. "Toby, this guy can't just show up here and think we can offer him a palace and a bunch of servants. He'll have to take what he can get. You have a pullout couch in the sitting room upstairs in your house, so put him on it. Lexie will be there, so you'll be fine. If he thinks he's too good for that, then he can sleep in somebody's car. Tomorrow Caleb or Victoria can find him a place to stay for a longer term. Prince or not, he's an adult and he can take care of himself. Now, how about some cake?"

"Sure," Toby said and motioned that it was okay for Jared to leave her, that she'd be fine. She knew he was right, but still, she did feel some responsibility for Prince Graydon.

She looked around the tent at the many guests. Alix and Jared were cutting the cake and everyone was focused on them. Lexie was behind the caterers, and Toby had an idea she was still hiding from the men in her life. She maneuvered around the crowd of guests and went to her friend. "Could I talk to you?"

"Gladly," Lexie said as she grabbed two plates of wedding cake. "Get the forks."

Toby got forks, napkins, and two cups of punch and they went outside the tent. "I want to know what's going on," Toby said as soon as they were out in the clear, clean, salty Nantucket air.

"I should ask you the same thing," Lexie said. "That scene in the tent with that guy was out of a novel. Candlelight and chocolate. All you needed was a rose in your hair."

"Are you trying to avoid telling me what you're up to?"

"Completely," Lexie said, and gave a great sigh. "Toby, I feel really bad about this, but Plymouth said he needs someone to stay with his fourteen-year-old sister in the south of France and he asked if I'd consider doing it."

"I thought you didn't want to travel with him."

"He won't be there. He's going off to do something with a car, race it somewhere, I guess, but he promised his sister he'd take her to France."

"Doesn't the child have parents?"

"Plymouth's dad is on his fourth wife. This one is barely twenty. She doesn't want to be stuck babysitting for three months."

"Three months?"

"Yeah," Lexie said, looking guilty. "It's until the first of September, so technically it's only two and a half months, but still . . ."

Toby knew that this was one of those times when she had to work to be unselfish. This was a great opportunity for Lexie. And she didn't believe for a moment that Roger wouldn't show up. And on some level, Lexie probably knew it too. But maybe if she got away from Nantucket she'd be able to figure out what she wanted to do with her life.

On the other hand, the backyard of the house they shared had been made for their business of raising flowers to sell. There were a greenhouse and many raised beds, all of them needing weeding and fertilizing and constant care.

"I'll send you my half of the rent," Lexie said. "Plymouth is doubling my salary for these weeks, so I'll be able to afford it."

Toby would have liked to tell her to forget about the rent, but she couldn't. Jared owned the house, and he let them have it for much less than it would bring if he rented it to an off-islander. But still, Toby's half took a lot of her pay.

"Jilly can help you with the flowers," Lexie said, her expression pleading with Toby to agree to this. "I know I'm letting you down, but I would really like to do this. I met Plymouth's sister last year and she's a sweet kid. She likes to read a lot and he says she wants to visit museums. Can you imagine Plymouth in a museum?"

Since Toby didn't know the man at all, she couldn't imagine anything about him. As for Jilly, she was in the early stages of being in love and all she seemed able to see was Ken. And besides, Ken's teaching job was off-island, so they'd be there a lot of the time. Toby didn't think Jilly would be much help at all.

But she knew her friend needed this time away. Toby took a deep breath. "Of course you should go. You can't miss an opportunity like this. Maybe things will happen that will help you decide—"

"Thank you!" Lexie said as she set her plate on the ground and hugged Toby hard. "I need to go pack. Can you handle things here?" She nodded toward the tent and the wedding.

"Sure," Toby said as she picked up the plate and watched Lexie disappear into the darkness.

For a moment Toby stood outside the tent, holding the empty utensils and letting the warm air soak into her. This had to be the most unusual day of her life. It was as though from the moment she and her friends had walked into a bar and seen that man sitting in the back, surrounded by women, everything had started changing.

She looked inside the tent. They were dancing, eating cake, drinking, and laughing. It looked perfectly safe to return.

Rory had changed his clothes and was now wearing a tuxedo identical to the one his brother had on. After Gray went back to his little blonde, it hadn't taken Rory long to find Roger Plymouth. He was in a corner of the big tent chatting with three pretty girls. Rory motioned for him to come outside.

When they were alone, Roger spoke first. "I thought I saw you in the back hiding behind those people. So you and your brother both are here? What's the occasion? Some royal shindig coming up?"

"We're related to the Kingsleys," Rory said quickly. He didn't have time to make small talk. "Is it true that that bridesmaid Lexie works for you?"

"Yeah," Roger said, and shook his head. "She's a handful. Right now she can't stand me, but I'm working on her. Give me another couple of months and I'll soften her up." He gave a humorless laugh. "But I said that a year ago and I haven't made any progress. A man can dream, can't he?" He narrowed his eyes. "You aren't thinking of going after her, are you?"

Rory knew he'd never get used to the American way of telling everyone everything. "No, not at all."

"I get it," Roger said. "You're asking me about Lex because

your brother is interested in her roommate. I saw the way he was staring at her all through the wedding. At first I thought he was you, but I know you're not going to hang it all out for everybody to see. Your brother stared at her like he was the snake at the end of a flute."

"I think that's a little strong," Rory said stiffly, wanting to protect his brother.

"Yeah, right," Roger said. "I know he's the one who'll be king. I like that country of yours. Best skiing in the world and the food's not bad either. But I think I better warn you that, from what I've heard, he'll have an easier time being king than he will conquering pretty little Toby."

"What does that mean?"

"That half the male population of this island has tried with her. The scuttlebutt is that she's 'saving herself for marriage.'"

"You're saying that she's . . . ?"

"A virgin is what everybody says," Roger said. "Whatever is true, I can tell you that a lot of people like that girl. If your brother decides to go after her just so he can put another notch on his bedpost, many people are going to be angry at him, including Jared Kingsley."

Yesterday Rory would have said that his brother wasn't like that, but today everything seemed to have turned upside down. "My brother wants to stay here on Nantucket for a week and he would like the young lady to spend some time with him, but I fear that her roommate will interfere. She—"

"You don't have to tell me!" Roger said. "You wouldn't believe the things I have to do to make Lexie stay with me. I have to hide things then pretend I've lost them." He grimaced. "She thinks I'm a moron, but if I don't do that, she says 'Toby needs me' and runs off."

"So there's no chance that you could occupy the roommate for just a week? A trip somewhere, maybe?"

"I know she wants to travel and I've asked her to go with

me, but she just laughs. Hey! Maybe I can get my little sister to help. They like each other. When do you need this?"

"Now. Immediately," Rory said.

"I'll try to do it," Roger said, then looked at Rory. "Maybe next time I visit your country I can stay in your house."

A business deal, Rory thought. "We'll put you up in the oldest part of the palace. It's haunted and girls squeal when you take them there."

Roger grimaced. "I wish that would work with Lexie but she'd probably make friends with a ghost. You should hear the Kingsley stories that float around this island!"

Rory had no idea what that meant, but he didn't have time to find out. He had other things to do. He said thanks, they exchanged goodbyes, and they parted.

When Rory went back toward the small tent, he saw that his brother and the young woman were still in there together. The candles inside the tent and the darkness outside made a sort of movie screen in shadow and he could see them clearly. They were leaning toward each other, heads close together, and Graydon was talking with more animation than Rory had ever before seen him use around an outsider. There were very few people Gray relaxed around—and they were all blood relatives. But there he was with the girl he'd just met and moving his hands about as they talked.

But no matter how much his brother liked this girl, there was one thing that Rory knew he absolutely had to do. He must see if she actually could tell the brothers apart. Forget the family legend about people who could tell the Montgomery-Taggert twins one from the other. Rory needed to know the truth.

He'd called his assistant and minutes later he was dressed just like his brother. Quietly, he stood on the sidelines of the party, sipping champagne, while he waited for Graydon's dinner to end—which is where Roger Plymouth found him. With a grin of triumph, Roger said his sister had come up with a way to get Lexie off the island for most of the summer, and as far as he could tell, Lex was going to agree to it. "I had to promise that I wouldn't be there, but I predict that I might break a bone or two and have to recover around them," Roger said, laughing. "This is my chance with Lexie, and I plan to make the most of it. Let's hope that when I stay at your place, she'll be with me."

When Rory went back outside, he was just in time to see Lexie run to the tent where Graydon and Toby were dining, and he heard her excited voice. Rory knew that as soon as his brother heard that Toby's roommate had been called away by her rich playboy boss—a man Rory was likely to know—Graydon would know who had done it. Graydon didn't believe in coincidences, especially not when his brother was nearby.

Sure enough, when Rory's phone buzzed, it was a single word from his brother. NOW! That meant Graydon wanted to talk now. Rory wrote back. I'M AT KINGSLEY HOUSE. MEET ME THERE. Since his brother had sneaked away, leaving all his staff in Maine, that meant he was without transportation. It was a long walk from the site of the wedding, through town, and up Main Street to Kingsley Lane. Even if Graydon got a ride with someone, it would still give Rory time to find out what he needed to know.

He straightened his jacket, put his shoulders back, adjusted his face to the I-am-going-to-be-king expression, and started toward the big tent. He was going to do his best to impersonate his brother.

Chapter Five

Rory saw Toby standing by a large round table full of guests and asking them if they needed anything. He stood to one side and waited for her to finish, as that's what Graydon would do. If he were being himself, Rory would have pulled her onto the dance floor and swept her away. If she protested, he would've kissed her into silence. But that wasn't Graydon's style.

When she turned and saw him she looked a bit startled, but then she gave him a warm smile.

"May I please have the honor of this dance?" he asked with his brother's exaggerated politeness.

"Of course," she answered and took the hand he held out.

Rory reminded himself to stay rigidly straight and distant. He was glad it was a slow dance, as he didn't trust himself to hold back in a fast one. It was the first time he'd been so close to her and she was prettier than he'd thought. A sort of Grace Kelly, with her blue eyes and quiet features. Her makeup was subdued, meant to look like she wore none. He thought that if her eyes were emphasized more and she added some red lipstick, she could be a knockout.

He gently led her in a circle, constantly reminding himself that he was his brother. "I enjoyed our dinner tonight very much."

"Oh?" Toby said, smiling. "And with whom did you eat it?"

"With . . ." It took him a moment to understand what she was saying, then he laughed and relaxed his shoulders. "Did I fool you at all?"

"Not for a second," she said, and the smile left her face. Anger flooded through her blue eyes. "Tell me, did your brother send you in here to test me?"

Immediately, Rory saw his mistake. "No," he said seriously. "Graydon knows nothing about this. I sent him away so I could—"

"Find out if I'm a liar? See whether I'm after something?" Toby's eyes were very angry. "Would you please tell me why the ability to tell you two apart matters?"

Rory avoided that question. "How much did Graydon tell you about himself?"

"That he's to be king, that he's to marry some highborn young woman—at least I assume she's young—and that he wants a bit of peace before then. I promised I'd find him a place to stay while you take over his duties. However, in light of this very unpleasant game of the two of you, I may rethink that offer. I don't like to be on the receiving end of anyone's practical joke."

Rory could feel the blood draining from his face. It looked like his brother had set up everything on his own, but now it seemed possible that Rory was going to ruin it all. He did not want to anger Graydon more than he already had.

"I think I need to tend to the guests," Toby said and started to pull away from him.

But Rory held firmly on to her hand. "Miss Wyndam, please, my brother is innocent in this." He was looking into her eyes and she saw the pleading in them. "Would it help if I explained things to you?"

"Truth would certainly make for a change," she said.

He turned her around in the dance. "I'll tell you, even though it is at my own expense. You're a good dancer."

Toby glared at him. "If you start flirting with me, I'll leave."

"All right," he said, "but first you have to understand that Graydon covers for me because I never live up to anyone's expectations. I seem to have been born with an endless ability to make our parents angry. But then, you see, I don't care if I do. My brother does. In fact, Gray cares about everything. People without homes, injured animals, whether children can read or not. If there's a good cause, Graydon cares about it. So when I'm not where I should be or doing what I shouldn't, he covers for me. My personal opinion is that he should let me take the consequences for my own actions but . . ."

Pausing, Rory took a breath. "The real problem is that my brother cares about me too. But this time his taking of my sins on himself is about to rob him of some time off that he deserves, and that's not fair. Even I have limits."

By the time he'd stopped talking, they were standing still on the dance floor, his arm about her waist, and he waited while she thought about what he'd just said.

"All right," she said at last. "I'll help him."

Rory turned her hand in his and kissed the back of it. "Thank you," he said, then began to move again. Only this time he was himself and there was a lot more energy in his movements.

"You can't dance like this while you're pretending to be him," Toby said, nearly out of breath from following him around and around so fast.

"I know," Rory said. "Do we really look so different to you?"

"Oh, yes." She put her head back a bit. "You two are quite different. His reticence is natural, but yours is forced. And there's a feeling about you that you don't know where you belong. Graydon knows exactly where he fits into the world."

As they moved quickly around the dance floor, the others began to stand back to watch them. Both of them had had a lot of dance lessons and they made a beautiful, graceful couple. "I wanted to protect him from you," he said, "but now I want to protect you." He gave her a look that seemed to come from deep inside. He was no longer laughing or teasing. "Don't fall in love with my brother. He takes his responsibilities very seriously, and no matter how much he loves a woman, he will always put his duties to his country first."

Toby knew what he was saying but she wasn't worried. Graydon was too exotic, too much from a completely different world, for her to even think about loving him. "Do his duties include his soon-to-be princess?"

"Yes, they do."

"What's she like?" Toby asked.

"Tall, beautiful, dark hair and eyes. Intelligent. Her parents hoped she'd get the position, so they've trained her for it since she was a baby."

He spun her out to arm's length, then back.

"Is he deeply in love with her?"

"Answering that would be a betrayal of my brother. You'll have to ask him." He whirled her so her back was to his chest, his arms around her. "But I warn you that he doesn't like personal questions, even from me."

"I've seen that. He tends to freeze up."

When the dance ended, the people around them applauded the performance. Rory gave Toby a bow and she couldn't resist going into a curtsy to him. "Your Royal Highness," she murmured so only he could hear her, and they laughed as he led her off the floor.

"What in the world is going on with the girls?" Victoria asked Jilly as she took a chair beside her. The two women were new friends but they'd bonded strongly after Victoria helped Jilly get together with Ken, the man she loved. "First I hear that Lexie is going away for the rest of the summer, then Toby keeps disappearing and no one can find her, and now she's dancing with that man who I thought she didn't like."

Jilly looked at the beautiful couple on the dance floor. For a while they'd been talking quite seriously, but now they were gliding across the floor as though they were on ice. "I don't know anything about Lexie, but Graydon—whom Toby is dancing with—is a Montgomery, so he's probably skirting around whatever it is that he wants."

"What does that mean as it concerns Toby?" Victoria asked. As usual, she looked quite dazzling. Her auburn hair and emerald eyes were set off by her green silk suit—and she couldn't stop looking at Dr. Huntley, who was dancing with her daughter, Alix. Victoria was sure that she'd never been happier in her life.

Jilly waved her hand. "It's nothing, just a family joke." When Victoria stared at her, she continued. "In our family there are Montgomerys and there are Taggerts. I'm a Taggert, and according to my brother Michael, we're honest, forthright, courageous, and brave, while the Montgomerys are . . ." She shrugged.

Victoria frowned. "Slimy as snakes? I don't like that. Toby is a sweet girl." She started to get up but Jilly put her hand on her arm.

"No," Jilly said, "it's okay. Graydon won't do anything bad. He'll just take forever to get around to whatever he's after, that's all."

"And you think that what he wants is Toby?" Victoria was still frowning.

Jilly sighed. "I'm not sure, but he seems to be so curious about her that he's planning to stay on Nantucket for a while. You see, Toby can tell the twins apart, and in our family that's important. Too important, if you ask me."

Victoria was an internationally bestselling writer and she loved a good story. Her lovely face smoothed out and she leaned back against her chair. "Now you have to tell me everything."

"It's nothing," Jilly said. "It's just a family saying. Whoever can tell the twins apart is supposedly a person's True Love."

Victoria didn't reply but looked across the room at Toby and the very handsome young man she was dancing with. Around them people were beginning to stand aside to watch, but Toby and the man seemed oblivious. "Have I seen him somewhere before? He looks familiar."

"You may have seen Graydon's photo in some magazines."

"Is he an actor?" Victoria asked.

"Sort of. He's the Crown Prince of Lanconia."

Turning, Victoria looked at Jilly with an expression Jilly couldn't quite read. "Are you saying that the prince has an identical twin brother and Toby can tell them apart? And that she can tell one from the other is supposed to be a sign of True Love?"

"Yes," Jilly said cautiously. She didn't know Victoria very well, but Ken said he thought Victoria had been behind this entire wedding, that it had all come about due to her efforts. Well, actually Ken had said, "Victoria's underhanded, devious, conniving interference," but then he used to be married to her so he was allowed some exaggeration.

"Why are you looking as though you disapprove?" Victoria asked.

"I know it's silly but what if that legend is true? What if Graydon and pretty little Toby fall in love? Then what? His mother is a terror and she'd never allow the marriage. And even if she did, how could Toby give up all privacy to go live in a foreign country to be a princess? I've been there several times and the isolated way Graydon lives isn't something I'd want. And his daily work schedule is a killer!"

Victoria was looking at Jilly in consideration. "Maybe being in love would make his life easier."

"I don't think—" Jilly began, but then shook her head. "Who am I to judge? Because I wouldn't like the job doesn't mean no one would."

"Where is the prince booked to stay tonight?"

"He's with the young man who picked him up at the airport."

"Wes?" Victoria asked, horror in her voice.

Jilly didn't know the man but she followed Victoria's glance to the back of the tent. In the darkest corner, behind a table, Jared's cousin was wrapped around a very pretty young woman, and they were kissing more deeply than should be done in public. They were a living illustration of the phrase "get a room."

Abruptly, Victoria stood up and looked down at Jilly. "I believe in True Love," she said, her face quite serious, "and if there's a possibility of it, I think a person should find out. I feel that it's my duty to help this along."

"You'll tell me everything?" Jilly asked.

"Oh, yes," Victoria said. "You've taken that poor-miserable-me look off Ken's face, a look he believes that I gave him, so I owe you." She made her way through the crowd.

"Darling," Victoria said as she slipped her arm through Toby's as she left the dance floor. Toby was still a bit breathless. "Whatever is going on with you and those two delicious young men?"

Toby looked toward the tent door and saw Princes Graydon and Rory standing together, both of them wearing tuxedos and looking quite handsome. Right now Rory looked as though he feared his brother might hit him, and Graydon was looking as though he just might do it. Since she had an idea this was about her, Toby had an urge to start giggling. "It's just boy stuff," she said as she turned back to Victoria. "Nothing important."

Victoria lowered her voice and put her face near Toby's. "In this case, it seems to be the battle of the princes. Can you really tell those two apart?"

"Yes," Toby said, and she didn't ask how Victoria knew who the young men were. "But I don't see what difference that makes." She changed the subject. "Are you having a good time?"

"Marvelous," Victoria said, squeezing Toby's arm. "You did a truly wonderful job and no one can thank you enough. In fact, I want you to plan my wedding."

Toby looked at Victoria with wide eyes. Victoria was a very famous person, with a great many equally famous friends. She wouldn't want a wedding with bouquets of what looked to be wildflowers hanging from the top of tent walls. Victoria would want crystal chandeliers and orchids flown in from Hawaii, Kobe beef from Japan, and—

"Toby!" Victoria said. "Come back to earth!"

Toby tried to refocus, but she still couldn't speak properly. "I . . . I can't . . ."

"Of course you can, dear," Victoria said. "I must be married in my daughter's chapel, and since it's here on Nantucket, that's where I'll be married." Her daughter, Alix, was an architect, and fresh out of school, she had designed the perfect little chapel. Her father, Ken, and Jared, both builders as well as architects, had finished it in time for the wedding.

Toby was beginning to recover herself. "You'll want more than I know how to do."

"Nonsense!" Victoria said. "Toby, dearest, you just need to dream big, that's all. And believe in yourself."

"What kind of wedding do you want?" Toby asked softly, even as she told herself that she should firmly and irrevocably say no to this.

"I'll leave that to you. You're clever, so come up with a theme. I'd help you, but I'm months late on my next book, so think of something and I'm sure I'll love it."

Toby had a vision of presenting thirty-one possible wedding themes to Victoria and her turning them all down. "I think you need a professional at this. I've done just this wedding, so I'm not—"

"Did you know that your prince is spending the night at Wes Drayton's house?" Victoria nodded toward the far end of the tent to the two people who were kissing with so much enthusiasm that they were sliding out of their chairs. "Oh, good! Jared is going over there to break them up. Have you ever seen the tiny two-bedroom bungalow Wes lives in? I do hope your prince can sleep tonight. I wouldn't want him to go back to his own kingdom— Where is it?"

"Lanconia."

"Oh, yes. I've been there. Lovely place. They mine some metal the U.S. needs to keep the country running. But I'm sure diplomatic relations won't be hurt because the future king spent a night listening to . . . well, to fornication. The prince has probably heard it before. Well, dear, I have to go." Victoria released Toby's arm and turned away. "Oh, and Toby, dearest child, the wedding has to be by the last day of August. My Nantucket friends leave the island at the start of September and I want them all to come. That's just over two months away, so let me see your plans as soon as possible. Oh!" Her fiancé had taken her hand and was pulling her toward the dance floor. "Eager, isn't he?" Victoria said to Toby, who was still unable to speak.

"What are you up to?" Dr. F. Caleb Huntley said as soon as he had Victoria in his arms.

"Why, nothing at all."

"Don't give me that," Caleb said. "Toby is as white as a new sail. You knocked the wind out of her."

"I just gave her a little project, that's all. Lexie is going to be away and Toby's going to need help, so . . ." Victoria smiled as Caleb waltzed her across the floor.

"What does that mean?"

"I'm going to see if I can get her some help," Victoria said. "It may not be exactly what she thinks she needs but it will be there."

Caleb was looking at her hard. He knew the woman he loved very well. While her schemes always had good intentions, sometimes they backfired. "What did you ask Toby to do?"

Victoria was looking over his shoulder at the two princes, who were by the doorway. They seemed to have finished their discussion, as one was leaving and the other one was heading toward Toby, who still hadn't moved.

"What did you say?" Victoria asked.

"Your project," Caleb said. "What have you asked Toby to do?"

"Oh, that. I want her to plan our wedding. I do hope you don't mind, but I told her that we had to be married by the end of August." She looked at him in question. Since the two of them hadn't so much as mentioned marriage, maybe she should have consulted him first.

"The end of August?" Caleb asked, frowning.

Victoria stopped dancing and looked at him in silence.

"Why so far away? Why not tomorrow?" he said, and Victoria's laugh echoed around the room as he whirled her in his arms.

Chapter Six

"Miss Wyndam," Graydon said when he reached Toby, "I fear that I owe you yet another apology. My excuse for not intercepting my brother is that he said he would meet me at Kingsley House. I was halfway there before I realized what he was planning to do." He was looking at her, but Toby was staring straight ahead at the people on the dance floor. "Has something happened?" he asked.

Toby tried to bring her mind back to the present. "I need to learn to say no."

"Please tell me you aren't referring to my brother."

What Victoria said had shocked Toby so much she had no idea what Graydon was talking about. She looked at him but didn't see him.

"Come with me," he said as he took her arm and led her to

the door. As they passed the buffet table, he picked up a bottle of water and an empty champagne flute.

He led her through the people and into the cool night air, neither of them speaking. They walked far enough away that the music and noise were in the background. A fallen tree blocked their path. Graydon took off his jacket, draped it across the log, and nodded for Toby to sit down.

"Your jacket will get dirty."

"That's not important," he said.

Toby wanted to sit down in the cool darkness but the seat was a little high for her.

"May I?" He was holding out his hands toward her waist.

She nodded and he put his hands on her waist and lifted her to sit on his jacket. He opened the bottle, filled the glass, and handed it to her.

Gratefully, she drank half of it and handed the glass back to him. "Would you mind?" He nodded toward the log.

"Please do."

Graydon took a seat next to her. "If my brother didn't upset you, what did?"

"Victoria wants me to plan a wedding for her."

"I can understand that. You did a splendid job on this one."

"But Victoria is a famous author! You may not have heard of her in your country, but in America, Victoria Madsen is quite well known."

"Of course I've heard of her. My grandmother reads all her books and I think maybe my father does too. Why would planning another wedding bother you?"

"She'll want something grand, something beyond perfect. She told me to come up with a theme and I don't know how to do that."

"A theme? You mean have everyone dress in costumes?"

"I guess only the bridal party would, but all the decorations would follow through on it. Like having seashells running down the center of the table, except that Victoria would never want anything that mundane. She'd want . . . I have no idea what would please her."

"How about a Lanconian theme? All the men could wear bearskins and carry spears, and the women would wear short tunics with a quiver of arrows on their backs."

For a moment Toby looked at him like he'd lost his mind, but then she smiled. "I'm sure Victoria would love to dress like that, but can you imagine some of those men in bearskins?"

"Big bearskins," he said. "Maybe grizzlies."

"What food would we serve?"

"Whole roasted goats."

Toby was starting to forget her anxiety. "Will we have a jousting match?"

"We could have an Honorium. That's where the women fight each other and the winner marries the king. In this case I guess it would be the groom."

"No one would dare go against Victoria. Was that a real event?"

"Oh, yes," Graydon said. "In my country, that's how a king got a wife. Until King Lorcan stopped it, that is. He was won by a woman who was so ugly that he couldn't . . . Well, they never had any children."

Toby smiled. "You're making this up."

"I'm not. There was only one Honorium after that, and that's when the beautiful Jura won Rowan the Great. It was a love match and they had six children, who married into the different tribes. The kids finally fulfilled their father's dream of uniting the tribes into one country."

Smiling, Toby looked at him. "You're making me feel better, but I still think I should say no to Victoria's offer. I'll wait until Lexie decides on a boyfriend, or maybe your aunt and Ken will get married. Those weddings will be smaller and I can handle them—if they ask me, that is."

"Aunt Jilly is a Taggert."

"What does that mean?"

"The Taggerts are a big, loud, rambunctious family and most of them will descend on Nantucket for the wedding. You'll have to deal with eighteen to twenty little girls. The ones that carry the baskets?"

"Flower girls?"

"Yes. And Aunt Jilly has many brothers and sisters, and they all have produced many more Taggerts. To accommodate that family, you'll have to evacuate most of the residents of Nantucket or the island might sink under the weight of the Taggerts."

"So Jilly's wedding wouldn't be easier?" She was trying not to laugh.

"Have you seen the Taggert men? Each one will eat an entire cow. You'll have to dock an aircraft carrier beside the island just to bring in enough food for one Taggert meal."

Toby couldn't hold in her laughter any longer. "You make them sound like trolls."

"And who do you think Tolkien modeled his characters on?"

Toby laughed so hard that Graydon handed her the water glass and she drained it. "Okay, I do feel better. I can do this, can't I?"

"Of course," he said as he looked at the moonlight on her hair. Rory said that she'd known who he was the second she saw him. When they were dressed alike, with Rory doing his annoying imitation of Graydon, Graydon couldn't believe anyone could tell them apart. But this young woman had.

Graydon's face changed to serious. "Did my brother's charade cause you any difficulties?"

"No," she said. "After the first few moments, he was quite pleasant." She looked at Graydon. "He loves you very much."

Graydon was glad for the darkness that hid the redness of his face. "I asked him not to bother you."

"He was just looking out for you," she said. "He warned me of your sense of duty."

"I'm sure he exaggerated everything."

"Perhaps," she said as she slid to the ground. Graydon immediately stood beside her and put his jacket on. "I better go back in," she said. "It's getting late and people are beginning to leave. And I need to find a place for you to stay tonight."

"I told you that I have a bed for tonight."

"At Wes's house," Toby said, "but I don't think that's a good idea." She turned away but then looked back at him. "What metal does your country have that mine needs?"

"Vanadium," he said. "It's for hardening steel, among other uses. Who was talking about vanadium at a wedding?"

"Actually, it was Victoria. She seems to think that if you have to spend a night at Wes's house, it will be so horrible that your country will stop exporting to mine."

Graydon started to say that was absurd but he didn't. "Where did Victoria suggest that I stay?"

"She didn't, but Jared said I should put you on the pullout couch in my upstairs sitting room."

Years of practice at hiding his emotions was the only way Graydon could keep from bursting out that Jared was his new favorite relative. For all his bravado of saying he wanted to remain on Nantucket, being utterly alone was not something he relished. He didn't say a word, just waited for Toby's decision.

"Lexie will be there, so I guess one night will be all right. Tomorrow I'll find you somewhere else to stay."

"I thank you for your generosity," he said and gave her a small bow.

"I rather like these Lanconian manners," Toby said.

He held out his arm to her. "May I escort you back?"

"Only if you promise to attack any grizzlies we encounter with your vanadium-hardened steel sword."

Graydon smiled. "I swear it on my honor as a prince of the realm."

Laughing together, they walked back to the tent. After they parted, Graydon stayed outside and called his brother. "I want every piece of clothing you brought with you. Find out where Toby lives—somewhere on Kingsley Lane—and put everything in her upstairs sitting room."

"That was fast work," Rory said. "I hope you understand that if you hurt this girl, a lot of people are going to be angry at you. Montgomerys, Taggerts, Kingsleys, everybody. Why don't you take this week and go to Vegas instead? You could—"

"The plane back to Maine will be ready for you at six tomorrow morning. And remember that the fewer Lanconians who know about this exchange the better. You think you can do this?"

"Sure," Rory said. "The question is whether you can handle it."

"Don't worry about me." He paused. "Thank you. This means a lot to me. And Rory?"

"Yes?"

"Thanks for whatever you said to Toby about me."

"I only told her the truth." Rory hesitated. "I have a question that I need answered to be able to pull this off." He took a breath. "Are you and Danna lovers?"

Graydon was glad his brother couldn't see the smile on his face. He had to work to sound offended. "By Naos! Cut out your tongue! I've never touched her."

"Yeah?" Rory said. "I mean, that's only right, but I thought maybe the two of you had . . . Anyway, I needed to know."

"Keep it formal with her," Graydon said. "The truth is that I rarely see her, certainly not in private. Maybe you could put in a good word for me, like you did with Toby."

"Possibly," Rory said.

Graydon could feel his brother's grin even through the phone. "If you need any help with anything, let me know. And Lorcan will always be with you."

"Sure," Rory said, and for a moment the two brothers held their phones in silence.

They'd never before done an exchange on this scale. They hadn't discussed the repercussions if their parents found out or if the Lanconian nation discovered what the brothers were doing.

There could possibly be legal ramifications. If nothing else, there would be the extreme embarrassment to the throne of Lanconia.

"Good luck," Graydon said.

"Same to you," Rory answered. "And I'll take good care of Danna. She won't suspect a thing."

"Thanks," Graydon said, and they clicked off, but he didn't move. He well knew that his brother was in love with Danna. The way he looked at her, the way he was silent when Danna was around, hadn't been difficult to see. For Graydon's part, he would have gladly stepped aside and let Rory have her, but he couldn't do that.

For all that he spoke of wanting a holiday, the truth was that Graydon needed to do a lot of thinking. Country or brother? was his dilemma. If he didn't marry Danna there would be a huge uproar in his country. To toss her aside to his younger brother would cause anger and deep resentment.

The truth was that he could see no solution that didn't involve his abdication—and even that would solve nothing. Rory would be put on the throne in his place, and his brother would hate being king.

Right now, the best Graydon could do was give his brother this week with Danna. Maybe during that time something would happen, or Graydon would figure out a solution.

He'd been lucky with this girl, Toby. Her ability to tell him from his brother fascinated him. Was it all physical? Some body language the men couldn't disguise?

Whatever her abilities, she was certainly a kind and generous young woman and he deeply appreciated her help. He'd already decided that he was going to do all that he could to be allowed to stay with her rather than get dumped into a hotel room.

Peace and calm so he could think about his problems: That was his goal. Toby laughed at his jokes and he enjoyed her company. And it might be pleasant to involve himself in her life for the short time he had on this pretty island.

At least that's what he told himself. Actually, the young woman confused him. He still didn't understand why he'd struck out at his brother over her. Didn't know why he'd been so angry when he realized that Rory had sent him away so he could test whether the girl really could tell them apart. Maybe it was some genetic throwback to when Lanconian men wore bearskins and carried swords and fought over women.

That thought made him smile. He'd loved making Toby laugh about his ancestors. In fact, making her laugh was already becoming one of his favorite things to do.

He put his phone in his pocket and walked back to the tent. People were leaving and he saw Toby going from one person to another and making sure they'd had a good time. They were taking away boxes of food and cake and smiling at her.

He had a feeling that if someone didn't step in and physically remove her, she might stay there all night. He could imagine her there at three A.M. making sure the place was clean.

Maybe for the next week, when he didn't have a country and army and charities to look after, he could take care of one overworked young lady.

Smiling, he stepped into the tent.

Chapter Seven

Graydon had to practically drag Toby from the wedding. As the people left, she began to clean up trash, fold empty chairs, and set centerpiece flower arrangements on one table. Tomorrow they'd be picked up by a local charity. But Graydon caught her arm and pulled her away. "You need to get some rest," he said. "My aunt and Ken are going to give us a ride to your house."

"But I have to—"

"It can be done in the morning and I'll help you," he said.

The idea of a crown prince on garbage detail almost made her laugh, but it would be rude to say so. Besides, now that the band was gone and the guests were leaving, Toby felt the tiredness that she'd been fighting. For days she'd been working on adrenaline and little else. Tonight, if it hadn't been for Graydon, she wouldn't have had any dinner.

"All right," she said. "I'm ready to go."

He motioned toward the tent door, where Jilly and Ken were waiting for them. Jilly looked from Graydon to Toby and back again, but she said nothing.

As soon as Ken started the engine, Toby fell asleep in the back of the big SUV, and her head leaned against Graydon's shoulder. When he put his hand on her cheek to steady her, she snuggled closer to him.

Jilly turned in the front seat and looked at Toby, then at Graydon. She couldn't quite keep the frown off her face.

"Trust me," Graydon said softly. "I won't hurt her."

Jilly turned back around and Ken squeezed her hand. Minutes later, they stopped in front of a small house.

"This is it," Jilly said, looking back at them. "Maybe Ken should—"

"Oh! I think I fell asleep," Toby said as the car light came on, and she sat up straight.

"You're exhausted," Ken said as he got out and opened the door for Toby. He put his hands on her arms. "I can't thank you enough for today. You did a wonderful job. Everything was perfect."

"Victoria wants me to plan a wedding for her and Dr. Huntley," Toby blurted out.

"Does she?" Ken said, and he knew Toby was warning him. Sometimes men reacted strangely about the remarriage of their ex-wives. "I'm glad for her," he said, "and you'll do a great job." Bending, he kissed her cheek and whispered, "Will you plan my wedding to Jilly? Our secret? At least until I ask her."

Toby nodded.

Ken got back in the car, Toby waved to Jilly, and they drove away. She turned to Graydon. It was dark around them, with only the porch light on. "Mind if we go around to the back? The front stairs lead past Lexie's bedroom and I don't want to wake her."

"I'll follow you," Graydon said.

They went around the far side and there were only a few feet between the house and the fence. A narrow stone path went between shrubs and flowers and a couple of small overhanging trees. At the end, the vista opened up to reveal the shadows of what looked to be several raised beds full of flowers, a greenhouse, and a tall ironwork gazebo. It was all lit very subtly, with soft golden spots that made the garden look like a place of enchantment.

"This is beautiful," Graydon said. "Did you design this?"

"Heavens, no! Jared did. Lexie and I had to nag him for months but he did it."

"I can see why he's famous."

Toby opened the back door to the house and they stepped inside. She switched on the light by the door and he saw a very pleasant—and very old—room. The ceiling was low. Another few inches and his head would graze the overhead beams. White plaster was between them. There were some built-in cupboards that he guessed to be original. "Early 1700s?" he asked.

"Yes," Toby said, pleased by his knowledge. "Jared bought the house with his first commission as an architect and he restored it on weekends. He's a firm believer of 'gut fish, not houses.' "

"What does that mean?"

"Nantucket's historical commission is fierce on keeping the exteriors of the old houses intact, but you can tear out the inside and replace it with anything you want, even if that means stainless steel and Plexiglass."

"I take it you like the old things?"

"Yes," Toby said, "I do." She started up the stairs with Graydon behind her.

"My favorite part of my house was built in the 1200s," he said. "I even found some furniture from then. It has a lot of sword cuts on it."

"That vanadium certainly is useful."

"It is, or else my ancestors were bad marksmen. 'Brocan! Strike your fellow Lanconian, not the table.' "

Toby laughed. At the top of the stairs, she pointed to a door and whispered, "Lexie is sleeping in there."

Graydon nodded. They turned the corner and saw a pile of luggage left by Rory.

"My goodness," Toby said softly as she looked at the stack, four high, three deep. It took up half the wall against the stairs. There were two leather cases big enough to transport a person, several duffel bags, a couple of attaché cases, three thick garment bags, and things on the bottom that she couldn't see.

"My brother doesn't travel lightly," Graydon said.

"What about you? What do you usually travel with?"

"Half an army," he said with a grimace.

She looked at him. "How did you get away?"

"By lying. Right now all my staff except for my head bodyguard believe I'm locked away with a highly contagious virus. One of my Montgomery doctor cousins verified it. If I'm found out, it won't be pleasant."

"You risked all that just to come to a wedding?"

"It was more to get away from scrutiny for a few days." He smiled, his eyes having a faraway look. "But to think of an entire week! It's more than I thought possible and it's all because of your extreme generosity. I can never thank you enough."

Toby was a bit embarrassed by his praise.

"I can certainly never fully repay you," he said, his voice soft and so low it was more of a feeling than a sound.

Toby realized that it was turning into an awkward moment. A very attractive man, the dim light . . . "Invite me to your wedding," she said.

"I would be honored. Front row?"

"Perfect," she answered. The reminder of who and what he was cleared the air. He helped to remove the cushions from the big old couch and pull out the bed. They halted once when it let out a loud squeak, but it was silent behind Lexie's door so they continued. There were clean sheets on the bed, and Toby got a couple of blankets out of the closet.

"Sorry, but you and I share a bathroom," she said. "Lexie has a private one, but mine opens into this room."

"I spent three years in the Royal Guard and I shared the baths with hundreds of men."

"I hope I'm not quite as bad as that," Toby said.

Graydon's instinct was to say something flirtatious, flattering, but he didn't. He didn't want to ruin this before it started. He'd made promises to his brother and to his aunt Jilly, and he meant to keep them.

"All right," she said when the bed was ready. "I'll go first." She nodded toward the bathroom.

"Of course," he said politely.

Toby took a shower, washed away all the sprays and foams the hairdresser had put into her hair for the wedding, and scrubbed the layers of makeup off her face. She took longer than she meant to, but it felt good to get clean. She dried off, then put on lots of moisturizer and a freshly laundered nightgown.

She wasn't sure what to do next. What was the proper way to tell a prince that the bathroom was free? She told herself she was being ridiculous. Prince or not, he was still a human being. She opened the door into the sitting room a bit and looked out.

He was sitting in the old wing chair in a far corner of the room. The reading lamp was on and he had a book open. It was one of Nat Philbrick's exciting nonfiction accounts of Nantucket.

Toby didn't say anything, but looked at Graydon. Even when he was alone he sat up very straight, and even though he'd removed his jacket, his shirt was buttoned almost to the collar.

At first glance, he seemed very formal, but there was something about him that made her able to imagine him with a rough fur thrown across his shoulders and wielding a heavy sword. Maybe it was what his brother had said about Graydon doing anything for his country. If saving it meant brandishing a sword, that's what he'd do.

He looked up at her, as though he'd known she was watching him, and smiled.

"Bathroom is yours," Toby said, and she went into her bedroom before he could see her red face. How awful it must be for him to have people staring, she thought.

She got into bed and was asleep instantly.

Chapter Eight

*I*n spite of Lexie's excitement about going to the south of France for the rest of the summer, last night she'd slept like she was half dead. Maybe it was all the champagne and how, when she got home, she'd run up and down the stairs about a hundred times as she packed. Whatever it was, when she fell into bed, she was out of it. She vaguely remembered hearing Toby in the sitting room and the creak of the old sofa bed being pulled open. It looked like someone was spending the night. Lexie didn't think any more about it and went back to sleep.

This morning, she got out of bed and went into her bathroom. It was barely daylight and she was to meet her boss at the airport at seven. They were flying out on his private jet—her first time on it.

In the summer, the little Nantucket airport looked like a parking lot for private jets.

There were so many smaller ones by the fence that they looked common, like something every family had. The big ones were parked farther back on the tarmac. There was a saying about the two big islands off Cape Cod: The millionaires went to Martha's Vineyard and the billionaires went to Nantucket. Her boss, Roger Plymouth, fit into the second category.

The upstairs of the small house they rented from her cousin Jared was meant to be three bedrooms, two baths, but Toby and Lexie had scoured Kingsley attics until they found the furniture needed to convert the middle bedroom into a sitting room with an office. Now and then they allowed someone to sleep over on the old couch's pullout bed.

She heard the shower running in Toby's bathroom, and Lexie was glad her friend was awake, as she wanted to say goodbye to her. She felt bad about leaving Toby with the garden to take care of, but last night Jared had assured her that he'd find someone to help.

As Lexie put paste on her toothbrush, she thought how she was going to miss Nantucket in the summer. The light, the salt-filled air, the sunsets, cursing at the tourists who never looked where they were going—she would miss it all.

Most of all, she was going to miss Toby. Right now Lexie wanted to hear every word about that private dinner at the wedding. Candles and champagne and Nantucket bay scallops. What little Lexie had seen of it had been beautiful. She wondered if Toby—

Suddenly, she accidentally knocked her drinking glass off the counter. It hit the tile floor and shattered, sending slivers of glass all over her feet. "Damnation!" she said loudly.

"Don't move," said a male voice and she looked up to see the most extraordinary sight. The man Toby had dined with last night was standing at her bathroom door—and he was wearing only a small white towel tied above his left hip. On that side he was nude from stem to stern, from foot to head.

"I apologize for my dishabille," he said, "but if you move you'll cut your feet."

Lexie couldn't have moved if she'd been told a bomb had been planted. Since the man she worked for was considered "beautiful" and often ran around half dressed, she would have said that a nearly naked man wouldn't affect her. But this man had a body like an Olympic athlete, with lean muscle and no fat on him. And there was something different about him, as though he might do the unexpected at any moment. Throw a woman over his shoulder and carry her off?

Lexie stood there, immobile, toothbrush in hand, and stared down at him as he began to pick up pieces of glass. The open side of the towel showed quite a long stretch of honey-colored skin. His garment made her think of a Native American loincloth.

Looking up through thick dark lashes, he nodded toward the box of tissues beside her. She pulled out a few and handed them to him.

"There, that should do it," he said as he slowly came up from the floor. Lexie was presented with his bare chest inches from her face. Abs you could count, pecs like steel, and very little hair until the line that disappeared down into the towel.

She just stood there staring.

He put the broken glass in the trash bin, then turned and smiled at her. "Shall I make breakfast for you before you go?"

All Lexie could do was nod and he left the room, his long legs striding out.

It took her a moment to recover. It wasn't every day of your life that you broke a glass and a nearly naked man of mythical beauty appeared out of nowhere and rescued you.

Turning, she saw herself in the mirror, toothpaste foam on her lips, her hair a disheveled mess, and wearing an old T-shirt that she'd stolen from Jared. Yet he'd looked at her like she was a princess in a satin gown.

"Toby," she said into the mirror, "you are in way, way over your head."

"Good morning," Lexie said as she entered the kitchen. He was standing by the stove and it had three pans on it, each one sizzling, and the smell was divine.

"*Tavar nuway,*" he said. "That's 'good morning' in Lanconian."

"I knew that," she said, joking, as she stepped farther into the room. She was very aware that this man would someday be a king. And she was even more aware of her vision of him in a teeny tiny towel.

Graydon smiled. "Somehow, I doubt that. Few people can even find my country on a map, but I understand. We're buried in the mountains and overshadowed by some major world powers." He glanced at the stove. "I didn't know what you like to eat, so I have eggs, bacon, and griddle cakes."

"I like anything I don't have to cook," Lexie said, still staring at him. He was wearing dark blue trousers that looked like they came from a hand-tailoring shop in London and a tan shirt that had initials on the cuff: RM. "Where did you learn to cook?"

He piled a plate high and motioned her through the kitchen. There was a little sunporch on the back of the house. It was a pretty room—or would be if she and Toby didn't use it for storage. But this man had cleared a place in the corner by the kitchen, removed all the bags and boxes off the table, and set it with the good china they kept in the top cabinets.

"When did you do all this?" she asked in astonishment.

"I don't sleep much, so I came down early. This is a nice room."

"It is," Lexie said. "But Toby and I each have two jobs so we tend to dump things in here."

"What are your second jobs?"

"That," she said, nodding out the window to the greenhouse and the raised beds. She looked at the single plate he'd put on the table. "You aren't eating? Or maybe you want to wait for Toby."

"I would be pleased to join you," he said and went to the kitchen to fill a plate. He sat down across from her. "I apologize for this morning. I heard the glass breaking followed by your exclamation. I feared there would be cut arteries."

"No, just feet in danger. Thank you for rescuing me."

"My pleasure," he said.

"I think I'm the one with the pleasure," she said with her eyebrows raised.

He glanced at her across the table and his eyes were so warm that Lexie felt like fanning herself. But she didn't. Instead, she frowned. "I don't know what you have in mind with Toby, but I'd better warn you that she isn't one to fool around with some man just to have a good time."

Graydon's face changed in an instant. He went from hot to an expression so remote, so reserved, that Lexie began to doubt what she'd seen. "Miss Wyndam has been nothing but a friend to me and it will stay that way. I'm here for a short time, then I must return to my own country and resume my responsibilities. I would never be so crass as to cause problems for the young woman who has been so helpful to me."

As Lexie chewed, she thought about what he'd said in his very formal manner. "You hurt Toby and I'll tell the newspapers."

"Fair enough," he said, and between them passed an understanding. "Would you like more eggs?"

"No, thanks. All this tastes great. So where did you learn to cook?"

"In the Lanconian Royal Guard. It's our army, navy, and air

force combined—not that we have many ships or planes. But I served for three years, and my loyal subjects thought it was a great joke to give me the lowliest jobs and the hardest training."

"To see what you're made of?"

"Precisely. One of the tasks assigned to me was to cook for a hundred or more guardsmen at a time. It became a challenge to prove that I could do it, so I learned quickly—and I found that I rather enjoyed cooking. When I got home I wandered down to the kitchens and started asking questions. I'm quite good at stuffing game birds."

She took a bite of one of his griddle cakes. It was delicious and also unusual, as if a liqueur had been added. "You almost make me sorry I'm leaving—for more reasons than one." At her flirty tone, he gave her a cool, polite smile. She didn't have to be told that there would never be anything between the two of them. He'd never look at her as he had at Toby in the tent the night before. There was a knock on the front door. "That's the car for me."

"Is your luggage upstairs?"

"Yes," she said. "Would you mind asking the driver to wait for a moment? I want to tell Toby goodbye." When she stood up, he did too. He went toward the front door and Lexie ran up the stairs.

She paused for a moment to stare at the mountain of luggage against the wall. It looked like the prince planned to stay for months, not just a week.

It was dark in Toby's bedroom and she was buried deep under the covers. "Hey!" Lexie said as she sat down on the side of the bed, and Toby rolled over and opened her eyes. "I'm about to leave and I wanted to say goodbye."

Toby put a pillow behind her and rubbed the sleep from her eyes. "Already? I haven't adjusted to the idea of your being away."

"I know," Lexie said, "and I'm eaten up with guilt over it. Maybe I should stay and—"

"Miss out on the opportunity of a lifetime so you can help me cut flowers? Sure. That makes a lot of sense, and Nelson will be ecstatic."

Lexie laughed. "I'm going to miss you so much!"

They hugged for a moment, then Lexie pulled back. "What are you going to do with this prince?"

"I have no idea," Toby said. "It's like being asked to babysit a two-hundred-pound infant."

"Infant he is not and I don't think he's helpless at all."

"You know what I mean."

"Toby, this guy is very smooth, and he's sexy beyond belief. Roger is pretty, but he doesn't smolder."

"What are you talking about? Smolder? Graydon? What in the world have you been reading? He's a nice man who dedicates his life to his country. The truth is that I feel a bit sorry for him."

"I don't think he needs anyone's sympathy. I know you made a vow to wait until you're married before you get into bed with a man, but things happen."

"I still feel the same way," Toby said. "It's just a personal choice."

"True, but men have a way of changing a woman's mind. Broken glass and towels that barely close—and 'barely' is the key word here—can make a woman rethink any and all vows."

"What happened between you two to make you say these things?"

"Nothing. Not really. It's just that when it comes to men you're an innocent."

"I'm not as young or as innocent as you think."

"Toby, I'm saying that you should have a good time with him. A great time even. In my opinion, it's okay to forget your self-imposed vow and spend every minute in bed with him. I have a feeling that he would give you a very good time. But don't—whatever you do—do not fall in love with him."

"Of course I won't. There's no future for us. And I don't plan to get into bed with anyone."

"I wish I could stay and talk about this but I have to go." Lexie stood up. "Email me every day?"

"Yes," Toby said and got out of bed to hug her friend again. "Now go! I need to get dressed and feed the prince. What do you think he eats? Hummingbird tongues?"

Lexie didn't smile. "I think you're going to be surprised by him. By now he's probably cleaned up the basement and the attic."

"You have to write me about what happened between you two."

"I will," Lexie said, then left the room. She wasn't surprised to see that her four suitcases were gone. She had no doubt that the prince had carried them downstairs. "Tell me everything that happens!" Lexie said loudly.

"I will," Toby called through the doorway. "Every word."

Downstairs, Graydon was waiting for Lexie by the front door with her jacket over his arm.

"Let me guess. My bags are in the car."

"They are," Graydon said.

"You know, I thought my boss was slick but you're much worse. Tone down the charm, will you?"

Graydon didn't smile but his eyes were twinkling. "I play the lute."

Lexie groaned. "I don't know whether to pity Toby or envy her. Just promise me that when you leave she'll be smiling."

"That I can promise," Graydon said, and kissed her forehead in a brotherly way. "I'll take care of her."

"That's what I'm afraid of," Lexie said as she went to the waiting car.

When Toby got downstairs it was already late. She'd meant to be back at last night's wedding site by now, as there was a lot to oversee and do. The kitchen smelled very good. Roger probably sent food for Lexie, she thought. Toby looked around for the prince but didn't see him, but then she glanced through the window and a movement outside caught her eye. He was wandering around in the back garden, looking at the beds of flowers.

"He probably has a dozen gardeners who work for him," she said aloud, then went to the stove and helped herself to one of the warm pancakes. They were unusual: small, and they seemed to have oatmeal in them. The flavor was of some fruit that she didn't recognize. It was truly delicious.

"Good morning."

She turned to see Graydon standing in the doorway, and for the first time she noticed the sunroom. It had been completely cleared out! Only the table and chairs remained and she was surprised to see a built-in seat against the far wall.

"Wow!" Toby said. "I guess Lexie really was feeling guilty if she cleaned up this room before she left. It looks great, doesn't it?"

"It does," he said.

"Sorry," Toby said. "I've forgotten my manners. Good morning." She looked him up and down, and saw that he was dressed as though for a garden party, while she had on an old pair of cotton pants and an even older T-shirt. Whatever was she going to do with him today? And since nearly everyone she knew was off-island, how was she going to find a more permanent place for him to stay?

"Did you try these pancakes?" she asked. "They're really good. I'll have to ask Roger where he got them."

"I did have some," he said. "Are you planning to go to the chapel site this morning?"

"I have to."

"I was wondering because it seems that your car was exchanged." He pulled back a curtain to show Jared's old red pickup in the narrow drive beside the house.

"Oh, no!" Toby said. "I bet Wes did this. He was taking people to the airport and the ferry this morning, so he'd need the extra seats. But he knows I have to clean up. Now what am I supposed to drive?"

"You weren't left the keys to the truck?"

"I'm sure they're in there, but it's a standard shift and I can only drive an automatic. Maybe Ken can help."

"I'll drive you," Graydon said.

"You? But you said you didn't know how to drive."

"I said I wasn't cognizant of all the road signs, but I have driven a few larger vehicles. Besides, I told you that I'd help you clean."

Toby hesitated. "You're not exactly dressed for garbage duty."

Graydon's face lost its humor. "This is what I could find in my brother's luggage."

Toby thought about looking for a pair of jeans for him, but she couldn't spare the time. As for driving, it was either him or spend an hour trying to find someone else. "All right," she said. "I'll direct you."

"I would appreciate that."

Outside, Toby checked in the back of the pickup. All her supplies had been removed from her car and put in the truck bed. Graydon opened the door for her and she stepped up into the old truck. He got in the driver's seat, took the keys from over the visor, and started the engine.

"Everybody who drives this truck complains about it," Toby said. "Except Jared, that is, but then it's his truck. People say it's hard to get it into second gear, and I think the clutch sticks sometimes. And this driveway is very narrow. If you don't back straight out, you can tear off the mirrors. And it's hard to see into the lane so if anyone's coming you have to be careful not to get hit. For that matter, the lane is also very narrow and it's two-way. When I first got to Nantucket, I had a really hard time driving around. I was afraid of hitting people or parked cars, or of crashing into vehicles that were coming toward me and . . ." She trailed off because he had his arm across the back of the seat, ready to reverse, but he was waiting for her to finish.

"Anything else I should know?" he asked.

"I guess not." As he began to back out of the drive, she held her breath, sure that between the tall fence and the side of the house, he'd at least scrape a mirror. But he didn't.

He stopped to let a car pass, then smoothly backed onto the lane.

"Be careful," she said. "It's summer and there are thousands of tourists here who are looking at the scenery and not at the road." Just then a big black SUV came toward them. A woman was driving, a cell phone plastered to her ear, and she didn't even seem to see the truck. Toby drew in her breath and grabbed the seat with one hand and the armrest with the other.

Graydon easily moved to the right, so close to a wall that Toby could have touched it, but he didn't scrape anything. When she looked at him, he didn't seem to be perturbed at all, as though two vehicles passing with only inches between them was an everyday occurrence.

He stopped at the end of the lane, looked both ways, then took a left onto Main Street. Toby's hands relaxed as she watched him smoothly slide the old transmission from one gear to another.

"I thought we'd go down Centre and onto Cliff Road," he said. "Or do you have another way you'd like to go?"

"No, that's fine," she said, watching him. "Did you memorize a map?"

"On the flight here, yes, I did look at one." He turned left onto Centre Street. "I haven't really had time to look at the island, but this is quite beautiful."

Toby glanced around at what was a familiar sight to her. The old houses, so perfectly preserved, the exquisite shops, a feeling in the air of the history of the island, were all there. Past the two candy stores, he knew to go left at the JC House—Jared Coffin—and she glanced down the street at the beautiful whaling museum. Beyond that was the sea. "You've done a lot of driving, haven't you?" she said.

"A fair bit. Much of it has been on dirt roads, sheep tracks, that sort of terrain. Two of the Lanconian tribes have small towns high up in the mountains along a narrow road with a drop-off on the side. When I go up there I like to drive, although I give my bodyguard Lorcan heart attacks."

"I can understand that," Toby said. "You can do that but you've never used a credit card?"

"Never," he said, smiling. "I wonder if Rory left me his?"

"Do you know how to use a computer?"

"Not very well," he said, but there was a tiny smile on his lips that made her suspicious.

"Does that mean you don't know how to turn one on or that you write programs as a hobby? I got the impression you weren't good at driving but you seem to do rather well at it."

"You sound as though I've disappointed you," he said as he pulled into the driveway where the chapel was.

She didn't answer him as she got out, pulled her metal toolbox out of the back, and looked around. There were four trucks at the site. Chairs and tables were being packed away, generators were being loaded onto a flatbed, and the big tent was coming down. Toby started toward the middle of the commotion.

Graydon moved to stand in front of her. "I seem to have done something wrong," he said. "Or are you disappointed that I'm not actually a fairy-tale prince who can't do ordinary things?"

When he said it like that, Toby saw how ridiculous she was being. But still . . . "Yeah, I think maybe I am," she said. "People like their illusions."

Graydon looked surprised for a moment, but then he laughed. "Does this mean I can stop trying to impress you? My brother's valet packed his luggage and there seems to be a system to it, but I can't figure it out. It took me half an hour to find a shirt and trousers. And what I went through to be able to shave! For a while I thought I was going to spend the day wearing only a towel. When your roommate dropped a drinking glass I had nothing to put on."

" 'Broken glass and towels that barely close,' " she quoted. "I'm beginning to understand some things now. I—" She broke off because there were loud voices and she turned to look. There seemed to be an argument between one of the tent people and a caterer.

Graydon looked at Toby. "I am rather good with staff, so perhaps I could be allowed to handle this."

She remembered how he'd commandeered three people to set up the dinner for them. "It's yours," she said. "I'll be in the chapel."

Graydon left to go to the men and for a moment she watched him. Would he be autocratic and order people about? But no, he listened to the problem, then said a few quiet things to the two men and they walked away, seeming to be satisfied with his solution.

Smiling, Toby went into the chapel. It was a mess! Yesterday there had been over two hundred people at the wedding and most of them had been jammed into the little building. There were scuff marks on the walls, the floors were filthy, and every flat surface had candle wax stuck to it. It wasn't going to be easy to return it to the pristine state it had been in before the wedding.

There was a tall water spigot at the front of the property and she was going to have to go there to fill the buckets to start cleaning. But first she needed to get at the wax. As she scraped, she tried to think of a theme for Victoria's wedding.

She went through the usual ideas of hydrangeas—they grew magnificently well on Nantucket—and seashells, but she needed something different, an idea that might intrigue Victoria.

At one point she remembered what Graydon had said about how he wasn't really a fairy-tale prince. And that thought led her to thinking of the old stories. Cinderella. Snow White. Fairy tales were so in right now!

The door to the chapel burst open and Graydon stood there, the light behind him.

"Fairy tales," he said.

He didn't have to explain what he meant; she knew. "Just what I was thinking. Do you know any Lanconian tales?"

"None that don't involve the spilling of blood and internal organs. What about something from Victoria's books?"

"They're full of adultery and murder, that sort of thing. They are bestsellers," Toby said.

"Hey, Gray!" a man called. "Where do you want this?"

"I have to go. What's that glass slipper one?"

"Cinderella. It was my first choice, but Victoria would probably say it's too common."

He glanced to the side for a moment then back at her. "There's a truck stuck in the mire and I must pull it out. What about a medieval theme with a great deal of velvet? I could have Rory send me my lute. That would give some atmosphere." With a wave, he left.

"Velvet's too hot for August," she called after him, but he was gone. She went back to scraping wax. "Your lute?" she said, smiling. At least something he did fit in with his being a fairy-tale prince.

Chapter Nine

Graydon and Toby worked to put the whole area back to the way it had been before the wedding. It took her hours to clean up the chapel, while Graydon took care of the outside.

After all the service people left, the two of them wandered around the acreage carrying plastic trash bags and picked up everything from cigarette butts to a shoe that had been left behind.

When they finished it was four P.M. For lunch they'd had sandwiches from Something Natural, during which they'd talked only of the work yet to be done. Now they looked at each other, unsure of what to do next.

"In the back of the truck I saw a canvas bag full of large towels," Graydon said.

"Beach towels," Toby said. "Jared loves to swim, so I guess he stays prepared."

Graydon looked toward the ocean, which was just a few feet away. "To me, the sea is a rarity since Lanconia is inland. I don't want to keep you waiting, but would you be appalled if I stripped to the bare essentials of clothing and swam for a while? Perhaps you would join me?" Toby wasn't sure what he was leading up to. When she was silent, he turned toward the truck. "I could drive you home and return here."

Part of her thought this was probably an attempt to get her in a compromising position, and she should say no. But she didn't. "I am grimy," she said, "and I'd love to have a swim."

She walked to the water, and before she could change her mind, she started removing her clothes down to her underwear. She couldn't help thinking that sometimes it seemed that the whole world was leaping into bed with one another. From what she heard, dates nearly always included going to bed together. Toby wanted something deeper in her life. She wanted to experience an emotional relationship as well as a physical one. Lexie said she was missing out on a lot of life, but Toby didn't think so.

And the truth was that Toby had never met a man who'd made her forget herself so passionately that she was blind to everything else in her life.

Whatever her thoughts, with this man she was glad she'd worn her lacy blue bra and matching underpants. She hurried into the water. It felt not too cold, not too warm—just perfect after the hot, sweaty work they'd been doing.

When Graydon showed up, she was up to her neck in the water. "It might be colder than you like," she said.

"The climate in my country makes this island seem tropical."

As she treaded water, she couldn't keep from watching him undress. Shoes, socks, shirt. Her eyes widened. The muscles on his upper body showed that he did a lot of physical activity! When he started to unfasten his trousers, Toby dove under the water. When she surfaced, he was at the edge, about to enter. "Boxers" was the answer to the old question.

"Wonderful," he said as he slid into the warm water and parted his arms to swim.

Toby moved back to watch him. He sliced through the water with the ease and grace of an athlete. Long, slow strokes that hardly made a wave. He went so far out that Toby began to be concerned. She meant to call out to him to be careful, but he did a dive and went underwater.

She waited for him to come up, but he didn't, and there was no sign of him. No ripple in the water, no movement at all.

Frowning, she turned around, looking for him, but saw nothing. On her third spin around, his head appeared next to her, his face inches from hers. "You scared me!" she said.

"Sorry. Guard training. Silent underwater espionage. I think it was made up just for me. A sort of 'Let's see if we can terrify our future king.'"

Toby laughed. "Did it work?"

"Oh, yes. I spent six months shaking in fear. I still have nightmares about underwater battles."

She wasn't sure if he was teasing or telling the truth.

"What about you?" he asked.

"No battles," she said as she went onto her back and began to float, her body just on the surface. "Just summers lolling about in a swimming pool."

Graydon moved onto his back and seemed to be trying to float, but he sank into the water. "That's not easy to do."

"It's all in your mind," Toby said. "Think slow, calming thoughts." She jackknifed into the water and looked at him.

For a moment there was something in his eyes that she couldn't read, but it was gone in an instant. "Not possible," he said and tried it again, but his middle sank. "I start thinking of all I should be doing and I become a lead weight."

Toby put her hands on the small of his back and pushed him

upward. "There! Now relax. Clear your mind and think of how beautiful Nantucket is."

He closed his eyes. "I'd rather think of a mermaid with a long blonde braid who holds me aloft," he said softly.

"Think Victoria would like mermaids as a theme?" Toby asked.

Graydon opened his eyes to see that she was several feet away. Instantly, he went underwater—and came up coughing. "You abandoned me!" he said.

"I heard the call of a merman and went after him. He offered me pearls. I couldn't resist." Turning, she swam away.

Graydon dove under and caught her by an ankle to pull her down.

Toby had always been good in the water—and in high school she'd had some experience getting away from testosterone-laden boys. She put her free foot on his shoulder and pushed away to do an underwater somersault. She went up for a gulp of air, then back down.

Graydon went to the surface but she was nowhere to be seen. She grabbed his foot and pulled him down. When they were under the water, he looked at her for a moment. She was clad in her two pieces of thin cotton, her body sleek and creamy, her long braid across one shoulder. She looked like some divine, mythical sea creature. When she turned and swam away, he followed her, staying behind so he could look at her. The women of his country had dark hair and eyes, and Toby's blondeness was exotic to him.

Yet again, he thought how he'd like to stay in the house with her. He knew that all he'd have to do was contact Rory and a place for him to stay would be found. If Plymouth was out of the country, his house was probably empty. It would have a housekeeper-cook, access to a nice car, maybe a boat. Plymouth could arrange for people to visit, so there could be dinner parties with some of the illustrious visitors to the island. There would be beautiful women, laughter, wine. It could be a bachelor party in the truest sense of the word.

As he watched, Toby left the water and walked onto the shore. Her wet underwear was transparent, making her attempt to pull it into place useless—which made him smile.

Graydon went onto his back, his arms out, barely moving. He'd always been good at floating. Not as good as he was when she had her hands on his body, but enough to stay on top of the water.

He felt comfortable with her, enjoyed being with her. Today had been ordinary to her, but to him it was a rarity. As soon as he'd finished at the University of Lanconia, he'd gone into military service. Three years later he'd been released and had returned home to find that separate quarters had been set up for him in the palace his ancestors had built. It had been a shock to go from busy campus living and barracks to a rambling apartment where everyone addressed him as "sir."

He was given a full staff and a calendar of engagements so packed it made him tired just to look at it. It hadn't been easy, but he'd gradually adjusted. Only when Rory came home or when he was in Maine did Graydon get any relief from the day-to-day tedium—and the loneliness that went with the job.

But today had been a true pleasure—and he didn't want it to end. Not yet. He just needed to figure out a reason to stay with this beautiful young woman. He needed to find a way to make her need him.

He watched Toby wrap herself in a towel and sit down on another one. He swam for a while longer, and got out. "A merman theme?" he said as he picked up a towel. "With pearls everywhere?"

"That's possible," Toby said. "Maybe I could hire costumed bodybuilders to carry Victoria down the aisle."

"Think the groom would like that?"

"Good point." She looked at him. "Victoria's daughter calls her mother's bedroom in Kingsley House the Emerald City because it's all green. To match Victoria's eyes. Dark green, light green, yellow, pale, even a kind of greenish red. It's quite nice, really, but a bit . . ."

"Over the top?" he said. "But that's a good idea. We'll do something green. I was wondering how you're going to present these ideas to her."

"I hadn't thought of that," Toby said. "I guess I'll just tell her."

"On the other hand, it might be nice to present sketches with colors on them. It's my experience that people react to visual presentations better than to just words."

"I don't think I can do that," she said hesitantly. "I have to go to work tomorrow and I don't know if I'll have time."

"I'll help," Graydon said. "Is there an art supply store on the island?"

"Yes. There's a very good one on Amelia Drive."

"What if I go there tomorrow, pick up some supplies, and when you get home we work on the designs together? And maybe you could show me what to do with your garden and I could help there too."

She knew that he was asking to stay in the house. Not finding a new place, but remaining with her. She shouldn't. Someone could find him a place to stay. But not tonight. It was getting late and they hadn't even looked for lodging. So maybe he'd stay tonight, and tomorrow at work she could ask around.

"That would be nice," she said as she got up, a big towel wrapped securely around her. When Toby got back to the truck she had some difficulty pulling her clothes on over her wet underwear but she did it. "Bath," she mumbled as she struggled with the damp elastic that didn't want to move.

She looked in her bag for her phone and saw that she had an email from Lexie.

I'M IN NEW YORK NOW. PLYMOUTH WENT TO CA SO I'M STAYING AT HIS APARTMENT. IT'S NICE, COZY EVEN. WHO WOULD HAVE THOUGHT THAT OF HIM? I FLY OUT TOMORROW MORNING.

HOW DID YOU LIKE THE PRINCE'S COOKING? AND DID YOU LIKE WHAT HE DID TO THE SUNROOM? HE COULD STAY IN PLYMOUTH'S BIG HOUSE, AS IT'S EMPTY. BUT THEN, ARE YOU STILL PLANNING TO SEND YOUR PRINCE AWAY? TELL ME ALL! LEXIE.

He cooked the breakfast? Toby thought. He cleaned up the sunroom? She was beginning to see why Lexie had said she didn't think Graydon was helpless.

When Toby looked up, she saw him walking toward the truck. His clothes were so clean and unwrinkled, his hair perfectly groomed, that he could have been going to a dinner party.

They got into the truck, with Graydon driving, and started toward home. "Want to get sandwiches for dinner?" she asked.

"That sounds fine."

"Or would you like to cook something? Or clean a room?"

Graydon laughed. "How was I found out?"

"Lexie ratted on you. If you're such a busy person, what are you going to do while I'm at work all day?"

"Read? Find a beach and lie on it for hours?"

"You couldn't stay still for even an hour this morning, but you think you're going to do nothing for days at a time?"

"You need any help at your florist shop? I work cheap."

Toby shook her head. "How are you going to last for a whole week?" She didn't wait for his answer. "Maybe you should stay somewhere that has some entertainment. With a boat maybe." She was looking straight out the truck window.

"Speaking of staying someplace, I don't mean to complain

but the mattress on the couch upstairs is like trying to sleep on steel coils. They cut into a person."

"Maybe that's the reason that couch was tossed into a corner of the Kingsley attic." She smiled. "This is a bit like the Prince and the Pea."

Graydon started to laugh, but then they looked at each other.

"I don't think so," Toby said, reading his mind. "Lots of mattresses around? Strings of peas? Not very wedding-like. Will your wedding have a theme?"

"I have no idea. I won't be asked. It's a national event, so I'll just be told when to show up and what to wear."

"A uniform? With lots of medals?"

"Scads of them. All on the left side. Four weeks beforehand I'll have to lift weights with just my right hand to be able to balance myself."

"You always make things sound funny," Toby said.

"Not to most people. My brother thinks that I'm incapable of what he calls fun."

"Mmmm," Toby said. "Let me guess. His idea of fun is fast cars, steep mountainsides, jumping out of planes, all with barely clad women hanging on to him."

"I think you know my brother well."

Toby hesitated before replying. "You could have some of that on Nantucket," she said softly.

"And miss out on coming up with some ghastly theme that would please the very discerning Victoria for her wedding? No, thank you."

Toby couldn't help the grin that spread across her face. Never in her life had she lived alone and she had no desire to find out what it was like. "All right," she said. "You can have Lexie's room."

"That's very kind of you. I never imagined that—"

"Are you kidding me? Of course you imagined staying at my

house. You've worked at it. Your hints weigh about a ton each. Whales are lighter than your hints."

Graydon was laughing. "I thought I was being subtle, but it is true. I meet so many strangers and—"

"Spare me the Poor Prince act," Toby said. "You cook, you drive, you boss people around, you settle arguments. You even run around half naked in front of my roommate—"

"And you."

"And in front of me," she said. "It's my opinion that you're more than competent at everything. In fact, it's my guess that you could probably run an entire country all by yourself. So why do you want to stay with me? And your answer better not be about sex."

"You wound me," Graydon said, his hand melodramatically over his heart. "I'm not my brother. I do thank you for the remark about the country, though. I'm going to try to do just that." He pulled into the drive of the house they shared and shut off the engine. When he turned to look at her, she saw not one trace of humor. "I don't know the answer to your question," he said. "Right now nothing in my life makes sense. I have some problems that I don't know how to deal with— I won't bore you with them—but there's something about you that makes me feel calm enough to believe that I can eventually solve them. I know I could go elsewhere and have some so-called excitement but . . ." He motioned toward the little house. "This is what I need now. Solitude with a garden and a young lady who makes me laugh and talks to me of mermaids. Does any of this make sense?"

"It does," she said. "When I left my parents' house to be on my own, I was quite scared. Lexie took me in and—" She broke off. "All right. We'll be friends and you can stay here while you're on the island." She reached for the truck handle but looked back at him. "If you ever want to talk about what's bothering you, I'm a good listener." She got out.

He watched her walk toward the house. Right now the only thing bothering him was the vision of her in her wet underwear.

He took his time before he got out of the truck, then began to remove the supplies from the back. Toby's red metal toolbox was on the bottom and it made him smile. Not many women had a toolbox of their own. He carried everything back to the little storage shed by the greenhouse.

He didn't know much about gardening but to him it looked like everything in the greenhouse needed to be watered. He picked up the hose that was coiled on the floor, turned on the water, and went from one plant to another. It was soothing work and he thought he should use the time to think about Lanconia and Danna and Rory and what his future was going to be after he was married and . . .

He couldn't seem to focus on any of that. All he could think about was Toby in her lacy blue underwear.

Chapter Ten

When Toby's cell phone rang, she and Graydon were at the dining table eating the frittata he'd made and a salad she'd put together. The ID said it was Victoria. "She can't possibly already want to know what we've come up with," Toby said as she answered.

Graydon was so pleased by her use of "we" that he didn't reply.

"Darling," Victoria said, "I hope you know that the island is buzzing about the mysterious man who's moved in with you."

With a glance at Graydon, Toby put her napkin on the table, got up, and went into the living room. She didn't want him to hear whatever Victoria was going to say. "We're roommates and that's all."

"I know that but they don't. I fear that your reputation has been damaged beyond repair."

"Good," Toby said. "I'll no longer be some plastic trophy the boys want to win."

Victoria laughed. "That's a beautiful way of looking at it. Anyway, dear, I have something to ask you. Yesterday I spent hours with Jilly and found out a great deal about your prince. His country is very important to ours since they have that metal we so desperately need. I think you should stay with him while he's here."

"How could I do that? I have a job."

"I have many friends on the island and I'm sure I could find someone to temporarily take over your job at the florist shop. If you approve, that is?"

Toby walked to the doorway to look at Graydon, who was still sitting at the table. He'd stopped eating and was waiting for her to return.

"Toby, darling, could you stand some vacation time so you can be with your prince? Show him around Nantucket, that sort of thing?"

"Yes," Toby said. "I could."

"I'm so glad," Victoria said. "And how are you doing on the wedding plans?"

"When we have more ideas, we plan to make a presentation. Maybe in a few days we can all get together and—"

"How wonderful! I'll see you tomorrow at two. I must go now. Kiss your prince for me." She clicked off.

For a moment Toby stood in the doorway in silence.

"Bad news?" Graydon asked as he got up from the table and went to her, but she didn't respond. "Come and finish your dinner before it gets cold." Taking her arm, he led her back to the table. When they were both seated, he said, "Tell me what Victoria said."

Toby picked up her napkin. "She says she can get someone to take my place at the florist shop so I can have time off while you're here."

Graydon couldn't hold back his grin. "I like that idea very much. Perhaps tomorrow we can see some of this pretty island."

"No. Victoria is coming here at two to see what we've come up with for her wedding. By the way, I'm sorry I took the phone call at dinner. Now that I'm to—according to Victoria—help your country and mine get along, I think I should mind my manners."

"Let me guess. It's your job to save the vanadium?"

Toby nodded.

"I'm beginning to imagine Victoria as a charging horse. It goes wherever it wants to."

"More like twenty of them, and their riders have drawn swords."

"Shall I fight her for you?"

Toby narrowed her eyes at him. "You wish! You have to help me come up with more ideas. Tonight while we tackle that mountain of luggage of yours we can brainstorm wedding themes."

After they'd cleared away dinner, working easily together, they went upstairs to unpack Rory's luggage. Never in Graydon's life had he packed or unpacked a bag and he had no desire to learn how. When he asked Toby about art supplies, she told him to search in the desk and he found an old sketchpad and pencils.

Lexie's bedroom was large and in the corner there were a love seat and a coffee table. Graydon sat there and started making quick sketches of every idea they'd had, while Toby took over the luggage. They came up with as many concepts as they could, some of them ridiculously far-fetched. He made her laugh when he drew a Lanconian warrior complete with bearskin and lance.

"Don't show that one to Victoria because she'll love it,"

Toby said. "She'll try to make Dr. Huntley wear that. What in the world is this for?"

Graydon glanced at the heavy wool uniform she was holding up. "First Lancers. Rory sometimes reviews their troops."

"Why would he take this on a pleasure trip to the U.S.?"

"If there were a disaster, he'd have to—"

Toby held up her hand. "I don't want to hear the rest of that. I think I'll put things like this way in the back. Jeans and casual shirts will go in front. We'll have to get you some T-shirts that say *Nantucket* on them." Her head came up. "Maybe we could do a Lanconian theme that's not ancient. Something modern. What do people in your country wear today?"

"Jeans and T-shirts with *Nantucket* or wherever they've visited written on them."

"Too bad," Toby said. At the bottom of the pile she found a hard-sided case that held a laptop, an iPad, and an eReader, as well as several Bluetooth gadgets. On the bottom, inside a little box, was a leather wallet.

As Toby took it out, she started to say something, but Graydon was bent over the sketchpad. She opened the wallet to see if the credit card was inside. It was, along with about three grand in American hundreds. But what interested her was a beat-up old photo of a beautiful young woman. She had long dark hair and sultry-looking eyes, as though she'd just stepped out of bed—or was about to get into it.

From the wear on the photo it looked as though Rory had been carrying it for years. So Graydon's brother was in love, she thought, and wondered how that fit in with his playboy antics.

She glanced at Graydon, meaning to make a comment, but it was too soon for this kind of revelation. When they got to know each other better, she'd ask about his brother's love life.

"Catch!" she said and tossed the wallet to him.

He caught it in his left hand, opened it, and pulled out the card. "Is this any good?" It was a platinum American Express card.

"Unlimited credit," Toby said. "We could go buy a Rolls." She expected him to laugh but he didn't.

"Is that something you want?" he asked seriously.

"No," she said. "For my last birthday my dad wanted to buy me an expensive car but I asked for a refrigerator for the flowers."

"I saw it in the greenhouse."

Toby's eyes widened in panic. "I forgot to do the watering." She stepped over three suitcases and started for the door.

"I did it," Graydon said. "When I put away the tools, I thought the plants looked a bit dry so I watered them. Was that all right?"

She smiled in relief. "Very all right." It looked like he wasn't going to be the burden she'd thought he would be. She went back to unpacking, putting his shaving gear in the bathroom. He didn't use an electric shaver but an old-fashioned brush, a little tub of soap, and a safety razor.

By the time the luggage was unpacked, Graydon had nearly twenty sketches of their different ideas. With a great sigh of relief that the job was done, Toby flopped down on the little couch beside him and went through the drawings. There were historical themes, from medieval to the 1940s, and places ranging from barns with banjos to a fake mansion a la *The Great Gatsby*. They'd done four fairy tales, one of them Lanconian that involved fairies and dwarves. (They left out the evisceration parts of the story.)

"Your drawings are good. What did you study in school?" Toby asked as she checked her phone messages. Victoria had sent a text saying she'd found someone for Toby's job and she'd start in the morning.

"Everything," he answered. He was looking at her, so close

to him, her skin warm and pink, her hair in its long braid. She was in profile and he could hardly keep his eyes off her lips.

He looked away just as she turned to him. "Eclectic," he said. "I studied a bit of everything but nothing in depth. I had a drawing master from the time I was a child, as well as tutors for music and dance, horseback riding, and fencing. What about you? What did you study?"

"Mostly art history. My mother wanted me to study 'husband catching' but she couldn't find such a course, although she did search."

"That sounds like something you truly need to learn how to do. So tell me, how many proposals of marriage have you turned down?"

She laughed. "Three, but don't tell my mother." She looked at him. "How did you know I'd had proposals?"

"There are women you spend time with and women you marry. You are the latter."

"And you know this how?"

"I can't give away universal male secrets, now can I?"

Smiling, Toby got up. "On that note, I think I'll call it a night. Tomorrow I have to . . ." She smiled. "I don't have to do anything, do I?"

"We need to get some watercolors so I can finish the green theme."

"That's easy, and after we get them we can go to a beach. And this time you can work while I do nothing." She nodded toward the empty cases.

"I'm a prince," he said haughtily. "I don't do luggage."

"Why, you—!" Toby took a step toward him but stopped herself. "Just be warned that I put a pea under your mattress."

"Oh, my aching back!"

They laughed together and for a moment it was a bit awkward between them. How did they say goodnight?

Graydon solved the problem by getting up, taking her hand in his, and kissing the back of it. "Goodnight, my lady," he said softly.

Toby looked at him for a moment, the soft light of the room, the deep sound of a foghorn outside the open window, and she almost stepped toward him. But she didn't. "I put your toiletries in Lexie's bathroom and the sheets are clean and . . . I'll see you in the morning."

"It will be my pleasure," he said.

Toby went into her bedroom and closed the door, but she felt too restless to sleep. She wasn't sure, but she thought maybe she was beginning to feel what the girls in school used to giggle about. Graydon wasn't like other men she'd met. He wasn't making little excuses to touch her, to reach across her. He wasn't giving her long looks that he hoped would send her flying into his arms.

The truth was, he seemed to think of her as, well, a friend, or maybe a relative.

And that's good, Toby thought as she put on her pajamas. He's a man who is about to become engaged so he shouldn't be even looking at other women. On the other hand, it would be nice to think he had, well, a little bit of desire for her.

Graydon was in the shower. He had his head against the wall and the water pounding down on him was ice cold—but it wasn't cold enough to stop the furnace that seemed to rage inside him.

"Irial, Zerna, Poilen, Vatell, Fearen, Ulten," he said, reciting the names of the six tribes of Lanconia. It was a trick he'd used since he was a boy. When his mother—never his father—was bawling him out about some minor infraction, he'd distracted himself with the chant.

But right now it wasn't helping. All he could think of was how close Toby was to him. Just a few feet away. One wall separated them. He had visions of slashing through that wall with a broadsword and going to her.

"Too much Lanconian," he muttered as he got out of the shower and stood there for a moment. He'd opened the window and the cool night air felt good on his wet, bare skin.

He reminded himself that a quarter of him was American. "And I must be politically correct," he said aloud. American men didn't slash down walls, didn't jam swords into beds, and most certainly didn't rip off a woman's clothes.

He dried off and got into bed, but it was a long time before he slept.

In the morning Toby quietly dressed and tiptoed down the stairs. She thought she'd make corn muffins before Graydon got up. But when she entered the kitchen she saw him sitting at the little round table in the newly cleaned sunroom, a laptop open before him. "Good morning," she said.

Looking up, he smiled as though she were the person he most wanted to see. "Good morning. I thought I'd look online and see whether or not my brother has brought about the downfall of my country."

"Has he?" Toby asked as she got a box of cornmeal out of the pantry.

"So far, no. He has a factory opening ceremony tomorrow, so later I'll check to see if he set fire to the ribbon and kissed three pretty girls while it burned."

Again, Toby wasn't sure if he was kidding or being honest. "Did you have any new ideas about the wedding?"

"Pirates? What about American gangsters?"

"That's possible. The bridesmaids could wear flapper dresses with long pearls. Victoria would like that."

"What about you? If you were getting married, what theme would you want?"

"No theme," she said. "I just want a beautiful white gown with yards of lace and all my best girlfriends wearing dresses in shades of blue. I'd have white and blue flowers everywhere. Pale blue tablecloths and white dishes, and a cake with icing cornflowers falling down the side."

Suddenly, she stopped, embarrassed at having gone on in such detail. "Sorry. At the shop we deal with weddings all the time so I've thought about mine." She shrugged.

Graydon got up and walked to stand behind her. "I think your wedding sounds more beautiful than all the themes we've come up with."

"Thanks," she mumbled, still embarrassed. When he didn't move, she looked up at him. For part of a second there was a look in his eyes that made her step toward him.

When Graydon turned and stepped away, Toby couldn't help her frown. All right, so he wasn't interested in her that way. Good. Didn't that show he loved the woman he was to marry? And wasn't that good?

She turned back to the stove.

After breakfast, they bought watercolors, then drove to the Jetties and walked for a long way by the water. At first, they came up with a few more themes for the wedding, but then they began to talk about their lives—at least Toby talked about hers. Graydon asked her questions about her childhood, her schooling, her friends, what she liked and what she didn't.

She answered everything, but she was cautious and careful not to reveal anything that was truly private. When it came to her mother, she told how efficiently she ran the household, but Toby left out how much her mother's constant criticisms hurt.

But if Toby was concealing the truth about her life, she knew that Graydon was worse. He'd said he had some life problems he needed to solve. But no matter what she asked him, he never came close to revealing what they were.

After lunch at Brant Point Grill, they drove back to the house. While Graydon finished with the watercolors, Toby took a shower and changed before Victoria arrived.

When Graydon saw Toby come down the stairs, for a second that look was there again. She'd taken her time in dressing and put on a blouse that she'd been told matched her eyes. Graydon seemed to appreciate it, but in the next second his eyes cooled and he put back on what she was beginning to think of as his "prince face."

He saw that she was nervous. "I'm sure she will love so many of these ideas that tomorrow you'll be ordering flowers."

Toby sighed. "All I hope is that she will like one of them." The drawings were spread across the dining table, twenty-six sketches, some simple, some elaborate. Graydon had put color on a few of them. Based on what Toby had told him, he'd bought every color of green the store sold and later he'd mixed the paints so there were even more shades.

At a knock on the door, Toby took a breath and was shocked at how anxious she felt.

"I'll be right here with you," Graydon said and for a moment he held her hand, then he released it to open the door.

Victoria was there, the sun glinting off her auburn hair, her outrageously curved figure clad in a green silk blouse and perfectly tailored dark trousers. "Prince Graydon!" she said as she walked past him and into the house. "How good to see you again. Toby, darling, I don't think I've ever seen you looking better."

"It's good to see you too," Toby said as she kissed Victoria's cheek.

"Do either of you need anything? I can send my dear Caleb to visit, as he knows everything that can be known about this island. Or would you two rather be alone? So where is this fabulous presentation of yours?"

Graydon was behind Victoria and he looked over her at Toby with his eyebrows raised. He wasn't used to people pushing past him and not waiting to be introduced. His exaggerated expression of surprise made Toby stifle a laugh.

When Victoria looked into the dining room and saw the sketches on the table, she lost no time going to them. With Toby on one side and Graydon on the other, she slowly moved along the table, looking at each one. "Pirates, how imaginative! And fairy tales. Rather a lot of them. Green. I like that very much. Banjos, harps, violins, quite a variety of music."

At the end of the table she stopped and looked at Graydon's and Toby's expectant faces. "No, my dears, I think not. While they're all quite interesting, there's nothing that actually appeals to me. You'll just have to come up with something else. Now, I have to go."

She kissed Toby's cheek, then turned to Graydon and kissed his cheek also. "Welcome to the family. Toby, dear, let me know when you can present your real ideas to me. I'll let myself out. Goodbye." She left through the front door.

Toby collapsed onto the couch and Graydon dropped down beside her.

"I once went through a hurricane that had less force to it," Graydon said.

"Did you say even one word while she was here?"

"None. And to think people wait in line to be presented to me."

"Not Victoria." Toby looked at him. "So what are our real ideas?"

"I don't know," Graydon said as he stood up and held out his hand to her. "Right now you and I are going to walk into town and I'm going to see some of Nantucket. It may be our only chance before Victoria decides that we're to dedicate our lives to the wedding of her and her beloved Caleb, the man who knows everything."

Laughing, Toby took his hand and let him pull her up. "Thank you," she said and meant it. "I don't want to fail at this."

Graydon lifted her hand and kissed the back of it. "You won't. I promise. Do you have ice cream in America?"

"Americans invented ice cream," she said with a straight face.

"Actually, it's not a well-known fact, but it was first made by Rowan the Great. He was charging a wild boar through the forest and needed to cool off. Ice cream was his solution."

"That's totally untrue," Toby said. "It was Martha Washington who left milk on a doorstep."

Laughing, they pretended to argue all the way down the lane.

Chapter Eleven

Only one more day, Toby thought, and glanced at Graydon. They were sitting at the little table in the sunroom and looking at the sketches for Victoria's wedding. In just one more day he'd have to return to Lanconia and she'd probably never see him again. Except at his wedding, she thought, and yet again imagined sitting in the front row and watching him marry someone else.

It wasn't as though she and Graydon were in love, she reminded herself, but in six days they'd become friends. They hadn't been apart all that time. They'd explored Nantucket, walking around beautiful 'Sconset, seeking out unique shops.

Graydon was excellent company. He was always cheerful and smiling, and he knew how to talk to anyone. Only once had there been any difficulty. A woman had recognized him as the

Crown Prince of Lanconia and had loudly said so. Toby had frozen in place, unable to speak. They were in a store by the wharf and everyone had stopped and stared. But not Graydon. He turned to the woman and grinned—and showed that he had what looked to be a missing front tooth. "Honey," he said in a heavy Southern American accent, "she thinks I'm a prince. That ain't what you say about me."

It took Toby a second to catch on, but she said in the same accent, "You a prince! Ha-ha. Now, your cousin Walter, he could be."

"Always Walter!" Graydon said, his voice angry. "Don't start on me again." Toby threw up her hands and headed out the door, Graydon close behind her.

They kept going until they reached the fountain on Main Street, then stopped and started laughing. "Your tooth!" Toby said, and Graydon held up the packet of chocolate-covered cranberries they'd bought earlier.

"Think she believed it?" Graydon asked.

"Not for a minute, but her husband thought she was crazy so maybe he'll talk her out of what she thinks she saw."

"My opinion too," he said.

It had been like that all week, she thought, the most pleasant of experiences, laughing, agreeing on everything. But to Toby's mind, there were two things missing. One was that Graydon never, ever came close to revealing anything private about himself. He told her where he went to school, who his friends were, but he never really confided in her. Any questions she asked about his private feelings, he stepped away from, deflecting them with a joke or a glib little remark that revealed nothing.

Toby told herself that he had to do that. He was a prince and there was the press and he had to be careful. He couldn't risk telling a stranger his true feeling about anything.

But Toby didn't want to be thought of as a stranger. She

wanted . . . She wasn't sure how to fill that in. All she knew for certain was that when he became The Prince, that made her The Peasant.

The other thing missing was how she was coming to feel about him physically. She remembered her last phone call with Lexie.

"So?" Lexie asked in her usual blunt way. "Have you leaped into bed with him yet?"

"No, and he hasn't asked," Toby said, trying to keep her voice light but not succeeding. "He's not interested in me that way."

"I don't believe that," Lexie said. "Why would he go to all the trouble of staying with you if he weren't dying to get into bed with you?"

"Friendship," Toby said. "We're great friends. And besides, he's about to become engaged. Really, Lexie, could we talk about something else?"

"You haven't fallen in love with him, have you?"

"No," Toby said. "He's a friend but nothing more. When he leaves, we'll wave goodbye and that'll be it. What about you?"

"Bored," Lexie said. "When I met this kid before, I liked her, but now she's a dud. I can't even get her to go on a driving trip to see some of the countryside. She says she's seen it all."

"Too bad," Toby said. "The poor child has probably been dragged around everywhere in her short life, while you want to see the world. If you get too lonely, you should come home."

"But only after Saturday," Lexie said. "After he leaves, right? Will you drive him to the airport or will a limo pick him up?"

"He's not a limo sort of guy," Toby said. "Sometimes it's hard to remember that he's a prince."

"Especially since he spends his days helping you with Victoria's wedding."

Toby knew Lexie was trying to make her feel better with her

insinuation that maybe Graydon didn't like any females. But she'd seen him smile at pretty waitresses, seen his eyes widen at some girl in a nearly nonexistent bikini. He seemed to like every woman on earth except her.

She and Lexie promised to keep each other informed and hung up.

"I think I'm going to have to admit defeat," Toby said to Graydon. They were looking at the pile of sketches, and so far, they hadn't come up with any new ideas that they thought would intrigue Victoria.

Graydon leaned back in his chair. "I wish I could say that we can do this, but I'm beginning to agree with you."

She looked back at the drawings. They'd come up with everything from having the pastor skydive in, to drawing the wedding Toby always envisioned for herself. They'd set up the table with the watercolors and she'd done most of the painting.

"I'm beginning to think that the wedding has to be personal to Victoria," Graydon said. "Unless we know more about her personally, all we can do is guess at what will please her."

As soon as he said it, they both knew. They looked at each other, their eyes locking, their minds in complete harmony.

"Where?" Graydon asked.

She knew what he meant. The person on island who knew the most about Victoria was the man she was going to marry, Dr. Caleb Huntley, and Graydon was asking where he could be found.

"He's the director of the NHS, the historical society." She looked at her watch. "He's probably at work now." She looked down at her jeans and T-shirt. "I'll change," she said as she headed up the stairs.

Graydon was right behind her. "Should I wear a tie?"

"Heavens, no! You'll look like an off-islander. Put on that light blue denim shirt and the dark brown trousers." She went into her bedroom and stripped down to her underwear. "And put on those shoes that lace up," she called through the open doors.

"Brown or black?" he called back.

"Brown," she said as she stood there looking in her closet. It was less than a third the size of Lexie's big walk-in, so all her clothes were jammed together. Where was her pink and white dress?

"Which shoes?" Graydon said from the doorway. He had on trousers and an open shirt, and he was barefoot and holding two pairs of shoes. "Oh, sorry," he said when he saw her in her underwear. He turned around but he didn't leave the room, just held the shoes out behind his back.

"The ones on my left, your right." She pulled the dress out and held it in front of her. Graydon was still standing inside her bedroom, his back to her. "Do you mind?"

"No, go ahead and get dressed." He didn't move.

That wasn't what she meant. She stepped into the bathroom, leaving the door half open.

Graydon sat down on the end of the bed and put on his socks. "So what do we ask this man?"

"I don't know," Toby said. "To tell us Victoria's innermost secrets, I guess. Her fantasy wishes." She pulled her dress on over her head and looked in the mirror to start applying makeup.

"That should go over well," he said sarcastically. "You wouldn't have a shoehorn, would you?"

"Bedside table," she said. "Maybe we should be more subtle and lead up to what we want to ask. My worry is that he won't want an inexperienced person like me overseeing his wedding."

Graydon pushed the bathroom door all the way open as he began to button his shirt. She was applying mascara. "What do you know about this Dr. Huntley?"

"Not much. I didn't even know he and Victoria were serious

about each other until Alix's wedding. There they were, holding hands and looking at each other with big cow eyes. It was a shock to me. My hair is a mess! I'm going to have to take it down and rebraid it." She was referring to the strands that were hanging down the sides of her face.

"Here, let me," he said and took her hairbrush from her. Gently, he began to smooth the strands back.

All Toby could do was stand there and watch him in the mirror. This, she thought, this simple but incredibly intimate act of a man brushing her hair, was the kind of thing she'd always imagined as marriage. She'd never wanted the frantic tussles in the back of a car that girls giggled about. When she was growing up, a man brushing her hair was the kind of thing she'd dreamed about. Graydon had his head down, his eyes on her hair, and she thought how much she'd like to turn and slip her arms around his neck and kiss him.

She made herself look away. He's not yours, she told herself. He isn't; he can't be. Besides, in the last week she'd seen how he ignored anything that could lead to any physicality between them. There'd been a couple of times when she'd turned toward him in the hopes that he'd kiss her, but he'd always moved away. She'd been pursued by boys since she was fifteen years old and to suddenly have a man step away when she got too close hurt. Actually, it was crushing her ego.

When she looked back up at Graydon she was smiling, determined to not let him see that she wanted more than he was willing to give.

Graydon looked at her in the mirror. "Better?"

"Perfect, and thank you," she said, then slipped away from him to go back into the bedroom. She pulled a little heart locket necklace out of her jewelry box and started to put it on.

Graydon brushed her hands away and fastened it around her neck. "A gift?"

"From my father for my sixteenth birthday." For a moment they both looked into the mirror, and again Toby wanted to turn to him.

As always, Graydon stepped away. "Excuse me for a moment. I'll meet you downstairs." He went back to his own bedroom, closed the door, and leaned against it. What the hell was he doing?! When he saw Toby in her undressed state he should have left the room but he couldn't make himself do it. A lifetime of discipline seemed to disappear in a moment. He was so aroused at the sight of her seminude state that he'd been tempted to fling her onto the bed and tear off her clothing. But then what? Tomorrow he'd fly away and never see her again? Maybe she'd recover from a one-night stand, but he wasn't sure he would. He'd be condemned to a lifetime of living with another woman, while Toby . . .

He closed his eyes. He had to go home. Next week a couple of ambassadors were visiting Lanconia and Rory knew nothing about them. It wouldn't take long for the exchange of twins to be found out. Graydon could see the headlines now. "Royal Twins Fool the World." Lanconia would be an international joke. It would go down in Lanconian history books, and a hundred years from now schoolchildren would laugh about it. Would Toby's photo be beside Graydon's? Worse, would the textbooks tell how Graydon's scheme had brought down the Lanconian throne?

He knew he had to return home, but the idea of leaving tomorrow made his heart ache. It took a lot of work on his part to get himself fully under control before he could go downstairs.

Toby was waiting for him, looking very pretty in her pink and white striped dress and her little sandals. "We can walk to Dr. Huntley's office," she said, then looked at him. "Are you all right? You look like something has upset you."

"No, nothing," Graydon said curtly.

Toby knew he was yet again, as always, not confiding in her. When he opened the front door, they both came to a halt. Standing there were two magnificent-looking people, a man and a woman. "Your Royal Highness," they said as they bowed to Graydon.

When Toby looked at him, he wore the expression of a man whose life had just come to an end.

He opened the door wider to let them in.

Chapter Twelve

Less than an hour after the accident in Lanconia, Lorcan and Daire got on a private jet to New York. At JFK airport they'd been hurriedly escorted to a small jet that took them to Nantucket. Daire was concerned about Lorcan's injuries, but he'd not directly asked her about them. For one thing, there were too many people around them and too much secrecy involved for either of them to speak freely. And besides, Lorcan wouldn't have liked his implication that a few bruises had lessened her abilities as a royal bodyguard. Prince Graydon needed her, so she would be there.

It was Daire, who was always at ease with people, who chatted about the weather and thanked them for their help.

As for Lorcan, she was mostly silent during the long journey halfway around the world. Very tall, with her long black hair slicked into a ponytail that reached halfway down her back, she was a woman who caused heads to turn. But she didn't respond to any of the glances. Even though it was her first trip out of Lanconia, she didn't let her eyes stray from Daire. She followed him through airports and did what he told her was needed. When she winced in pain, he saw it, and his eyes asked if she was all right. She didn't speak, just gave a curt nod.

Daire had to turn away to hide his smile of pride. He had taught her well.

When they got to the Nantucket airport, they waited for the wide doors to open and their crates and trunks to be put onto the ramp. Against Lorcan's protest, Daire dealt with the bulk of it. They had brought what was needed to stay in contact with Lanconia, as well as training equipment and personal items. When it was all collected, they put it into a rented car.

It wasn't until they were inside the vehicle that Lorcan felt she could speak. "What do you think she's like?" she asked as Daire drove out of the airport.

He didn't have to be told who she meant: the woman who had caused so much trouble with Prince Graydon. "He doesn't have a type. If it were Rory, it would be easy to say. Tall, blonde, beautiful, and willing to follow him into any dangerous situation he wants to blindly run into. But Gray . . ."

Daire was a royal cousin, sixth in line for the throne, so he could call Prince Graydon by his given name. But Lorcan was not of their class. She was a descendent of the Zerna tribe, orphaned young and taken in by her elderly grandparents, who were very happy when, at the age of twelve, she won a palace scholarship. From then on, she'd been fed, clothed, educated, and above all trained at government expense. Martial arts, boxing, swordplay, weaponry of all sorts were mastered by her. When she graduated in the top five of her class, she was hired by the royal family. Three years ago, after her quick thinking and decisive action had saved the life of a royal cousin, she was assigned to Prince Graydon.

"I have no idea what kind of woman he prefers," Lorcan said. There was no jealousy from her in that area. She and the prince had become friends, and she aspired to no more than that. "Certainly not Danna."

Daire laughed. "How many times in the last week has she had a private meal with Rory?"

Lorcan grimaced. "If she had fallen down the stairs with the king, I wonder who Prince Rory would have tried to save?"

Just a few hours earlier the King of Lanconia had fallen at the top of some wide marble steps. Rory—who people thought was Graydon—had leaped in front of his father to break his fall. Rory had landed on his left arm and broken his wrist. He would have been hurt worse, but at the first sign of movement, Lorcan had thrown herself in front of both men. Without a thought for her own safety, she'd used her body to cushion their landing. When everyone settled, Lorcan had been on the bottom, Rory on top of her, and the king at the crest of the pile. He was the one least hurt—at least physically. What the press didn't know, and what everyone at the palace was working hard to conceal, was that the king had fallen because he'd had a stroke.

"Rory said Gray became fascinated with her because she could tell the twins apart," Daire said.

"I wonder how she pulled off that trick." Lorcan looked at him. "What do you think her game is?"

"I have no idea. Maybe she fell in love with him at first sight." They looked at each other and scoffed.

"My guess is that she's trying to get pregnant," Lorcan said. "Needles in the condoms, that sort of thing."

Daire shrugged. "But then, it's a fashion for royals to produce a love child. It hasn't hurt Albert of Monaco."

"I thought our prince was smarter than that."

"Smart has nothing to do with it," Daire said, his voice almost angry. "Gray is facing a loveless marriage and a job nobody in his right mind would want. I hope he did fall for her, or her for him. It doesn't matter which way it is, but I plan to help him all I can. And if a child is produced, good!"

"I reserve my judgment until I've met her," Lorcan said. "I figure she's either the lowest class produced in this country or she owns a mansion and the prince is her . . . her . . ."

"Plaything? Wild, with endless sex? Something for him to remember when he's in bed with Ice Queen Danna?"

"Put that way, I hope he is being used by her," Lorcan said.

"And since we'll be staying there, I hope she has a mansion with multiple bedrooms. I don't relish sleeping on the floor."

"You're getting soft as well as old."

"Think so?" he said as he glanced at her. He and Graydon were the same age and they'd started training together when they were children. After Rory had been sent away to the first of several boarding schools, Daire was the only real friend Graydon had left. For years they'd schooled together, played sports, traded secrets. But as they grew up, Graydon's mother, the queen, began to separate the boys. There was specialized education that Graydon needed, so he was gradually moved into royal duties in preparation for his future role.

It was only after university and after they'd both served in the military that they got back together. But then, Daire was the only person the queen considered sufficiently high ranking enough—and fit enough—to go through the rigorous training that Graydon preferred.

When Lorcan became his bodyguard, she fit in easily with the two of them and they'd been a team since then. At least they were until Graydon said he was flying down to Nantucket to be in a wedding. After that, everything had changed.

And now things were changing even more. Prince Rory's arm was in a cast and the king was hidden away in a hospital in Switzerland, while Daire and Lorcan had been sent to Nantucket with orders to keep the man believed to be Rory away from his own country.

"There it is," Lorcan said. "Kingsley Lane. Turn here."

Toby could only stare at the two people as they entered the house. To say they were magnificent was an understatement. They were both very tall—he was six feet three or four, and she had to be at least six feet. They were both dark, with hair and eyes as black as midnight, their skin honey-colored. He was about Graydon's age, early thirties, while she was quite a bit younger, maybe Toby's age. They were wearing all black, a combination of leather and wool, with a bit of silver here and there. Their dress and their extremely erect posture would have been remarkable in itself, but their faces were beautiful: eyes slightly slanted, long, narrow noses, and full lips. Altogether they seemed to have come from a time long ago.

When they stepped inside, Graydon and the man started talking in what Toby assumed was Lanconian. She'd heard only bits of the language. It was deep, with words pronounced inside the throat, an old sound—and a beautiful one.

But it was obvious that something was wrong, as Graydon's frown was growing deeper with every word the man spoke.

Toby stood to one side, waiting to be told what had happened. After a few moments, she reached out to put her hand on Graydon's arm to ask him what was wrong, but the woman slashed a look at Toby that made her drop her hand and take a step back. She got the impression that if she dared touch The Prince the woman would strike her.

At last Graydon formally greeted the two people. He and the man clasped arms, with hands at the elbows, their heads bent forward. Graydon didn't touch the woman but they smiled at each other with great warmth. Obviously, the three of them knew one another well.

Graydon turned to Toby. "I must . . ." he began, but he seemed to be so overwhelmed with what he'd heard that he couldn't finish.

"If you need me, I'll be outside," she said softly, and gave him an encouraging smile. He looked at her with gratitude.

She went through the kitchen to the back door. Her guess was that something bad had happened in Lanconia and these two had come to tell Graydon about it. She truly hoped no one had died. In most people's lives a death in the family was a tragedy, but in Graydon's life it could mean that he was now a king.

She went to the greenhouse and began the daily watering. Now and then she'd glance toward the house but she saw no one. Whatever had happened, she felt sure that Graydon would soon be leaving. By now they'd probably gone upstairs and one of them—the woman?—was packing his luggage. She smiled as she remembered Graydon saying that he didn't do luggage. Would they know that about him? That woman didn't look like someone who knew how to fold sweaters properly.

Toby lifted the leaves of a scented geranium to water underneath. Wet leaves under glass tended to burn.

Of course Graydon would have to return a day early, she thought. He was a prince and he had duties. That she'd nearly forgotten that in the last few days didn't matter. She hadn't thought of it before, but now she'd have no one to help her with Victoria's wedding. She could ask . . . Well, actually, right now there wasn't anyone on the island whom she could ask for help. Toby had never been one of those people who had a thousand friends. No, she had a few close friends and when she was away from them . . .

She moved six pots of camellias to the floor and began to scour and disinfect the bench. Maybe Jared or Lexie would know someone she could get for a summer roommate. But where would she find someone who could help her cook and help with Victoria's wedding? Someone who'd make her laugh?

She was putting the plants back on the shelf when she glanced up to see the man from Lanconia walking toward the greenhouse. He certainly was beautiful! And he walked as though he might spring into action at any second.

She went to the door, wiping her hands on the big apron she wore, and stepped outside.

"How bad is it?" she asked, then stopped. "I didn't mean to be rude, but I could see that something is wrong. Could I help pack?"

The man was looking at her as though puzzled by something. "His Royal Highness has sent me to inform you of everything."

For a moment Toby didn't know who he meant. "When is Graydon leaving?"

"He is not. He must stay longer, and we'd like to remain in your house. With your permission, that is. Perhaps my colleague and I could use your second bedroom."

Toby felt such relief that Graydon wasn't going away, that she wasn't going to be left alone, that she smiled deeply. "Mr.—?"

"Daire," he said, not giving his title or even his last name.

"Appropriate," she murmured. "Why don't you sit down there"—she nodded to a raised bed—"while I tend to the garden and you tell me what's going on? Oh! And we'll have to make a place for you downstairs—unless you share a room with Graydon." She looked at him. "Or does he share with . . . with her?"

Daire's eyes widened in surprise. "With Lorcan? She is his protector. I believe the American term is bodyguard."

Toby gasped. "Is there some danger? Has someone threatened Graydon?"

"No," Daire said, his voice lowered.

Toby thought it was a nice voice, but she couldn't help thinking that it wasn't as rich and deep as Graydon's.

"There is no danger and no threat. Lorcan and I know about the exchange of twins, so we volunteered to come here to guard the man believed to be Prince Rory. But there are things that Prince Graydon will need to oversee in the coming weeks."

Toby, her hand on the faucet, halted. "Weeks? Why can't they just exchange back?" She put up her hand before Daire could speak. "Unless something changed to keep them from being identical. Please tell me Rory didn't ride a motorcycle up the palace steps and break his leg."

At that Daire laughed, and when he did, his body relaxed. He took the hose from her. "Please sit and I will tell you all. But first, why would I need to share a bedroom with Gray?"

Toby looked at him. "I don't know Lanconian customs but I can assure you that you're not sharing a bedroom with me."

Again, Daire laughed as he turned on the water and began on the rows of flowers along the fence.

Toby didn't sit but went to walk beside him, pulling weeds as they moved down the bed. He told her how Rory had put himself between the falling king and the marble stairs and had come out of it with a broken wrist. "And Lorcan was bruised," he said, then he told of her heroic act.

Toby saw the way his face softened when he spoke of the beautiful young woman. "And she is to you . . . ?"

"My student. I have trained her since she was a child."

The way he spoke made him sound like an old man—which she could see was far from the truth. "That makes you what? Fifty-two, fifty-three?"

For a moment Daire looked shocked, then his eyes twinkled. "My age seems to depend on the day. My hope is that Lorcan will take time off from her training so my old body can have a rest."

Toby looked at him. It was easy to see that under his clothes was a well-toned body. Like Graydon's, she thought. "I can see that you are a very lazy man."

When he looked back at her, his eyes had a slow, easy fire in them that made Toby's breath catch in her throat. She hastily pulled out three weeds and tossed them onto the pile. Graydon had certainly never looked at her like that, she thought, and suddenly, a surge of anger went through her. This man she'd just met let her know he found her desirable, but Graydon never had! She kept her head turned away. "So what happens now?"

"Prince Graydon needs to stay away from Lanconia until Rory's wrist heals. We could fit Gray with a cast but the doctors would know. And right now we don't want anyone knowing the king is incapacitated or that the brothers have . . ." He seemed to be trying to find the right words.

"Have played some crazy, juvenile trick on the entire country?" Toby finished for him.

"You seem to understand well."

"Just common sense," Toby said, then her head came up. "If the king is away, who will handle his duties? I'm sorry but I don't know much about Lanconia. Are the royal family's duties all ribbon-cutting or more serious?"

Daire sighed. "If they were only what the public sees, this would be easy, but every visitor who is important to our country wants to deal with royalty. They want to say they negotiated a contract with the king or his son, not with a committee of old men and women. They want to be wined and dined and entertained in the palace."

"Oh," Toby said as she sat down on the rim of one of the raised beds. "Graydon could handle that, but from what I understand, Rory hasn't spent enough time in Lanconia to know all the things he'll need to." She looked up at Daire. He was holding the hose and looking down at her. She put her hand up to shield her eyes from the sun behind him. "Graydon is going to have to do the king's job as well as Rory's, isn't he? And all from the other side of the world."

"I think you do see the problem."

She couldn't help smiling at his tone. He sounded as though he was quite proud of her. "Wait a minute! What about the engagement ceremony? Rory can't do that, can he? And does the woman know about the exchange?"

Daire turned away to hide his smile. Lady Danna was "the woman," was she? "No, she doesn't. She has been very solicitous of Prince Rory's injury and she calls him Graydon. She cannot be allowed to pledge herself to the wrong man, as once the engagement is finalized it is as good as a marriage. But Lorcan and I have planned for this. We will secrete Graydon back into the country the night before the ceremony, then out again afterward."

"But wouldn't Rory go see his father in the hospital?"

"It has been publicly reported that the king is relaxing at a spa, so Rory's unscheduled visit would draw attention to the matter. It is better that no one know of the king's stroke. After the ceremony, if the king has not shown significant signs of recovery, he will step down and Graydon will take over."

Toby looked toward the house. Which meant that very soon Graydon could be a king, she thought. "What's he doing now?"

"Instructing his brother in how to deal with the president of a country few people had heard of until six years ago. A sheep fell down a hole and when they pulled it out, it had four lavender diamonds stuck in its wool. Since then, the inhabitants have ravaged their country looking for more of them."

"Did they find any?"

"Several," Daire said. "Lady Danna's engagement ring contains one."

"How nice for her," Toby said but there was no enthusiasm in her voice.

Daire was watching her. "Lady Danna knows nothing about

any of this. We are entrusting only you with our country's secrets."

"Don't worry," she said. "I'm no snitch."

Daire started to reply, but the back door to the house opened and the formidable-looking Lorcan appeared. She seemed to be glowering in disapproval.

"I believe I am wanted," Daire said and gave a small bow. "It has been a pleasure."

"For me too," Toby said and they smiled at each other.

He took a few steps toward the house, but then turned back. "Perhaps tomorrow we could train together."

"I'm not very athletic," Toby said.

"I will teach you," he replied. His eyes were very dark.

"Yes" was the only thing she could think to say.

"I will give you first choice of weapons." Turning away, he hurried into the house.

"Weapons?" Toby said as she rolled up the hose, then thought, Maybe Victoria would like a Lanconian wedding. Maybe two lines of these glorious men could form a tunnel of swords and Victoria could pass under them. It would certainly be dramatic.

"You were out there a long while," Graydon said when Daire entered the dining room, which had been set up as an office.

Rory was on the screen now. "Hey, Daire!" he called out. "How do you like Nantucket?"

Daire moved the screen around to face him. "I haven't seen much," he said in Lanconian, "but the streets are nice and wide."

The two of them laughed together. It would be difficult to find narrower streets than in Lanconia or Nantucket.

"How's Toby?" Rory asked.

"Truly lovely. She guessed the problem was you and asked if you'd ridden a motorcycle up the palace stairs and broken your leg."

"I am wounded!" Rory said, his hand to his heart. "Tell her that I was injured while being a hero."

"Ha!" Daire said. "You were cushioned by Lorcan. If she hadn't acted so quickly and so well, both of you would probably have broken your necks."

Rory stopped laughing. "How is she?"

Daire sat down in front of the screen. "Injured worse than she allows anyone to see."

"Tell her thank you and that I'm sorry Dad is so fat."

Daire smiled. "I'll be sure to."

"I know Gray is worried about all of this." Rory lowered his voice. "Tell him I'll do the best I can, but some ambassador from Russia is coming tomorrow. By Naos, I don't know what I'm doing!"

Daire leaned closer to the microphone. "The man likes vodka and very tall women," he said quietly, then looked up to see Graydon listening. He raised his voice. "My advice is that you listen to your brother and obey him."

"That's what I plan to do," Rory answered just as loudly and Daire moved away.

"Go to bed!" Graydon said to his brother. "We'll talk more tomorrow." He clicked off the screen, then leaned back in his chair and looked at Daire. "What did you talk to Toby about for so long?"

"Why we're here, sleeping arrangements, that sort of thing. I was surprised that you two have separate bedrooms."

"She is a maiden and I plan to leave her that way."

"Then why the hell are we here?!" Daire asked, truly confused.

"I . . ." Graydon began but couldn't think of a plausible answer. "I've been helping her come up with a theme for a wedding."

Only Daire's eyes showed his amusement. "Have you chosen your colors yet?"

"How about black and blue to match what I'm going to do to you when I get you on the field?"

"I look forward to it. Shall we eat? Or have these Americans turned you into a veggen and now you live on tofu and kale?"

"It's vegan and Nantucketers eat quite well. I'll go get Toby," Graydon said, but his—Rory's—cell phone rang and the ID said it was from the palace. "I have to take this."

"Then it will be my pleasure to get Miss Toby," Daire said and he left the room before Graydon could protest.

When Graydon got off the phone, he went to the kitchen and saw Daire and Toby seated side by side at the small table that he had cleaned off, in the room he had cleared out.

The table was covered with food from Lanconia that Daire and Lorcan had brought with them: roasted meat, sausages, pâtés, loaves of multigrain bread, cheeses, olives, pickled grapes, raisins, nuts, and even some Lanconian beer. Since they'd traveled with diplomatic immunity, they'd been able to get everything through customs.

"Try this one," Daire said, and when Toby had her hands full, he put the tidbit into her mouth.

"Delicious," she said. "What herb is that? I've never tasted anything like it."

"It grows high up in our beautiful mountains. Maybe someday I can take you there."

"I'd love that!"

What Graydon felt at the sight of them was the same as on the first night when he'd struck out at Rory for talking about Toby. But now, with Daire, he wanted to go for his throat.

Graydon took a step forward but Lorcan came up behind

him. She firmly put her hands on his shoulders and began to massage the back of his neck with her thumbs. Part of her training had been how to deal with the tension before a match and the injuries afterward.

"It is just Daire," she said into his ear. "He flirts with every pretty girl. It means nothing."

"Toby is more than just a pretty girl," Graydon growled.

"I'm sure of it," Lorcan said and tried not to sound patronizing. Prince Graydon might think of the American as someone unique, but it looked as though she didn't feel the same about him. Obviously, she went from one man to another easily enough.

Maybe, Lorcan thought, she could get this flirting woman to show her true motives. If that happened, perhaps when Prince Graydon returned home he wouldn't be so very unhappy.

While Lorcan wasn't a fan of Lady Danna, she was certainly preferable to this girl, who seemed to like any man who crossed her path.

As for Daire, now with his head so close to the blonde woman's that they were nearly touching, Lorcan had the idea that his motives might be the same. Perhaps he too wanted to show Prince Graydon what he was risking so much for.

When Toby looked up and saw the beautiful Lorcan with her hands on Graydon's neck, she realized that Lorcan's eyes were on Daire. How interesting, Toby thought. She smiled at Graydon and motioned to the chair beside her. "You must be starving. Come and eat."

When he sat down by her, she could see by his eyes and his silence that he was quite upset. Was he worried about his father? she wondered. Or was his concern about Rory and what he could do to the country with no one there to guide him?

"Try this," Toby said as she spread a pale yellow cheese on a rye cracker.

"No!" Lorcan said from across the table.

It was the first English word Toby had heard her say. "What's wrong?"

Lorcan said something in Lanconian.

"She says Prince Graydon does not like that cheese," Daire said.

"Oh. Sorry." Toby looked from one face to the other and finally understanding came to her. Daire's flirting, his questions about bedrooms and his obvious surprise, Lorcan's sneering, and now Graydon's silence had nothing to do with Lanconia. All of them had made assumptions about her, and they were showing the conclusions they'd reached. As far as she could tell, the two newcomers thought she was some sort of femme fatale who was trying to lure their beloved prince away from his country and his duties. While Graydon . . . It was hard to believe, but he looked as though he were jealous! Did he think she was about to run off to bed with the beautiful Daire?!

Toby put the cracker down and pushed her chair back. "You know, I think I've had enough to eat. I'll leave the three of you to discuss business." She got up and went to the front door.

When she left the house, she didn't know where she was going. She just knew that she had to get out.

It had started to rain, a nice, quiet summer shower, which meant that no trees were coming down and no roofs were flying off. On Nantucket, "storm" was a relative term.

Toby stood outside the door for a few seconds, but when she heard a sound behind her, she hurried toward the lane. When she reached it, she saw that the door of the big old house across the road, the one Graydon's relatives had under contract, was wide open. She didn't think anyone was there, which meant that someone hadn't closed the door properly. The wind and rain were sure to get inside. Besides, Toby wanted a place to go, somewhere where she could think.

The rain pounded at her as she ran toward the house and

inside. The marble floor of the foyer was wet. Grabbing the door, she pushed it closed.

For a moment she leaned against it. Before her were doors to her right and left, with a wide staircase in the middle. She chose to go up.

At the top of the stairs were two open doors. A flash of lightning showed a bedroom to her right, so she went in there. The room was dirty, with cobwebs and thick dust, and in the center was a huge mahogany bed frame. The size of it made her think that to remove it, it would have to be sawn in half. A wide fireplace was on one side of the room, its wooden hearth carved with swags of roses and leaves.

At the end of the room were two doors and Toby instinctively went to the one on the left. She found herself in what looked to have been a library. It was a small room. Cozy.

There was a little fireplace against one wall and it was surrounded by bookshelves. The two flanking walls also had shelves, all of them empty and very dusty. In the fourth wall was a double window and beneath it was an old sofa with a curved back.

With the rain outside, it was dim in the room, but there was something about the place that made Toby feel calm. When she sat down on the old sofa a cloud of dust went up around her, but she didn't mind.

She put her head back, and as she looked about her, she could almost imagine the room as it had once been. The shelves would be full of leather bound books, the fireplace would have a cheerful little blaze in it, and she would wear a long dress of white cotton. In spite of the fire, it was cool in the room and she drew her shawl closer to her. She knew it was of red paisley and someone—Captain Caleb?—had brought it back from his last voyage to China. Smiling at the clarity of the image, Toby closed her eyes and drifted into sleep.

She dreamed of someone touching her hand, kissing it, and holding it to his whisker-stubbled face. She smiled a bit, for she knew he was someone she loved very much.

"Toby," said a deep voice.

She opened her eyes to see Graydon bending over her, his face full of concern. For a moment she couldn't seem to clear her mind. Her dream had been so vivid she was surprised to see that there were no books on the shelves, no fire in the fireplace, and she didn't have on a white dress with a beautiful red shawl over her shoulders.

She sat upright. "Go away."

Graydon stepped back and his whole body stiffened. "If that is what you wish," he said formally and turned toward the door, but he stopped and looked back at her. "Toby, I—"

When she looked up at him, there were tears in her eyes. "Do you realize that they think I'm a woman of low morals who is trying to make you desert your country? Or maybe I'm a spy trying to wheedle classified information out of you. Whatever it is, I'm judged to be the guilty one!"

"I know," he said softly. "I will straighten this out. I will take the blame for every bit of it."

She looked up at him. "I can't figure out anything that's going on in my life right now. Since the moment I met you, everything has been turned upside down. My friend Lexie suddenly left the island, I was given a huge event to plan, and my day job was taken from me. And there you were through all of it. It's like you made everything happen."

Graydon was standing by the door and his posture seemed to stiffen with every word she spoke.

"But why?" she said. The tears were running down her cheeks. "What is between us? For days you were like the best girlfriend in the world. We went places and did things together. I loved every minute of it. But there was nothing . . ." She took a breath. "There was never even a hint of intimacy between us.

Nothing physical, no sharing of secrets. Not one bit of real closeness. For all that we've been living together, we are strangers."

At that, Graydon's stiffness—his protection from the world—left. "Is that what you think?" he said, and he sounded both shocked and offended. "I have never shared what I have with you with anyone else, not even my brother."

She stood up. She'd not been aware of it but anger had been building in her for quite a while. "That's not how I see it."

Graydon frowned as he seemed to be trying to figure out what had triggered this outburst. "Lorcan should not have told you of my dislike of the Ulten cheese. It was not her place."

Toby made her hands into fists. "That isn't about cheese. That woman was letting me know that you belong to her."

Graydon looked shocked. "Lorcan and I have never—"

Toby threw up her hands. "How can men be so dumb? How are you able to dress yourselves when you have no brains at all?"

Graydon's eyes widened.

Letting out her breath, Toby unclenched her fists. "Has a woman ever yelled at you before?"

"No," he said. "And may I say that I find it quite confusing? I have tried to be courteous at all times. I have had a few lapses in decorum. You in your . . ." He motioned up and down with his hand. "I should not have stayed in the room with you when you were so scantily attired, but I could not make myself leave."

"You just don't get it, do you?" She wiped away the tears. She no longer felt like crying. Now only anger ran through her. "Is Daire married?" she asked abruptly.

"No, he is not."

"I just wondered because he let me know that if I'm willing, he is. Right now, I'm thinking that I'll take him up on his offer." With that, she went to the door and stepped into the old bedroom.

Graydon caught her by the arm. His face was fierce. If she didn't know him she would have been frightened. "You will not bed my man."

She glared at him. "The last I heard, I have free will." She jerked away from his grasp, took a step forward, then looked back. "You want to know a truth about me?" She didn't give him time to reply. "I'm not a virgin because I'm 'saving myself for marriage.' That was something I said because it's fashionable. The truth is that no man has ever made me feel that passion I read about. When I was in college the girls would come in with their clothes on backward, then giggle about it. But I didn't! Never once was I tempted by any of those boys. But when Daire looked at me, I did consider it. But then I realized that since you're just a shorter, paler version of him, it was really you who I wanted, but—" She threw up her hands. "Oh, what does it matter? It's not like you have any interest in me." Turning, she started for the stairs down.

"Is that what this is about?" Graydon said from behind her. "You think I don't desire you?"

She looked back at him, glaring. "Of course it isn't. You're engaged to someone else. Or you almost are. You're going to marry someone who I bet is an overly tall woman with black eyes who would look down her nose at a washed-out blonde like me. I bet she can fight with a lance or any other weapon. Hey! Nantucket has a harpoon-throwing contest, so maybe Lorcan and your beloved Danna could enter. I'm sure they'd win."

Toby ran down the stairs and he caught her at the bottom, his hands on her shoulders. "Let me go!"

But he didn't release her. He put his face close to hers. "How can you not know?" he said, his eyes nearly as angry as hers. "How can you not feel what I go through every day with you? To be so near you yet not be allowed to touch you tears me apart. I lie awake at night, in the room so close to yours, and dream of going to you, of slipping into bed with you and pulling you into my arms."

"But you've never said or done anything to make me think that's true."

"I dream of kissing your neck." His eyes seemed to turn to black coals and every spark showed his desire for her. As his fingertips cut into her upper arms, she saw a different man from the one who laughed so easily. This man didn't seem to laugh about anything. This man looked like one of his Lanconian warrior ancestors.

He pulled Toby against his hard chest, not gently but with force. "In the morning I lean over you so I can smell your hair. Just one soft whiff is all I ask."

"Graydon," she whispered, but he didn't let her speak.

"I have seen women of all nationalities, all shapes and sizes, but I have never desired any of them as I do you." His voice was more of a growl than a human sound. "I have wanted to touch you, caress you, make love to you, since the first day."

Toby was blinking up at him, her eyes wide. He was making her feel as she'd never felt before. For the first time in her life she was experiencing what other girls did, what made them sigh and giggle—and it felt glorious! Powerful, really. Never in her life had she felt . . . well, so very pleased to be a woman.

It was tempting, like original-sin tempting, to hold her lips up to his and . . . Then what? They'd go at it on the floor?

With a bit of an inner smile of triumph, she pushed him away and it took more than a little force. There, at last, was that look in his eyes that she'd wanted to see. Heat radiated from him like fire, drawing her to him. He made Daire seem like a boy. At this moment she could see how Graydon's ancestors had won the kingship.

"No," she said softly. "I'm not going to give in to you. You're as good as a married man."

Graydon fell back against the big newel post. "You thought

I didn't desire you and I showed you that I do, but now you're saying no?"

"Yes, that's right. But at least now I know where I stand with you and what all this is about. I'll tell you something, Graydon Montgomery, I am not going to fall in love with you." She flung the front door open, then stood back and looked at him, waiting for him to leave.

He looked as though he wanted to say something but couldn't think of exactly what. Mostly, he looked bewildered.

It took a great deal of discipline on her part, but Toby didn't comfort him. He'd hidden his true feelings for her since they'd met, which made her very angry. And now that he'd revealed himself he seemed to think she'd give in to him instantly.

No, she valued herself a great deal more than that! Graydon put his hands in his pockets and left the house.

Chapter Thirteen

As soon as Graydon was outside, Toby slipped on the rain-soaked marble floor and hit her head on the edge of the door. She caught herself before she reached the floor, and for a moment she stood there, watching Graydon walk down the path toward the lane. Never before had she seen his shoulders slumped, but they were now. The rain was pounding down on him but he seemed oblivious to it.

She watched him until he crossed the road and went inside her house. Part of her hoped he'd turn and look back and see her standing there, but he didn't.

She closed the front door and leaned against it for a moment. It was going to take a while for the anger inside her to calm down. And she needed to think about everything in her life right now. One thing she knew for sure was that if she had any sense she'd tell all the Lanconians to leave, and this included the almost-married Graydon. Kingsley House was free of guests now so maybe they could stay there.

But she needed time to figure out what to do. A flash of lightning momentarily illuminated the entryway and she looked at the two doorways that led into the rooms. As had happened upstairs, she knew which door to go through. Inside the door on the right was a large room with a big fireplace along one wall. Beside it was a cabinet door. "It's been built over the old oven," she said aloud, then frowned. Obviously, she'd been going on too many of the old house tours on Nantucket.

At the back was another door and she went to it. Inside was a small room with a little fireplace along one wall.

Suddenly, she felt dizzy, and when she put her hand to her head, it felt wet. Another burst of lightning showed blood on her fingertips. When she slipped she must have cut her head. She knew she should go home and bandage it, but the thought of confronting Graydon right now made her hesitate. She needed to consider all aspects of this situation. What happened after what had been revealed between them? Was their friendship over? In the coming weeks should she do what Lexie had advised and have a rip-roaring good time in bed with Graydon— even though she now had an idea of the pain she'd feel when he left? And besides, would they carry on this affair with the flirting Daire and sneering Lorcan downstairs?

The more she thought, the dizzier Toby felt.

She looked about the little room. The only furniture in it was a hard little cot pushed against the wall. "Where's the card table?" she whispered. And that hard little sofa that her great-aunt Marjorie had needlepointed the upholstery for? But then, she'd had the time to do that, since she'd been widowed at twenty-four.

"The same age as me," Toby said aloud and again she felt dizzy. How was she making these things up? She really did need to get the cut on her head looked at.

It was as she put her hand on the door that she turned to look at the old paneling on one wall. She couldn't really see it, but she knew there was a narrow door there. It was hidden by the paneling. In fact, you could look at that wall and not even see that there was a door.

But Toby knew not only that it was there, but how to open it. The brass catch was hidden behind a piece of wood that had to be pushed to one side before you could see that latch.

It was as though she was drawn to that side of the room, pulled toward it, but at the same time she fought against touching it. She knew that inside was something horrible. No! Inside something very bad had happened.

She put her hand on the panel and tried to slide the wood to the side. Over the years—centuries, really—the wood had swollen and shrunk, and the finish that John Kendricks had put on there was gone.

It took both hands to push the wood back, and by the time she got it aside, she was crying—and the blood from the cut on her temple was running down the side of her face.

Here is where I died, she thought, then repeated aloud, "Here is where I died."

She put her hand out to open the door but she couldn't make herself do it. She turned away. "I must go home," she said. "To Garrett." Lightning struck outside. "No. To Silas."

She put her hand to her forehead and managed to make it to the cot. Her mind seemed to be twirling about with faces and images that were familiar but at the same time strange. Victoria was there, smiling at her, her red hair pulled high up on her head, and the front of her dress was so low cut that Toby was almost blushing. And Victoria was young, Toby's age.

"Are you well?" Victoria asked. "Or did you have too much cider? Or too much dancing?"

Toby touched her temple, but it no longer seemed to be bleeding.

"Why don't you stay in here and rest for a while?" Victoria said, smiling down at Toby. "Come out when you have recovered."

Toby sat up on the sofa and looked around her. The room seemed familiar, but it took her a moment to place it. "Am I in Kingsley House?"

"Oh, my! You have had too much of that brew the Kingsleys are serving. You don't remember that this is Captain Caleb's new house? Not that I've met the man, but everyone wonders what he'll say when he returns and finds his builder has used the house for his own wedding before the captain has so much as spent one night in it. But then, no one seems overly concerned about injuring the pride of a Kingsley. After what I've heard, my opinion is that someday a woman should say no to one of them just for the pleasure of it." Victoria leaned toward Toby. "But I need not tell you that, do I? Do you mean to tell the family tonight?"

Toby's head was beginning to clear somewhat but that didn't take away her confusion. She looked down at herself and saw she was wearing a dress similar to Victoria's. It was all white, with short, puffy sleeves, a low neckline—but she was showing only half as much as Victoria was—and a long skirt that was beautifully embroidered around the hem. Vaguely, she seemed to remember that she had done the embroidery, which was absurd since she'd never sewn anything in her life.

"Do you mean I'm to tell Jared something?" Toby asked.

"Dearest, there are a dozen Jareds on this island. Which one are you talking about?"

"Jared Montgomery Kingsley the Seventh," Toby said, giving her friend's full name.

Smiling, Victoria took Toby's hands and pulled her up from the little sofa. "The only Montgomery on this island is me, and

I can assure you that there's no Kingsley who I'd attach my name to. Arrogant bunch of swaggering . . ." She broke off. "I am telling you nothing that you don't already know."

Victoria looked Toby up and down and seemed satisfied with what she saw. "I have changed my mind. There will be no more hiding in here. Come and join the celebration." She put her arm through Toby's and led her out the door.

"What are we celebrating?" Toby asked tentatively.

Victoria laughed. "You are inebriated! It's John and Parthenia's wedding, but I know how you feel. It's all rather plain, isn't it? When I get married I shall wear a gown of silk, with blue satin ribbons on the sleeves. And I shall marry a man who will love me for all eternity."

"That's asking a lot," Toby said.

"You think that because all you ask of a man is that he stay alive." When Victoria opened the door there was a burst of light and sound: music, laughter, and the blaze of what had to be a hundred candles. Before them was a scene out of a period drama. They were in the large back parlor of Kingsley House and it was full of people who were all dressed as though for a Jane Austen movie. The women had on dresses like the one Toby was wearing: high waisted, with long, flowing skirts. The men wore jackets that stopped at the waist, with trousers that were like tights.

Three men stopped in front of Victoria, silently waiting for her to notice them. Toby wasn't surprised by that, for Victoria was a ravishingly beautiful woman, and the very low cut of her dress left little to the imagination.

"Will you be all right?" Victoria asked.

"Of course," Toby said, even though she was feeling as though she wanted to run away and hide.

Victoria leaned toward her and whispered, "Remember that tonight you must tell them."

"Tell who what?" Toby asked, feeling a bit of panic that Victoria was leaving her side.

Victoria laughed. "If I had to say what you must, I would also try to forget." She stepped toward the dancers. "Eat something. It will clear your mind and give you courage."

Victoria turned away and Toby stood where she was. This is a dream, she thought. A very vivid dream caused by too much emotion in the last few days.

She took a step back, moving behind some women who were watching the dancers. They smiled at her as though they knew her, but Toby didn't remember ever having seen them. When she was in the shadows she felt safer, not overwhelmed by this much too realistic dream.

A couple walked by. He was holding her arm tightly and leaning over her as though he feared that she might fly away from him. With a jolt, Toby realized that they were Jilly and Ken, who'd only recently met but were already a couple.

The familiarity of them made Toby relax somewhat. It looked like she was putting people she knew in her dream. Victoria and now Ken and Jilly. That they were all wearing Regency clothes made sense, as Toby loved any Jane Austen movie and owned all the DVDs. "Wonder who else I've put in my dream?" she said aloud.

"Did you say something, Tabby?" an older woman in front of her said as she turned to look at her.

Toby smiled. "Is that short for Tabitha?" she asked.

Two other women turned to look at her, frowning. "I think you should seek out your mother," one of them said.

"No," Toby said pleasantly. "This is my dream, so I think I'll skip that encounter." She moved around the women and went to the doorway. She had to let three people pass—none of whom she recognized—before she could go through, and found herself in the back hallway of Kingsley House.

The house looked so new! Everything was so clean and fresh, as though it really had just been built instead of being over two hundred years old. At the end of the hall, she came to the front parlor. It had always been the most formal room in the house, where all the best furniture was, where the beautiful things that Captain Caleb had brought back from his voyages were kept.

The room was much like Toby knew it, but there was half as much in it. And everything looked sparkling new. The old couch that she and Lexie had sat on many times wasn't there. In its place was a long settee upholstered in needlepoint of a seafaring scene: a harbor with a ship; ladies holding on to the arms of gentlemen; men in big shirts, tight trousers, and boots; and workmen moving huge bales of goods about.

There were a few people in the room and they smiled and nodded at Toby.

"Tabby, be sure to get some cake before it's all gone," a man said as he and the woman with him left the room.

Toby answered that she would, then returned to looking about. There was a long, narrow lacquered box on a corner cabinet and she recognized it from having seen it in the attic of Kingsley House. When she'd tried to open it, Lexie said, "There's no key. It's been lost over the years."

"You could get a locksmith," Toby said.

"Top of my list of things to do," Lexie said and they'd laughed.

Now Toby saw that the key to the box was sticking out. It made sense that it would be in her dream since she'd been curious about it. She turned the key and opened the box. Inside, perfectly fitted in satin-lined compartments, were twelve jade figures of animals. She recognized them as Chinese zodiac symbols. "What a beautiful collection," she whispered aloud as she closed the lid and turned the key.

"There you are!" came a woman's voice so familiar that it made the hair on Toby's neck stand up. This is my dream, she thought as she closed her eyes very tightly. Go away! she said to herself. Go away right now!

"Tabitha?" the woman said. "Valentina said you weren't feeling well."

Toby's fingers closed over the key to the box, and when she turned around, she looked into the face of her mother.

But as alike as the face was, there was a difference. For one thing, she wasn't glowering at her daughter as though Toby had yet again committed some great sin. That had been the expression she'd grown up with, the look her mother had given her all her life. As far as Toby remembered, she'd never pleased her mother in anything she'd ever done.

But this woman in her dream wasn't looking at Toby like that. While it was true that there wasn't any genuine happiness in the woman's eyes, there was concern. It was as though she really cared whether or not Toby was feeling well.

"Mother?" Toby whispered.

She gave a small smile. "You look as though you've never seen me before."

"I'm not sure I have, actually," Toby said.

The woman laughed—a sound Toby didn't think she'd ever heard before. Her mother was a very serious person. Taking care of her household, helping her husband with anything he needed, and, above all else, finding her daughter a husband were jobs that consumed her.

"Come along, dear, and get something to eat."

When she slipped her arm through Toby's, Toby's eyes widened in shock. Casual affection was not something that her mother demonstrated. Toby couldn't help that her eyes began to grow teary.

"Valentina was right. You are a bit off tonight. Come away.

Silas will be here soon. He is delivering a coffin. People die at the most inopportune times, don't they?"

At that callous statement, Toby laughed. This was the mother she knew. "Valentina is the red-haired woman?"

"You know that."

"Yes, of course I do," Toby said and remembered hearing that long ago Captain Caleb and Valentina had been lovers.

As they walked toward the doorway, another woman entered the room. "Lavinia, Tabby," she said in greeting and they nodded to her.

Outside this vivid dream, in the real world, her mother's name was Lavidia. "Lavidia, Lavinia, Toby, Tabby," she said aloud.

"No more cider for you, dear," Lavinia said, patting her daughter's hand.

They went across the hall to the dining room, where a long table was laden with food. Several people were around it, holding beautiful plates that Toby had seen on display in the Nantucket Whaling Museum.

"Did Captain Caleb bring these back from China?" Toby asked.

"You helped unpack them." Her mother was looking at the food, picking over it.

It was when Toby reached for a plate that she realized she still had the key to the box in her hand. But then, it made sense that her dream was reconciling the lost key. Maybe if she put the key back in the box it would be there when she woke. Smiling at that idea, she picked up a plate and reached for a piece of fish with mushrooms on it. "So how is Captain Caleb?"

To Toby, it was an innocent question, but her mother turned to her with the angry face Toby had seen all her life. "No sea captains!" she said in a voice that was more a hiss than human.

Toby took a step back. "I didn't mean anything by my question. Isn't this his house?"

Lavinia seemed to need a few breaths before she could speak. "Of course it is, but don't let his riches fool you. You know as well as anyone what it's like to marry a man of the sea."

"I guess so," Toby said as she picked up a little bowl full of what looked to be custard. "I take it Silas has nothing to do with the sea?"

Lavinia looked at her daughter across the table. "What has happened to you tonight? You do not seem to be yourself."

"I'm just reevaluating my life, that's all. I want to know what you think of Silas and me. Are we truly in love?"

"Really, Tabitha! You do ask embarrassing questions! I assume you are since you have pledged yourself to him."

"We're engaged to be married?"

Lavinia looked hard at her daughter for a long moment. "You're not thinking of . . . of him again, are you?"

"No, certainly not!" Toby said. "He's not in my mind at all." *Whoever "he" is. What a marvelous dreamer I am,* she thought. *I had no idea I was so imaginative.* As far as she could tell, she—as Tabitha—seemed to be in love with one man but engaged to another—whom she might or might not be in love with at all.

It certainly beat her current life! "What year is this?" she asked.

"Tabitha, you are beginning to frighten me."

"I don't mean to. I just need some reassurance that I'm doing the right thing in choosing Silas over . . . him."

Lavinia squinted her eyes. "That will not be a concern, because you will be married by the time his ship returns. He and that brother of his will not be able to turn your head with their looks and their swagger."

"And who is his brother?"

She leaned toward her daughter. "Mark my words, Tabitha

Weber, but Captain Caleb will be dead before long. He's too reckless, too full of his own importance. His crewmen tell stories of the chances he takes when he's on the seas. Someday that will take him down—and when he goes, he'll take young Garrett with him."

Toby raised her brows in interest at this rather romantic, swashbuckling story and her mother saw it.

"Do not imagine yourself with him!" Lavinia said and there was desperation in her voice. "We are a house full of sea widows and we need what Silas offers." Lavinia put her full plate down on the end of the table. "Now see what you have done to me! My heart races. I must lie down."

As Lavinia rushed past her daughter, Toby said, "I'm sorry. I didn't mean—" Her mother was gone. Toby looked at the other people in the room, who were staring at her with eyes of disapproval. She had no doubt that they knew the whole story behind whatever was upsetting her mother.

Toby put down her plate of food. "I'd better go see about her." The women looked at her as though to say indeed she should, and Toby left the room.

She felt a pang of guilt for not trying to find her mother and soothe her, but then, what could she say? That she promised that Tabitha would marry Silas and not the rascal from the ship? But since her mother seemed to have set the wedding before the sailor was to return, there was no need to make a vow that she knew nothing about.

Instead, Toby went back to where there was dancing and music, wondering when she would wake up. She truly hoped that she hadn't suffered a concussion when she fell on the slick floor. This dream was taking so long she was beginning to think she was in a coma.

Not that any of this is real, Toby thought as she looked around at the dancers. There were a few people she'd seen around the island but didn't know their names. If this was her own dream, made up by her, why was Jared excluded? Victoria/ Valentina had never heard of him, but that made no sense.

When the dancers parted, Toby saw a little girl curled up on a window seat on the other side of the room. She was bent over a board with drawing paper on it, and something about her looked familiar.

Toby made her way around the dancers and sat down by the child. "What are you drawing?"

"The windows," she said.

Toby smiled, for she knew exactly who the child was. In contemporary times, she was Alix Madsen, who was an architect down to her very bone marrow.

"Let me guess," Toby said. "Your father is Ken. I think that here he's John Kendricks, and today he married Parthenia, who is Jilly."

The girl turned to look at Toby as though trying to figure her out. "My sister is Ivy and our mother died."

"I'm sorry," Toby said softly. "Do you like your new mother?"

"She made my father give me blocks of wood to build with."

"High praise indeed!" Toby said and for a moment she watched the dancers. "Do you think Captain Caleb is going to be angry about his house when he returns?"

The girl was bent over her drawing. "He is here now. I saw him. He went up the back stairs."

"Oh, dear," Toby said. "Just home after a long sea voyage and his house is full of people. No wonder he's hiding out. I seem to remember Alix telling me something about Captain Caleb and Valentina meeting in an attic. Maybe I should help things along by suggesting that she take a break up there." She looked at the child. "I'm sure I know your name, but what is it?"

"Alisa, but everyone calls me Ali."

"Perfect," Toby said. "You wouldn't know who Silas is and why my mother is so afraid of men of the sea, would you?"

"You live with sea widows. Your mother and sister and the women married to your three brothers all live there with you. All the men went down on ships. My father says they would all starve without you to look after them, as they are a silly bunch of girls."

Toby would have laughed except for the thought of so much death near Tabby. "I think I'm beginning to understand things. I guess Silas does something here on the island."

"He owns a big store. Only Mr. Obed Kingsley's store is bigger."

Toby was digesting this information—that she'd made up, she reminded herself. All of it was based on bits and pieces of history she'd heard from several sources in the last few weeks.

She leaned toward Ali. "You wouldn't know of another man whom I like, would you?"

"Everyone knows that. He is Captain Caleb's brother Garrett, and he wants to marry you, but your mother says no. You have to live at home and make sure the girls work."

"That doesn't sound fair," Toby said and she suddenly had the ridiculous idea that maybe she really was Tabitha and her modern life was a fantasy she'd created to escape "the girls."

"Ali, I want you to promise me that you'll keep drawing houses. Get your father to teach you about building, and someday you'll design homes that people will love living in for centuries to come. Promise?"

"Yes," the girl said but she looked puzzled. Just like Alix in the twenty-first century, she couldn't imagine not designing buildings.

When Toby stood up, she heard a faint clatter and realized she'd dropped the key to the lacquered box behind a cushion. She felt behind it but didn't find the key.

"My father has not finished building the house yet," Ali said.

Toby told her about the key being to the box in the front parlor and asked the child to tell her father to look for it. Ali nodded.

"I think I might go look at where I live. What's the name of the house and where is it?"

"At the end, by Main Street. It is called NEVER TO SEA AGAIN. The widows named it."

"Thank you," Toby said as she left the room. What a sad name, she thought. They had never seen their men again so they wanted men who never went to sea. She had an idea that the house was the one where she was sleeping, and she wondered if dreams like hers had caused it to be renamed BEYOND TIME.

As Toby made her way through the people and toward the front door, she saw Valentina and suggested that she slip away to the attic for a few moments of peace. As always, there were several young men around her. Valentina said that sounded like an excellent idea.

The clear, cool, salt-laden air outside felt good and Toby breathed deeply of it. There was some movement in the shrubbery outside and she smiled. It looked like some trysts were happening.

She left Kingsley House and took a left. In modern times there were three houses between this one and the house the Montgomery-Taggert family had bought. But now there was just land, and across the road was empty also. Nantucketers were good at moving houses from one place to another, so maybe some were brought in later. Or maybe young Ali would grow up and design houses that would be built on the vacant lots. She liked that idea best.

The narrow lane was full of horses and carriages and people on foot, all of them heading toward the light-filled Kingsley House.

When she got to the end of the lane, to the house where she'd hit her head, she paused, her hand on the gate. Across the road was the much smaller house she was sharing with Graydon—and now the Lanconians. Turning, she looked at it. It was completely dark, with no sign of life, and she wondered who lived there now.

She opened the gate and walked along the side of the big house. She didn't think she should just throw open the front door.

There was a big tree near the house. It wasn't there in her century, but its branches hung low, and she walked toward it.

"I knew you'd come to me," said a voice she knew well. He looked like Graydon, and it was as though he was and wasn't the man she knew.

Before she could speak, a strong arm caught her about the waist and pulled her to him. Toby's first instinct was to push away, but the night, the air, the stars, and the familiarity of this man prevented her movement.

She couldn't help herself—or didn't want to—as she put her face up to his and he kissed her, his lips on hers.

She'd kissed boys in her life, but as she'd told Graydon, she'd never felt anything in those encounters. It wasn't that way with him. His body against hers, his lips on hers . . . It was like their souls were melding into one. At that moment she was someone else, probably Tabby, and she knew she loved this man very, very much.

"Did you miss me?" he whispered. His hands were removing the pins from her hair and letting it fall down past her shoulders. "Did you think about me? Remember me?"

"I thought you no longer wanted me," she said and wasn't sure whether she was talking about her own life or Tabitha's.

"You always think that," he said, laughing.

She could see he was teasing her. She put her hand to his cheek. "Just today I said that I'd never love you."

"How could you not when I love you so much?" He kissed her palm. "Who is your mother trying to marry you to now?"

"Someone named Silas."

Smiling, Graydon began kissing her face. "I'm here now and you'll only marry me."

"But what about the widows?"

He pulled away to give her a very serious look. "I have been in countries where a man has many wives." He sighed. "So I will do my duty and take them all. Except your mother. She is too much for any man!"

"You!" Toby said, laughing, and again she caressed his cheek. She could feel the stubble of whiskers and knew he was the man in her first dream. "Did you bring me back a red paisley shawl?"

"I did, but how did you guess?"

"I dreamed of it. I was in the little room upstairs, the library, and I dreamed I was wearing the shawl. And you were kissing my hand."

"I would like to kiss all of you. Come, lay with me now, and tomorrow we will be married."

"I don't think I have a right to do that," Toby said. "It's not my body and not my future."

Graydon pulled back to look at her. "Are you now owned so fully by your mother that you cannot claim even your own body?"

"I meant that Tabitha owns it."

He didn't pause in holding her, just kept smiling. "If you are not Tabitha, who are you?"

"Toby. At least that's the nickname my father gave me. My real name is Carpathia."

"I like that. Good name for a ship," he said. "And I love you whatever your name. Will you marry me this day? I will build us a house here on my family's lane and I will love you forever."

"Unless you are made a king," Toby said.

"I do not understand you. When I left we said that we'd marry no matter what objections there were. All your letters to me have said that. I know your mother doubts me, but I will be a good husband."

"Will you give up the sea for Tabitha?"

Graydon laughed. "I am the sea; the sea is me. It is in my blood, in the veins of all my family."

"Like Lanconia is in Graydon's," Toby said.

"I have heard of that place. Wild and full of men who carry spears. It's said that in Lanconia even the women fight. It is not somewhere I want to go. And who is this Graydon?"

"What is your name?"

Laughing, he picked her up to twirl her around. "I have missed you every minute I was away. I bought you so many gifts that my brother Caleb laughed at me. He says that loving a woman would unman him and he vows to never do it."

"Don't worry, Valentina will fix him."

"And who is she?"

"She's — Actually, I'd rather you didn't meet her. She's too beautiful for any man to resist."

"I doubt that. I saw some Chinese women who took my breath away. They have tiny feet and—"

"I'd just as soon not hear about them."

He held her to him. "No one makes me laugh as you do. Marry me now. This minute. I brought you back a lavender diamond."

She pushed away to look at him. "But that's what you're giving to Danna."

"I know no one of that name. I got it from a trader. He said that a man's sheep fell down a hole and—"

"Came out with four lavender diamonds attached to its wool," Toby said. "How did you know that?"

"Toby! Toby! Wake up," she heard, then turned to him and said, "I think I'm leaving. I don't know if I'll ever be back again. Kiss me again."

"Gladly," he said.

But his lips never touched hers because she woke up to find herself back in the house that Graydon's relatives from Maine had bought.

Chapter Fourteen

When Toby woke up, she expected to see Graydon hovering over her and looking as forlorn as he had when he'd left the house. But to her surprise it was morning and no one was in the room.

But someone had been there. Her head was on a pillow in a clean case, which was good on the beat-up old cot, and a blanket had been spread over her.

Sitting up, she saw a basket on the floor. Inside was a bottle of water, a nicely wrapped rolled-up sandwich, and some fruit. Beside it was a set of her workout clothes and shoes. And there was an envelope made of the heavy kind of paper that was probably still only used by royalty.

Toby took a bite of the sandwich. Lanconian, she thought, recognizing the herb she'd had the day before. Inside the envelope was a note from Graydon. His handwriting—which she'd

seen on his drawings—was odd, with *r*'s shaped differently
from the American way.

Come home and you will be allowed to strike all of us.
We are at your mercy.

Your most humble servant, Graydon Montgomery

The note made her laugh, and what she liked best was that
he wasn't sulking because of what she'd said to him yesterday.
She'd always despised sulkers! Sitting with their lips stuck out,
wanting people to beg them to tell what they thought you had
done wrong. Then you had to plead, explain, and grovel to get
them to forgive you for something they had misunderstood.
No, thank you!

She went upstairs to the big bathroom and was glad the
water had been turned on in the house. Her hair had come out
of its braid, but then she remembered that it had been
Graydon—no, Garrett—who had taken it down. Smiling at the
memory of her dream, she rebraided it. Ten minutes later she
was dressed in her workout clothes. There was a mirror on the
back of the door and she glanced at herself. While it was true
that she wasn't athletic and didn't belong to a sports club, her
job entailed a lot of lifting of heavy garden flats and terra-cotta
pots. All in all, she was glad she looked good in her tight clothes.

When she went back down to the sitting room to get the
basket, she glanced at the paneled wall that she knew concealed
a door. She would have thought that in the bright light of day
the hidden room would hold no fear for her, but it did. In fact,
a part of her felt that if she opened the door and stepped inside,
she would not come out alive.

Grabbing the basket, Toby left the big house and hurried
across the lane. She couldn't help wondering how Graydon

would react after the way she'd bawled him out. Maybe she shouldn't have been so harsh. She could have modified her words. Actually, she should have sat down with him and, in an adult manner, told him what her complaints were.

She hoped he wasn't too depressed over their argument.

When she got to the front door, she was about to open it, but a sound from the back made her turn to the path. As she got closer to the backyard, the sound was louder, almost like steel striking steel.

She ran the last few steps, then halted.

Graydon and Daire were both wearing loose white trousers tucked into black boots that laced halfway up their calves—and their upper bodies were bare. They were fighting each other with what looked to be heavy medieval broadswords.

Toby stood under a tree and watched them. Daire was a bit taller, a few pounds heavier, and his skin was a few shades darker than Graydon's. He was indeed beautiful, but it was Graydon whom she couldn't take her eyes off. She'd seen him wearing very little when they'd gone swimming but they had been mostly underwater.

The early morning sunlight glinted off his bare, sweat-glistening upper body. His dark hair and eyes seemed to gleam. There was no fat on him, just long, lean muscles, and very little hair on his chest. His pants hung so low that the V that led downward was exposed.

The way he moved took her breath away. He and Daire circled each other, and when Daire swung his sword as though he meant to cut Graydon in half, Toby took a step forward, meaning to stop the fight. But Graydon leaped up and came down two feet away, missing Daire's sword by no more than an inch.

Laughing, Graydon said something in Lanconian. Daire replied with what seemed to be a threat and a ferocious swing of his sword. Again Graydon easily leaped away.

For all that their fight showed enormous skill and beauty, Toby wanted it to stop. If Daire hit Graydon, he could injure him badly.

It was Lorcan who saw Toby. The tall woman had just come out of the house. She was wearing the same white trousers and black boots as the men, but a tight black tank top covered her large breasts. In her hand was a sword like the men had.

When Toby turned to look at Lorcan, she grimaced. Heaven only knew what the woman was going to think since Toby had been away all night. That she'd been out partying? Spending the night with a dozen men?

Silently, Lorcan walked to Toby, her beautiful face expressionless.

"Look," Toby said, "I don't want any problems. You and I—" She broke off because Lorcan went down on one knee in front of her. In a movement that looked as though Lorcan had rehearsed it a thousand times, she extended her arms straight out, her hands into fists, the palms down. Across her outstretched arms was the wide sword, and her head was bent forward so far that the back of her neck was exposed.

In astonishment, Toby looked across the garden toward Graydon. He saw her just as Daire's sword was flying toward his middle. When Graydon didn't jump out of the way, Toby let out a little scream, her fist to her mouth.

But Daire stopped his sword just in time to keep from slashing into Graydon.

"Holy Jura!" Daire shouted, then said something in Lanconian that Toby felt sure was a string of curse words.

But Graydon ignored the invective as he stood there looking at Toby.

She started to say something but Daire strode forward to take his place beside Lorcan. They were in identical stances, both of them in one-legged kneeling positions, arms extended, heads bowed, their swords across their arms. As far as Toby could tell, Lorcan hadn't moved an inch since she'd gone into the position.

Graydon, moving to Toby, spoke. "They are offering their swords for you to use if you wish to remove their heads."

She looked at him to see if he was joking, but Graydon's face was absolutely serious. "They have offended you and misjudged you," he explained.

"And I guess since I'm connected to their king, they deserve the ultimate punishment." In answer, Graydon gave a curt affirmative nod.

Toby's impulse was to immediately tell them to get up, but that would seem insulting to their formality. She looked down at them. "I am impressed with your great loyalty to your future king and your country," she said. "But you really should understand that not all women in this world are trying to get him. I just felt sorry for him for having no place to stay and . . . well, I'm not sure how the rest of it happened, but I can assure you that I do not have any plans to upset your country. That's all. You can get up now."

But they didn't move.

Toby looked over them at Graydon. "You must say you forgive them."

"It's you I don't forgive," she said. "So shouldn't you be down there with them?"

Graydon's eyes showed he was suppressing a smile. "Kings only surrender if there's a war."

Toby looked back at the two kneeling figures and thought that they must be aching from their stance. "I forgive you. Get up! Please."

Daire and Lorcan raised their heads. Lorcan looked solemn but Daire's eyes were laughing. They stood up.

"Come on," Graydon said to Toby. "I'll let you have a chance at beheading me."

"That's the best offer I've had this year."

"I have weeks before I leave, so there's still hope for better to come." She tried not to laugh but wasn't successful.

"Let's see what you can do," Graydon said.

She took the sword he held out to her, but then nearly fell backward. "How much does this thing weigh?"

"About thirty-two pounds," Graydon said as he held his straight out toward her.

"I choose Daire to be my champion," she said.

Graydon was bending forward and beginning to circle her. "You're confusing England with Lanconia. In my country each man is his own champion."

Toby lifted the heavy sword and stuck it down into one of the raised flower beds. "I have a wedding to plan, and now I know exactly what Victoria wants." She started toward the house, but Graydon caught her by the waist, her back to his front. His lips were by her ear.

"Do you want a surrender from me? A groveling apology?" he asked.

She knew she should push him away but there was something so primeval, so visceral, about his sweaty bare chest against her back that she didn't move. "I'd rather hear the truth. Did you send Lexie away?"

"That was purely Rory's idea." There was pride in his voice. "I saw no reason to say no to his scheme."

"Did you give me Victoria's wedding to plan and were you involved in relieving me of my job?"

"No. That was all from Victoria. I owe her a great deal. I like that you're not gone all day. Any chance you could take the whole summer off?"

"Why ask me? You and your brother and Victoria seem to be in charge of my life." She twisted to look at him. "It's hard to believe that I was beginning to think you were a sweet, gentle man. You seemed so mild that I was starting to wonder if you could handle being a king."

Smiling, he put his face on her neck, his lips not kissing but grazing her skin. "Kingship is born into a man."

"Or a woman."

"In my country a woman can be queen only if she marries a king."

"How very medieval of you. Tell me, do you pay women employees half the wages of men?"

"Our women have no jobs outside the home. It is forbidden."

Toby glared. "Are you kidding me?"

"You have seen Lorcan. What do you think she would say if a man told her she must stay home?"

"His head would roll across the floor?"

"Exactly."

"Arrogant, swaggering Kingsley," she said. "That's what Valentina said you were."

"And who is she?" Graydon asked, his arm tightening about her waist and his face more deeply buried in her neck. Against her backside she could feel his arousal.

"Be careful or you're going to embarrass yourself in front of your companions."

"To show I am a man with manly desires is an honor."

With a quick movement she twisted around to face him and he put both his arms loosely around her.

"You have issued me a challenge and I accept it," he said.

Toby was realizing that it was a mistake to have turned around. Graydon in an open shirt standing behind her in the bathroom was bad, but him shirtless with her front almost, just about, touching his bare flesh was very bad. But she didn't want to let him know that. Two could play at his flirting game.

"Last night I had a very vivid dream and you were in it." When he bent as though to kiss her neck, she moved her head away. "You were kissing me and begging me to marry you but

I was saying no. I was going to marry Silas, a man who owns a big store."

"Tell me his name and I will cut him to pieces."

"No, this dream was in civilized times, when Kingsley House was first built. Actually, I saw a lot of people I know."

"I like this that you have on." His hands went up her bare arms, feeling them, as though testing for muscle. "You have some strength here."

She took a quick step back and got out of his embrace. "You're more like your brother than you seem."

"To the world we are identical."

"Ha!" Toby said. "He's better looking than you are."

"Not as short and pale as I am?" His eyes were teasing as he picked up some bright yellow, long, narrow straps. He took her hand in his and began to wrap the cloth tightly around it.

"What's this for?"

Graydon nodded toward Daire, who was standing nearby holding some red leather boxing gloves. "I am going to honor your challenge by letting you hit me."

"Sounds good, but what challenge did I give you? No. Wait! It isn't what I said about not falling in love with you, is it?"

Graydon had one of her hands done. The binding was very snug and wouldn't allow her wrist to bend. "I like the other one better."

At first Toby didn't know what he meant. "You mean that I've never wanted to . . . you know?"

"Yes, that one." He had both her hands wrapped and he inspected them, turning them over. Leaning forward, he whispered, "Do I have your permission to seduce you?" With that, he stepped back and nodded to Daire, who came forward with the boxing gloves and began to put them on Toby.

She looked around Daire to see Graydon slipping his hands into some big leather pads. "So what would you do?" she asked.

"Rose petals on my bed? Riding black horses at midnight? Or maybe long, flowery love letters?"

When Toby's gloves were on, Daire stepped away.

"Have they all been tried on you?" Graydon asked as he stood before her.

"That and much more. It started when I was sixteen and didn't stop until I moved in with Lexie, with Jared nearby."

"Hit this pad with your left hand," he said. "Do it quickly and pull back fast. Good," he said when she'd done it. "Now come across with your right."

After her second hit, he took off the pads, went behind her to put his body close to hers, and ran his hand down the length of her arm. "When you hit with your right, turn your hand this way. Come back quickly. Don't leave your arm extended so your body is unprotected."

He put the pads back on and stood before her. "Back and forth. Ten times."

It was an unusual exercise to Toby but already she was beginning to catch on.

"Is such vigorous pursuit of a young girl usual in America?" he asked when the round was done.

"No!" Toby said, then slammed her right glove hard into his hand pad.

She didn't see the way Graydon looked at Daire. She had some strength in her body!

"My father is rich and my mother is cooperative," Toby said as she stopped to take a breath. Boxing was an all-out sport that took every bit of a person's mind and body.

Graydon went behind her and again put his arms around her. This time he showed her how to do a left hook. He stepped away. "Left jab, right cross, left hook. Got it?"

"I can try," Toby said as she did the combination ten times.

"I don't need your father's money or your mother's approval," Graydon said when she'd finished and he began to untie her gloves.

"Good thing," Toby answered. "If my mother knew about you, she'd be here screaming at me to run away. You're not exactly available for marriage."

With her hand in his, the teasing left Graydon's eyes and he looked at her seriously. "I don't believe I've ever heard of a modern mother who is so intent on getting her daughter into a suitable marriage."

Toby started taking the wraps off her hands. "If I believe the dream I had last night, she has a reason to be so particular about who I marry. She lost a husband, three sons, and a son-in-law to the sea, and I—I mean Tabby—was fooling around in the garden with a man who said that the sea was in his blood. I bet Tabby married him, he died on his ship, and yet another sea widow was stuck in that old house. Whoever she married, I'm pretty sure that Tabby died in that room off the back of the big living room. Even today the place makes my skin crawl in fear!"

When she looked up, the three Lanconians were all staring at her in wide-eyed silence. "Sorry," she said. "I didn't mean to go into a tirade. It's all from a dream I had, that's all. It was just that it was so very real, I felt like I was there. Why are you looking at me like that?"

Graydon smiled at her. "We are a superstitious country, that's all. Shall we have something to eat? Why don't we all go out to Seagrille? I find that all this talk of the sea has made me want some fish. Is that all right with you, Carpathia?"

Toby looked at him. "How do you know that's my name?"

"You told me."

"No, I didn't," she said, "but I told Garrett and he called me that last night."

Graydon was frowning. "Is this the man in your dream who looks like me? Who you were kissing?"

"Yes," she said. "Usually, a dream fades during the day, but this one keeps getting stronger in my mind. It's like I'm supposed to do something about it or with it, but I don't know what."

"How about if we go out to lunch and you tell us all about your dream, every word of it? These two love a good ghost story, don't you?"

Obediently, Lorcan and Daire nodded, but they said nothing.

"Who said anything about ghosts?" Toby asked.

"No one, just a guess. What's your favorite alcoholic beverage?"

"I'm not much of a drinker but I do like a good frozen margarita now and then. And I need to talk to my boss about when I'm supposed to return to work."

"We'll do all of it," Graydon said, then stood there looking at her.

It took her a moment to understand what he wanted: an answer to his question. As she turned away, smiling so he couldn't see her, she said, "You may try," then went into the house.

Chapter Fifteen

Graydon carried Toby up the stairs to bed, but then, it was late and she'd had a long day. After lunch they'd gone to a beach to swim. There'd been a vigorous Lanconian ball game that the three of them were good at while Toby had to work to keep up. Afterward they'd walked around town and Toby had been a tour guide.

At five, Graydon had started plying her with drinks and asking her more questions about her dream. The four of them had dinner, then Toby and Graydon went for a long walk along the water, followed by champagne.

When Graydon saw Toby's eyes drifting shut, he knew it was time to go home. She fell asleep in the car.

Graydon put her on top of her bed and turned to leave, but he paused at the doorway. This wasn't a situation he'd ever dealt with before. Drunken females only happened when Rory was around, and all Graydon had to do was tell someone to see that those young women got home safely.

But as he looked at Toby curled up on the bed, still with her clothes and shoes on, he didn't want anyone else to touch her.

"Come on," he said softly as he stood at the end of the bed, picked up her feet, and removed her shoes.

She smiled, half asleep, and looked up at him for a moment. "My very own prince."

"I'm beginning to think that may be true," he said, wondering how he could undress her more yet keep his sanity. "If I get your nightclothes, will you get into them?"

"Sure," she said and began to unbutton her blouse.

Reluctantly stepping away, Graydon rummaged in her chest of drawers and withdrew a long white nightgown of soft cotton trimmed with rows of lace. "This all right?"

Toby was lying on the bed with her blouse off, wearing one of her lacy bras. Her cotton trousers were unbuttoned, and she was sound asleep.

Graydon's first thought was that he should leave the room, but he didn't. Instead, he lifted her to a sitting position, slipped the gown over her head, put her back down, then wrestled her trousers off from under the gown. He folded the big coverlet over her and stepped back to look at her.

She was changing his life, he thought. She complained that he had taken over her life, but it was nothing compared to what she'd done to him. From the moment he'd first seen her he hadn't been the same person. It was as though everything that had ever been important to him had abruptly been taken away.

His country and all it meant seemed to have been pushed to the background. Never in his life would he have believed that he was capable of setting duty aside so he could spend a week with some woman he hardly knew. Had it been a week of wild sex that he'd wanted before marriage, he could have understood. But he'd spent an entire week with Toby planning some other woman's wedding. He would never have believed himself capable of such a thing.

But he had enjoyed it! What was it she'd said? That he'd been her "best girlfriend." That idea made him smile. At night, alone in his bed, the last thing he'd felt like was a female.

He wanted to believe that at the end of the week he would have said goodbye to Toby and flown home to his real life. He would have invited her to his wedding with Danna and maybe even smiled at her as he stood at the front waiting for his bride.

But he'd made no plans to return home, and when Daire and Lorcan showed up and Graydon was given an excuse not to leave, he'd taken it instantly.

He should be in Lanconia now. Even if he had to put on a fake cast when he appeared in public, he should do it. Their family doctor would cover for him. Rory could run off to wherever he went when he wanted to retreat and Graydon could carry on with his duties.

But he wasn't doing that. Instead, he was still on this island, still with this young woman, and downstairs were his two trusted friends, who were trying to understand why Graydon wasn't doing what he should.

He had no explanation for them because he didn't understand it himself.

"Don't leave," Toby said.

"You need your sleep."

"Why were you so interested in my dream?" she asked.

"It's a haunted house." He was standing over her and looking down. Her hair had come loose and was flowing out around her. Moonlight came into the room and he could see her blue eyes. With her golden hair and the white gown, he knew he'd never seen anything more desirable. He could no more leave the room than he could teleport himself back to Lanconia.

Even while telling himself that he shouldn't do it, he stretched out on the bed beside her and pulled her into his arms, her head on his chest. When she looked up at him as though she meant for him to kiss her, he moved her head back down.

"Why won't you kiss me?" she whispered.

"I am afraid of what will happen," he said.

"Afraid I'll fall so hard in love with you that when you leave my heart will break?"

"No," he said. "Afraid my heart will break."

"But today you said you wanted to seduce me. You don't seem to be making any progress."

"You are here now, in my arms, there is moonlight and darkness. Is that not success? Or would you prefer that I ride a horse up the stairs?"

Toby snuggled against him. "I like this better. I find you very attractive. Do you know that?"

"Yes," he said.

She ran her hand over his chest, putting her fingertips inside his shirt to touch his warm skin. She moved her leg over his. "I'm here and it's now."

He pushed her leg off his and kissed her fingertips. "You are most tempting, but you have consumed a great deal of alcohol. You might regret this in the morning. In my country we take the losing of a maidenhead very seriously."

"In my country it tends to be in the backseat of a car."

"But not for you," he said. "You are different."

She relaxed against him. "Why have you stayed?"

"I don't know. It's as though something is compelling me to remain here. As though there's something I need to do."

"No time like the present," she said suggestively as she ran her leg against his.

Graydon laughed. "You are a very happy drunk, are you not?"

"I've been happy since you came into my life."

"Except when you were shouting at me."

"Did I hurt your feelings very much?"

"No," he said. "It was wonderful. I've been afraid to be myself, afraid that you were such a fragile, delicate little thing that I could easily break you, snap you in half."

"Ha!" Toby said. "My mother has hardened me so much that nothing anyone says to me gets through my skin."

"At least your mother doesn't wear a crown and rule a couple of armies."

Toby drew in her breath. Never before had he said anything so personal. "Does she demand a lot of you?"

"More than I know how to give," Graydon said.

Toby slipped her fingers through his, intertwining them. "We're alike in that."

"I think perhaps we're alike in many ways," he said softly.

When Toby put her face up to his, he couldn't resist. He put his lips on hers, meaning to kiss her sweetly and gently, but at the first touch, the kiss deepened. His hand went to her head, burying in her hair.

He kissed her lips, her eyes, her cheeks, then back to her lips. His tongue touched the corner of her mouth, a tantalizing bit that made her want more.

Toby's hands went around his chest and pulled him on top of her.

It was as though some memory was stirring inside her. This wasn't the first time, she thought. This man, his breath, his face, his body were familiar to her. She knew him. She knew how he worried about living up to the heavy responsibilities that had been placed on his shoulders. He worried about her and her family, about whether she would love him as much as he did her. If anything happened to her, she knew his soul would go with hers. "Tabby, don't leave me," she seemed to hear inside her head. Or had Graydon said that?

She pulled back to look at him and for a moment she thought she saw tears in his eyes, but surely it was a trick of the moonlight.

He rolled onto his back and pushed her head down onto his chest. "Sleep, my lovely one," he whispered.

"Don't leave me," she said as she clung to him.

"I'm not sure that I can," he said.

They fell asleep together, wrapped in each other's arms.

Toward morning, Toby began to dream.

"I can't marry you! Do you not understand that? I have too many people depending on me. Silas can help support us. He will—"

"I'll burn his store down before I let you marry him!"

Tabby drew in her breath. The houses on Nantucket were close together and nearly all of them were wooden. Fire was a very dangerous threat. "You wouldn't," she whispered.

"How can you think I would?" Garrett grabbed her upper arms. "Tabby, you must marry me. I love you more than life."

"More than the sea?"

When he moved away from her, his face was filled with anguish. "I have to make a living and the sea is what I know. Would you have me open a store like that truck-bellied, brocky Silas Osborne? Is that what you want of me? To emasculate me? Would you cut off the parts of me that make me a man?"

"I don't know," Tabby said. "I don't know what to do."

Chapter Sixteen

The ringing of a phone woke Toby, and for a few seconds she was disoriented. Was she with Garrett wearing a long brown dress or was she in Nantucket in her nightgown?

She looked at the other side of the bed and saw the indentation where Graydon had slept—or had that been part of her dream? When she sat up, her head hurt, her mouth was dry, and her stomach was queasy.

The phone stopped, and she pulled on jeans and a T-shirt, but when she left the bathroom, it started ringing again. It was Graydon's phone and there was a photo of a crown as the ID. Probably Rory, she thought. "Hello?" Her voice was hoarse.

There were some unintelligible words spoken by a woman and Toby recognized the Lanconian language. "Sorry," she said, her hand to her aching head. "He isn't here right now."

The woman's voice changed from strident to sweet, from Lanconian to English. "Oh, my goodness, you sound as though my son has given you a difficult night."

Toby could feel the blood leaving her face. She was talking to Graydon's mother—who was a queen. Toby was glad she hadn't said Graydon's name and exposed the exchange.

"Yes, ma'am," she said. "I mean, no, ma'am. He . . ." She couldn't think of anything else to say.

"Well, dear," the queen said, "perhaps you could find my son and give him the phone. I doubt he's very far from your side."

"Of course," Toby said. As much as it hurt, she started running, the phone held tightly in her hand. When she heard the shower she went into Lexie's, now Graydon's, bedroom. The bathroom door was open and she peeped in. He was behind the foggy curtain, steam rolling upward.

Toby started to say his name but couldn't. Graydon was supposed to be Rory. "Your mother is on the phone," she said as loudly as she could without being heard all the way to Lanconia.

Instantly, Graydon shut the water off and put his head and arm around the curtain. Toby started to hand him the phone but he shook his head. He was too wet. She turned it on speaker and held it up for him.

"Hello, Mother," Graydon said formally, sounding as though he were in a tuxedo at a formal reception.

The sweet-voiced woman who'd spoken to Toby was gone. "Roderick," she said in English, her voice as sharp as a whiplash. "I have something important to say to you, and for once in your life I want you to listen to me."

"Yes, ma'am, I will."

"I assume you have been told of your brother's heroic act in saving your father." Graydon nodded toward a towel hanging on the rack. Toby reached for it with one hand, phone in the other. He took it from her, wrapped it around his waist, and stepped out of the tub and from behind the shower curtain.

"Yes, ma'am, I have and may I say that he—"

"No, you may not say anything," his mother snapped. "Just listen. I don't want you to come here to this country and pile more work on your brother. He has enough to do without you here being a demon of temptation and trying to get him drunk. And with his engagement coming up, he can't have you throwing your mindless girlfriends at him. Your father needs to heal, and the less stress put on him, the faster that will happen. Am I making myself clear?"

"Yes, ma'am, you are."

Toby could see the shock on Graydon's face. When he started to take the phone from her, she grabbed the falling towel and tied it around his waist.

The phone was still on speaker and Graydon was holding it away from his head, as though he couldn't bear it to be near him.

"I am pleading with you," his mother said, "to stay away. Graydon takes his coming rulership very seriously, while you have only contempt for what we stand for." She made a sound of exasperation. "You and I have been through this many times before. Do I have your word that you will remain wherever you are and put as little stress as possible on your father and brother?"

"Yes," Graydon said, his voice hard and cold. "I can assure you that I will not interfere with my brother's obligations."

His mother wasn't bothered by his tone. "As for that American strumpet who answered the telephone, get rid of her. If the media find out your father is ill, there will be plenty of negative press about us without your dangling one of your cheap harlots in front of the journalists. And Danna doesn't need to be insulted by having to meet whomever you've picked up this time. Do we understand each other?"

"Perfectly," Graydon said, and without a further word, she hung up.

For a long moment he stood there, immobile. Toby gently pushed him out the door and into the bedroom to the little couch by the fireplace. There was an old quilt over the back and she draped it around his bare shoulders, which were still wet.

"Was that the first time you heard that?" she asked as she sat down beside him and took his hand in hers.

"Yes. Rory never told me that our mother speaks to him in that way. No wonder he so rarely comes home." He turned to her. "What she said about you . . . I can't apologize enough."

Toby raised her hand. "My mother says about the same things to me. I never live up to whatever she wants me to do and be." She didn't add that in his case it was his brother who was the disappointment.

"Sir?" Daire's voice came to them from the sitting room. "Prince Rory asks that you call him."

"We're in here," Toby said.

When Daire, with Lorcan close behind him, saw them sitting so close together on the sofa and Graydon with little clothing on, they turned away. "I beg your pardon."

"Graydon just heard the way his mother talks to his brother," Toby said.

Graydon looked at her as though she had betrayed his confidence, but Daire shrugged as though to say he'd heard it many times.

"Does everyone know?" Graydon asked.

"Within a close circle of people, yes," Daire answered, and Lorcan nodded.

"But no one, not even Rory, told me." Graydon looked at them. "Were you protecting me from the truth?"

"Yes," Daire said as he went to the closet to get Graydon some clothes.

"Get the blue denim shirt," Toby called to him. "And jeans.

He'll want to stay in today and talk to Rory about damage control."

"And his sneakers," Lorcan said from the doorway. She
went to the big chest of drawers. "Socks?" she asked as she
looked at Toby.

"Top left. Get the white ones."

Graydon was beginning to recover himself. "I believe I'm
capable of dressing myself," he said.

With a curt nod of their heads, Daire and Lorcan put the
clothes on the bed, then left. "I'll let you get dressed," Toby said
and started to leave, but Graydon stopped her.

"No. Please stay," he said as he stood up, the quilt falling
away. "Unless you want to go, that is."

For a moment she looked at him standing there in just a
towel and she seemed to remember being in his arms last night.
Was it real or one of her dreams? She took a step toward him,
her hand extended as though she was going to touch him, but
he turned away and the moment was lost.

Graydon got underwear out of a drawer and Toby looked
away as he put it on. When he had his jeans on but not fastened,
she looked back at him. "What are you going to do about this?"

"I don't know. I don't like anyone talking to my brother like
that." He was frowning. Toby sat down on the end of the bed
and watched as he got dressed. He was striding across the room
as though he were marching into battle but he was saying nothing.

"Can your mother tell you twins apart?"

"As proof that it's True Love? Not quite," he said, a sneer in
his voice. It took Graydon nearly a minute before he realized
what he'd said. He came to a halt, his shirt on but hanging
open, and looked at Toby.

Only a paleness of her skin showed that Toby had heard
him. She leaned back on her hands and looked up at the ceiling.
"I see. I could tell you weren't your brother, so you—the king to

be—decided to stick around and see if I could be your True Love. You know, like in a fairy tale. Only in this story the prince is going to run away and marry the princess, not the strumpet who has a hangover."

Graydon put his shoulders back, his body went rigid, and his face became expressionless.

Toby, still sitting on the bed, glared at him. "So help me, if you turn yourself into The Prince and freeze me out, I'll show the lot of you to the front door."

Graydon's eyes widened for a moment, then he flopped down onto the bed behind her. "Oh, hell! I don't feel much like a prince. My mother just cut my brother and my girl to pieces. I'd like to tell her what she can do with her opinions but she's a queen. It's not done."

Toby stretched out on her back beside him but not touching. "What's this about the True Love thingy?"

Graydon laughed. "How American. A 'thingy.' It's just a family legend and ridiculous—except that it keeps coming true. Aunt Cale loves to tell how her husband, Uncle Kane, hated her when they first met. But she could tell him from Uncle Mike so they were doomed to be together."

"Interesting," Toby said, then rolled to her side to look at him. His shirt had fallen open and she did truly love the sight of his bare, muscular chest. All those fights with Daire certainly paid off! "So you set up dinner in a tent in order to find out what your True Love was actually like?"

"Mmmm," Graydon said. "More or less."

"And that's what Rory was so angry at you about? You said you two argued about me. Wait a minute! I bet you weren't even going to tell me what you do for a living."

Graydon, with his eyes on the ceiling, tried not to smile. "Sometimes my, uh, 'occupation' tends to overwhelm people."

Toby flopped back on the bed. "Sure it isn't your ego that smothers them?"

Graydon rolled onto his side, his face close to hers. "I just wanted to present myself as me, a man, and nothing else." He picked up a strand of her hair and twirled it around his finger.

"You and your Poor Prince act," Toby said. "Did you think I'd get giddy at the mere mention of you and a palace?"

"Some girls do," he said and rolled onto his back—but he didn't let go of her hair.

"Ow!" Toby turned toward him and with a twist from him, she ended up on top of him. "Is this more of your seducing?"

"Yes. Do you like it?" He had his hands in her hair.

"I rather do," she said softly.

"Do you know how beautiful you are? Your skin is like cream and takes my breath away. Your eyes are the color of a mountain stream, your lashes like butterfly wings, and your lips are like the ripest cherries."

She put her lips almost on his, and when he parted his to kiss her, she rolled off him and sat up. "You make me sound like a cross between a forest and a farmyard."

She started to get up, but Graydon caught her hair, began to wrap it around his wrist, and pulled her back to him. He pushed her onto the bed, then straddled her.

"How about this? If you were the king's daughter I'd kill everyone to win you."

"Better," she said. "But you certainly talk a lot."

In a quick motion Graydon put his arms around her, pulled her on top of him, and kissed her.

The intensity of what went between them surprised both of them. It was sparks, a merging, a flowing—a union.

They broke apart and stared, then came back together with a force that nearly shattered them. Graydon opened his mouth over hers, and rolled on top of her, covering her.

Toby reacted in the age-old way of wrapping her legs around his waist, her hands digging into his back, pulling him closer and closer.

It was Graydon who broke away. He pulled his mouth off hers and buried his face in her neck. "I can't. We can't. When I leave . . ." He didn't finish his sentence.

Toby's heart was pounding. She'd never been this close to a man before. Feeling a bit embarrassed, she put her legs down on the bed. "I understand," she said. "We can't take a chance that ol' True Love will rear its head and . . ."

He rolled off her but stayed near, his hand stroking her cheek. "How about if today we go explore that old house? Aunt Cale has to finish a book before she can take possession of it, so she wanted me to see if the roof was okay, that sort of thing. If I'm with you, maybe when you're there you won't fall asleep and dream of kissing another man."

Toby couldn't get her mind off his closeness, but it didn't seem to bother him. Did this happen to people, that lovemaking became blasé after a while? Something that was easy to turn off and on?

"Sure," she said as she tried to still her heart. "But I need to sketch Victoria's wedding from what I saw in the dream. Oh! I forgot. This morning I had another one."

Graydon got off the bed, took her hand, and pulled her up. "I have to shave. Sit with me while I do it and tell me of this dream. Did I kiss you and ask for your hand in marriage?"

"This time you were so angry at me you threatened to burn the town down."

"I guess that means this one's about Silas," he said heavily.

"What do you think 'truck-bellied' means?"

"If I said it and it was about the other man, my guess is that it's not good."

"You think?" she said and followed him into the bathroom.

Chapter Seventeen

The four of them worked together in the dining room. Toby and Graydon took the ends of the table, laptops open before them, while Lorcan and Daire were in the middle. Graydon had to walk Rory through a meeting with an ambassador from Lithuania. Graydon had played golf with the man and had met his family so Rory had to know everything his brother did. Instead of memorizing facts, Daire and Graydon came up with the idea of strapping a phone onto Rory's cast. He kept it on so Graydon could hear what was said and quickly tap out a reply. It caused some delays in the conversation, but Rory was good at coming up with distractions before he answered.

Toby was researching what she'd seen in her dreams. Maybe if she showed Victoria some drawings or photos of dresses of that time period, she would like them, which would mean that Toby could go ahead with planning the wedding. Food, flowers, all of it was going to take a lot of work, and she needed to get started. When what she saw in her research was so much like her dream, she had to remind herself that it wasn't real.

Graydon was by the kitchen door, his phone to his ear. "How many of those dreams have you had now?"

"Three," she said. "Is this a Lanconian thing, because Americans don't pay much attention to dreams?"

"Last year I—" Graydon broke off as Rory spoke to him. "Tell her," he said to Daire, then went through the kitchen to the sunroom to talk in private.

"Last year His Royal Highness—" Daire began.

"You mean Graydon?"

Daire smiled. "Yes, of course. Gray's father—the king—sent his son up into the mountains to a remote little village. It seemed that some of the Ultens had decided a woman in the village was a witch. They wanted to stone her."

"Were their goats dying, that sort of thing?" Toby asked.

"No. She was a very pretty young woman and the husbands found her irresistible. When we investigated, we found that the problem was that she never said no."

"Some witchcraft!" Toby said, smiling. "So what did Graydon do?"

"He gave her a one-way ticket to Los Angeles and an introduction to a movie producer. So far, she's been the pretty girl who gets killed in four horror movies."

Toby laughed. "*Cold Comfort Farm* comes alive," she said, and went back to work.

Unfortunately, all these jobs left Lorcan with nothing to do. So far, Toby'd had little interaction with her. They had advanced to there being a sense of both of them working to help Graydon, but it hadn't moved past that.

Toby did a computer search for Regency costumes and came up with some beautiful examples from various museums. She printed them out, then spread them on the table to look at them.

Graydon was still on the phone and Daire was absorbed by the computer, so Toby pushed them toward Lorcan. "What do you think?"

"They are nice," Lorcan said.

Toby was disappointed by her reticence. Not exactly girlfriend material. She pulled the photos back.

"They are better in person," Lorcan said.

"Oh? You've seen them in museums in Lanconia?"

"No, in the . . ." She looked at Daire.

"The attic," he said without looking up. "That family never throws anything away. They just build onto that palace so they can store more old oddments."

Toby looked at Lorcan. "I wish we could borrow a dress and show it to Victoria. Maybe she'd remember it," she said, laughing. "Of course she can't remember my dream but she looked so good in that dress. She's quite large on top." She glanced at Lorcan. "You'd be a knockout in one of them. Soft white muslin with a red ribbon right around here." She put her hands on her own upper rib cage.

Daire snorted. "Lorcan sleeps in leather."

Toby saw a shadow go across Lorcan's eyes at that remark, but she said nothing. The Lanconians were certainly good at hiding their emotions! she thought.

"Perhaps you could wear one of the dresses," Lorcan said politely.

Toby got up and went behind Lorcan's chair. After a nod of permission, Toby lifted Lorcan's long ponytail to the top of her head and studied it. "Yes, quite beautiful. You know, in high heels, you're probably taller than Daire."

That made Lorcan smile, the first one she'd directed at Toby, while Daire shook his head as he typed something on the computer.

"Do you really think we could do this? I mean, would Graydon agree?" Toby asked the both of them. "And even if he did, would it be possible to borrow clothes and get them here in a short time?"

"Of course," Daire said, "but Gray won't like being told what we want him to do."

"Especially where you are concerned," Lorcan added. "And if Prince Graydon thinks Daire suggested it, he will say no."

Toby started to ask for more information about that concept, but when Graydon appeared at the doorway, Toby said, "Come look at these pictures."

He picked up one of a lady in a long white dress that was low cut and clung to her legs. "I like it," he said.

Daire looked up from the computer. "It says here that a problem at the time was the 'muslin disease.' It seems that the women wore dresses of such thin fabric that they caught their deaths of cold." He seemed to consider that. "I think maybe it was worth it."

"Are you planning to dress like this for Victoria?" Graydon asked.

"Heavens, no! That's impossible to achieve," Toby said, looking at him. "Wait a minute! This was Jane Austen's time. Not that we could pull this off, but that would mean that you . . . drumroll please . . . could be Mr. Darcy."

"Are you talking about that priggish man who everybody thought was a snob?"

"You're talking about the most romantic man ever put on paper, so have some respect. If I were to wear a dress thin enough to give me pneumonia, you would have to wear those breeches." She handed him a picture of a man wearing tan trousers that were like a second skin and a tight black jacket with a high collar.

"Are you saying that if I wore tights, you'd agree to wear a dress like this?"

"Sure. Why not? But where are we going to get some eighteenth-century costumes?" She batted her eyelashes at him in a very innocent way.

"We'll search the closets of my ancestors," Graydon said. "I'll ask Rory and— No. I'll call my grandfather and he'll have everything here as fast as jets can fly."

Toby bent her head over the picture to hide her smile. The clothes in the photo were romance personified. "Does this mean that I might wear a gown that was once worn by a queen?"

"Yes," Graydon said. "A prince doesn't impress you but a queen does?"

"Makes sense to me," Lorcan said and they all laughed. For the first time, Toby and Lorcan exchanged looks of camaraderie.

"So when are we going to wear these ridiculous clothes? And I wonder what the food was like then?" Graydon's phone rang. "I have to take this," he said tiredly and left the room.

"What a great idea," Toby said. "We'll put on a Regency dinner party and be in costume. Why don't you two join us?" She smiled at Daire's look of horror and Lorcan's surprise.

"No," Daire said in a quiet voice, and Toby could tell that it was a final statement. She looked at Lorcan. "Rory's iPad is in the bottom right drawer in Gray's bedroom." Lorcan was up the stairs before Toby finished speaking.

⌘

It was five P.M., Lanconian time, when Graydon pushed the button to reach his grandfather's private number.

"Graydon? Is that you?" In spite of his advanced years, J. T. Montgomery's voice and spirit were strong—and he didn't give his grandson time to answer. "I want to know why the hell Rory is pretending to be you and taking over your duties. Your grandmother is beside herself with worry that you're secreted away in some hospital somewhere like your father is and your mother won't tell us about it."

"Granddad, I'm fine, and Mother knows nothing about this. I just wanted a week's holiday, that's all, but then Rory broke his wrist and . . . Well, things happened. Besides, I met a girl who—"

"I told Aria that was the problem," J.T. said.

"It's not like that. I'm just staying with her for right now and—"

"What do you mean 'it's not like that'? Is she pretty?"

Graydon's voice softened. "She's beautiful. She has long blonde hair—natural blonde—and—"

"There's only one way a man can be sure of a woman's natural hair color," J.T. said. Graydon couldn't help laughing. Age hadn't killed his grandfather's love of life!

"The young lady and I spent the day cleaning up after a wedding, and afterward we went swimming in our underwear. It didn't leave much to my imagination. Toby and I are just—"

"So help me, if you tell me that the two of you are just friends, I'll disown you. The real question is, Does she make your blood boil?"

"Oh, yes!" Graydon said, and he suddenly realized that he wanted to say the truth out loud. "Sometimes I feel like one of my warrior ancestors and I want to throw her across my shoulder and run off with her. That I can't touch her, can only look at her, makes me crazy. Granddad? She can tell me from Rory."

J.T. was quiet for a moment. He was of a different generation than his grandson and he strongly believed in the old family legends. "You're sure?"

"Yes. When I said I was Rory, she got angry because I was lying. Then later Rory dressed up like me and put on his bad imitation of me and . . . Anyway, she knew who he was instantly."

"I'm sorry," J.T. said, his voice barely a whisper. They both knew what was involved in this. When he was a young American soldier, J.T. had nearly killed himself fighting against centuries of tradition within the Lanconian royal family and their retainers. He'd made a lot of progress, but he hadn't changed the system of whom his grandson would marry. That Graydon had found a woman who might mean more to him than just someone to sit beside him on a throne made J.T. feel deeply, deeply sad. "How can I help you?"

"I want you to get someone to send me some clothes from the early 1800s." J.T. couldn't help a snort of laughter. "And here I was thinking you wanted me to tackle your mother on your behalf."

"How could I do that to you, Granddad? I love you, and I want you to continue living."

J.T. laughed. "If your mother realizes what's going on between you and your brother, nobody will live through it. Will you be back for the . . . you know?" He couldn't bring himself to say "the engagement ceremony."

"Yes," Graydon said. "I plan to return in plenty of time for that. But what about the clothes? Can you get them for me?"

"Sure. I'll have your grandmother send one of those girls she bosses around to search."

"Good! I'll send you the details of sizes and such later, but mainly I just need something that will dazzle Victoria Madsen."

"The writer? Aria loves her books and when I tell her who it's for she'll have the whole palace working for her."

"Just so Mother doesn't hear about it and get suspicious," Graydon said. He wanted to talk to his grandfather about how his mother spoke to Rory, but not on the phone. He'd do that in person.

"Don't worry. She's otherwise occupied. I take it you're instructing Rory, because he's dealt well with two ambassadors."

"I'm on the phone and Skype with him hourly."

"Yeah, well, don't let duties take away time with your girl. Send me a photo of her, will you? And, Gray? I love you too."

"Thank you," he said. "I couldn't do this without you." They said goodbye and hung up.

It wasn't until three P.M., ten in Lanconia, that Graydon could get away from the phone. He turned it off, tossed it to Daire, and said "Let's go!" to Toby, and they left the house. As soon as they were outside, he told her of the call to his grandfather. "So you'll be able to put on your pretty dress and I'm sure Victoria will agree to the wedding."

"I hope you're right." She walked ahead of him and looked back. "Too bad Daire won't wear the costume. He'd be gorgeous!"

"Not pale and short like me?"

The sun was at his back and it seemed to form a halo of light around him. Whether it was the light or just her growing familiarity with him, right now she didn't think she'd ever seen a better looking man. She turned away, afraid he'd read her thoughts on her face. He's not mine, she reminded herself.

When they reached the front door of the old house his relatives had bought, Graydon pulled from his pocket a key that was as big as his hand.

"Where did you get that?" Toby asked.

"Aunt Cale sent it to me. My question is how you got into the house without it."

"The front door was standing open."

"As though it were beckoning you to enter?" He was teasing.

"No," Toby said, "as though the wind had blown it open. You have to remember how old houses are. Doors and windows and floors creak."

"My bedroom at home was built in 1528 and it's one of the newer rooms."

"But the question is whether or not it's haunted."

"Swords clash every night," Graydon said as he shut the door and handed her the key. It had two dolphins on the top of it.

She held it up. "Is this so I can escape if your seducing of me gets too passionate?"

"That's to lock the door so no one can come inside and interrupt us. Where should we start?"

"The bedrooms, of course," she said as she put the big key in the lock. Laughing, they went up the stairs.

The old house was well lit even through very dirty windows, and they saw no sign of damp on the walls or the floors.

The main staircase led the way up to two bedrooms with large fireplaces and en suite bathrooms. "This is my favorite," Toby said, and led him into the room where she'd had the first dream. In spite of the dirt, it was easy to see it had once been beautiful.

Graydon sat down on the dusty little sofa. "I like this too. I'd like to fill those shelves with books."

She sat down by him. "And what would they be about?"

"I think that for here I'd like a collection of books about Nantucket. I'd like to know more about this island. What about you? What would you like to see in here?"

"Novels that I like to read and reread, gardening, and I agree, history books. I think I would like to know some more about this house."

"Did you tell Daire all the details of your dreams?"

"Yes," she said seriously, "and he was especially interested in hearing the kissing parts."

There was a flash of anger across Graydon's face before he realized she was teasing him. "You devil!" he said and made a lunge for her, but Toby was on her feet and running.

She went out a side door that Graydon hadn't noticed, took a right down the hall, and he heard her footsteps on what sounded like stairs—but he didn't see any. He opened doors to two bathrooms and two bedrooms before he found the narrow stairs tucked between walls. It was so dark he could hardly see his feet, and he wished he'd brought a flashlight.

At the top of the stairs was a solid door and when he opened it he saw a big, bare attic. The wide, thick, roughly sawn floor-boards attested to the age of the house. The steep roof made a sharp pitch in the ceiling height. Toby was standing at the end, in front of a window.

"It's as though I know this room. Wet laundry was hung over there."

When Graydon looked where she was pointing, he saw some big iron hooks in the beams. Perfect for a clothesline.

"Herbs dried over there. There were a lot of them needed for the candles." There were holes where smaller hooks had once been.

"We . . . I mean, they sold candles. The children played in that corner. Young Thomas cried because the toy his father made him fell through the boards and we couldn't find it." Toby threw up her hands. "This is strange. Why do I keep making up these things? Maybe I should tell Victoria and she can use the stories in her books."

"Or you could write them yourself."

"No, thanks!" Toby said. "Being a writer is too isolated for me."

"So what do you want?" he asked, his face serious.

"I'm an American. I want it all. Husband, kids, nice house, a career that makes me feel that I'm doing something to help people. You ready to go downstairs?"

"After you." As he followed her downstairs, he said softly, "That's exactly what I want out of my life too."

They spent half an hour looking in each of the four bed-rooms and three baths, checking for water damage or mold, but saw none.

Toby flipped light switches and turned on faucets, but nothing happened. "The utilities were on the night I slept here. Did someone turn them off?"

"Not as far as I know," Graydon said as they went downstairs. What he hadn't told her was that he was most curious to see the room that she said frightened her.

They went down the large main staircase and he followed as she went from room to room. He never remarked on how familiar she seemed to be with the house. On the day they argued—well, actually, Graydon hadn't said much—he got the idea she hadn't done much exploring.

"The dining room. Wouldn't this look wonderful with half a dozen Oriental carpets? All of them on top of each other. Brought back from faraway places and shiny new. A Queen Anne dining set with seats upholstered in red plush, brought over from London, would be in the middle of the room."

Next was what she called "the stair room." "The family would use this. It would keep the children off the front stairs, which meant that no adults tripped over their games, shoes, and dropped mittens."

"And Young Thomas's lost toy?"

Toby laughed. "He was a corker. Lost everything as he walked." She went through a door to a narrow room full of cabinets, with a tiny powder room tucked against the wall. "Of course this wasn't here," she said of the modern plumbing.

"What was the room used for?"

"Concoctions," she said quickly. "Anything that could be made to sell. Candles, face creams, cordials—and soap. But then, Valentina and her transparent soap took that market away from everyone else."

Graydon followed her and listened. She went to a room she called the back parlor, to a bedroom, and finally into the kitchen. "This is all new," she said.

Since the kitchen didn't look like it had been remodeled since the 1950s, what she was saying was odd.

Again, Graydon was glad to see no sign of leakage about the house. It may not have been lived in for years, but someone had done a good job of maintaining it. They went back to the front and into the big parlor. The fireplace, with its carved surround, was beautiful. In the back was the sitting room where Graydon had found Toby sleeping. He hadn't wanted to disturb her, so he'd returned to the house to get food, a blanket, and a pillow. And he'd not let her know that he had slept on a hastily prepared pallet just outside the door. He wasn't about to let her spend the night alone in that big, empty house! Just as he'd hoped, the next morning she'd awakened in a better mood.

"That's all of it," Toby said. "There's a cellar, but it's not very big and is only used for storage. If you want to see it, we can." She started to leave the room.

"Wait," he said. "Where is the room you're afraid of?"

"I don't know what you mean," Toby said and began to walk faster.

Graydon stepped in front of her and put his hands on her arms. "It's all right. I'm here and you're safe."

"I don't know what you mean," she repeated, louder and stronger. She twisted away from him. "I think I'll go back home. I'll see you later."

She hurried out of the house so quickly that Graydon was reminded of a cartoon character going so fast he couldn't be seen. He was torn between wanting to go after her and staying in the house to find what had so upset her.

It didn't take him long to find the hidden room. But then the palace had rooms and closets and stairs hidden everywhere, so he knew what to look for. Finding the way to open the door that was so cleverly hidden in the paneling took longer. Slide, push, lift. He had to do them all to get the door open.

What he saw was a small room with a window in the far wall. To his right was an old cabinet that looked original to the house. There was a frame for what looked to have been a sort of chaise longue.

He wondered what the room had been used for originally. Maybe it had once been a place to store wood for the many huge fireplaces in the house. But no, that would have been outside. What he didn't see was anything about the room that would cause fear in anyone.

But as he stood there, it was as though a feeling of sadness began to come over him. He needed to leave and see if Toby was all right, but he didn't move. Slowly, he was beginning to feel that his life was ending, that everything he'd ever thought and felt, all he'd ever wanted to do, all that he'd ever accomplished, meant nothing.

A low light seemed to fill the room and he could hear a woman weeping, then two women, then more. It was as if the whole room was full of women crying in grief.

When Graydon felt like there was a weight on his chest and he couldn't breathe, he turned and left the room. He slammed the old door, then bolted it. For a moment he leaned against it, his heart pounding. The little room he was in, with the old cot and the fireplace on the far wall, seemed very normal. And the whole house was quiet. Yet he had just felt the most extreme sadness he'd ever known in his life.

As he stepped away from the panel, he decided to call his aunt Cale and see what she knew about the history of the house. Knowing her, by now she'd thoroughly researched every year of its existence. And Graydon wanted to know every bit of it.

He slowly walked back to Toby's small house. The front door was open and for a moment he stood in the small entryway. He needed some time to calm himself after being in that room in the old house.

"You have to help me with these party plans," he heard Toby

say. "I do not know how to do this," Lorcan said, sounding confused. "I'll show you," Toby said.

Graydon smiled, as he had an idea that Lorcan wasn't used to the easy chatter of female friends.

He well remembered Lorcan when she was twelve and had just qualified to enter the government program. She had been a tall, thin girl in clothes too short for her, but her grandparents couldn't afford more. Their faces had shown their love and hope for their only grandchild.

Graydon had attended the welcoming ceremony, then, as always, had hung around for a few days to watch the students. It amazed him that you couldn't predict who would succeed and who would fail. He and Daire had long ago seen that, even more than muscle and training, it was heart and will that made a champion.

For three days the students were allowed to wrestle, fight with rubber swords, train in a gym, and attend a few academic classes. During those days, little instruction was given, and few rules. The idea was to see what each student was capable of, without interference.

On the first day, Graydon had been called away by his mother to be charming to some women who were making new cushions for their private chapel. It had been difficult for him to say the empty phrases of flattery, as his mind was elsewhere.

That night, over beers, Daire said, "I have a champion."

"Which one?"

"I'll not tell you. Come and see if you can guess."

"It's the big kid with the snarl," Graydon said. "He frightened even me."

Daire smiled. "Can you stay tomorrow or does your mother have you scheduled for flower arranging?"

"I would laugh if that weren't real. Was it the lad with the heavy brows?"

Daire didn't answer, and the next day, Graydon saw why.

Within hours, he saw that the tall girl with the long black hair was Daire's future champion. She was fast, lithe, and smart. It was as though she knew what her opponent was going to do before he did it.

By the end of the third day, every student had tried to hit Lorcan, but none of them had succeeded. One large boy got so frustrated at Lorcan's dips and dodges that he ran at her to try to pin her against a wall. For a second her eyes widened at the sight of two hundred pounds of muscle coming at her.

Graydon took a step forward, meaning to stop the boy before he crushed the girl, but Daire put his hand on Gray's arm. A split second before the boy hit Lorcan, she dropped to the ground into a ball, head down, arms around her knees.

The boy slammed into the wall hard.

Daire gave Graydon a look to stay back. As the teacher, Daire wanted to see the reaction of these new students to what Lorcan had done. Who would get angry and cry "Foul!"

It was the biggest boy, the one Graydon had said would scare him, who started the laughter. Daire's eyes were on the student who had slammed into the wall. How would he react to Lorcan having made everyone laugh at him? His nose was bloody, he'd cut his forehead, and he had his hand to his chest. With a dazed expression, he looked down at Lorcan, still in a ball between his feet.

Reaching down, he picked her up by her shoulders—and Daire stepped forward, meaning to protect her. This time it was Graydon who stopped him.

The boy, nearly twice as big as Lorcan, held her up by her shoulders and stared at her. "It's like fighting my cat," he said at last, and everyone laughed even harder.

The big boy threw his heavy arm around Lorcan's skinny shoulders and led her over to the other young men. The girls who were in the training program were left in their own group.

From then on, Lorcan was one of the boys—and she had to train twice as hard to gain the muscle and strength that came so easily to them. But she had an agility that they would never possess. They teased her about it, but they also envied her.

"Daire?" Graydon heard Toby say. "How are you doing on the menu? And when are we planning to host this dinner? How long will it take the clothes to get here? I need to make out an invitation to Victoria and Dr. Huntley's wedding, so I need a plan. And Jilly and Ken should come too, although Victoria and Ken tend to take potshots at each other."

There was silence in the room.

"I know no answers to these questions," Daire said.

"What are potshots?" Lorcan asked.

"A bit like machine-gun fire. No! Not for real, but Victoria and Ken used to be married. Sorry. I forget that you two don't know anyone here. Let's see if we can make a plan and a schedule."

"Where is Graydon?" Daire asked and there was what sounded like fear in his voice.

"Go on," Toby said. "Find him. I left him across the lane in that old house. Why don't you two have a boys' night out? Lorcan and I can do all this. Since Graydon's grandfather knows about the twins' exchange, do you think it would be all right if I emailed him the measurements?"

"I'm sure he'd love that," Daire said, heading quickly toward the door.

Graydon was waiting for him outside. "You look like you just escaped a fate worse than death."

"You have no idea," Daire said.

"Shall we see what there is to do in Nantucket at night? Unless you want to help plan a wedding, that is. I warn you, if you do help you get called a 'girlfriend.' And if you don't—"

"Let me guess. I'm insensitive," Daire said, then sighed. "I miss the days when a man just showed up on his wedding night." There was such longing in his voice that they both began to laugh.

"To the beer!" Graydon said.

"Yes! Forward to the beer."

That night, while Graydon was out, Toby did what she'd wanted to for days. She looked on the official website of Lanconia. What did the blue-blooded Danna look like? When the photograph came up and Toby saw that the woman was the one in the photo Rory carried in his wallet, she shut the lid of her computer. "Oh, my goodness," she whispered. Graydon was to marry the woman his brother loved?

All in all, it was something that Toby did not want to think about.

Chapter Eighteen

Graydon and Daire were in The Brotherhood restaurant, where they'd eaten a huge amount of seafood and were now on their fourth beers. For the whole time they'd talked about all things Lanconian.

Daire told Graydon about his new students. "Of course there is no Lorcan in the group," he said.

"No star who shines brighter than all the others?" Graydon asked. He was staring at his glass, a faraway look in his eyes.

"You are homesick?" Daire asked.

"Not at all!" Graydon said. "I like this island very much. If I were here longer I'd get to know people. I'd like to work on my sailing and I hear they have good teachers. And some of my American family seems to be moving here."

"You cannot stay with her," Daire said softly.

"I know. I have never, even when I was a child, neglected my duties. Country always comes first."

Daire wasn't going to let his friend dwell in self-pity. He changed the subject. "What is it about that old house and the dreams of a girl that so intrigue you?"

Graydon was glad of something else to think about. "That house should be sealed off forever. There were things in there that shouldn't be." He paused a moment, then told Daire what he'd felt in the little room, the sadness and the grief that had run through him.

"What are you going to do about it?" Daire asked.

"When I left the house I thought I'd find out what happened there, but now I'm not so sure I want to. I have so little time here that I just want to enjoy it. Toby seems to have ensnared Lorcan into her wedding designing so perhaps tomorrow you and I can do some serious training."

"In between Rory's frantic calls?"

Graydon took his time in responding. "I don't know how I will do it, but my mother is going to stop speaking to Rory the way she does. He has sacrificed a lot for me and for Lanconia."

Daire knew that Graydon was referring to Danna. He was close enough to both brothers to know who loved whom. "How are you going to leave this American girl when the time comes?"

When Graydon looked up at Daire, what he felt and what he was going to feel were in his eyes.

Daire leaned back. "I would not trade places with you. Perhaps you could—"

"Do not say it," Graydon said. "If I had any sense I would have left days ago, but I cannot. I must stay on this island as surely as I have to breathe." He paused. "Let's get out of here and go get drunk. Do you have any money?"

"Not so much as a centime," Daire said.

"I have Rory's credit card. Toby showed me how to use it but I'm not sure I remember."

"Smile at our barmaid and let her show you," Daire said, "then let's go get so drunk that we forget all women everywhere."

"There's not that much liquor on the earth," Graydon said.

Toby was awakened by a crash and some loud cursing. Or rather some shouts in Lanconian that sounded an awful lot like curses. When she looked at the clock, she saw that it was just after three A.M. It seemed that Graydon and Daire were at last returning home. All evening she'd been worried about them, but the look Lorcan gave her made Toby keep her concerns to herself.

"He is with Daire," Lorcan had said in a tone that suggested there was no need for further questions.

But Lorcan's words didn't keep Toby from constantly glancing at the clock and the door. She was trying to concentrate on the wedding plans she'd present to Victoria, but she couldn't keep her mind on them. "I just hope she'll like these," she mumbled.

"Daire likes anything historical," Lorcan said.

"I didn't mean—" Toby began, but stopped herself. "Does he? I know so little about you two personally. Either of you have a boyfriend or a girlfriend?"

"Daire lives in the barracks with his students, but he sometimes returns to his parents' home for the   " She couldn't seem to remember the word.

"Weekend?"

"Yes," Lorcan said. "If there are women, he is discreet, although he does make all women feel at ease."

There was something about her tone that intrigued Toby. "What else does Daire like besides history?"

For fifteen minutes, Lorcan talked nonstop. In the entire

time she'd been on Nantucket she hadn't spoken so many words. She didn't seem to notice that a quarter of them were Lanconian. She just kept on going. She told Toby what Daire liked to watch on TV—American and English shows such as *Spartacus* and *Game of Thrones*—what he read—biographies— what movies he liked—anything with an intricate plot that used what, according to Lorcan, was his prodigious brain. She told of the foods he liked and disliked. It seemed that his favorite vegetable was asparagus.

Toby wanted to ask, "And how long have you been in love with him?" but she didn't. She looked down at her notebook to hide her smile. How very interesting, she thought.

At about ten she gave up waiting for the men to return and went to bed. But she didn't sleep well. Her worry made her rest- less. If something bad happened, how would anyone know to call her? But then, maybe someone from the wedding had seen Graydon and would realize that he was a Kingsley. But what if no one recognized him?

She flopped about on the bed, dozing off now and then but always just barely. When she heard Graydon and Daire on the stairs, bumping into furniture and cursing in Lanconian, she let out her breath in relief.

She lay there listening to their attempts to be quiet, then fi- nally, Daire went downstairs and there was silence. Toby told herself she should go back to sleep but she wanted to be sure Graydon was all right.

She had on her pink pajamas and thought of putting on a robe, but she didn't. Barefoot, she went to Graydon's bedroom. The door was open and she tiptoed in. He was lying facedown on the bed, the covers thrown back, with the tail of a blanket over the lower half of him. From the waist up he was nude, with his right arm hanging off the bed, his fingertips touching the floor.

Smiling, she reached across him to get the other half of the blanket to cover him. It was too cool to be so bare.

When his hand reached out and grabbed her thigh, she gasped in surprise. In a lightning fast movement, he pulled her off her feet so she landed on top of him, then he deftly rolled her over so she was stretched out beside him.

"Now you are mine," he said and began to kiss her neck.

"You smell like a brewery." She was pushing at him.

"Daire got me drunk."

"Held you down, did he? Poured gallons of beer into your mouth?"

"He did," Graydon said. "Think I should have him be-headed? What do you have on?"

"Pajamas, and stop unbuttoning them." She pushed at his shoulders to look at him. His eyes were so dark they were al-most black. "I don't want to be deflowered by a drunken prince."

"Good," he said and collapsed with his face on her shoulder. "We'll just be still and in the morning we'll work on the flow-ers."

Toby laughed. She knew she should let him sleep, but in his inebriated state he just might answer a few questions. "Do you love Danna?"

"Lanconia owes her father for businesses and jobs and schol-arships and . . . everything," Graydon murmured sleepily. He was on his stomach and had his arm around Toby so securely she wasn't sure she could move if she wanted to.

"And you're the prize? Like in a fairy tale? If a man does some great deed the king rewards him with the hand of the prince in marriage to his daughter?"

"Exactly like that."

His breath was warm on her cheek. "How does the word 'barbaric' sound to you?"

"Perfect," he said, "but I didn't mind until I came to Nantucket. Danna is beautiful."

"Oh?" Toby said. "Does she have the blonde hair that you seem to like so much? Can't keep your hands out of it, can you?"

Graydon went back to kissing her neck. "Natural blonde. I told my grandfather that."

She pulled away from him. "You did what?"

Graydon just smiled, his eyes closed.

"No wonder your grandfather was so flirty in his emails!" Toby said. "I thought it was cute but now I'm embarrassed. What else did you tell people about me? You didn't mention me to your mother, did you?"

"No," Graydon said and rolled onto his back.

When his merriment instantly disappeared, Toby wished she hadn't mentioned the queen. She moved to his side and put her head on his shoulder. "I didn't mean to sober you up with something bad. Did you know that Lorcan is in love with Daire?"

"Daire is highborn," Graydon said in a distracted way. He was staring at the ceiling.

When he said nothing more, she moved on top of him. "Think of happy things." She kissed his neck.

"Like you dreaming of being with other men? Or the fact that I can't touch you?"

"It's you in the dreams," she said as she nuzzled his neck. "It's not like I'm being unfaithful. Besides, you're the one marrying someone else."

"But I have to! Danna's father threatened to move all his businesses and charities out of the country if his daughter isn't made queen."

"Did anybody ask Danna what she wants?"

He held her shoulders back to look at her. "Of course not, but then, what woman would not like to marry me?!"

Laughing, Toby rolled off him but he went with her, his body over hers. He held himself up by one arm and looked at her face. It was fairly light in the room, as the curtains hadn't been drawn. "In that dream life of yours," he said, "you marry another, and in this one I must marry someone else. It seems that there are always obligations that pull us apart. You with your sea widows who need support, and me with a country that I must take care of. Do you think we'll ever be together?"

She liked his insinuation that he wanted to be with her, even though it was impossible.

"I tell you what, next time I have one of my time travel dreams, you should go with me. You can take over Garrett's body and I'll be Tabby."

He began to smile. "Since it all happened over two hundred years ago, I would make love to you and damn the consequences. Let them deal with what happens." He ran his hand down the side of her, slowly touching the curve of her waist and her hip. When he came up, his hand went under her pajama top to cup her breast.

Toby drew in her breath. Never had a man touched her so intimately.

"My darling Carpathia, you have no idea how much I desire you. To touch you, to hold you, to be near you, is all I want. To kiss your neck, your lips, your eyes, your ears. To run my mouth over every inch of you is all I seem to think about. But I cannot," he said, and moved onto his back.

Toby stayed where she was, looking up at the ceiling. So this was it, she thought. This was the way other girls felt when a man kissed them. "I didn't mean to, but I couldn't help myself," they said. "It just happened. There was nothing I could do to stop it." Toby had always felt disgust when she'd heard that because no man had come close to making her forget herself for even a second.

But this man did.

She turned toward him. "Graydon," she whispered.

"Go to your bed," he said, his voice firm. "I've had too much to drink to be in control of my actions."

When she started to protest, he said "Please" in a way that made her think he was in pain. Slowly, she got out of his bed and went to her own. It took her quite a while before she went to sleep.

Graydon didn't get up until eleven the next day. He tried to pretend that nothing hurt him, but when Toby held up two pain-reliever tablets and a glass of water, he took them. "Did I make a fool of myself last night?"

"You declared your undying love for me, we spent three hours having fabulous sex, and I'm probably pregnant."

He didn't so much as pause in draining his glass of water. "As long as it was nothing important," he said, his eyes sparkling. He left to go back to his computer, as he was working with Rory on a coming meeting. Since it was to be conducted in Russian—which Rory didn't speak but Graydon did—it was causing some problems.

Daire had just come inside, heard the exchange between them, and was looking at Toby with serious eyes.

"It was a joke," Toby said. "I'm still a maiden and your precious country is in no danger." She left the room.

But it seemed that the two nights spent nearly together had changed things between her and Graydon. Their movements and words were more free with each other.

For the next few days they were all very busy. The first thing they did was invite Victoria and Dr. Huntley, and Jilly and Ken, to dinner the following Saturday night, when they'd present the theme. Leaving the choice so late gave them less time to prepare for the wedding, but Jilly had already sent out the Save the Date cards. Besides, Toby and Graydon were so sure that Victoria was going to love the idea that they planned a lot of the wedding beforehand. The venue—Alix's chapel—was available, and Daire's love of history helped them with the food, flowers, and music. Even the invitations came from history. They decided not to tell their dinner guests of the plan for it to be in costume or that they would serve a meal of dishes that dated from the Regency period.

Jilly stopped by to accept the invitation. What she saw was a house buzzing with activity. Graydon's constant calls and video conversations with his brother ruled their lives.

"Right now, Graydon is prince and king and even the queen," Toby told Jilly. "It's just that he's doing it all through Rory."

"And Graydon can do that from here?" Jilly asked.

"Oh, yes. We help him, of course, but he manages." Toby told Graydon's aunt about his idea of strapping a phone to Rory's cast and sending text messages. Another time Graydon spoke to a Russian businessman directly on the phone and suggested that, for privacy, they speak English when they were together in person. "Russian is one of the six languages Graydon speaks," Toby said.

"I had no idea he was so accomplished."

"Graydon can do most anything," Toby said without a hint of humor.

"Can he?" Jilly asked, trying not to laugh.

When the back door opened and Graydon came inside, Toby jumped up to meet him in the kitchen. He'd been outside with Daire, the two men attacking each other with their heavy swords.

"Your aunt is here," Jilly heard Toby say, "and you are a sweaty mess."

"Since when don't you like that?" Toby's giggle could be heard from the hall. When Toby returned to the living room, one side of her face was damp and red from what looked to be whisker burn. Jilly stood up. "We'll see you on Saturday at seven," she said and left. She was frowning. It looked like someone was going to get her—or his—heart broken.

During the week, Toby put Lorcan and Daire together more often. She had no idea that what she was doing would cause her and Graydon's first real argument.

Since Lorcan had said that Daire liked history, Toby soon figured out that all she had to do was mess up the plans and Daire would take over. She proposed a menu for the dinner that looked like a New Age fusion meal. She said she was especially pleased with her idea of using lemongrass.

Daire told her she was an idiot, then apologized. Toby, in false anger, told him that if he didn't like her ideas, he could come up with the menu. She walked out the back door, slamming it just hard enough that she didn't endanger the old panes of glass.

Graydon was gracefully moving about the garden as he jabbed his heavy sword into the air. "What are you up to?" he asked.

"Nothing interesting. I'm going to water the greenhouse."

"I already did. Get the wraps and you can do some punching and tell me what you've done to Daire."

There was no talking during boxing, certainly not the way Graydon did it. He showed her how to duck the big pad that he directed at her face. When she forgot, he tapped her head. "Hit me again and I'll make you sorry," she said.

"Is that a promise?"

She tried to punch him, but he easily sidestepped her every move. After an hour, he wrapped his arms around her shoulders and pulled her back to his front and kissed her neck.

"What are you up to with Daire?" he asked as he let her go and began pulling off her gloves and unwrapping her hands.

"He's going to plan the menu for the dinner party."

"And what is Lorcan to do?"

"I have no idea," Toby said innocently, but when Graydon kept staring at her, she broke. "How long has Lorcan been in love with Daire?"

"The three of us are a team and we work well together. They are not 'in love,'" Graydon said in a patronizing tone.

She looked at him in astonishment. "Can you honestly tell me that you've never seen anything between them? She is in love with him. Why are you frowning so hard?"

"Daire is my cousin. His father is a duke and his ancestor was a king."

"I'm sure Lorcan can be persuaded to overlook his flaws." Toby was making an American joke about equality—but Graydon didn't stop frowning. "I see," Toby said. "Kings don't soil themselves by marrying commoners. Tell me, do you guys still have affairs with people like us?"

She started to walk away but he caught her arm.

"Toby, I know that none of this makes sense to you, but this is the way it's been in my country for centuries."

She pulled away from him. "I think you misunderstand me. I'm making no criticism or judgment. It's none of my business if you Lanconians want to spend your lives with people you don't love. I'll bet Daire's illustrious family has somebody picked out for him."

She could tell by his face that she was right. "All of you have my best wishes for what I'm sure will be a very happy future."

If she'd been wearing a long dress with yards of skirt she couldn't have swept past him more haughtily. By the time she got to the house she was so angry she could hardly see where she was going. It felt good to think of a romantic, even tragic, prince who was being forced to marry a woman he didn't love. It was noble of him to sacrifice himself for his country. But to hear that Graydon thought that because of some man's birth he couldn't marry a beautiful, intelligent woman like Lorcan was sickening.

She went upstairs, firmly closed her bedroom door, showered, and changed. When she was ready, she went downstairs, barely glanced at Daire and Lorcan at the dining table, grabbed her handbag, and went out the front door. Twice she heard Graydon call her name but she didn't respond.

She quickly walked into town and realized how long it had been since she'd been out of the house. Since she'd met Graydon Montgomery it was as though he'd taken over her life.

Maybe I should rename our house THE SEIZE OF MONT-GOMERY, she thought, and the play on words of "seas" and "seize" made her smile.

In the last two weeks she had neglected her real life—the one she would return to when HRH went home to marry the "highborn"—but beautiful—woman he didn't love.

Toby walked down to the end of Straight Wharf and looked out at the water. Right now she wished with all her might that she had someone to talk to about all this. She called Lexie in France. "I miss you," she said as soon as Lexie picked up.

"What's wrong?" Lexie asked.

"Nothing," Toby lied. "What's going on with you?"

When Lexie started talking, she didn't seem to take a breath. Her boss, Roger Plymouth, had arrived a few days before. He'd been injured in a car crash and his left arm was broken. "He can't drive," Lexie said, making it sound like the biggest tragedy on earth. "He brought a nurse with him, but—"

"A nurse? Was he that badly injured?" Toby asked.

"No, but Roger can't do anything by himself. It seems the nurse knows his sister and the two of them haven't stopped laughing together—in French, no less. I didn't even know the kid could laugh. With me she just does a lot of heavy sighing.

She's not at all the girl I met last year. I've ended up spending all my time with Roger."

"Oh?" Toby said and noted that Lexie was calling him Roger and not Plymouth. "You must have hated that. Did he have anything to actually say?"

"He does. I didn't know it, but he works on some philanthropical committees. He's opening a camp for inner-city kids and using his money and athletic abilities to—" Lexie cut off. "I don't want to bore you."

Right now Toby was so angry at Graydon that she wanted to hear what Lexie had to say. "You're beginning to like him, aren't you?"

"Maybe. He wants to go on a driving tour around the country. There are some places he wants to visit to get ideas for his camp. It was planned that he was going with a college buddy of his, but the guy backed out at the last minute. Roger can't drive his stick-shift car with only one hand, so he's asked me to go with him."

"You can't drive a manual," was all Toby could think to say.

"He's going to teach me. It's either go or stay here with his sister. If I don't go with Roger, I'm afraid I might be relegated to maid status by his sister. Besides, I might be able to help with ideas. Roger is no good at organization."

"Do it," Toby said. "Take any chance you're offered and be glad of it."

Lexie was quiet for a moment. "You sound bad. What happened?"

"I guess I took off my rose-colored glasses, that's all."

"Want to tell me about it?"

Toby thought of trying to explain the ideology of another country but had no idea where to begin. "Not yet," she said.

"You haven't committed the ultimate sin and fallen in love with him, have you?" Lexie asked.

"Far, far from it. In fact, I'm thinking that after the dinner party on Saturday I may kick the lot of them out of the house."

"What dinner party?" Lexie asked.

Toby was glad of a subject she could talk about freely and she launched into a description of her plans for a historical wedding. But she didn't tell Lexie about her dream encounters with Victoria/Valentina. That was too much to explain over the phone. Instead, Toby said the idea had come from Victoria's historical novels.

"I always knew you were brilliant," Lexie said, "and I think Victoria will love the idea. Is Dr. Huntley getting the costumes for you to wear?"

Toby told of Graydon asking his grandparents to raid the palace closets.

"Sounds like he's rather involved in your life. Have you been to bed with him yet?"

"Yes and no," Toby said. "Kissing, rolling around on the bed, but no sex."

"Sounds like high school."

"Yeah, doesn't it? What about you?"

"No, of course not. This is business. I have to go," Lexie said. "Toby, hang in there and let me know if anything, you know, happens."

"Same with you and Roger."

"There won't be anything. He and I—" She broke off because Toby was laughing and when Lexie joined her, Toby knew her friend was tempted.

Still laughing, they said goodbye and hung up.

Toby put her phone away and realized she felt much better. She walked to the florist shop where she worked and talked to her boss. Maybe next week she'd go back to her job. No more hanging out with Lanconians and trying to understand their ways.

But her boss didn't need her. The young woman Victoria had

found to replace Toby was doing exceptionally well. What he didn't tell Toby was that he'd made a deal with Victoria that all her wedding flowers would come through him if he didn't re-hire Toby until September.

"Sorry," he said and he was. All of them liked Toby and her work was excellent.

Toby spent some time with her coworkers, sharing hugs and stories of the work they'd been doing, but when she began to feel in the way, she left and walked to Jetties Beach. But it was where she and Graydon had walked together and there were too many memories.

She took herself to Arno's for lunch, then went shopping at Zero Main. Noël and her staff always made Toby feel better.

At five she started home. She knew she'd made some decisions, and she planned to stick with them. The first thing was that she was going to stop disparaging Graydon's country. It wasn't any of her business what they did. She was an American and had different views, but that didn't make them the only way or even a better way. It was Graydon's life and if he wanted to marry a woman he didn't love, he had that right.

The main thing Toby knew was that she needed to protect herself. She'd laughed about it to Lexie, but the way Toby was going, she was going to fall in love with Graydon. Then what? She'd kiss him goodbye as he went off to marry someone else? No, she wasn't going to do that.

By the time she got back to the house, she was smiling.

"Where have you been?" Graydon demanded as soon as she stepped inside. His hair was rumpled and his eyes were red. A deep frown creased his forehead.

She put her shopping bags on the floor and her handbag on the little table in the hall. "How did it go with your Russian businessman?"

Graydon stepped forward, his arms extended, as though he meant to pull her into them. But Toby took a step back, her body stiff, and her face wore what Lexie called the don't-touch-me look.

Graydon dropped his arms. "I apologize for what I said." His voice was so soft only she could hear him. "We Lanconians are too inflexible. We—"

"It's all right," she said. "Different countries; different ways. I had no right to criticize you or your country."

He smiled at her. "Shall we kiss and make up?"

"No," she said firmly, then took her shopping bags and went upstairs.

It was early morning on Saturday, the day of the dinner party, and Graydon was looking out the upstairs window as Toby watered the garden. It was cool and foggy, perfect Nantucket weather, and he would have liked to be with her, but he knew that things had changed between them. Ever since he'd explained to Toby why Daire couldn't possibly marry someone like Lorcan, it was as though she had closed a door on him.

She seemed to have left their private little world for two and returned to her life on Nantucket. Twice she'd been out to lunch with her girlfriends. At six one morning he saw her outside cutting flowers for a wedding. Graydon had asked if she needed help but Toby had politely told him no. No teasing or laughing, just her extreme courtesy—and it was getting him down. Every sentence she addressed to him was polite. She smiled at him, made small talk, and was always endlessly courteous.

"I don't know what you did to her," Daire said after a few days, "but if I were you, I'd be afraid to close my eyes."

The truth was that Graydon had no idea what he'd done to make her go from . . . well, almost loving to smiling at him as though she'd just met him that morning.

Twice he'd tried to talk to her. Both times he'd used his most patient—and certainly most charming—voice to explain his country and hers. He'd talked of how his homeland was very old and that it was based on centuries of tradition. He'd smiled as he told her that her country was so young that it couldn't understand having customs that went back hundreds of years.

She'd seemed to be listening—until he reached out to take her hand in his.

Toby drew back and stood up. "Lanconia sounds wonderful. Maybe I'll visit someday. Right now I have a date." Smiling at him in her cool way, she left the room.

Graydon wanted to run after her and demand to know who her "date" was. A man? That was the first time it truly hit him that on Nantucket he was just a regular person. He had no princely rights and no one was looking at him as though they lived to please him.

On the third day of Toby's never-ending courtesy, Graydon started watching Daire and Lorcan. His original objective was to prove that Toby was wrong. Maybe it was true that Lorcan was "in love" with Daire. After all, he'd been her teacher for many years. But Daire had taught a lot of people and never once had he hinted that he felt anything personal for any of them. At least not to Graydon.

He began to watch the two of them training together. Lorcan's bruises were healing from her fall, but still, Daire was quite solicitous of her.

When Graydon was working out with them, both Daire and Lorcan showed nothing personal between them. It was only when he went inside and watched them through an upstairs window that he began to see what Toby had.

Many times Daire put his arms around Lorcan as he showed her some movement that Graydon was sure she knew well. Twice he saw Daire close his eyes for a moment as Lorcan's body grazed his.

That night when they were alone Graydon asked Daire about the woman he was pledged to marry. "How is Astrie?"

For a moment Daire looked blank. "Well, I assume."

"You don't keep in contact with her?"

"My family does. That is enough."

"And when is your wedding?" Graydon asked.

"Why all these questions?"

"I was just curious, is all," Graydon said, then turned away. At meals he began to see the way Lorcan and Daire moved certain dishes toward each other. It was subtle, something he'd never noticed before, but it was there. One morning he glanced up and saw Toby looking at him as though to say "I told you so." It was the most personal she'd been all week.

When the historic clothes arrived from Lanconia, Graydon was sure that they'd melt Toby's coolness. His grandparents had sent a dress for her that was truly beautiful.

Gently, Toby held it up. "This should be in a museum."

"No, it should be worn by a beautiful woman," Graydon said in a voice that in the past had made several women look at him with dreamy eyes.

But Toby ignored him.

"Toby, I—" Graydon began as he stepped toward her.

But her cell phone rang. "It's Jared," she said as she went outside to answer it. Minutes later she returned, smiling. "He's given me a job! I'm to design an entire garden for his cousin's house. Alix is drawing the remodel now and . . ." She took a breath. "I have to go measure things. Lorcan? Want to hold the end of the tape?"

"I would like to—" Graydon began but his cell rang and it was Rory with yet another emergency. Their father was recovering and wanted to talk to him.

"Now I really have to be you," Rory said, panic in his voice. "Maybe you should come home for this one."

Graydon looked at Toby and Lorcan talking together, both

of them with their eyes alight, and he thought that if he left now he didn't think Toby would let him back in the house. "I can't do it," Graydon said in Lanconian. "I have business here."

"You think bedding some American girl is more important than your king?" Rory shot at him.

"I'm not touching her and don't try to bully me. You can do this! I'll walk you through it."

Rory seemed shocked at what his brother had said. "You've had weeks but you haven't won the girl? What's wrong?"

Graydon gave a half smile. "It seems that to Toby I'm not a prince by birthright. She expects me to *earn* the position."

Rory laughed so hard that Graydon rolled his eyes and very nearly hung up on his brother.

It was just before Rory was to go see their father—and try to fool him about his own sons—that Graydon asked his brother to do something for him.

"Besides try to be you?" Rory snapped.

In the past Graydon had been almost patronizing about Rory's reluctance to spend time with their parents. But since Graydon had heard the way their mother talked to Rory, he was much more understanding.

"Yes," Graydon said. "I want to ask more of you. I want a document drawn up and signed by our father."

"You're not asking much, are you?"

"I am asking a great deal of you," Graydon said, his mind on Danna. The night before he'd seen a YouTube video of Rory and Danna leaving a dinner party and they'd looked like two sublimely happy people. Graydon was beginning to question how he was going to be able to reconcile taking that away from his brother. "I think the American in me is coming to the surface," he said.

"What does that mean?" Rory asked.

"I don't know yet. I'll write to you about what I need and you can have it drawn up and get Father to sign it."

"Mother will give me hell."

"No, she won't!" Graydon said sternly. "If she says anything at all, don't back down. Stand up to her. Don't even blink. Father will back you."

Rory took a breath. "All right. Send me what you need and I'll try to—no! I'll do it."

"Good," Graydon said and they hung up.

In the remaining days before the dinner party Lorcan and Toby spent a lot of time planning the garden for Jared's cousin's house. They went on one of the many house and garden tours held in Nantucket and returned with photos and sketches.

"I've never seen Lorcan so easy with another woman," Daire said as he watched the two women bent over books and papers. "She's spent her life with men and the women were always jealous of her."

Toby had taken Lorcan shopping and outfitted her in Nantucket white linen. Gone were Lorcan's black leathers and wool, and her heavy boots. It greatly amused both Graydon and Daire that while Lorcan had learned a lot of English, Toby had learned just as much Lanconian. They talked to each other in a mix of the two languages. When Toby said, "By Jura, but I think this garden is going to be beautiful!" both Daire and Graydon had hidden their laughter.

What Graydon regretted about the friendship was that Lorcan had taken over training Toby. Compared to Lorcan, Toby was awkward in her martial arts skills, but then Toby introduced Lorcan to yoga. Both men glued themselves to the sunroom windows when the two women were outside doing their exercises.

One time Rory called in the middle of a session. His voice was frantic as yet another crisis had arisen.

"Rory," Graydon said calmly, "do you know what a 'downward facing dog' is?"

"One of the natural wonders of the earth. But that's just my opinion," he said.

"That's what Toby and Lorcan are doing right now."

"My problems can wait," Rory said and hung up.

But this was the day of the dinner party and Graydon hoped that tonight he could make up with Toby.

Chapter Nineteen

When Toby threw open her bedroom door, she had on a bathrobe, her hair was streaming down her back, and her pretty face was devoid of makeup. "I need help!" she said to Jilly. "I can't figure out any of this dress, and the corset is a monster—even though there's not much of it. And my hair! I didn't even think about it! I should have had it done and—"

"You'll be fine," Jilly said. "I'm rather good with my daughter's long hair so I can help with yours. In fact, I brought a few things with me." She had a duffel bag that looked to be packed full.

At Jilly's soothing words, Toby began to relax. This was how she'd always wanted her mother to be, how she'd imagined the two of them sharing events. She was almost twenty before she realized that it was never going to happen.

Early that morning, when Jilly had stopped by to ask if they needed any help with the party, Toby had revealed that they were presenting a wedding theme in costume. She'd even shown Jilly the dress she was to wear. Toby had carefully opened the flaps of the box to expose pale green tissue paper. Inside was a dress of sheer white silk, the bodice covered with what looked to be hand embroidery of intertwining flowers and vines, all of it white. The necessary undergarments for the gown were in a separate box.

When Jilly picked the dress up, the first thing she noticed was that it was nearly transparent. "Oh, my goodness," Jilly said. "Graydon got this for you?"

"He did," Toby said curtly, then looked away.

She certainly wasn't rhapsodizing over Graydon today! Jilly thought. "What are you planning to wear under this?"

"Red flannel underwear?" Toby said and the women laughed.

"The house smells great," Jilly said. "Who's doing the cooking?"

"Mostly the men," Toby answered. "Lorcan and I just cut up things. I've been trying to get her and Daire to stay for the dinner, but they won't do it."

Now, in the bedroom, Toby sat down on an ottoman as Jilly began working on her hair. She piled the thick blonde curls up, and held them in place with what seemed to be a thousand pins. Tendrils fell down prettily at the sides of Toby's face. Afterward, Jilly applied light cosmetics, letting Toby's pure skin show through.

After the hair and makeup were done, they tackled the corset. It encircled Toby's ribs and supported the lower half of her breasts, but it left the top half nearly fully exposed.

"I think they sent the wrong undergarments," Toby said as she tried to pull the top up so it would cover more, but it wouldn't move.

"This shows that every generation has liked sex," Jilly said. Nothing had been sent to wear under the slip, no underdrawers of any kind. Toby thought they'd made a mistake, but a quick computer search showed that there was no error.

"There's historical accuracy and there's common sense," Toby said as she pulled on a pair of modern cotton underpants.

Jilly held out the nearly transparent slip for Toby to put on, then handed over the white silk stockings with their garters. At last, she helped Toby slide the dress over her head. It was a perfect fit, with the high waist just under her breasts and the pretty, puffy sleeves showing off Toby's slender arms. The skirt barely grazed the floor, with the embroidery weighing it down enough that it clung to Toby's body when she moved.

When Toby looked in her antique full-length mirror, she thought she'd been transformed into a different person. The truth was that she thought she looked even more like Tabby from her dream. But this dress had once been worn by royalty and was richer and more beautiful than anything she'd seen before. She made a couple of tugs at the top of the dress to try for more coverage, but then let it drop. She turned to Jilly.

"You look beautiful," Jilly said. "Really, Toby, you are something out of a fairy tale." There was a knock on the door.

"Is it safe to come in?" Ken asked.

Opening the door, Jilly swept her hand back. "Behold what we have done."

"Toby!" Ken said. "You look fabulous."

"Thank you," she said. "Let's just hope that Victoria agrees."

"Based on what I know," Ken said of his ex-wife, "Victoria will love wearing a dress that shows so much of her—" He made a vague gesture around his chest area. "The sight of you nearly made me forget. Graydon sent this to you. It's from his grandmother."

Toby took the package he held out to her. It was wrapped in

a pretty pink silk fabric and tied with a cream-colored ribbon. When she opened it, she gasped, for inside were a pair of pearl earrings and a bracelet of tiny pearls and twisted gold wire. In the bottom were a dozen little pearl and gold pins.

"They're for your hair," Jilly said as she began to put them into the upsweep she'd created.

Ken took a small camera out of his pocket and began snapping. "Two beautiful girls," he said.

The sound of voices downstairs made them look at one another. Victoria and Dr. Huntley had arrived.

"Ken and I will go down first," Jilly said to Toby. "Gray asked if he could escort you down. He said he has something he wants to show you. We'll fix drinks and turn on the music, so come down when you're ready."

The two of them left the room and went downstairs.

It was just before their guests were to arrive, and Graydon was dressed in what Toby called "Mr. Darcy's clothes." When he sat down on the couch to put on the ridiculous little slippers that came with the getup, he found a note and a small package from his grandmother Aria.

My darling Gray,

The clothes I sent were worn by my grandmother's way-ward sister and her Groom of the Horse—who everyone knew was her favorite lover. But then, her foreign princely husband was such a dud! These are the jewels she wore with the dress.

My dear grandson, I know what you are facing in the future and how desperately you need this time to think and plan. Please be assured that whatever you do, whatever decisions you make, your grandfather and I will support you and love you.

With greatest love, Aria

The tone of the note made him miss his grandparents very much. Before he thought about what he was doing, he called his brother.

A sleepy, grumpy Rory answered. "Do you know what time it is here?" he asked in Lanconian.

"About one-thirty in the morning," Graydon said. "Since when do you go to bed before dawn?"

"Since I took over your life. Did you know they even schedule when I can use the restroom?"

"Discipline in all things," Graydon said.

"You didn't call to hear me complain. What's going on? Except that you're having to dress up like a Jane Austen book cover, that is."

"I wondered if you'd been told about that."

"Of course I was," Rory said. "The grandparents wanted to know all about your little girlfriend."

"What did you tell them?"

Rory was quiet for a moment. He knew this call wasn't merely social. "What's bothering you?"

"I like her," Graydon said. "I've never felt this way before. But right now she isn't happy with me."

Rory heard the longing in his brother's voice, but he wasn't going to give him any sympathy. "If you want to come home, let me know."

It was Graydon's turn to hear the underlying emotion in his brother's words. "And separate you from Danna? I value my life too much. I'll talk to you later." He hung up.

In Lanconia, Rory collapsed back against the bed pillows. So his brother did know how he felt about Danna. How long had Graydon known? What had given him away?

Getting out of bed, Rory went to the window and pulled aside the heavy brocade curtains to look out on the lawn below. To his shock, there was Danna astride that big gelding of hers, riding on the path toward the stables.

Rory knew he shouldn't go outside, but even as he thought it, he was pulling on a pair of jeans. He grabbed a shirt and slipped it on as he ran barefoot down the old stone stairs. He shouldn't do this. He knew that. Moonlight and Danna were not things he should put together. She was to marry his brother, not him. He was the UYB and he would never be able to give her what she deserved.

But his thoughts didn't stop him running across the lawn toward the stables.

When Toby opened the bedroom door into the sitting room, Graydon was standing there waiting for her—and she drew in her breath at the sight of him. If anyone had ever been made for Regency era clothing, it was him. The trousers, the jacket, it all suited him so perfectly that he looked like a time traveler. At the moment, she couldn't remember what she had been angry about.

As for Graydon, he was staring at her in a way that made the blood rush to her cheeks. He looked her up and down, slowly, lingeringly, and when their eyes met, his were blazing.

Usually, when a man looked at her like that, Toby turned and ran away. If possible, she would refuse to ever again get near him. But tonight, she took a step toward Graydon—and he opened his arms to her.

She didn't know what would have happened if music hadn't suddenly come blaring from downstairs. It was a waltz that

Graydon had found on the Internet. The sheer volume of the music jolted both of them out of their trance.

Stepping back, Graydon extended his hand to her. When she took it, he began to lead her in a dance. She'd danced with Rory and had enjoyed it, but dancing now with his brother was something else. Graydon was strong but graceful. He held her closely but not intimately. They moved together so perfectly it was as though they were one person.

It was several minutes before someone turned down the player, but she and Graydon could still hear the music clearly. He led her all around the sitting room, swirling about the furniture, close but never touching it.

Her dress was made for dancing. The thin, fine fabric didn't hinder her movements and it clung to her legs in a way that made her feel weightless, like she was clad in something made by elfin hands.

At one point, Graydon put his hands on her waist, lifted her up, and swung her through the air to the other side of him. Toby's laugh could be heard over the music.

When the music stopped, he pulled her to him, her cheek on his chest, and she could hear his heart beating. She wasn't sure but she thought he kissed the top of her head.

For a moment she and Graydon didn't move, just stood there with their arms about each other.

It was Graydon who broke away and held her at arm's length. "You are more beautiful than I imagined. You should dress like this every day." He glanced down at the very exposed top of her.

Toby smiled. "Cleaning the house, weeding the garden, all while wearing a dress with the top half missing," she said as she stepped away from him. "But you . . . You finally actually look like a prince."

"But I don't think I've been acting like one lately."

She pulled away from him. His words had broken the spell and she remembered their argument. "I think we should go downstairs."

"I have something to show you." He handed her a rolled up piece of parchment with a blue ribbon around it.

She unrolled it. It was a very pretty document, done in what looked to be hand calligraphy, but it was all in Lanconian. At the bottom was a wax seal and a bold black signature. "What is it?"

"Basically, it's Daire's freedom. He can marry whomever he wants and he'll still inherit the title and lands in his family. Daire's father is an irascible old man, and without threats from the king, he would disinherit his son if he married someone unsuitable. Everything would have gone to Daire's cousin, who is a nasty little character. Daire didn't want to be the one who destroyed his very old and distinguished family."

"You got your father to sign this?"

"Through Rory, yes," Graydon said. "I would have done it years ago if I'd had any idea that Daire was displeased with his family's choice of bride. But he never complained to me."

"And Lorcan has never talked to me about her feelings for Daire, even though I've tried to get her to." She looked up at him.

"I am sorry," he said. "These last few days have been . . ."

She put her fingertips to his lips. "Tonight we are Tabitha and Garrett and we have no differences in country policies."

"I like that," he said and put his arm out for her to take. "And tomorrow be damned."

When they got near the bottom of the front stairs, everyone suddenly stopped and stared—but Victoria reacted the most strongly. She looked at Toby as though she'd never seen such a sight in her life. Her expression seemed to be of shock, but also, there was . . . Was it recognition? Toby couldn't help wondering.

The other three stepped back and let Victoria absorb the sight of the two young people standing on the stairs. They certainly made a handsome couple! Graydon's black jacket showed his broad shoulders and trim waist; the trousers clung to thighs thickly muscled from years atop unruly horses.

As for Toby, she was breathtaking. The white, gossamer-thin gown suited her perfectly. The low-cut neckline, the way the fabric skimmed over her hips, the hint of transparency, all of it seemed to have been created just for her.

They all stood still, transfixed, as everyone waited to hear what Victoria was going to say. After several long moments, she turned to Caleb. "This is what I will wear when I marry you," she said softly. Victoria's eyes were so full of love that everyone felt they were seeing something very private.

Caleb gave a bit of a smile, then he bowed—as a man from Jane Austen's time might do. In return, Victoria performed an absolutely perfect curtsy.

After that pretty little vignette, everyone began talking, mainly about how great Toby and Graydon looked. Victoria took Toby's arm and led her to a corner of the living room.

"I knew you would come up with the perfect theme. But, darling," Victoria said as she lowered her voice, "next time, leave the slip off. Show what you have while you still have it." She looked up. "Caleb, dearest, have we run out of champagne already?"

The four older adults gathered around the cabinet where that afternoon Ken had set up a drinks bar.

"Did Victoria thank you for all your work?" Graydon asked from behind Toby.

"Yes. Sort of. And she told me I should have on fewer undergarments."

"Victoria is a very wise woman."

"Not going to happen," Toby said as she joined the others.

The dinner was a great success. As was the eighteenth-century custom, all the dishes had been put on the table, with desserts on the sideboard. As soon as the soup—pea with cucumber and mint—was finished, Ken took away the tureen. They helped themselves to meatballs with anchovies and cayenne pepper, sole in wine with mushrooms, vermouth-enhanced scallops, oysters on vol-au-vent pastries under a cream sauce, and little stuffed game birds that were crisp and tender. There were several vegetables, each with its own sauce.

Everyone ate ravenously, filling and refilling their plates.

"Now, this is food!" Caleb said, then began a diatribe against pizza, burgers, and even sandwiches.

Toby expected everyone to protest, but instead they all agreed with him. In fact, the four of them seemed to agree about everything. There was no sniping between the formerly married Victoria and Ken, no disagreements at all. Everyone spoke of what they'd been doing over the last weeks, but it was Dr. Huntley who stole the spotlight. He entertained them with the story of how Captain Caleb and Valentina met in 1806. The captain had returned early from a lucrative voyage to China and found his new house being used by the builder for his own wedding. "The captain was so annoyed he took a keg of rum and went up to the attic to . . . to meditate."

"Sounds like he wanted to get drunk and sulk," Ken said.

"It depends on how you look at it," Dr. Huntley replied, but he was smiling. "The captain had been up there just a short time when the very beautiful"—he looked at Victoria—"Valentina came upstairs. She had on a dress that . . ." He motioned with his hands to mean that it was very low cut. "Since the captain had been places that weren't as prudish as America, he thought she wasn't a respectable woman—which was quite understandable. He . . . Well, he . . ."

"He made a pass at her?" Jilly said.

"With a bit of, shall we say, 'passion' attached to it. And she agreed."

"Really?" Victoria, who had never heard the story, said. "Just like that, she said yes?"

"At least the captain thought she did," Dr. Huntley said with a funny little smile. "But it wasn't so. However, she was convincing enough that she persuaded the captain to remove all his clothing."

"Oh, my!" Jilly said.

"Then what did she do?" Victoria asked, leaning forward, her eyes alight.

"Valentina Montgomery took the captain's clothes, left the room, and locked the door behind her. The wedding downstairs was so loud that the captain wasn't let out until the next morning. By then, he'd nearly frozen to death." He looked around at the faces at the table with an expression as though he expected sympathy. Instead, he got an explosion of laughter.

When she could catch her breath, Toby said, "And I take it that from there they fell madly in love."

Dr. Huntley took Victoria's hand and kissed it. "Yes, they did." He raised his glass in a toast. "Here's to good food, to friends, and to life. But most of all, to love that endures forever."

They drank to the toast, then Ken said, "Shall we have dessert?"

Jilly made pots of Assam tea, and everyone filled their plates with lemon cheesecake, molasses cookies called Joe Froggers, slices of fruity yeast cake, and bowls of vanilla custard laced with brandy. Afterward, there were cheeses, raisins, and nuts, followed by more tea and glasses of port.

After the dinner, Caleb insisted that there be dancing. They went into the living room, with its low beamed ceiling. All electric lights were turned out, with only candles remaining. Caleb pulled Victoria into his arms and led her in a dance that had to be a few hundred years old. The others stood back and watched as they performed it perfectly. "It's your turn now," he said to the others when the music stopped.

He pulled a packet of pipe tobacco out of his pocket, then pushed on a corner of the old fireplace, and a door popped open—which astonished them all. Inside were three pipes that looked very old.

"How did you know that door was there?" Toby asked.

"Captain Caleb's son, the first Jared, didn't want a life at sea, so he stayed home and built houses that his wife designed. Unfortunately, what they did together has been lost to history." He sounded almost bitter.

That was an interesting historical tidbit, but it was no answer at all. "But how did you—" Toby began, but Caleb cut her off.

"I think you and your prince should dance," he said, showing that he had no intention of answering her question. He took one of the pipes, packed it, and sat down on the settee next to Victoria, while Jilly and Ken took chairs next to each other. The music began and the older people were content to watch Toby and Graydon glide about the room in their beautiful clothes.

It was late when Toby and Graydon finally sat down. She looked at Dr. Huntley. "You wouldn't happen to know if a couple of people named Tabitha Weber and Garrett Kingsley actually existed, would you? I'm not sure of the year, early 1800s by the clothes."

Caleb took his time answering. "They were real and their story was pure tragedy." When he looked up at Toby his eyes seemed to be very old—and there was grief in them. "Garrett was Captain Caleb's younger brother."

Toby looked at Graydon. "The captain was Jared's ancestor. And related to you, I guess."

"Through Valentina Montgomery," Jilly said. She was her family's historian and she was beginning to work on their connection with the Nantucket Kingsleys. "The captain never married Valentina, even though they produced a child together."

Dr. Huntley winced, looking as though someone had hit him. "Foolish, stupid man," he muttered, then looked at Toby. "But I believe you wanted to know about Tabby and Garrett. May I ask how you know of them?"

"I, uh . . ." She glanced at Graydon and he nodded encouragement. "I had a few dreams about them."

Caleb looked at his pipe. "In the house called BEYOND TIME? Did you know it used to be called—"

"NEVER TO SEA AGAIN," Toby said.

Caleb's eyes widened. "Yes, you are right. Not many people know that."

"What I want to know is whether or not she married the man she loved," Toby said, and she couldn't help glancing at Graydon.

Caleb took a breath. "There was a great scandal at Parthenia's wedding," he said. "You see, Tabby was seen under a tree with Garrett Kingsley, and both of them were half undressed."

"Oh," Toby said and her face began to redden. It had only been a dream, but she had been kissing Garrett. Had she given in to his entreaties and rolled in the grass with him?

Caleb, sitting directly across from her, was watching Toby intently. "The incident seemed out of character for Tabitha. It was more what a modern woman would do."

"I think you should tell us the whole story," Ken said. "Can I assume that the young lovers were forced to marry?"

"No, they didn't marry. At least not each other," Caleb said. "You see, Tabby had a mother who made sharks look kind. But then again that family had lost all their men to the sea. She didn't want Tabby to marry a Kingsley, as it was said that all of them were dedicated to the sea."

"She made Tabby marry Silas Osborne, didn't she?" Toby said.

"Yes," Caleb answered. "That night, there and then, at Parthenia's wedding, she made her daughter marry that—"

"Truck-bellied, brocky man," Toby said softly and she began to feel very sad.

"I'm confused," Ken said. "Who was this guy Osborne?"

"No one!" Caleb said and there was anger in his voice. "Tabby's mother sold her daughter. Lavinia Weber owed that little pencil pusher money and the ugly little bastard promised to forgive the debt and to support all those sea widows—but only if pretty little Tabitha would marry him. So she did. Her mother snatched her from Garrett's arms and wed her to Osborne that very night. Parthenia's wedding celebration went from happiness to tears. If the captain had been there he would have stopped it, but he was locked away in an attic and brooding. Stupid man!"

Dr. Huntley's vehemence and anger were so strong that for a moment they were all silent.

"Was her husband good to Tabitha?" Toby whispered.

"No," Caleb said, his voice calmer. "Osborne put a new roof on the house, but after that, he would do nothing else. He told Lavinia that Tabby didn't like him, so the bargain was off. Lavinia's screams of outrage were heard all the way to 'Sconset. She said that nobody liked him so it didn't count that Tabby didn't. But her words didn't matter because Osborne never gave that family another cent."

"What did Tabby do?" Toby said.

"Earned her keep and supported all of them. She ran Osborne's store and she never received a word of praise or thanks for all she did. She died when she was in her early thirties, with no children. Everyone said she willed herself to death because she never got over her love for Garrett."

"And what happened to him?" Graydon asked.

Dr. Huntley took a long breath before he answered. "Three years later Garrett went down with his brother Caleb, on the ship the captain had stubbornly led into a storm. He was trying to get home to Valentina." Reaching out, he took Victoria's hand in his.

Again, everyone was silent.

"How did we get on this depressing story?" Victoria asked. "It was all so very long ago. What I want to know about are Toby's dreams. Anything I can use for a book plot?"

Victoria's words broke the misery that had descended on the group. As Graydon got up and opened another bottle of port, Toby began to tell them about her dreams. While she talked, Caleb kept nodding his head. When Toby said she'd sent Valentina to the attic, he said, "So you were the culprit! Go on. I didn't mean to interrupt."

When Toby said Ken and Jilly looked exactly like John Kendricks and Parthenia, they smiled at each other. "I knew we were meant to be together," Ken said.

"Ha!" Victoria said. "If it hadn't been for me, you would never have come together." She looked at Toby. "What I want to know is if this was real. Did you actually visit that time?"

"Of course I didn't," Toby said. "I dreamed it all. I've spent every summer of my life on Nantucket so I probably read a journal of Tabitha or Parthenia, or someone. And I remembered it in my sleep."

They all looked at Dr. Huntley in question. As the director of the island's historical society, he would know about that. "It's true that there are snippets of the story in some of the letters and journals we have."

"See?" Toby said. "I'm sure that's how Dr. Huntley knows what happened. Right?"

He didn't answer her question. "Did you change anything while you were in any of your dreams?"

"No, nothing," Toby said, but then her head came up. "Actually, I did. I lost a key to a box. It's still in Kingsley House, keyless, but when I saw the box, it contained—"

"Jade zodiac symbols," Dr. Huntley said. "Captain Caleb bought them in China as a gift for the woman he loved. The key was lost at Parthenia's wedding, and the captain always thought one of those Starbuck brats stole it."

"How could you possibly know that?" Ken asked.

"Didn't I tell you that my Caleb knows everything about this island?" Victoria said, her voice full of pride.

"In my dream," Toby emphasized, "I dropped the key behind an unfinished window seat in Kingsley House."

"Shall we go look for it?" Caleb said as though it were the most ordinary thing in the world. No one hesitated in leaving.

It took them only minutes to reach Kingsley House, but when they got there, Caleb refused to enter.

"I'll wait out here for you," he said as he stood on the little front porch.

"But, darling," Victoria began, but even she could see that he wasn't going to budge.

Jilly put her hand on Caleb's arm, her face sympathetic. "If it's ghosts you're worried about, I have a bit of intuition about them. I'll warn you if—"

"Intuition?" Caleb said. "You can see them. Poor creatures have to hide from you. Ghosts hold no fear for me. It's just that I've seen enough of that house. Go and look for your key, then come back out here to me."

Everyone, even Victoria, gave up arguing and went inside. Ken flipped the light switches on as they went to the back parlor and Toby pointed out the cushioned window seat.

"I sat here with Alisa, or Ali, as she liked to be called, and I watched her draw pictures of the windows."

Ken pulled the cushion off and looked at the way the seat

was constructed. "I know how this was done. I'd not noticed it before but it's quite ingenious." He looked at Toby with teasing eyes. "But then that's rather vain of me to say considering that in another life I built it."

Toby knew he was making fun of her, but she didn't mind. However, part of her almost wished they would find the key.

Ken got Jared's big toolbox out of a closet and removed the bottom panel of the seat. He stretched out on the floor to take out the inner panel. When that was done, he had to slide the upper part of his body inside the opening to search with a flashlight and a long screwdriver.

No one said a word as they listened to the scratching and saw the light move about. When Ken scooted back out, he sat up and looked at them. He took his time before he opened his hand to show a little brass key.

"That's it!" Toby exclaimed as she took it.

It was one thing to laugh about finding a key that had been lost centuries ago but quite another to see it in real life.

Ken, Jilly, and Victoria were staring at Toby in openmouthed astonishment.

Graydon stepped forward, put his arm protectively around Toby's shoulders, and said, "Shall we look for the box full of jade?"

Ken was the first to recover. "Uh, ah . . . Does anyone know where it is?"

When no one spoke, Toby said, "I saw it in the attic but I don't remember exactly where it was. Maybe I should call Lexie and ask her."

Victoria was recovering from shock. "I'll find out." She went to the front door and told Caleb that Ken had found the key.

"I thought he would," he said. "Third row from the right, halfway down, inside the red lacquer box. When I danced with Alix I knocked the bulbs out, so take a light."

"I assume you're talking of the attic," Victoria said, blinking.

"I am. When you find the box, bring it outside so I can see it."

The five adults ran up the old stairs to the attic and the treasure hunt began. It took a while, but they found the box exactly where Caleb said it was. They'd had trouble agreeing about the meaning of "halfway down," and the lacquer box was so old the red was almost black.

"How did Caleb know where this was?" Ken asked in awe. "It was inside another box."

"He really does know everything about the island," Victoria said, but this time it didn't sound like she was bragging. She sounded as though she thought it was a bit creepy.

"Old soul; new body," Jilly murmured, and everyone was glad to turn their thoughts to someone other than Toby. "Shall we take the box downstairs and try the key?"

They met Caleb outside, then they all walked to the back of the property to the guesthouse, where Ken and Jilly were staying, and put the old box on the kitchen countertop.

"This place has certainly changed," Caleb said as he looked around. "Used to be where we kept the cow."

No one asked about that comment. Under the spell of the late night, and the wine and the port they'd ingested, no one questioned his odd statement. Toby gave the key to Caleb. "I think you should be the one to do this."

Considering that the box had been locked for over two hundred years, the key turned easily. Caleb didn't open it but picked it up and handed it to Victoria. "The gift was meant for you."

Victoria opened the box to reveal the jade carvings of the Chinese zodiac. Each figure was of a different color of jade: dark green, white, even lavender. Each was exquisitely and intricately carved.

"I'm a rabbit," Victoria said as she lifted that figure. "All about family and ambition." They all began to talk of the year they were born. Only Caleb was silent. When they looked at him in question, he said, "What was the symbol for 1776?"

There was a hesitation, then Victoria said, "Fireworks!" and they all laughed—and their laughter broke the tension. No one had said it, but the question hung over them all: Had Toby actually time traveled? Did the key prove that her dreams were real?

Victoria, Ken, and Jilly turned to look at the two young people standing there in their beautiful eighteenth-century clothes, and it was easy to imagine that they'd stepped out of the past.

Graydon was the first to break the silence. "There's a room in that house," he said softly, "where I felt a sense of misery, even tragedy."

They hadn't spoken of it, but Toby knew the room he meant. "The door is hidden behind the paneling."

They were all looking at Caleb, waiting for his answer. No one seemed to doubt that he would know. "The birthing room?" he asked. "Back then women gave birth often and they gathered together when the time came. A lot of the houses had birthing rooms. There was indeed much sadness in there, but there was also joy. Valentina gave birth to the first Jared Montgomery Kingsley in that room. He was a big, healthy boy." He sounded proud.

"Who grew up to marry little Ali," Victoria said. "Toby, since the book I'm working on is from Valentina's journal, I'll want to talk to you about her. I didn't realize Ali was older than Jared."

No one noticed that Toby and Graydon were silent and slightly frowning. While the others discussed Valentina and her life, Toby turned to Graydon. "You didn't tell me that you saw that room. I couldn't go inside it. I also felt a deep sadness—

grief—coming from it. I kept feeling that I—I mean Tabby—had died in there."

Graydon took her hand in his and kissed the back of it. He wasn't about to tell her that was exactly what he too had felt. "But you heard Dr. Huntley. Tabby had no children, so she probably wouldn't have died in that particular room."

Toby grimaced. "No, she just willed herself to leave the earth because her life was so unhappy. That poor, poor girl. When I was in my dream, if I'd known what happened to her, I would have tried to save her."

"By doing what? Marrying her to Garrett?" He was smiling as though that was a great idea.

"Then he goes off to sea with his big brother and gets himself killed? That would leave yet another widow in that house and probably more children to take care of. And if she was Garrett's wife, Tabby wouldn't have had Silas Osborne's store to help feed and clothe them."

"Are you saying that Tabby should have married that odious little man?" There was anger in Graydon's voice. "He killed her by not keeping to his bargain to support them."

"The real problem was that if Tabby couldn't stand him, she was stupid to let him know that. Maybe if she'd been nicer to him, it wouldn't have been so bad for her and her family."

"That is one of the dumbest things I have ever heard! Garrett would have taken care of her both physically and financially. He was a Kingsley. He had money! None of them would have starved."

"No, but she would have died of a broken heart!" Toby shot back at him.

"Which she did anyway!" Graydon replied in the same angry tone.

Suddenly, they became aware of the silence of the room. Toby and Graydon were leaning toward each other, nearly nose to nose, their voices loud and angry. When they saw the stares of the others, they stood upright, almost at attention.

"Tabby should have stood up to her mother," Graydon said stiffly, his eyes on Caleb. "Am I right?"

Caleb was the only one looking amused. The others were wide-eyed at this passionate argument over something that had happened so long ago. "Yes and no," he said. "Yes, Tabby should have told Lavinia what she could do with her ugly little storekeeper, but no, she shouldn't have married Garrett the way he was."

"What does that mean?" Graydon asked, and his voice was belligerent, challenging.

"My young brother—sorry, I mean Captain Caleb's brother—was a bad sailor."

"A what?!" Graydon said, sounding personally affronted. He took a breath, then sat down on a bar stool. "I apologize. All this seems to be getting to me more than it should. You said that all the Kingsleys went to sea."

"They did," Caleb said, "but that can manifest itself in many ways. What young Garrett should have done was stop trying to lord it over a few dirty sailors on a ship and stay home to run what could have been a Kingsley empire. Garrett was like you: meant to run something much larger than a single ship."

"Like an entire country?" Jilly said.

"We do have a parliament," Graydon said under his breath, but when he looked into Caleb's eyes, he knew what the man meant. He liked his country, liked traveling around it, getting to know the people. He liked being able to help people on a grander scale than what would be possible aboard one ship.

Toby broke the silence. "But when I—as Tabby—asked Garrett if he would stay home and not ship out, he got angry."

"That's because the captain had expressed the same desire several times on the last voyage. But the boy thought he would be letting the family down if he didn't get on a ship every few years. I think if he had married Tabby he might have used that as an excuse to never again leave the island."

"But her mother . . ." Toby began.

"Was scared," Caleb finished for her. "Lavinia was terrified out of her mind of the future. Seeing her grandchildren hungry was something she couldn't bear—and rightfully so. If keeping them fed meant sacrificing one daughter, she'd do it. I happen to know that she offered herself to Silas Osborne first but he only wanted pretty little Tabby."

"What happened to them after Tabby died?" Jilly asked.

"Osborne had become lazy over the years. What with his wife running everything, he had forgotten how to work. Garrett had made out a will leaving everything to Tabby and at her death it all went to her mother. Lavinia bought Osborne's store and made her daughters-in-law help run it. She lived to be eighty-something and died a fairly wealthy, but miserable, old woman. I don't think she ever really recovered from Tabby's death."

"Too bad you can't change history," Victoria said. "It's not like my books when my editor makes me rewrite a chapter and I change what people said and did."

Toby was staring at the box on the countertop and the others were looking at her. If she had truly gone back in time—which was, of course, impossible—there were possibilities. She looked at Caleb. "Tabby was caught in a compromising situation with Garrett, and her mother didn't give her time to think but rushed her into a marriage with Osborne. If, say, I had another dream, what could I do to change the situation?"

"Complete the deed," Caleb said. "Garrett and Tabby were caught kissing. If they were seen . . . well, past that, the whole island would expect them to marry each other. Besides, I think Osborne would certainly refuse to marry Tabby after something like that."

Toby didn't look directly at Graydon, but she did take a tiny side step toward him. For a while everyone was quiet.

"I don't know about anyone else," Ken said, "but it's past my bedtime." Since they were all in his house, he gave them a look that it was time to leave.

After goodnights, Victoria picked up the box of jade figures, and Caleb took her arm and led her to the front door. Toby and Graydon were right behind them. When they were outside, the four of them walked to the end of the lane together.

Caleb looked at the house BEYOND TIME. "That house has a strong history to it. The man who built it—" He broke off with a laugh. "I think I've done enough storytelling for one night. Toby, dear," he said, his face serious, "I think perhaps you should stay out of that house. Memories remain with a person for a very long time. We may not be conscious of them, but they're there, buried deep within our minds. It may seem sad to you that Tabby died so young, but it was a very long time ago. My suggestion to the two of you is to think about now, today, not the past."

Graydon picked up Toby's arm and slipped it around his. "My sentiments exactly," he said. "That room . . . It still gives me chills when I think about it." He looked at Toby. "We stay out of there? Agreed."

"Yes," she said. "Let your relatives take care of it."

The four of them said goodnight and parted. When Toby and Graydon got upstairs, they stood for a moment in the sitting room, just looking at each other. Their argument about Daire had been settled, but Toby didn't want to return to the ease that they'd shared before. She reminded herself that Graydon was going to leave; that hadn't changed.

It might have become awkward between them if Graydon's cell hadn't started buzzing. He'd left it upstairs for the evening but now he picked it up.

"Rory?" she asked.

"Who else?" Graydon said, his teeth clenched. With longing in his eyes, he looked at her in her beautiful gown. "He's left a lot of messages so I better take this."

"Of course," Toby said. "Goodnight."

"Goodnight," he answered as he pushed the button on the phone. "And may I again say that you—" He broke off. "Rory, calm down. I'm back now." With one last look of regret at Toby, Graydon went into his bedroom and shut the door.

Inside her own bedroom, Toby leaned against the door for a moment. She didn't want to take off the gown. She'd have to ship it back to Lanconia and would never see it again. But maybe she could wear it at Victoria's historical-themed wedding. But no, Graydon would be gone by then and it wouldn't be right to keep the dress when he wasn't there.

Her attention was taken by a light shining through her window. She hadn't thought to draw the curtains before she left so the beam was prominent. When she looked out the window she saw that it was coming from the house across the road. The forbidden house. Not only had someone left a light on inside, the front door was standing wide open. It wasn't raining but it might, and if it did, the floor and woodwork could be ruined.

Quietly, she opened the door and stepped into the sitting room. What she should do was tell Graydon about the door. After all, the house was owned by his family, but she heard that he was still on the phone and his voice seemed rather loud and fast. No doubt Rory was falling apart again. That seemed to be an hourly occurrence with him.

Toby tiptoed down the stairs, glanced toward the closed door of the family room, and wondered if Daire and Lorcan were home, but she didn't look. She'd just go across the road, close the door, ignore the light inside, and return before Graydon got off the phone.

But when she got to the door, it was stuck and she couldn't pull it shut. When she stepped inside to get a better grip, she heard voices upstairs. It looked like someone—probably kids— was in the house. She reached for her phone to call the police but she didn't have it with her. Turning, she started to leave, but the door shut in her face.

Across the road, Graydon was pulling down the window shade as he spoke on the phone to his brother. It was early morning in Lanconia. "Rory, I'm tired. I want to go to bed. You can handle this on your own. Just have some confidence in yourself and you can—" When Graydon spat out the vilest curse known in his language, even his brother was taken aback. "Toby just went into that house and slammed the door behind her. I have to go." As he took off running, he clicked off the phone and tossed it onto the couch.

Chapter Twenty

When Graydon got to the house, the door was standing open and he couldn't help sighing. Of course it was open, beckoning him to come in. If Toby weren't somewhere inside he would have walked away and never looked back. He couldn't help wondering if his aunt Cale was aware of what she'd bought. But then, she was a writer and as bad as Victoria. Aunt Cale would probably love hearing about whatever the house did to people.

When Graydon was fully inside, he stood still and waited. He knew what was coming. Only when the door closed on its own behind him did he shout Toby's name. There was no answer, but then, he'd expected none.

Upstairs, he quickly went from room to room. Four bedrooms, three baths, and the little library. Toby was nowhere to be seen.

Again downstairs, he took his time looking through the rooms. His fear was of the birthing room, that Toby was in there. His imagination made him worry that somehow the old house had taken hold of her and—

He ran his hand over his face. No more horror movies for him!

He went through the dining room and into the front hall. As soon as he stepped into the parlor, he heard music and laughter, and saw a light under the door to the small sitting room.

He covered the larger room in three strides and flung the door open.

What he saw was a great surprise yet no surprise at all. Two women, wearing clothes like those he and Toby still had on from the dinner party, were standing by the fireplace. The room was painted yellow, with a bright red wood-framed sofa and a few chairs with needlepoint upholstery.

Graydon stayed outside, looking into the room. He wasn't sure about entering this place that seemed to have a very flexible attitude toward time.

"Is Toby here?" he asked, but no one looked at him. "Is Tabby here?" he asked louder, but still no one reacted. Obviously they couldn't hear him.

Tentatively, he put his foot inside the doorway—and saw the slipper he'd been sent with the costume change to a square-toed boot. Ah, much better, he thought. When he looked up, he thought he saw Toby walking toward the stairs.

Without hesitation, he entered the little sitting room.

"Garrett!" one of the women said. "You have returned." She was a pretty young woman and smiling in a way that seemed to mean they were friends. "We didn't expect your ship to get in for another few weeks."

The other woman was older and she was frowning at Graydon. "Have you seen Mrs. Weber yet?"

Graydon was glad for his training in diplomacy because he

felt like saying that when he did see the woman he might strangle her. Instead, he smiled. "No, I haven't seen her. Is Tabby here?"

"I'm not sure," the older woman said.

The younger one stepped forward. "I just saw her with John Kendricks's daughter."

"On the window seat," he said and realized that he was now in Kingsley House and it looked like it was John and Parthenia's wedding—which made him smile. That meant Tabby hadn't yet been sacrificed to the storekeeper in an attempt to pay the bills.

As he headed toward the door that led to the big parlor, the young woman stopped him. "Garrett," she said softly so only he would hear, "I think you should know what's been going on while you were away. Mrs. Weber has arranged for Tabby to marry "

"That little sea urchin, Silas Osborne? I know that. I've come home to rescue her."

"How fortunate for her," she said. "I wish you luck."

"Thank you," Graydon said and turned away. The large parlor of Kingsley House was full of people dancing and laughing, and Graydon in his tan trousers and short jacket fit right in. Many people greeted him by the name of Garrett, most of them expressing surprise that he was there so much earlier than expected.

"Where's your brother?" a few asked.

Graydon covered himself by saying, "Which one?" He assumed they meant Captain Caleb, but he wasn't sure. He looked over the heads of the dancers to see if he could find Valentina/ Victoria, hoping she could tell him where Toby was. But he didn't see her.

In the far corner was the little girl Ali, with her drawing pad. She was sitting on the cushioned window seat that just an hour before Ken had taken apart. Graydon quickly made his way across the room. He didn't have time to make introductions. Besides, he assumed Garrett and the child were acquainted. "Was there a woman here with you?"

"Tabby," the girl said. "Her mother is angry at her. She doesn't want Tabby to marry you."

"I know," Graydon said, "but in this life, she can marry me. Do you know where she is?"

"I think she went home," Ali said, and he knew the child meant the BEYOND TIME house. Graydon started to leave, but then he turned back. "Ali, I want to ask a favor of you."

She was quite young and he doubted if she'd remember what he was about to tell her, but he could try. "When you are twenty-three years old, I want you to have your portrait painted and put it in a big frame. Have your father make it with secret compartments in it. I want you to write about and draw pictures of the houses you and your husband create and hide everything inside the picture frame. I want to make sure the future knows who you are and what you two did. Do you think you can remember all that?"

"Yes," Ali said and nodded in that way children do when something nonsensical makes perfect sense to them. "Who will I marry?"

"Valentina's big, healthy boy," he answered as he hurried toward the front door.

When someone handed him a beer, he took it and kept walking. It was beginning to hit him that right now he was not a prince. He didn't have the weight of a whole country on his shoulders. Who he married, where he lived, every word he spoke, was not going to be scrutinized, questioned, weighed, and measured. Any slip of his tongue would not be tomorrow's headlines in the Lanconian newspapers. Being seen with a pretty girl wouldn't show up on the Internet with the caption "Is This the Next Queen of Lanconia?"

And speaking of pretty girls, he saw a circle of men surrounding two of the most beautiful women he'd ever seen. In the modern world he was used to seeing women who'd spent hours making up their faces, but these young women had the faces they were born with and they were exquisite, almost too perfect to be real. As he looked, hardly able to blink, one of them smiled at him, and he was so enraptured he almost ran into a door.

A man nearby laughed.

"Who are they?" Graydon asked, still staring at them.

"The Bell sisters, and don't get too near or their father will go after you with a grappling hook."

"Somebody should paint their portraits."

"Garrett!"

Reluctantly, Graydon turned away and saw his brother. He wasn't exactly like Graydon, but enough like him that they must cause comment. "Rory," he whispered.

"Rory?" he said, laughing as he gave Graydon a masculine shoulder clasp. "I haven't heard that nickname in years." He turned to the woman on his arm. "Right after I was born, Cousin Caleb said I 'roared like the wind' and the name stayed with me. Until I was an adult, anyway."

Graydon hadn't at first noticed the woman with his brother, but when he looked at her, his eyes widened. Unless he missed his guess, she was Danna—and she was heavily pregnant. He very much wanted to talk to his brother, but he wanted to see Toby more. "I must—"

"I know. We all know," Rory said, laughing. "Just back from the sea, and all you want is Tabby. But have you heard what Lavinia Weber is up to?"

"In detail," Graydon said over his shoulder as he practically ran to the front door. It took him about a minute and a half to cover the distance from Kingsley House to BEYOND TIME. If his guess was correct, that was where Toby would be trying to find him.

She was standing under a huge tree at the side of the house, the white silk of her dress shimmering in the moonlight.

Halting, he watched her as he tried to let everything sink in. It was quite possible all this was a dream. For days they'd been inundated with everything of the early 1800s. Food, clothing, manners had all been studied. On top of that, Toby's dreams had filled their minds. And tonight, with Dr. Huntley's story of Lavinia and her unhappy daughter, it's no wonder that he would have the same dream.

That's what he consciously told himself. Inside, all he could think was that right now he wasn't fated to be a king, and with that came a great deal of freedom.

When he took a step forward, he felt taller, lighter, as though a great weight had been taken from him. He stopped a few feet behind Toby and waited for her to turn around and see him. When she did turn, she looked as though she was about to cry.

Graydon didn't say anything, just held out his arms, and she ran to him. He held her tightly, his face buried in her hair.

"Tabby's mother is going to—"

"I know," Graydon said softly. "I'll take care of it." He began kissing her neck.

Toby pushed away from him. "No! You don't know what's ahead. She's going to make Tabby marry Silas Osborne and he'll treat her badly."

When she referred to Tabby as another person, Graydon realized that she thought he was Garrett and he couldn't help smiling. It looked like he could never get away from having a doppelgänger. He should, of course, tell her who he was, but he didn't. "What should we do?" he asked, his face as serious as he could make it.

"Caleb said that—"

"My brother Caleb? He's been on the ship with me. When did you talk to him?" He sounded jealous.

"Years from now," Toby said and waved her hand. "That doesn't matter. We need to let them find us in . . . in a certain stage of undress so Tabby won't be forced to marry Osborne."

Graydon's eyes widened in shock. "You want me to undress you? Here? Now?"

"I know it's not the done thing but—" She broke off, and for a moment she looked at him in the moonlight. "The truth is that while you were away, Tabby—I mean I—fell in love with someone else. I'm sorry for it but I couldn't stop my feelings for him. In memory of what you and I once had, please help me."

Graydon stared at her. This was part of the story he hadn't heard. Maybe this was the reason Garrett Kingsley let her marry Osborne. But then, he saw a sparkle in Toby's eyes.

"You imp!" he said and drew her back into his arms. "I've been frantically searching for you."

She pulled back to look at him. "Is that why you smell like beer?"

He laughed. "I wonder if the food is as good as the beer? Maybe we could—"

"You think we were sent back in time to check out the food?!"

He was unperturbed by her tone. "Do you realize that here, in this place and time, I'm not a prince?"

She was puzzled. "What does that matter?"

"Everything," he said. "I can do whatever I want." He picked up her hand and began kissing it, and moving up her arm.

"Graydon," she said slowly. "I don't think you should . . ." She closed her eyes as his lips touched the inside of her elbow. The skin there was especially sensitive.

"Do you trust me?" he asked.

"I don't know. I guess so. I can't think when you're doing that." It took effort on her part, but she pulled out of his grasp.

"This is Tabby's life, not ours, and I think we need to solve her problem. Dr. Huntley said that Tabby and Garrett needed to be caught in a way so they'd be forced to marry."

"Naked under the elm tree? That sort of thing?"

"That's a little crude, but yes, I guess that's what we must do."

"No," Graydon said. "We—" He broke off as they heard the crunch of gravel and what sounded to be angry voices. People were rapidly approaching.

"Graydon! We have to do something now. Tabby can't marry that odious little man. She—"

He put his hands on her shoulders, his face close to hers. "Trust me. Part of my training has been in solving problems. Remember that Caleb said I was made to run kingdoms."

"That's not exactly what he said. He thought you should run the Kingsley family. I don't think they're the same as an entire country. They're just one small—"

"Stand behind me and be quiet!" Graydon ordered as his arm swept behind him and took Toby with it.

"Oooooh. Regency machismo," she said. Graydon had his back to her and was looking at the crowd of people coming toward them. She had the idea that if she moved he'd push her back again. "On the other hand, I think you and I should talk about this and decide—"

"You want to marry me or not?" Graydon asked under his breath. Toby was too stunned to reply.

"It's me or Osborne," he said. "So which is it?"

"Uh . . ." Toby said.

"Is that your mother at the head of that lynching party?"

Toby looked around him. Lavinia Weber had been relatively nice to her the first time they'd met, but the woman coming toward them was the mother Toby had grown up with. She was always angry and it was usually directed at her only child. No matter how hard Toby had tried, she didn't think she'd ever pleased her mother. It was that woman who was approaching.

"I'll take you," Toby said and moved behind Graydon more fully.

Lavinia stopped in front of Graydon and reached out to grab her daughter's arm, but he blocked her. Behind her were half a dozen people, all watching with undisguised interest.

"Now I see why TV was invented," Graydon said under his breath to Toby, and she almost giggled.

"My daughter is engaged to marry another man," Lavinia said, her teeth clenched. "Tabitha! Step away from him."

From a lifetime of training, Toby started to obey, but Graydon's arm wouldn't let her move.

"I ask your permission to marry your daughter," he said.

"Denied!" Lavinia said loudly. "Tabitha! Come!"

Toby took a step forward.

"I will give up the sea," Graydon said in his best, most authoritative princely voice. The reaction of the crowd was disbelieving laughter. Not what he was used to!

"Do I strike you as a fool?" Lavinia said, her anger rising. "You are a Kingsley. Your brother Caleb loves to say 'You can replace a woman but there's only one ocean.' I'll not have my daughter widowed within the year. Tabitha! Come with me this minute!"

Toby glanced up at Graydon and the calm on his face made her stand her ground.

"I'm afraid that my brother's geography is a little off," he said. "There are seven oceans but only one Tabitha."

That caused another burst from the crowd, but this time they were on Garrett's side. "I don't believe you," Lavinia said, glaring at her daughter.

The crowd's favor was building Graydon's confidence. When he spoke, his voice was louder, reaching the new people who were quickly adding to the crowd. "Get a lawyer to draw up a contract and I will sign it. Now, this night," he said.

Lavinia scoffed. "You will give up the sea?"

"Kingsley or no, I am a bad sailor," Graydon said. He expected the crowd to disagree, but instead they nodded yes.

"Good thing Lanconia is inland," Toby said and stepped close enough to take his hand in hers.

"Good or bad sailor," Graydon said, "I believe my family is known for its honesty. Our word is our bond."

People nodded their heads in agreement, then looked back at Lavinia. The ship was now in her port.

"A Kingsley who doesn't go to sea?" There was contempt in Lavinia's voice. "That is not possible."

Graydon could see that he was making no progress with the woman so he decided to take a chance. If Osborne was bad in the future, there would probably be evidence of it in the present. "Do you think Silas Osborne is going to honor his bargain with you? Is he known for his honesty?" The faces of the crowd showed him that he'd been right, and for the first time he saw Lavinia hesitate.

"What would you do if you stayed on this island?" she asked, this time with less venom in her voice.

"I will run my family's business. And if you give your blessing so that Tabby and I can marry this night"—there was a gasp from the audience—"I will fully repair your house and help support all the widows and orphans in your family."

For a moment there was only silence from all of them. Toby and Graydon didn't know if it was shock at what he was offering or the idea that a Nantucket male—a Kingsley no less!—could even think of giving up the sea.

A woman's voice broke the silence. "Will you find us husbands?"

"Only if I can ship you to Lanconia," Graydon said, making a joke.

"I'll be packed in an hour," the woman shot back and everyone laughed.

"Well?" Graydon said, looking at Lavinia. "Do we have a bargain?"

Toby moved to stand so close to Graydon that they were hardly separate beings.

"Mr. Farley!" Lavinia shouted over her shoulder, and a small man came forward, a pair of spectacles on his nose. "Get a pen and paper and start drawing up the contract."

"I've had too much to drink to do a lawyer's work. I'd have to " he began, but one look at the fury on the woman's face and he gave in. He made his way through the crowd, muttering, "When Captain Caleb hears about this, I'll be a dead man."

"What do you think they're doing?" Toby asked as she stood by the door and listened. She didn't exactly have her ear against it, but close. But all she could hear was laughter and music from downstairs. After Graydon's declaration that he'd sign a contract and marry Tabitha tonight, they had been half shoved back to Kingsley House and locked inside the room that would someday be Victoria's bedroom. It was larger than it would be in the twenty-first century because no space had yet been taken from it to put in a bathroom. The big fireplace looked well used, but now, in summer, it was covered by a pretty screen. There were only two candles in the room, so it was quite shadowy.

When Graydon didn't answer, Toby turned to him. He was stretched out on the bed, hands behind his head, and smiling up at the underside of the canopy. All the chairs had been taken downstairs for the wedding guests to use, so the bed was the only place to sit.

"I think they're plotting our future," he said.

She walked over to stand by him. "Why are you so calm about all this?"

"Because I like it."

He said it with so much enthusiasm that Toby laughed.

Moving over on the bed, he patted the space beside him.

She hesitated, but then she used the little wooden steps to climb up and stretched out beside him. She too looked up. "You aren't concerned that we're doing the wrong thing?"

"Couldn't be worse than what actually did happen."

"But then, we don't know all the facts, do we?" she said. "Maybe Tabitha did come to love someone else. Maybe she just doesn't want to marry Garrett."

"Think not?" he asked and there was amusement in his voice.

She rolled onto her side to face him and he put his hand in her hair. "What if we stay?" she whispered. "What if we never leave here?"

He put his hand on her cheek. "Would that be so bad?" he asked softly. Turning her head, she kissed the palm of his hand.

Smiling, he pulled her head down onto his shoulder and held her to him. "If we stayed here, I'd do my best to run the Kingsley family business, and I would send your sisters-in-law to Lanconia, where they'd be treasured as wives. I would buy and sell ships and—"

"What about us?" Toby asked.

"We'd have six children. At least that many. You could grow acres of flowers and fill the houses with them."

It all sounded so wonderful that Toby was afraid to move, scared that everything would disappear in a second.

"Do you like the idea?" he asked as he stroked her hair and ran his hand over her neck.

"We won't have a choice," she said, evading giving an answer. "I'm sure we're here for a purpose. I wonder why? Maybe Tabby and Garrett have a child who saves the world. Maybe

Lavinia messed with destiny when she forced her daughter to marry Osborne, so now the house has sent us back to right the wrong."

"That would mean we might leave as soon as it's sure that they'll conceive such a child. We say 'I do' and poof, we're gone? Think that's the plan?"

She heard disappointment in his voice, but also a bit of resignation. She looked up at him. "Maybe we'll stay longer. Perhaps until the morning after the wedding night."

That idea brought the smile back to his face and he kissed her.

What started out sweetly soon deepened, and when Graydon rolled on top of her, Toby pulled him closer. She opened her mouth under his as his hand moved over her bare shoulder to the top of her breast.

"Yes," she murmured as Graydon's lips moved down to her neck, then lower.

The two of them were so absorbed in what they were doing that they didn't hear the door open.

"Time for that later" came a voice that made Toby and Graydon reluctantly roll apart. The lawyer, Mr. Farley, was standing in the doorway, a piece of paper in his hand.

Garrett had a physical condition that made him reluctant to stand up. "Give me a minute," he said as he sat up facing the wall.

"Better not take too long," Mr. Farley said, "or Lavinia may change her mind. Osborne showed up and he's threatening to sue. Says his reputation has been forever ruined by an 'Almighty Kingsley.' He's offering money for Miss Tabitha."

"I'll deal with him. He better not—" Graydon began.

"How much?" Toby asked.

"You can't be serious!" Graydon said as he came around the bed.

"I'd like to know how much I'm worth, that's all," she said.

"Where's the paper?" Graydon asked and the lawyer handed it to him.

"Careful, the ink isn't dry yet."

Graydon scanned it, but the handwriting, so perfect, the *s*'s made into *f*'s, was quite difficult to read. The contract said he'd marry Miss Tabitha Lavinia Weber and support all the widowed women in the household, plus the children. A list of names followed. He would build Tabitha "a fine house" on Nantucket and never again go to sea.

Graydon didn't hesitate as he asked for a pen and ink. He had a bit of trouble with the quill, but he signed it as Garrett Kingsley. He handed it to the lawyer, who witnessed it, then held out his arm toward the door.

"Are you ready?" Mr. Farley asked.

Toby went first, Graydon behind her, then the lawyer.

"Are you sure you want to take on Lavinia Weber as a mother-in-law?" Mr. Farley quietly asked Graydon. "The woman will make your life miserable. Wouldn't you rather head out to a nice raging storm at sea?"

"I'd rather have Tabitha," Graydon said firmly.

"Your brother Caleb is the only sensible one in your family. He would never lose his head over a woman."

As Graydon started down the stairs, he gave a snort of derision. "Has my brother met Valentina yet?"

"Why, no . . . I don't think he has. She arrived after he sailed."

"Ah," Graydon said. "In a month tell me again what my brother says about love."

At the bottom of the stairs a dozen people were waiting to greet them, and he and Toby were separated. For all that the marriage was a hurried affair and in some ways forced, everyone knew it was a match of True Love, and they were glad of it. No one had wanted to see pretty little Tabitha married to Silas

Osborne. The day had been joyous, with the marriage of Parthenia and John Kendricks, and now this new excitement. The island would be talking about it for years to come.

Graydon was surrounded by people he didn't know and half pushed, half led down Main Street to the church.

All the wedding guests, even the original bride and groom, were there—and everyone was happily flushed from a lot of food and even more drink. Some of the men had their heads on the back of the benches and were snoring. If each man's wife didn't punch him awake, someone used a tall candle snuffer to reach out to do the job.

It was dark out, but enough candles were lit to give the church a glow that was soft and beautiful.

Graydon was positioned at the front of the church and Rory came to stand beside him.

"I figure you'd rather have Caleb but no one can find him."

"He's probably locked away somewhere with a keg of rum," Graydon said. Rory nodded in understanding.

Valentina came down the aisle carrying the same bouquet she'd held a few hours earlier for Parthenia's wedding.

Behind her came Toby in her dress that a queen had worn. Graydon knew there had never been a more beautiful sight in his life. She was on the arm of an older man whom he didn't recognize.

When they stopped at the front, Graydon stepped forward to take Toby's hand.

The words spoken by the pastor were different, but when Graydon pledged his love, his care, and his worldly goods to Tabitha, he meant every word he spoke.

As for Toby, she seemed a bit hesitant at first, but then she smiled and repeated her vows to him.

Rory handed them rings to exchange. "Jeweler was already here," he said to Graydon's questioning eyes.

"Would that it were a lavender diamond," Graydon whispered as he slipped the narrow gold ring on Toby's finger. It fit perfectly.

She closed her hand around it. She liked it just as it was.

After the ceremony, everyone on the island seemed to be happy—except for Lavinia, who still thought Garrett would renege and go back to the sea. She kept muttering, "I'll believe it when I see it."

As soon as they got back to Kingsley House, the second newly married couple was kept apart with everyone toasting them and whisking Toby into dances. Girls gathered around Graydon to tease him about the coming night.

At one point he escaped long enough to go to a long table to get a mug of homemade beer. Valentina stopped beside him.

"I'm so glad you saved Tabby," she said. "She was willing to sacrifice herself but it would have been a miserable marriage."

"Very bad," Graydon said, looking at her. She was exactly like Victoria, only years younger. Between her face and her outrageous figure, a lot of which was exposed by the low-cut neckline of the dress, he could understand why Captain Caleb had mistaken her for a lady of the evening. And if his time calculations were correct, she was the only one who knew that he was locked in the attic with no clothes.

"You wouldn't know what happened to my brother Caleb, would you?"

Valentina looked away. "I'm afraid I've never been introduced to him."

Graydon could see that her neck was turning red and the color was spreading upward.

"I was just thinking that after our lengthy sea voyage it might be good for him to have some time alone, time to remember that he's no longer the commander of men."

Valentina looked at Graydon with widened eyes, as though trying to figure out what he knew.

He lowered his voice. "Whatever you do, don't give in to him. Show him that you're worth more than all the seven seas combined."

Valentina just stood there staring, unable to speak.

Graydon put down his empty mug. "Excuse me while I go dance with my bride." He caught Toby's hand and pulled her away from a little man who looked old enough to be her grandfather.

The wedding guests were lining up on two sides as they prepared to go into some complicated dance that required everyone to know the steps. When the fast, energetic music of the dance started, Toby pulled away to go to the women's side, but Graydon wouldn't release her hand. "We have to—" she began.

But he pulled her into his arms in the traditional form of a waltz—a dance that wouldn't come to the U.S. for several years—and began to glide her about the room. Everyone stopped and stared at the scandalous close-body movement. The musicians quit playing, then frantically tried to come up with a tune that fit what the dancers were doing. The other guests stepped back to give the young couple room.

Graydon and Toby were dancing as they had before the dinner party—which now seemed so very long ago. A lifetime, centuries.

Toby closed her eyes and gave herself over to the sensation of being held by Graydon and of dancing with him.

When the music stopped, they reluctantly broke apart. He bowed to her and she curtsied to him.

When they looked away from each other, they saw how much they'd shocked the guests. But it didn't last long. For all that these people lived on an island, they were very worldly. Their houses were filled with artifacts from the far corners, brought back from their travels.

It was Valentina who first applauded, and the others followed.

Graydon took Toby's hand and didn't let go as he led her to the front door. He'd had enough of being with other people and he wanted to be alone with her. Once they were outside, he stopped to breathe. Now where did they go?

"I was told that NEVER TO SEA AGAIN had been cleared out for the evening. For us," Toby said, her voice hesitant. "But do you think you and I should take advantage of this night? After all, it isn't really ours." When she looked up at him, he had such an expression of Are you serious? that she laughed.

They held hands tightly as they walked to the house. As seemed to always be the case, the door was standing open.

"If we go in, we might find ourselves at home again," Toby said. "Maybe we shouldn't—"

Graydon's answer was to sweep Toby into his arms and carry her across the threshold into the house. For a moment he stood still. In the twenty-first century the house was nearly empty and it looked old and long unused. But what surrounded them now was a much newer house full of the needs of a large family. It was dark but they could see flowered wallpaper and furniture and children's wooden toys on the floor.

"Come on, Rhett," Toby said, "take me to bed."

Laughing, Graydon carried her up the stairs. At the top he saw that the bedroom connected to the little library had been prepared for them. Candles were lit and there were flowers everywhere.

When he put Toby down she couldn't help opening the door of the library. Moonlight shone through the window enough that she could see the room was exactly as she'd envisioned it. The shelves were full of leather-bound books.

Graydon came to stand behind her. "Shall we hide all the books under the floorboards and dig them out two hundred years from now?"

"They wouldn't hold up," she said. "Damp and dust and mice and . . . No, no hiding of anything." Turning, she looked up at him. "I don't know how long we have before all this ends, but while we're here I just want us to be together. No prince and commoner. No—"

He put his finger over her lips. "Never say that."

"You know what I mean."

"Yes, I do." He stroked her temple and smoothed back her hair. "Are you sure about this?"

She put her arms around his neck and kissed him. "Very, very sure."

For a moment his eyes searched hers and he seemed to be looking for reassurance.

He gently kissed her cheek, then her neck. His hand touched the shoulder of her dress and pushed it down an inch. He was so very gentle, so very sweet.

It was nice, Toby thought. She liked his kisses, liked being so close to him, but something was missing. Where was the man who'd stood up to Lavinia and told her how it was going to be? Where was the man who'd tossed her around in their boxing classes? Where was the passion?!

She didn't have to ask to know the answer. It was her blasted virginity that she'd held on to for so long. There were many times when she'd wished she lost it on prom night like most of the other girls. But her date had expected it, so she couldn't bring herself to give in, then later . . .

Toby stepped back to look at him. What she was seeing was Prince Graydon of Lanconia. His eyes were alight, but he was reserved, holding back, probably because he was afraid of hurting her. Sometimes, she thought, men needed a little help.

She turned her back to him and lifted her hair. "Would you please untie the back of this dress?" she asked rather formally.

"Yes, certainly," he said, just as formally. She let the beautiful gown slip to the floor.

One thing she'd learned this week was that historical clothing might be a bit dowdy on the outside—no hot pants or tank tops—but what was underneath was worthy of a stripper.

Turning to face him, she let him see her in the corset that Jilly had helped her into. Her breasts were pushed high up, the pink tips half showing. Her waist was pulled into a tiny circle and below that was a petticoat of cotton so transparent you could read through it. White silk hose covered her legs only to mid thigh, tied with garters with pink ribbons.

Toby had the delicious, soul-satisfying pleasure of watching Prince Graydon completely disappear. In his place was a man who was consumed with lust. For her.

He didn't speak but grabbed her about the waist and lifted her off the floor as his mouth met hers, his tongue exploring, thrusting. His lips, his hands, seemed to be all over her body at once.

It took Toby a few moments to react. The sensation of him, of what he was doing to her body, seemed to change her from human to a flaming column of desire.

While he kissed her, his hand went down to caress her thighs. When she went limp in his arms, he picked her up and put her on the bed.

In seconds, his coat was off, then his big white shirt. Years of training had given him a chest delineated by muscle—and all of it on top of those tight trousers that slid down into knee-high leather boots.

"Now I know why the Regency ladies swooned," Toby said, and Graydon gave her a grin that was appropriately rakish.

He took a few seconds to pull off the boots, then he stretched out beside her and very slowly began to undress her, covering every inch of newly exposed skin with his lips. Stockings and garters went first, then he slowly rolled the half-slip down her body to expose her modern underpants. Toby couldn't help thinking that she'd discovered why Regency women didn't wear anything beneath the slips. Between her corset and his tight trousers, there was an urgency created that made excess under-garments an unnecessary hindrance.

Toby ran her hands over Graydon's chest, his arms, marvel-ing at the hardness of his muscles, the curves of his body: so male to her female. She ran her hands down his body, over the backside of him, felt the power of him.

Feeling greatly daring, she moved a hand to the front and he groaned at her touch. She'd heard and seen all that she thought she should know, but the reality of it was different. She liked the way her touch made Graydon react.

"Toby," he whispered, "I can't wait much longer."

All she could do was nod. She wasn't going to let him know that she was a bit afraid of this unknown event.

He slid his trousers off and she was nude from the waist down. When he entered her, her eyes widened in surprise. She'd heard so much about the pain of the first time, but all she felt was pleasure.

"Am I hurting you?" he whispered.

"No," she said. "Oh, that's lovely." He was slowly moving inside her. Gently at first and watching to see if she was hurt. But Toby put her head back and gave herself over to Graydon's long, deep, slow thrusts.

Gradually, something inside her began to react and she raised her hips to let him deeper inside her. She was awkward but Graydon's hands cupped her buttocks and held her, then guided her as she began to move with him.

"Oh!" she said. "Oh, yes!" She opened her eyes to see him smiling at her, but then his eyes changed, darkened, he buried his face in her neck, and seconds later his body stiffened. Groan-ing, he collapsed against her.

Toby lay close to Graydon, snuggled in his arms. It was nearly dawn and there was a blueish light seeping in around the closed wooden shutters. They'd made love all night, exploring, caressing, holding each other. Weeks of being close but forbidden to touch had left them with an insatiable need to hold, to feel, to caress, just to be together.

There were minutes during the night when Toby had wanted to talk, to ask questions of Graydon, but the feel of him removed all words from her mind. Besides, Graydon was showing her other things to do with her lips besides talk.

Now, at dawn, they were clinging to each other. The question of What happens now? hung between them.

Graydon untangled himself and got out of bed to open a shutter. The light nearly blinded her and she put her arm over her eyes. When she peeped through them she had a glance of a nude Graydon before he threw back the covers to expose an equally nude Toby.

Her first instinct was to cover herself, but she didn't. He sat down on the side of the bed and she lay there quietly while he looked at her from toes to head. When he reached her face, he smiled at her, then gently turned her onto her stomach.

He ran his hand over her body and stopped along her left side. He caressed her ribs, and bent over and ran his lips along her side. "How did this happen?" he asked softly, sympathy in his voice.

"I was born with it," Toby said, perplexed by his tone. Were a few pale birthmarks offensive to him?

"This isn't . . ." he began but stopped. "Can you feel this?"

She reached back to run her hand along her side and felt the deep ridges of skin. Twisting, she tried to see what was there.

Graydon got up, removed a small mirror from the wall, and held it so she could see the long, wide scars down her side. "I think you were burned, and badly."

Toby handed him the mirror and sat up in the bed, pulling

the sheet over her. "I have no burn scars but I do have a row of small pink birthmarks running down my side. My dad used to say they were a map of undiscovered islands."

Graydon sat on the side of the bed holding the mirror. "You are in Tabby's body," he said softly. "Last night I could feel the ridges on you and I thought of what you must have been through to leave such deep scars. But it wasn't you who had endured the pain."

The idea that she was in someone else's body was almost more difficult to comprehend than the idea of time travel. Right now it seemed that she and Graydon were in some historic inn, with a very authentic bed—except that everything was new. Two hundred years hadn't passed, so the furniture didn't have that years-old patina that made it into antiques.

"What about you?" Toby asked. "Anything different?"

"I don't believe there is." His eyes began to twinkle. "But perhaps you would like to search."

"I think that would be best," Toby said solemnly.

When he leaned toward her, she ran her hand over his hard, flat abs, across his shoulder, and down a muscular arm. "I have nothing to compare you to, but you look and feel fine to me." She put both her hands on him. It was wonderful to see and touch him. "Do you feel any different to yourself?"

"No," he said, his eyes darkening with passion as she drew closer. When the mirror started to fall, he caught it and twisted to the side to put it on the little table by the bed.

"Oh, my!" Toby said, her eyes wide and her hand to her mouth. "Your back!"

"Is it scarred?" he asked as he turned his back fully toward her.

"No scars anywhere." Toby was trying to contain her laughter but couldn't help herself. He handed her the mirror and she held it so he could see. The entire left side of Graydon's back was covered in a truly magnificent tattoo. It was unmistakably

Japanese and in vivid color. The image was of a woman, her hair pinned up on her head. What was unusual was that her hair was a golden blonde and her eyes were blue.

Graydon twisted about as he stared into the mirror. "Is that who I think it is?"

"I'm not sure, but I think it's me as a geisha."

"That's what I thought," Graydon said as he put down the mirror. They looked at each other for a moment, then burst out laughing.

Graydon stretched out beside Toby and pulled her into his arms. "I can assure you that in real life I have no tattoos."

"Not even an ankle butterfly?" Toby was still laughing.

"I must say that this one is rather remarkable, isn't it?"

"And stupendously flattering." Toby looked up at him. "I'm glad you were able to negotiate this marriage for them. Any man who loves a woman as much as Garrett loves Tabby should spend his life with her."

Suddenly, she was feeling very sleepy, which made sense, as they'd been awake all night.

"I want to stay here," Graydon said. "With you. I want the life we could have here." He put his hand on her cheek and lifted her face to his. Her eyes were closed. "Toby, do you know how much I love you? Do you have any idea how much it's going to destroy me to leave you? I don't think I can—" He broke off because he saw that she was asleep.

He started to say more, but he too was overwhelmed with sleepiness. "No," he whispered. "I don't want to sleep." He was very much afraid that he'd wake up and all this would be gone. But he couldn't stay awake.

With their bodies tightly entwined, they slept.

Chapter Twenty-one

Toby awoke slowly and for a moment she didn't know where she was. It was full daylight but the shades were down so the room was dim. Hanging from the door hinge was the beautiful gown she'd worn to the dinner party last night and she was glad she'd taken the time to put it on a padded hanger. For a moment she looked up at the ceiling, remembering the party. It had certainly been a success! Victoria had agreed to the theme and . . .

She sat up in bed. Had they really gone to Kingsley House and torn apart the window seat? She rubbed her hand across her eyes. Surely that had been one of her dreams. She also seemed to remember arguing with Graydon over something to do with Tabby and Garrett but she couldn't remember exactly what.

Feeling a bit confused—too much to drink?—she got up,

took a shower, and washed her hair. Last night it had been sprayed and gelled and moussed in an attempt to make it stay up, and she wanted all of it out. She dressed in jeans and a pink cotton shirt and went downstairs. It was going to take some work to clean up after the party.

But the house was in perfect order, with no sign of the previous night's gathering. Nor was there anyone around.

On the table in the sunroom were a bowl of fruit and a note from Graydon. "Yogurt in the fridge. I'm outside. Take your pick."

What an odd thing to say, Toby thought as she scooped yogurt onto the fruit and began to eat. Anyone reading it would think there was a great deal more between them than there was. But then, maybe it wasn't what he'd written but the note itself that was unusual. She seemed to remember Graydon writing something with a quill pen. There had been candlelight and some old document—only it wasn't old. Some man was saying that the ink wasn't yet dry.

The vision seemed to come and go in seconds and she couldn't think where it had come from. When she heard the clash of steel on steel, she went to the window and looked out.

Daire and Graydon, their upper bodies bare, honey-colored skin glistening with sweat, were, as usual, attacking each other. Nearby, Lorcan was watching them intently. Toby started to raise her hand to wave but someone knocked on the front door so she went to answer it.

She opened the door to see her friend Alix standing there.

For a full three minutes there was nothing but hugging and laughing and talking on top of each other. It was the first time Alix had been back to the island since her wedding.

"Did you have a wonderful time?" Toby asked.

"Fabulous. All of it! Has anything happened that I missed out on? Have you heard from Lexie?" Alix asked. "Dad said you have some interesting visitors."

"Come and see." Toby linked arms with Alix and led her through the kitchen to the sunroom windows. Outside, the two beautiful men were now wrestling, their strong bodies clad only in loose white trousers that were hanging so low they looked to be in danger of falling off.

"This is what you wake up to every morning?" Alix asked. "Talk about honey on toast!"

Toby sighed. "Yes. Honey. Acres of it."

"So remind me which one is yours."

Toby turned away. "Neither of them. Daire, the taller one, is in love with Lorcan." She nodded to the woman on the sidelines.

"I didn't even see her there," Alix said.

Toby laughed. "I know what you mean. See that flower bed on the far left? It gives me the best view of the men. I water the flowers in that poor bed for so long they're in danger of being waterlogged. But then, whenever Lorcan and I feel we're being ignored, we get the men back by doing yoga—with lots of rear-end-up poses."

Alix was watching Toby. "It sounds like you've set up a family here, but Mom said they're all going to leave soon."

"Yes," Toby said, her voice showing her dread of that event. "In about two and a half weeks Graydon will return to his country and announce his engagement to another woman."

Alix put her hand on her friend's arm. "Mom said you and Graydon were becoming . . ." She didn't finish that sentence because she thought it was better not to tell everything her mother, Victoria, had to say about Graydon and Toby. "He's going to break her heart!" Victoria had said, anger in her voice. "He's going to ride away on his black stallion, sword in hand, and leave dear little Toby crying so hard her life will be destroyed."

Since her mother tended to dramatically exaggerate at times, Alix hadn't paid a lot of attention to what she'd said. But now, looking at Toby's face, she thought maybe her mother was right.

Looking back out the window, Alix saw that the men had stopped trying to kill each other and were picking up equipment. They'd soon be coming inside.

"Why don't you and I go to Kingsley House and talk?" Alix said. "I want to hear every word of what's been going on while I was away. Besides, I have a few things I want to tell you."

"Your dad said you were terrorizing Jared's whole office."

"No, of course not," Alix said as they walked toward the front door. "Well, maybe a little."

The two women laughed all the way to Kingsley House, and it was only later that Toby realized she hadn't left a note to tell Graydon where she was. But she shrugged. It wasn't as though there was anything permanent between them. They were roommates and that was all.

"Graydon," Toby said for what seemed to be the hundredth time, "I don't know anything about the history of Japanese tattoos. I'm really glad that, in their quest to find more goods for importing to the U.S., sailors sometimes endured the pain of having them done. That's all deeply interesting, but I've been a little too busy to give tattoos my full attention."

She was glaring at him, her eyes letting him know that she'd had enough of his very strange behavior in the week since the dinner party. After she'd returned from spending the day with Alix and Jared and other friends, Graydon had greeted her as though she'd been away for a year. He'd swooped her into his arms and kissed her in a very intimate way.

It hadn't helped that for that entire day, she'd been lectured by members of the Kingsley family about how she must not get too close to Graydon. As if she weren't already deeply aware of it, they repeatedly told her that he was going to leave soon and she'd probably never see him again.

"You will be devastated when he leaves," Victoria said, her lovely face full of fear as well as warning.

Their words reminded Toby of what she already knew, and by the time she was ready to leave, her resolve had hardened. The dinner party had brought her and Graydon closer, but she knew she must stop it. It didn't help when she entered her house and Graydon pulled her into his arms and kissed her as she'd never been kissed before. In the past his kisses had been reserved. Nice but not full of . . . well, of passion. But the man who met her at the door didn't seem to be Prince Graydon but someone else. Her lover, was the first thought that came to her mind.

The truth was that if Lorcan and Daire hadn't been there, every word Toby had heard that day, every warning of the dire consequences of falling for Graydon, would have flown out the window. She had no doubt that she would have given in to his kisses to the point of losing her virginity on the dining room table.

But Lorcan and Daire were there, both of them staring in openmouthed astonishment, their Lanconian reserve overridden by their shock.

It was Daire who dropped a stack of books, thus reminding the two people who were so deeply kissing, with Toby's leg around Graydon's hip, that they weren't alone.

"Put me down!" she hissed.

"Yes, of course," he answered. "Later, in private, we'll be together."

He moved away too fast for her to answer him that they would not "be together" later. When Toby looked at Daire, she saw his disapproval.

Embarrassed, Toby ran up to her room. When throwing cold water on her face didn't cool her, she stripped off and stepped into an icy shower. As she shivered under the water, she began to have visions of Graydon's hands on her, of her hands on him.

At one point, she seemed to see his smile as he promised to spend his life with her—then he slipped a gold ring onto her finger.

She put her hands over her face and let the cold water beat down on her. This had to stop! It couldn't go on. She must do whatever it took to halt these fantasies about him. He belonged to another woman. No! His body, his mind, his very soul belonged to another country. He loved that place so much that he was willing to marry a woman he didn't love, which would probably alienate his beloved brother. If Graydon had such firm principles that he was willing to do all that, then Toby was going to help him by not further complicating his life. She wasn't going to make his parting harder for him—or her—than it was already going to be.

Besides, she had her own sanity to protect.

By the next morning she'd strengthened her vow to just be friends with Graydon. The way to do that was to bury herself in work—and maybe that would put a stop to her ridiculous visions. She had two jobs and she dove into them, trying her best to fill her mind with tasks that needed to be done.

Over the next week she spent a lot of time in the garden that Jared had given her to landscape. However, the first time she went there alone she had visions of the garden at the BEYOND TIME house. But she could imagine only a part of it and she kept thinking that there was a full grown tree missing. She thought of asking Dr. Huntley if he knew anything about that garden, but she decided it was better not to dwell on it. The house wasn't hers and truthfully, she had no desire to ever enter it again.

In addition to the garden, she was busy with Victoria's wedding. Now that she had a theme, she could move forward. And daily, things were added to her long list of what she had to do.

One evening Toby was deep into designing what would be historically correct flower arrangements when Graydon said, "Too bad you're working so hard to make everything accurate when only the bride and groom will be in costume. Perhaps everyone should dress in that manner."

Toby glanced at the guest list Victoria had given her. There were some very famous people, especially authors, on it. "How could we get the guests to dress in costume? That's not something Americans like to do."

"At home, I'd just tell them to," Graydon said. "If they want to come to a ball at the palace, they dress up in whatever they're told to wear."

"But that was when you were a prince," she said, looking down at her laptop. She didn't see the way Daire and Lorcan exchanged smiles.

Graydon picked up his phone. "I think we should ask the American queen how to get the guests to do this."

"Victoria," Toby said, and Graydon nodded as she took his phone and tapped out HOW DO WE GET YOUR ILLUSTRIOUS GUESTS TO DRESS IN COSTUME? and sent it.

It was only a minute before Victoria replied. OFFER PRIZES. THEY'RE ALL CUTTHROAT AMBITIOUS SO MAKE THEM COMPETE.

"Sounds good to me," Graydon said. "Should we commission medals to be awarded?"

"How about dances with a prince?" Toby said.

Graydon's eyes sparkled. "I'll see if Rory can attend."

Laughing, she went back to the planning, and again she didn't see the look Daire and Lorcan gave each other.

When people responded just as Victoria said they would, Toby was deluged with calls. Every author wanted to know what every other author was going to wear. They said it was so there wouldn't be duplicates. Victoria said it was so they could outdo one another. She explained that the number two *New York Times* bestselling authors wanted to make sure their costumes were more elaborate than the number one bestsellers. "But simplicity was the cornerstone of Regency dress," Toby said.

"Tell that to number three on the list," Victoria answered.

Between the garden and the wedding, Toby was nearly overwhelmed with work. Lorcan helped so much that she soon became Toby's unofficial assistant. Toby loved to hear Lorcan on the phone with Victoria's famous author friends. Lorcan was no-nonsense, gave no sympathy, and revealed all. She encouraged the competition with vivid descriptions of everything from hand-sewn pearls to shoes with crystal-encrusted buckles. When she clicked off, she gave Toby a wicked smile. It looked like Victoria's wedding was going to sparkle!

Toby relayed everything to Victoria via email, as she was deep into writing her latest novel—this one about the misfortunes of Valentina Montgomery Kingsley.

"Does she cry while she's writing?" Graydon asked at dinner.

At first Toby thought he was joking, but he wasn't. His face was serious. "I don't know," Toby replied, "but I'll ask Alix."

"How did you know that?!" Alix said over the phone. "The last three times I talked to Mom she'd been crying while writing. She says it's as though she's lived this book and it's tearing her heart out." Alix gave a little sound of exasperation. "Of course her editor loves this! She says that if authors cry, readers cry, and tears sell books."

"A bit callous," Toby said, "but understandable. So what are you and Jared up to?"

That's when Alix dropped the bombshell that Victoria wanted Toby to design the wedding dress.

"No," Toby said firmly. "That's the bride's job, not mine."

"That's a good way to start," Alix said, "but I bet you a dinner at Languedoc that Mom will win."

"You're on," Toby said. "There are limits to planning a wedding for someone else." Victoria won.

Days after the dinner, Victoria called Toby and said she wanted her to "deal with"—as she called it—her wedding gown.

"But I'm sure that is something you'll want to do yourself," Toby said, her voice as firm as she could make it.

"I would love to," Victoria said, "but I didn't get Valentina's journal until recently, and I'm months behind on my deadline. My readers have never before had to wait this long, and besides, in this economy I can't very well stop working, now, can I? You don't want to disappoint millions of readers all over the world, do you?"

"I guess not," Toby said, "but how am I to choose your wedding gown?" Her eyebrows were so high they were about to disappear into her hair.

Victoria didn't hesitate. "Send me photos of appropriate dresses of that time period, I'll choose one, then Martha and her marvelous ladies will make it for me."

"Martha?" Toby asked. "Is that . . . Martha Stewart?"

"Heavens, no! I mean the real Martha. Pullen, of course. The Queen of Sewing. She has all my measurements and she can make anything. I have to go. Send the photos today." She hung up.

Toby clicked off her phone and looked at Lorcan, but she was already on the Internet. She'd found Martha Pullen's website of products, history, and exquisitely crafted garments.

"Now we just have to find a gown beautiful enough to please

Victoria," Toby said. An hour later, using two laptops, they'd copied and pasted a file of twenty-two dresses from museum sites, each of them breathtaking.

"Here goes," Toby said as she saved the photos onto a flash drive. Later she'd deliver them to Victoria.

"I'll wager on the green one," Graydon said.

"In that case, I'll take the blue," she responded.

"The one with the red ribbons," Daire said.

"The pure white gown for maidenly virtue," Lorcan said, and they all looked at her for a moment before bursting into laughter.

All in all, it would have been a very pleasant week—except for two things. Toby continued to have lightning quick visions of herself with Graydon, and he did some rather odd things.

Sometimes Toby would look at Graydon and "see" him in Regency dress. She'd seen him in those clothes at the dinner party and he'd worn them well, but her brief visions were different. Instead of the elegant little slippers that he'd worn at the dinner party, he had on tall leather boots. And the clothes didn't look like a costume but like something he was used to wearing. One night Graydon was standing by the fireplace and she suddenly saw him in just the shirt, the skintight breeches, and those tall boots. The sight was so erotic that it had made Toby feel downright dizzy.

There were numerous other quick visions of food, of a big bed with rose petals on it, of rows of leather-bound books, and Graydon saying, "Shall we hide all the books under the floorboards and dig them out two hundred years from now?"

One morning before she was fully awake, she reached out for Graydon and was disappointed when he wasn't in the bed beside her.

She hid all the visions from Graydon. Nor did she tell Alix about them. And when she talked to Lexie on the phone she didn't mention them. But then, all Lexie could talk about was

Roger Plymouth and all they were doing on their long car trip. "I thought he'd insist that we stay at five-star hotels," Lexie said, "and there I'd be in jeans and a T-shirt looking like the worst of the American tourists. But we stop at places that have only three or four bedrooms and usually the food is grown and cooked by the owners. It's all wonderful! But how are you doing? Been to bed with him yet?"

"Not for sex, no," Toby said. "What about you?"

When Lexie hesitated, Toby gasped. "You *have* been to bed with him, haven't you?"

"It just happened," Lexie said. "Too much wine, too much moonlight. But it was just sex, no love. And you?"

"I think my problem may be the opposite: love but no sex."

"Yeow!" Lexie said. "Tell me everything."

"Not yet," Toby said, "but I will later."

With promises to each other, they hung up.

Besides the visions, Graydon was acting very strangely. One day he invited her on a walk, then took her to a Nantucket church that Toby had decorated for several weddings. At first she thought he just wanted to see the beautiful old building, but no, he'd wanted her to envision the church as it probably was in 1806.

Toby didn't understand his meaning. Since it was the year she was using for the wedding, that's what she thought he meant. "Victoria wants to be married in the chapel Alix designed, not here."

Graydon gave a great sigh, as though she'd disappointed him, and took her out to lunch.

Over the week he'd played some very old-sounding music for her, cooked some unusual dishes, and said he should give up the sea to run the Kingsley family. He'd asked her what made

Regency women swoon. He'd ordered a big book of slick photographs on Japanese tattoos and asked Toby to look at it with him.

By Saturday she was so tired of his strange actions that she got Lorcan and Daire to agree to go on a cruise around the island—knowing that Graydon had business in Lanconia and couldn't go with them. The enthusiasm of their agreement made her think they too were glad to get away from Graydon.

They left early in the morning, all of them hurrying out the door, leaving a very sad-looking prince behind.

Graydon knew he was trying too hard to make Toby remember their time together. And he also knew that he shouldn't do it. It was better that she didn't remember. Better that she wasn't going through what he was, being tortured daily by vivid, clear, relentless memories.

At first he tried to make himself believe it had all been a dream. A product of his imagination. He had lusted for Toby for so long that he'd dreamed about her. And with all the planning for a historic wedding, it was understandable that his dream would have ladies in semitransparent dresses. Since Toby remembered nothing, surely it was his fantasy alone.

But he didn't believe it. Inside of him was the soul-deep knowledge that what was in his mind had actually happened. But how to prove it?

On that first day after the dinner party, he'd waited for Toby to wake up. He imagined how she'd slide into his arms and . . . well, she'd tell him she loved him.

But she stayed in bed so late that Graydon went out with Daire to work off excess energy. While he was outside sweating, Toby got up and ran off with Alix. Not that she'd left a note for

Graydon, but his aunt Jilly stopped by and told him where Toby was.

"Everyone is worried about her," Jilly said. "They think she's too close to you and that when you leave she'll be crushed."

Graydon opened his mouth to defend himself, but how could he? Would he tell the story of how he'd been back in time with Toby? Admit that those were the happiest hours of his life? That he wanted to stay in a time when the barber was the dentist? When so-called doctors bled sick patients to get rid of "ill humors"?

But he knew he'd go back in a minute. Without a second thought—and his vehemence scared him. Before he met Toby, he would have said he was a happy man. He had everything anyone could want. But now . . . Now he was becoming more dissatisfied with his life, his future, by the hour.

That first day after their night together, he'd waited impatiently for Toby to return. He'd tried to keep his mind on the business of Lanconia, but he couldn't do it. At one point Rory bawled him out, saying he didn't seem to remember what it was like to work 24/7. "You get the vacation and I get the work," he said, and hung up.

Usually, his brother's anger would have upset Graydon. He would have called him back, apologized, and put his mind fully on the needs of his country. But he didn't do that. Instead, he'd gone outside to water the greenhouse and the flower beds. His mind was full of Toby—of when she would return and what they would do about what had happened to them. About their night together.

All that day he went over and over every second of their time together. He thought of every moment, every word, every touch.

By the time Toby returned, Graydon was frantic with worry. He planned to politely ask her to go upstairs with him so they could talk in private.

But that's not what happened. Instead, when he saw her, all courtesy, all reserve, fell away and he grabbed her in his arms. It seemed to be months since he'd touched her and he couldn't get enough. He didn't know what he would have done if Daire hadn't dropped a pile of books onto the hard floor. The resulting boom had startled him enough to let up on his grip of Toby.

Graydon had stepped back to look at the faces of everyone. Lorcan was shocked, Daire was disgusted, and Toby was looking at him as though she'd never seen him before. That was when he realized that she remembered nothing of their time together.

In the following week he'd done everything he could to make her remember. He'd searched the Internet until he found music such as he'd heard that night. He cooked food like he'd eaten, then retold the story of Tabby and Silas Osborne and said how much better it would have been if she'd married Garrett Kingsley. He recited bits of dialogue. He sketched people and scenes, including the wedding ceremony, and showed them to Toby. He'd even asked her to walk to the same church with him, but the sight of it brought back no memories. Nor did a visit to Kingsley House. The only obstacle he encountered was when he tried to get her to go inside BEYOND TIME with him. She refused to step a foot inside.

But it didn't matter because she remembered nothing. She looked at, listened to, tasted all that he offered, but nothing jogged her memory.

By the end of the week, Graydon began to think that it had indeed been a dream.

By the weekend, he was beginning to settle down and he could joke with Toby about all that Victoria was giving her to do.

On Saturday afternoon Jared stopped by to tell them he and Alix were leaving, but Graydon was the only one home. Daire, Lorcan, and Toby had gone on a sailing tour around the island.

Daire had never been on a boat before, and the women had teased him about whether a whale would come up under the boat and turn it over. "I hear they swallow people," Toby said, straight-faced. "It's their revenge for all that harpooning."

Lorcan had been on a boat only once before but she joined Toby in the teasing. Graydon had to remain behind because some American businessmen wanted to talk about possibly opening a shoe factory in Lanconia. Graydon had done all the preliminary work with them and had to be there to answer their questions, through Rory, about water, materials, and labor.

Jared's knock came just as Graydon had finished the fourth call with his brother, and it was a welcome relief. "Alix and I have to get back to New York," Jared said, "and I wanted to see if everything here was all right." He was looking Graydon up and down, as though he was trying to figure out what he was still doing in Nantucket and if he was intentionally trying to break Toby's heart.

Graydon offered Jared a beer, and they took the drinks outside. "How are you and Toby doing?" Jared asked bluntly.

"Great. I'm in love with her but she thinks I'm the best girlfriend she's ever had. She asks me about wedding dress designs and whether I like yellow roses or pink ones better. I've kissed her but she tells me to behave myself."

"Yeah?" Jared asked and his face began to relax a bit.

"When we leave I think all three of us Lanconians are going to be crying, but Toby will be glad to get her house back."

Smiling, Jared drank from his beer.

Graydon knew that what he was saying wasn't fully the truth, but it wasn't exactly a lie either. Maybe he was just voicing what he'd been feeling in the last few days.

"You leave when?" Jared asked.

Graydon winced at his cousin's tone. He wasn't used to people trying to get rid of him. "Week and a half," he said.

Jared didn't say "Good," but his eyes did.

As they went back into the house, Graydon suddenly remembered talking to young Alix—Ali—about her house designs. "Is there a portrait in your house of a young woman, about twenty-three, possibly in a large, heavy frame?"

"Yeah, there is. It's one of the pictures in the attic. My grandfather wanted it hung downstairs, but all the women said the frame was big and ugly so it stayed hidden away. How do you know about it?"

Graydon had to come up with a lie quickly. "Dr. Huntley said—"

"Say no more," Jared said. "If you want to see it, Toby has a key to the house. Feel free to look. I haven't seen that picture since I was a kid. Last I knew, it was leaning against the very back wall and there's probably a lot of stuff in front of it. My attic is poorly lit, so if you want to bring it over here, do so. Actually, I'd like to see that picture again."

"Thank you," Graydon said. The men said goodbye and Graydon watched Jared walk down the lane to Kingsley House.

On Sunday morning, the women went to church services. Graydon begged off, saying he had some work to do, and he nudged Daire to stay with him. They were going to go through the Kingsley attic.

Chapter Twenty-two

When Toby and Lorcan returned from church, Daire and Graydon were in the family room staring at a huge, sheet-covered package leaning against the wall.

"What's that?" Toby asked.

"One of Jared's ancestors," Daire said, then explained how they'd spent all morning in the attic of Kingsley House, armed with big flashlights and searching for the portrait. "We had to move heavy boxes, old furniture, a big birdcage, and . . ." He looked at Graydon.

"And what looked to be a basket full of shrunken heads," Graydon said, "but we didn't stop to investigate to make sure."

Curious, Toby went to stand beside him. "Were you looking for something specific or just exploring?"

"I was trying to find the portrait of Alisa Kendricks Kingsley, and I think this is it."

"Ali," Toby said softly. "The little girl in my dream. But what made you think she'd had her portrait painted and that it was stored in the Kingsley attic?"

"I told her to have it done, and since Dr. Huntley said she and her husband were never credited with building houses on the island, I asked her to leave proof inside the frame."

Lorcan and Daire were looking at him in puzzlement but Toby's mouth opened in astonishment.

"When did you see her?" Toby's voice was barely a whisper.

"I had a dream the night of the dinner party." Graydon sounded as though it didn't matter at all. "Shall we see what we have?" He nodded to Daire to take the other side of the old, yellow, dusty sheet and they lifted it off.

It was a portrait of a young woman. It was what was known as a primitive painting, probably done by one of the itinerant painters who roamed America making portraits of anyone who could afford them. The boards the picture was painted on had warped a bit, but they didn't take away from the prettiness of the young woman with her strawberry-blonde hair and her bluish-green eyes. However, the surrounding frame was too heavy for the size of the picture and nearly overwhelmed it. You could hardly see the young woman's face for the carved dark oak that surrounded it.

"She looks like your friend," Lorcan said.

"Alix." Toby was looking at Graydon. He hadn't said a word about having a dream in which he'd met the young Ali. But maybe in a roundabout way, he had. Had all his comments about tattoos and churches and historic recipes come from his dream?

Graydon didn't look at Toby. If he had, she would probably have asked him about his dream. Was she in it? Why hadn't he told her about it? She stared at him but he wouldn't meet her eyes.

She watched as the men turned the portrait to the wall and

Graydon began to inspect the back of the big frame. Oddly, it was carved in the back almost as much as in the front. Intricate vines and leaves, with little flower buds peeping out here and there, covered the back. Graydon ran his hands along the edges as though he were searching for something.

Whatever he was trying to find didn't seem to be there. But then, a ray of light hit the frame and Toby, standing a few feet away, could see the design more clearly. "I think parts of the wood used to be painted, or maybe dyed."

When Graydon moved to stand beside her, he saw that the little flower buds had a faint reddish tint to them. The color was hard to see over two hundred years of darkened wood, but it was there.

Kneeling, Graydon took one of the buds in his fingertips and twisted. It moved. Just a bit, but it did move. It took three more twists before a little door opened to expose a tight roll of papers. He took it out and handed it to Toby.

She held the roll out on her open palm. "Maybe we should take this to Dr. Huntley and let the archivists open it."

Graydon was from a much older country. A mere two hundred years didn't impress him. He took the papers from her and unrolled them. There were three sheets of what looked to be a good linen bond, two of them filled with tiny writing, obviously done with a quill pen. The last sheet had sketches of houses drawn on it.

By the time Toby had looked at all the papers, Graydon had pulled four more rolls from inside the frame.

"This is proof that Alisa designed the houses and that the first Jared built them," Toby said. "Dr. Huntley will like this."

"Wait!" Daire said. "There's another one." In the top right corner was a tiny carved flower that looked as though it had once been blue. "I can't figure this one out," he said as he stepped away.

It took Graydon several tries as he twisted, turned, and

pushed the little blue flower. He was about to give up when a long, thin door sprang open. Inside was a single piece of paper rolled to the size of a pencil. When Graydon opened it, his face seemed to lose all color and for a moment he wasn't able to move.

Daire looked over his shoulder, his eyes wide.

"What is it?" Toby asked.

"It's a picture of a girl." Daire was looking at Graydon, puzzled by his reaction.

"I think it's Japanese," Lorcan said, "except that the young woman is blonde." The three of them looked at Toby.

"What's wrong?"

Graydon handed the paper to Lorcan, then left the house. They heard the door close behind him.

Toby took the paper from Lorcan. It had rolled itself back up so she sat down on the couch to open it on the coffee table. As she unrolled one end of it, at first she didn't know what she was seeing. It was a watercolor, quite beautifully drawn, of what looked to be a Japanese geisha, but indeed, her hair was blonde, her eyes blue—and the woman resembled her. There were a few marks beside the picture and when she opened the top she realized she was looking at a drawing of a man's back.

"It's a tattoo," she said as she looked up at Daire and Lorcan. She couldn't help wondering if this had something to do with why Graydon showed her the photos of the Japanese tattoos.

"Look at the rest of it," Daire said as he held the bottom of the long, narrow paper.

At the top was Graydon's face. He was smiling and looking over his shoulder at the artist. It was Garrett's back that had a full-color tattoo of Toby as a blonde geisha.

"I remember," Toby whispered.

That's all she could think to say. She remembered all of it.

Every second. Every word, every taste and smell, every person and thought.

"Marry," she said, her voice weak with emotion. She looked up at Daire and Lorcan. "We got married. I think—"

She didn't say any more as the blood seemed to be draining from her body.

Daire caught her as she fell forward in a faint. He turned her to stretch out on the couch, her head on a pillow. "Get Graydon," he told Lorcan.

She didn't hesitate in obeying, her long legs eating up the distance to the back door. When she shouted in Lanconian for Graydon to come, there was urgency in her voice.

Graydon was in the greenhouse, but at Lorcan's call, he began to run. He ran past her, into the house, and through to the family room, where Toby was lying on the couch, Daire sitting beside her.

When he saw Graydon, Daire moved away and the prince took his place. "Call an ambulance," he ordered.

"No," Toby said weakly as she tried to open her eyes, but the truth was she was almost afraid to look at Graydon. Her mind was flooded with images. Her mother threatening Graydon—Garrett—and the way he'd stood up to her.

And the night! Hands and mouths, touching, caressing. Feeling him inside her! She remembered every bit of it.

Graydon had his hand on her forehead, as though feeling if she had a fever. "Toby," he whispered, "it's all right. It wasn't really us."

She didn't know if that thought made her feel better or worse.

When Graydon lifted his shirt up, Daire and Lorcan left the room. They didn't know what was going on, but obviously it was private.

Graydon turned his bare back to Toby. "Open your eyes and

look at me. I'm Graydon, not Garrett, and you are Carpathia, not Tabitha."

Slowly, Toby opened her eyes and saw Graydon's bare back. Nothing but honey-colored skin over deep muscle. No markings of any kind.

Tentatively, she put her hand out and touched him. He drew in his breath, but he didn't move. She ran her hand over his side, vividly remembering that the last time she'd touched him the tattoo was there. But she also remembered kissing his skin and how he'd turned, pulled her into his arms, and made love to her.

Abruptly, Toby sat up and wrapped her arms around Graydon, her cheek against his nude back. "It was wonderful there. I didn't want to leave—and now I wish I didn't remember that I'd been there."

Her hands were on his stomach and he clasped them. He didn't dare turn around, as he knew he'd pull her into his arms and lie down beside her on the couch. He'd so very much wanted her to remember what they'd experienced together, but now he realized that she was sharing his pain. It would have been better if she'd never remembered.

"You were trying to remind me, weren't you?"

"Yes, but I shouldn't have. Toby," he said, and his voice was full of what he felt and was going to feel. "My life in this century is different and I can't stay here."

"I know." There were tears beginning to come and she knew she was wetting his back. "I know all of it, but . . ." She didn't want to say what she felt.

"Tell me you'll be all right after I leave. Promise me that you'll be well and healthy."

"And fall in love with another man?"

For a moment Graydon's hands tightened on hers, then he turned to pull her into his arms, holding her so tightly she could hardly breathe. "I'll send my Royal Guard to execute him."

She was clasping him hard, her face pressed against his bare chest. "I'll go to Maine and pick out one of your Montgomery cousins."

Graydon didn't laugh, just stroked her hair. "They could not love you as well as I do." His words of "I do" and not "I could" made her tears fall freely. She wasn't sobbing, just had tears flowing from her eyes. "You couldn't stay . . . ?"

She left the rest of the sentence unsaid, but he knew what she meant. He couldn't abdicate and turn the throne over to his brother, could he? But then, these weeks had proven how bad Rory was at the job—and how much he hated it. Unlike Graydon, Rory had not been trained to survive day after day of protocol and monotony and of being a figurehead rather than a person. And then there was Danna, and her father's interests in the country. "No," Graydon whispered. "I cannot stay here. I must return to my home. It's what I am."

Graydon knew he couldn't continue to hold her. The night they'd spent together was becoming more clear by the second. Right now he needed to put something good, something happy into their lives.

Smiling, he held Toby at arm's length. Her eyes were full of tears and he wanted to kiss them away, but that would defeat the purpose. "Do you realize what we did?"

"You mean that I lost my virginity but I probably still have it?" She took a tissue out of the box on the coffee table. "Maybe it's an incurable disease. Think there's a pill for my problem?"

Graydon couldn't help laughing as he put his hands on her face and kissed her eyelids. "Do you think I'm too old to become a pharmacist?"

"Don't make me laugh! All this is horrible. You and I—we can't—" She was about to start crying again.

"Toby, my dear, sweet love, we changed history. Don't you see that what we did changed everything? Tabby married the man she loved, not the little store clerk but a big, handsome sea captain and—"

"Who was a very bad sailor," Toby said as she blew her nose. "So what happened to them?"

"I didn't search their history because I was waiting for you to remember me—which I thought you were never going to do." Taking her hand, he pulled her up, then started toward the kitchen. "I can't figure out how you forgot so much." He took a packet of fish out of the fridge and handed Toby a bag of carrots.

She was beginning to recover herself. He was right to try to lighten the mood between them. She could either cry about their coming separation or she could enjoy every minute of the time they had left. "Oh, well, you know, there was nothing monumental to make me remember." She was teasing him back, but Graydon didn't smile.

"Is your mother today like she was then?" he asked softly.

"Yes," Toby said as she began to run a peeler over the carrots. "I've always disappointed her." She looked at him. "Maybe it all has to do with what happened back then, in the past."

Graydon put the fish fillets in a baking dish and began to season them. "That's what's puzzled me. Garrett was going to give up the sea and stay home to manage the Kingsley future. If he did a good job at that, wouldn't there be something different now? And if he was able to show your mother that she was wrong, maybe you'd have different memories of her."

"If I knew they were different," Toby said. "But my mother has always been frantic, always worried about someone 'taking care of' me. She's never thought I could do that on my own."

"Just as Lavinia believed," Garrett said. He put the fish back in the fridge and began to peel potatoes.

"Why are you frowning?" she asked.

He didn't want to answer her question because he knew in his heart that something was wrong. He didn't know what it was, but it was there, haunting him. "Maybe it actually was all just a dream and you and I imagined it together."

Toby was thinking about what he'd said about changing history. "Tomorrow I think we should go see Dr. Huntley and ask him about Tabby and Garrett. If what happened really did change anything, then his story will be different." She put the cleaned carrots on a cutting board. "Did I tell you what Dr. Huntley was like before Victoria agreed to marry him? He was a widower and he had a sadness in his eyes, in his whole body, that was heartbreaking to see. He seemed more dead than alive."

"But the glorious Victoria said yes and now he's a man whose glance can command a room," Graydon said, smiling.

Like you, Toby thought but didn't say. He had his back to her and it was as though she could see through his shirt. She could almost see her face imprinted on his skin. If any of what they remembered actually did happen, that meant they'd been in love for a very long time. Centuries. She thought of when they first met and how Graydon had stared at her. It was almost as though he knew her. When you met someone you felt as though you'd known forever, had you?

"Stop it," Graydon said quietly, but he didn't turn around. "If we're to get through these last days, you can't think what's in your mind." Turning, he looked at her and his eyes were hot with all the desire he felt.

Toby took a step toward him, but the back door opened and Lorcan and Daire came inside.

"We can leave if you want," Daire said as he looked from one to the other.

"No," Graydon said firmly as he reluctantly took his eyes off Toby. "Anyone hungry? And how about we all go sightseeing later?"

Toby knew what he was saying, that they needed to keep busy and stay with other people. To be alone would cause too many . . . complications. "Yes, we'll be tourists for today, and tomorrow we'll go see Dr. Huntley."

"We won't take the picture of . . . ?" Graydon trailed off, not saying "me" out loud. A two-hundred-year-old picture of him might cause too many questions.

"I don't think we should," Toby said, and Graydon smiled, glad they were in agreement.

The NHS headquarters was in a beautiful old house on Fair Street and Toby asked the woman at the desk if they could see Dr. Huntley. They hadn't brought the papers from Alisa Kendricks Kingsley, as they didn't want Dr. Huntley's attention to be diverted to them. Besides, answering "How did you find them?" might be a bit awkward.

Dr. Caleb Huntley came out to meet them almost immediately. "Toby! Graydon!" he said as he put his hands on her shoulders and kissed her cheek. "How good to see both of you again. Come with me to my office."

A young woman holding a stack of photos of old paintings was waiting inside Dr. Huntley's beautiful office. There were shelves filled with books and interesting artifacts. "Excuse me," he said as he motioned for them to sit down, then took the pictures from the young woman. "Phineas Coffin," he said. "Died about 1842. Was married to one of the Starbucks. Eliza, I think. Six unruly brats." He switched photos. "Efrem Pollster. Worst captain who ever lived on this island. Let his crew rule him." He changed pictures. "The *Elizabeth Mary.* A very good ship. Went down off the coast of Spain in a storm. 1851. No. 1852." He looked at the young woman. "Did you get all that?"

"I think so," she said. "I have four articles for the journal that you need to read, and three donors called this morning. They want to speak directly to you."

Caleb waved his hand. "I'll get to them later." His tone was that of dismissal, and as the woman left the office, he sat down behind his big desk.

"You do seem to know an extraordinary lot about Nantucket," Toby said.

Caleb shrugged in dismissal. "They have stacks of unidentified pictures, so I've been putting names to faces." He looked from one to the other.

Graydon nodded at Toby for her to begin. "Remember the dinner party?" Toby asked.

"And your glorious food?" Caleb said. "That was a truly magnificent evening. You, young man, should get a job as a cook."

Graydon smiled. "I take that as a great compliment, but I do have other employment."

"We could call it The Prince's Wharf," Toby said, her eyes encouraging.

Both Caleb and Graydon laughed, then the older man looked at Toby. "So what can I help you with?"

"You told a story about Tabitha Weber," Toby said, "and we were wondering about that. Did she marry Silas Osborne?"

"No," Caleb said with a bit of a smile. "It's interesting that you know of the connection between those two. Tabby's mother, Lavinia, wanted her to marry him. But Garrett talked the woman out of it, made some promises, that sort of thing. Osborne wasn't happy about it and for a while he talked about suing, but . . ." Caleb shrugged. "He sold his store to Obed Kingsley and left the island. No one ever heard of him again."

Toby didn't look at Graydon but she saw that he was beginning to smile. It looked like they had changed history.

"So Tabby did marry Garrett Kingsley?" Graydon asked.

"Yes," Caleb said, but then the smile faded from his handsome face. "Garrett . . ." He almost didn't seem able to go on. He took a breath. "They married, but nine months later Tabby died in childbirth. Not long afterward, Garrett shipped out with his brother Caleb. The ship went down and took everyone on board with it." His face suddenly looked older. It was almost as though he'd lived through the tragedy himself.

"No!" Toby said. "That's not right. Tabby and Garrett got married and lived happily ever after." Her voice was rising. "Nobody died! Everyone was happy!"

Graydon reached out to take her hand in his. The strength of his grip was the only sign of what he was feeling. "What happened to Lavinia and the widows?"

"Tabby's death tore the family apart," Caleb said, his voice heavy. "Lavinia sold the house, but it was in such bad shape that she didn't get much for it. She tried to keep the family together, but she couldn't. All the widows took the grandchildren and left the island." Caleb sighed. "I don't think Lavinia was invited to go with them. She ended up alone in 'Sconset, a victim of the drink. Poor woman. She'd lost her husband and three sons, all her grandchildren, and her daughter. She didn't hold on to her sanity."

Graydon squeezed Toby's hand. He could feel her beginning to slump. "You're sure Tabby died in childbirth?"

"Oh, yes. Both Valentina and Parthenia were there with her." Caleb looked at Toby. "It was a miserable time then. Tabby was a well-loved young woman."

"She died in that house," Toby whispered. "In the birthing room."

"Yes," Caleb said. "Garrett was planning to build them a house on the North Shore but he didn't have time before Tabby . . ." He paused, his eyes full of sadness.

There was a quick knock at the door and the young woman opened it. "Dr. Huntley, sorry to bother you, but people are waiting."

He waved his hand and she left, but he didn't move. He sat

behind his desk and looked at Graydon and Toby, seeming to have all the time in the world. But then, he was a man who knew what was important in life.

"The baby?" Toby whispered.

Dr. Huntley shook his head. "Tabby and her son went together."

"Oh, God," Toby said, her words half prayer, half anguish.

Graydon stood up quickly and pulled Toby up to stand beside him. He put his arm firmly around her shoulders. "One other thing," he said to Caleb. "How did Tabby's body come to be scarred?"

Caleb looked surprised at the question, but he got his face under control. "When she was three she tripped on her skirt and fell into the fire. Her father pulled her out and rolled on her. He got some burns too."

"And Garrett's back?"

Caleb smiled. "That glorious tattoo? He was the envy of all of us. As for getting it, let's just say that when in a foreign port even a Kingsley can sometimes drink too much rum."

"Thank you," Graydon said, and he walked with Toby out of the office, and out the front door. He didn't let go of her until they had gone down Main Street, onto Kingsley Lane, and were inside the house. He put her on the couch in the living room and poured her a double shot of whiskey.

"Drink it," he said.

"We killed them," Toby whispered.

Graydon put the glass up to her lips and made her drink some.

"We destroyed Tabby and her baby." She looked at him. "Garrett's baby. Our baby. I know in my heart that you and I made him on that night. We created him, then we killed him." Graydon sat down beside her and pulled her into his arms.

"You can't think like that."

"We changed history, but when we did, we murdered three people."

"It was a very long time ago," Graydon whispered, holding her head on his chest. She pulled back to glare at him.

"They'd all be dead now anyway, so what does it matter? Is that what you're saying?" Her tone was belligerent.

Graydon started to defend himself but his eyes turned cold. "That's exactly what I meant."

She knew he was lying. He felt as bad about this as she did. She fell back onto his chest. "I don't understand. The first time I went into that birthing room, I knew I'd died in there. But I hadn't! That only happened after you and I changed things. How could that be?"

"Well," Graydon said slowly, "the rules of reincarnation, time travel, and changing history work differently. Shall we consult the textbook on the subject?"

His attempt at a joke didn't make her laugh but it did make her feel a bit better. "How do we fix this?"

"I think we should leave it alone."

She pulled back to look at him. "We have to return to that time."

"And do what?" he asked, his voice angry. "I've thought of nothing else since we left Caleb's office. Do we go back and allow Tabby to be sold to Osborne? That didn't work." His eyes locked with hers. "Toby, maybe there is such a thing as destiny. Maybe we could change the past a thousand times and no matter what we did, Garrett and Tabby would end up apart, either by marriage to others or by death."

"Like now?" She pushed away from him. "Their destiny— our destiny—is to find each other, then be separated forever? The sea, childbirth, your country, your future wife? It's our destiny to never be together and I should accept my fate? Is that what you expect me to believe?!"

Graydon didn't like what she was saying, but he did like that she was angry and not crying. "In my country—"

Standing up, Toby glared at him. "Your country is causing all the problems. Who has arranged marriages today?"

"Most of the world," he said calmly. "And they do not have a fifty percent divorce rate."

"That's because the women can't get away from the men. They're trapped."

Graydon sat where he was, knowing that her anger wasn't about his country, wasn't even about him.

His calm brought Toby back to reality. She collapsed onto the couch beside him. "I don't believe in destiny. Why couldn't we change history for the better? Maybe Garrett and Tabby could make a child who is more important than any of them. Maybe he or she will cure cancer. Maybe we'll change history so much that we return to find out there was no World War II." Her eyes were pleading with him for help.

He picked up her hand and kissed her palm. He was glad to see color coming back to her face. "I will do all in my power to help us bring this about. I pledge all that I have to you. Now, shall we go exploring?"

She knew he meant that they should go look inside BEYOND TIME. Perhaps there they'd find the answer. "Yes," she answered, smiling with her heart in her eyes. "Let's go."

"How do you seduce a man?" Toby asked Lexie on the telephone. Usually Lexie dominated their calls as she excitedly told of all she and her boss were doing on their long road trip. But today Lexie was unusually quiet. Toby knew she should ask Lex what was wrong, but she couldn't. At the moment, Toby's own problems were too urgent.

"I don't know," Lexie said. "Breathe. Be. Exist. It doesn't seem to be too difficult to get one of them to make a pass at you. You aren't after your prince, are you?"

Toby took a breath. "Yes."

"Don't do this!" Lexie said. "He's going to leave and— Wait a minute. You want to and he's telling you no?!"

"Yes. That's exactly what's happening."

"That's insulting," Lexie said. "Does he think he's too good for you? He's a prince and you're a peasant? That sort of thing?"

"No, no, no," Toby said. "It's not like that at all. I think he wants to but I'm cursed with a second virginity and he doesn't want to take it again."

"Toby," Lexie said slowly, "you need to explain that remark."

She started to, but Toby knew she couldn't. Maybe if Lexie were there and surrounded by the mystique of Nantucket, what she had to say would be believable, but not over the phone. Not to someone who was in the sunny south of France. "It doesn't matter," she said at last. "It's just that Graydon leaves in two days and he refuses to go to bed with me again, and I want him to. And before you protest, let me remind you that you told me to have an affair with him."

"Yeah, well, that was before I learned how serious affairs can be."

Toby heard what sounded like misery in her friend's voice. "How's Roger? Are you two still just having fun sex, with no commitments?"

In other circumstances, Lexie would have said yes to the sex but admitted that feelings were being added. But Toby sounded so down that Lexie decided against it. "Have you tried exceptional underwear?"

"Aubade," Toby said. "I ordered it online."

"You are serious. Booze?"

"He insists that I drink with him, I fall asleep after two drinks, and I wake up in my own bed. Fully clothed."

"Do you spend time together?"

The answer to that question made Toby's mind spin. It had been a whole week since they'd gone to see Dr. Huntley, and since then she and Graydon had rarely been apart. They were both obsessed with fixing what they'd done wrong. They wanted to save Garrett and Tabby. It had been Graydon's idea that when—if—they returned they could leave a letter behind explaining how to prevent death in childbirth. But before they could write such a letter, they needed to do some research. They'd ordered out-of-print books on the history of childbirth, downloaded books on their eReaders, and done online searches. When they went back they wanted to know all the possibilities so they could prevent Tabby's death no matter what. Their conclusion was that if she'd died from something simple—dirty midwife hands?—they'd be able to fix it. But if it was something like preeclampsia, there was no hope.

In addition to their research, they slept at the Beyond Time house. The first night they'd used sleeping bags they'd found in the attic of Kingsley House. But Graydon said his back couldn't take more of that so he'd bought mattresses from Marine Home and had them delivered.

Mattresses. Plural. Two of them, twin size.

At first Toby had laughed. She thought he'd done that to make Daire and Lorcan believe they weren't lovers—which, to Toby's mind, they were. But no, Graydon made the ridiculous comment that he wasn't going to take her maidenhood a second time.

"This isn't Lanconia," Toby said to him. "This is America, and any virgin over the age of twenty is put on the cover of *People* magazine, or they go on *Ellen* and explain themselves."

Graydon didn't give in. In the ensuing week Toby did everything she could think of to entice him onto her mattress, but he wouldn't budge.

She finally answered Lexie's question. "Yes, we're together whenever he isn't working with his brother. I've neglected Victoria's wedding and haven't seen my friends for a week, but Graydon is wonderful. He holds me when I cry; he talks me out of sadness. He does everything except make love to me."

"Toby," Lexie said, "what do you mean he holds you when you cry? What is that man doing to you?!"

"It's not like that," Toby said, her voice hesitant. "It's . . . You see, he and I are working on a historical project for, uh, for Victoria's 1806 wedding and I keep reading about things like medical practices back then and, well, I get a bit teary about it."

"It doesn't sound to me like you're neglecting Victoria's wedding at all. It sounds like you're obsessing on it."

If you only knew, Toby thought, but didn't say. During the day she and Graydon watched the old house. When he wasn't working out, he took calls from Rory while in front of the window, always watching.

On the second day, Daire asked Graydon what he was trying to see.

"When the door to that old house opens by itself, it's an invitation to enter, and I want to be ready to accept."

That afternoon, Daire and Lorcan left Toby's house and walked across the lane. When they returned, they reported that every window and door of the old house was shut tight.

They'd jiggled the front door, and Daire had rammed it with his shoulder, but it didn't budge. There was no way that door was going to open by itself.

They told their future king what they'd seen, but that didn't stop Graydon's vigilance. As doubtful as they were, they joined in watching the house. While Graydon was busy helping Rory and Toby was involved with the minutiae of Victoria's wedding, Daire and Lorcan kept watch. At night Toby and Graydon stayed in the house and waited for it to invite them back into the past.

"I have to go," Lexie said. "Roger wants . . ."

"What does he want?" Toby asked.

"Nothing, it's just that . . ." Lexie didn't think she should talk to Toby of what was becoming the happiest time in her life, when her friend was so obviously unhappy. And she was frustrated by Toby's lack of confiding in her. But then, she wasn't exactly forthcoming about her and Roger.

"You sound like you have problems. Is everything all right?"

"Yes. Very much all right. Roger isn't like I thought he was. The outside of him doesn't allow a person to see the inside."

"What does that mean?"

"I'll tell you later, but I have to go now. Send me emails, okay?"

"Sure," Toby said and they hung up.

"We're failing, aren't we?" Toby said to Graydon from her mattress. They were physically close to each other but as far apart as two countries separated by oceans could make them. It was dark in the old house, and there were often creaks and groans, but they'd grown used to them. Moonlight came through the uncurtained windows so they saw each other in silhouette.

Graydon didn't know which failure she was referring to. That he was in love with a woman he couldn't marry? Yes, that was a complete failure. That he'd begun to doubt what his true purpose was in life? Yes. Or was she thinking about how they had changed history so three innocent people died and others had had their lives destroyed? Yes to that too.

"I'd say we are," he said. "Toby, I never meant—"

"Please don't apologize. I can't take any more guilt." She took a breath. "What are you going to do after the ceremony?"

He knew she was talking of his coming engagement. Before he could think of an answerless reply, she said, "And how is Rory going to stand seeing you marry the woman he loves?"

Graydon's heart seemed to stop. "How do you know that?"

"When I was unpacking his luggage, I found his wallet. Danna's photo was in there. A man doesn't usually carry a picture of his sister-in-law-to-be."

When Graydon didn't answer, Toby wanted to shake him. "Don't shut me out! We have so little time left." She lowered her voice. "Please."

It wasn't easy for Graydon to talk about such a deep secret. From childhood he'd been taught to keep things to himself. As it was, he knew some diplomatic secrets that could cause, if not wars, certainly some ferocious battles.

"Honestly, I don't know how to handle any of it. I saw them," he said softly. "When I went back in time, before I found you, I saw Rory with Danna. I haven't done any research on them, and I didn't ask Caleb, but I assume they lived a long and happy life." He smiled in the moonlight. "My brother wore an earring in his left earlobe. If Dr. Huntley told me Rory did a little pirating on the side, I wouldn't be surprised."

"He's not suited to being a king," Toby said, and they both knew she was talking about the endless trouble Rory'd had over the last weeks. "But you are."

Graydon rolled over onto his side to face her. "I've missed what I do. This time away from it has shown me what Rory has always said, that the job suits me. He finds diplomacy and having to talk for hours about things like trade agreements boring, but I . . ." He trailed off and turned onto his back.

"It makes you feel like you're doing something for your country, for the world even."

"Yes," he said, then gave a great sigh. "I love my work, but I dread going home. How do I keep my brother from hating me? How do I leave you?"

Toby wanted to tell him she had the perfect solution, but she had none. Graydon was going to leave, marry another woman, and eventually become the king of a country. There would come a time when this moment, of the two of them alone in an old house, would become a distant—and beloved—memory.

The air between them seemed heavy with their gloomy thoughts and Toby wanted to lighten the mood. "Your brother will probably be so bitterly unhappy that he'll turn to drink."

"No," Graydon said, his tone serious. "Rory's more a speed junkie. He'll race cars with Roger Plymouth. It's you I worry about."

"I'll be like the woman in the movie *It's a Wonderful Life*. If you don't want me, I'll become a librarian and let my eyebrows go unplucked. And I'll never get rid of this blasted virginity."

Graydon gave a little laugh. "I should be so lucky! Once Daire and I are out of here, a hundred men will come after you. You'll choose some short, ugly man who adores you and will buy you an estate in Connecticut and you'll grow acres of flowers. You'll tend your gardens with a fat, blond baby strapped to your chest and two others following you, all of you laughing and singing."

She knew he was trying to make a joke but the image he'd conjured was so perfect that it brought tears to her eyes. The only thing missing was Graydon beside her—probably on his cell phone telling someone how to do something.

"Not helping, am I?"

"No," Toby said, "you aren't. But then you and I don't seem able to help anyone, do we?"

"No, we don't. If we just knew exactly what had killed Tabby, maybe we could change things. As it is now, if we went back it would take weeks to write down all that we've learned about the disgusting childbirth methods of the past. Cupping and bleeding!"

"If we both write it, it won't take that long."

"Considering that I'm going to be making love to you for twenty hours a day, that doesn't leave us much time to write."

"Graydon," she said and her voice was a combination of tears and pleading. She went to him.

When he opened his arms to her, Toby started to fall into them. But suddenly, she halted, his hands on her shoulders, hers on his. "That's it."

"Toby," he whispered as he started to pull her down to him. "I can resist you no longer."

She pushed away to sit on the edge of the mattress. "We've been researching childbirth in general, but maybe there's a way to find out specifically what caused Tabby's death."

"We didn't find a mention of a journal anywhere," Graydon said, his hands running up her arms.

"Dr. Huntley said Parthenia and Valentina were there at the birth and they wrote letters to each other."

Graydon struggled to regain control. For a whole week Toby had nearly driven him insane with her not-so-subtle attempts to get him into bed with her. From underwear so seductive it made him dizzy to looks so suggestive he broke into a sweat, he'd survived it all. But then he'd done his best to exhaust himself with constant, hard workouts. At the end of one that had lasted four and a half hours, Daire jammed his sword into the earth and said in Lanconian, "Burn her, not me!" and walked away. Graydon, sweat rolling down his face, asked Lorcan what she was doing. "Ordering tents," she'd said and fled into the house. Graydon had too much pent-up, frustrated energy for either of them to handle.

But now, when he'd finally succumbed, Toby was talking about the damned past spirits. It wasn't easy to get his mind back to what she was talking about. "If they were both here, they wouldn't have been writing letters to each other," he managed to say.

"This island was a hotbed of letter writers," Toby said, "so maybe we could find something somewhere."

Not in two days, Graydon thought, but didn't say. He purposely hadn't answered Toby's question of what he was going to do after the engagement ceremony because he knew it was better if he didn't return to Nantucket. He needed to sort out things with Rory. And as Toby had suggested, he should ask Danna what she wanted. "Aunt Jilly," he said. "In the morning we'll visit her and ask if she knows anything about Garrett and Tabby."

"She would have told us when we mentioned them at the dinner party," Toby said. "But wait! Back then, Tabby had married Osborne."

She turned on the table lamp sitting on the floor and picked up her cell phone. "What are you doing?"

"Calling Jilly."

"It's nearly eleven P.M. This can wait until morning."

She punched a button and put the phone to her ear. "No, it can't. We need every hour before you leave." She looked at him. "Before I never see you again."

Graydon didn't want to confirm what they both were dreading. "Call her," he said.

It was Ken who answered, his voice heavy with sleep. "Toby! This better be important."

"It is. Please let me speak to Jilly."

"Sorry about the time," Toby said when Jilly answered, "but we need some information about the past. I know you've done a lot of research about your own family's history, but because Valentina and Parthenia were part of that I thought . . ." She looked at Graydon.

He took the phone from her. "Aunt Jilly, I'm very sorry about the late hour, but I was wondering how complete your database on our family is. Is it possible that you could find a mention of Tabby and Garrett Kingsley?" He listened. "Yes, yes, I see. Excellent. Yes, thank you." He clicked off the phone and looked at Toby in silence.

"What?!"

"She doesn't remember reading of those names specifically, but then, over years of work she's transcribed thousands of letters, as well as photos and other documents, into a massive database. She bookmarked every name and place, object, house, whatever was in them so she can quickly reference them."

"Let me guess," Toby said. "It's all in Maine and it will take her days to access it."

Graydon kissed her cheek. "Not that it matters but Jilly is a Taggert and lives in Colorado, and yes, it's all there."

Toby sighed.

"However, you do underestimate my family. She has a backup of everything on flash drives and she has a set here. She just has to plug in the correct drive and do a search, then she—" He broke off when the phone rang. "Let's see what she says."

Toby put the phone on speaker.

"Yes," Jilly said, "I found them mentioned in a letter Parthenia wrote home to her mother." She hesitated. "But I'm afraid it's not good news. Poor Tabby. Her husband meant well, but his good intentions killed her."

Graydon took Toby's hand in his. "What did he do?"

He and Toby listened to the horrible story Jilly told of how a Dr. Hancock had, in essence, murdered dear Tabitha.

Chapter Twenty-three

*T*omorrow they leave, Toby thought, then tried to shut the idea out of her mind. But it was impossible since all she and Lorcan had done lately was prepare for their departure. Clothes washing, sorting, finding things, organizing.

At breakfast the four of them were silent, eating the meal the men had prepared without saying a word.

Toby and Daire reached for the plate of Lanconian cheese at the same time. "You take it," Toby said politely.

"No, it's the last of it and tomorrow I can get more."

She and Daire looked across the table at each other, both holding the dish, and the reality of parting became real. No more would the four of them be in the little house together. No more laughing over shared jokes. Toby would never again clash swords with a Lanconian. She and Lorcan would never put on a yoga show with the men watching. She wouldn't go shopping with Lorcan and get her into Nantucket whites. Toby would have no more use for the Lanconian she'd learned to speak.

Graydon looked at the unhappy faces of the others, took the plate from Daire, and set it by Toby. "I will send you cheese," he said, his voice almost harsh.

Lorcan gave her king-to-be a look of reproach and put her hand on Toby's. "I will send you some lace that they make in the mountains. The Ulten women are good at crafts."

Toby nodded. "I'll send you seeds for those tomatoes you like, and when those shoes we ordered arrive I'll send them too." There were tears in the eyes of both women.

Graydon stood up so fast his chair tipped backward. It would have fallen if Daire hadn't caught it. "Daire and I will spend the day out," he said and his voice was cold, sounding uncaring. He looked at Lorcan. "You will prepare for . . ." Graydon's voice nearly broke but he recovered himself. "For tomorrow."

Through all this he didn't look at Toby but kept his eyes on his fellow Lanconians. He didn't even glance at her when he left the room, Daire behind him.

"He is in pain," Lorcan said.

"I know," Toby whispered. "Shall we clean this up and start on the packing?"

It took hours to get all Rory's clothes back into the many bags he'd left for Graydon to use. The packing was hard for Toby, as every item conjured up bittersweet memories. This was the shirt Graydon had worn when they cleaned up the grounds of the wedding. He wore these trousers when they'd grilled hot dogs and Graydon had squirted mustard on the leg. His workout clothes were just out of the dryer, and for a moment Toby buried her face in the soft white cloth.

It was three weeks until Victoria's wedding and Lexie wasn't to return until after it, so Toby would be alone in the house. She dreaded it. She wouldn't even have a job to go to every day. But then, the way she felt today, she might spend the three weeks crying.

Congratulations! she thought. She had joined the millions of women who knew what a broken heart felt like. It was a very, very bad feeling. No wonder people had tried so hard to keep this from happening to her!

"And I should have listened to them," Toby muttered as she jammed Graydon's workout clothes into a duffel bag. She looked at Lorcan. "I bet he has a valet to unpack for him."

"Yes," Lorcan said. "He has everything a future king needs."

Toby grimaced. "No sand in his shoes like he's had here. No dishes to wash, no greenhouse to water, no one asking him what color ribbons Victoria would like."

"No," Lorcan said as she put Graydon's shoes into their protective bags. "And no one to yell at him when he gets too full of himself. There will be no one who would dare tell him that what he just said was stupid."

"He'll be glad of that," Toby said.

"No one to tease and laugh with, to share every meal with, to listen to his whispered stories of his life, to hear of his problems with his students or of his father's threats, which he's endured all his life."

Toby was watching Lorcan, realizing that she was talking about her and Daire. They'd shared a room for all these weeks, but never had there been a hint that anything private went on between them. But Toby had learned that it wasn't natural to Lanconians to let their feelings show.

Stepping back, Toby looked at the huge pile of luggage. It was two o'clock and they still had a lot to do. "Come on," she said. "Let's leave this for later. You and I are going out on the town. We'll have a huge lunch, then go shopping. We'll buy so many souvenirs for you to take back that people will call Lanconia the new Nantucket."

Lorcan smiled. "I like that idea very much."

The two women didn't return until six P.M. They were laden with many shopping bags full of all they'd bought. In spite of their good intentions it had not been a happy outing.

Lorcan had looked at Toby over the lunch table. "I have never before had a woman friend, a B . . ."

"A BFF. Best Friend Forever. I understand. Men like you, so women don't."

"You are right," Lorcan said. "But you are different."

Toby smiled at the compliment, and she wanted to say that they'd have to get together in the future, but she didn't think it would happen. There was no way Toby could visit Lanconia. And see Graydon with another woman? No, she couldn't bear that. And Lorcan would probably get involved with protecting people and never take a vacation.

After lunch they walked around the old, twisted, beautiful sidewalks of Nantucket and acted like tourists, stopping in every shop and looking at everything. They discovered that they both loved mermaids and purchased little boxes, letter openers, even buttons with mermaids on them.

They also bought T-shirts, sweatshirts, and jackets with *Nantucket* emblazoned on them. That all of the garments were in a size to fit Daire and Graydon was not something they commented on.

At five they stopped to have drinks made with tequila.

"You and I should get Virgin Marys," Toby said in disgust and raised her glass. "To the last of our kind."

"I hope we are the very last," Lorcan said.

Both women looked so miserable that they burst out laughing. What followed was a conversation of what each woman had done to entice the man she loved.

"Black lace bra and tiny matching underpants," Toby said.

"I arranged to be caught getting out of the shower with only a hand towel to cover me," Lorcan said rather proudly.

"I wish we'd compared notes. But did it work?"

Lorcan raised her glass, their second one. "Still a virgin."

"Me too," Toby said sadly and they drank deeply.

By the time they picked up their many shopping bags and headed home, they were feeling much better. Lorcan went into the family room she shared with Daire, and Toby went up the back stairs to the private sitting room she and Graydon used. To her shock, all the luggage was gone.

"They've left," she whispered, then dropped the bags and yelled down the stairs, "The men are gone!"

Lorcan, with her long legs, took the stairs two at a time. Toby and Lorcan had left the room in a mess, with some bags packed, some half empty. Clothes and shoes had been on every piece of furniture.

"Do you think Daire and Graydon finished the packing?" Toby asked.

Lorcan sat down in a chair. "No. Not possible. Someone from Lanconia has come and carried everything away. Perhaps Prince Rory's valet."

Toby sat down opposite her. She didn't have to say her thoughts, that it really was all over. Maybe this morning had been their last meal together.

Lorcan glanced through the open door into Toby's bedroom. "What is that?"

They went to look. Spread on Toby's bed was the beautiful Regency dress. Beside it was a notecard with a crest on it. Oh, great, she thought. Graydon had left her a goodbye note and the gift of a dress. Was vellum any better than a Post-it?

When Toby didn't pick up the note, Lorcan did and held it out to her, but Toby didn't take it. Lorcan raised her eyebrows in question, and when Toby nodded, Lorcan began to read. "My dearest wife, Tabby."

Lorcan closed the card and handed it to Toby, who read it in silence.

My dearest wife, Tabby,

Please join me in the small parlor of our home for dinner and dancing.

Your husband, Garrett

"How are you with corset fastenings?" Toby asked. "I have a date." Smiling broadly, Lorcan opened the box of undergarments.

As soon as Toby saw the small parlor in BEYOND TIME she knew what Graydon had done. In secret, he'd arranged for the little room to be transformed into what they'd seen in the past. There were candles everywhere: on wall sconces, on tall frames, on small tables that had been set along the walls.

Flowers flooded the room: bouquets were in glass vases, swags hung along the ceiling and draped the back of chairs. The colors were all the pale, creamy ones that Toby so loved.

In the center of the room was a little round table covered with a pristine white cloth; crystal and silver sparkled in the candlelight. Beside it was a cart with silver domed covers.

Graydon stood beside the table, wearing his Regency suit. When she looked at him, he bowed, an arm in front, one in back. "My lady," he said.

"It's all very beautiful," she whispered. "When . . . ? How did . . . ?"

He pulled out a chair for her. "A man does not divulge his secrets. Will you join me for dinner?"

She took the seat and waited as Graydon sat across from her. "You have taken my breath away. I didn't expect this. When I saw that the suitcases were gone, I thought you'd left."

Graydon just smiled at her and removed a dome to show a platter filled with a circle of tiny roast birds. "Do you like squab?"

"Very much so," Toby said and closed her eyes as she inhaled. The flowers, the candles, the food all went together to make a heavenly fragrance.

Graydon opened a bottle of champagne and filled their tall flutes. "To us," he said and they clicked glasses.

When they looked into each other's eyes, they made a silent agreement that they wouldn't talk about tomorrow. There'd be no mention of separation, no discussion of what Toby was going to do when she was left alone. Nor would they speak of what was coming in Graydon's life. Above all, they would not speak of Tabby and Garrett. They'd done all they could to repair the damage they'd done but they'd not succeeded.

Instead, they talked only of good things. Toby told of her and Lorcan's shopping excursion and how they both loved mermaids.

Graydon told of a long phone call he'd had with his family in Maine. "Uncle Kit has returned," he said, then entertained Toby with outlandish stories the children used to tell about Uncle Kit's adventures.

"Are any of them true?"

"We have no idea," Graydon said, "but we always believed James Bond was based on him, which wasn't possible as Uncle Kit is only about sixty. But then we kids probably thought that because he looks like Sean Connery."

"Tell me more. Please."

It was a lovely dinner of squab, little timbales of truffle-scented rice, and glazed carrots, with chocolate mousse for dessert. Through the meal, soft music played in the background.

When they'd finished, Graydon got up, pulled Toby's chair out, and took her hand. "May I have this dance?"

When she was in his arms—and he pulled her so her cheek was on his chest—she began to again think of the reality of his leaving.

"Graydon, I want to say—" she whispered, but he pulled her closer and she said no more. Yes, she thought, it was better not to think ahead, not to remember the past. Enjoy this moment. Right now.

She smiled a bit, feeling his heart against her cheek. His face was pressed into her hair and she could feel his breath. For all that he seemed to be calm, the pounding of his heart showed that he wasn't. What did it take to not show his true feelings? she wondered. To suppress anger, hurt, sexual desire, even love? This was what he'd done all his life. All Toby seemed able to think about was her own misery, her own grief at his leaving, but Graydon was going to marry someone he didn't love.

With her face full of what she was thinking, she looked up at him, and he brought his lips down to kiss her.

It was a kiss she knew she'd remember all her life. What they were feeling, all the longing, the desire, the need of each other was in that kiss. But the pain of the coming separation was also in the kiss.

Tears mingled with happy thoughts as their lips held. Graydon put his hand on the back of her head and turned her so he had a deeper access to her mouth. His tongue touched hers, locking together, exploring.

Her body moved closer to his and she could feel his desire for her through the thin fabric of her gown. Her bare shoulder felt the heat of his body. His thighs, hard from his training, pressed against hers.

It was as though the room around them began to spin. They were standing still, but everything around them was moving. Around and around, faster and faster. The lovely scents intensified, the music became louder and quicker, but all Toby cared about was the man who was kissing her. She never, never wanted to break apart!

"Garrett!" came a low voice that sounded like Rory's. "Crack it down! The admiral is coming."

"Tabitha!" came a loud voice that Toby would know anywhere. It was her mother. But that made no sense, as this summer they were on a cruise and not in Nantucket.

It was Graydon who pulled his lips away and tucked Toby's face against his chest. She stood there, her eyes closed, his strong arms around her, she didn't want to see what was going on. Obviously, their private dinner had been invaded by others. Her heart was pounding, her breath shallow. Even her stomach felt odd.

Graydon loosened his hold on her. "I think you should look at this."

Toby did not want to open her eyes. Didn't want to see who was intruding on their dinner. Their farewell meal.

Graydon put his hand under her chin to lift her face to his. "Trust me," he whispered, then pulled back so she could see around her.

Glaring at the two of them was her mother. Toby was still stunned from Graydon's kiss, her mind and heart filled with the sadness that was to come, so it took her a moment to register that the frowning woman was in a simple dress of dark green, a ribbon at its high waist.

Toby took a step back from Graydon and looked around her. They were back in the past! People were in a circle around them, some faces she knew, some she didn't. There was Rory with his gold earring, standing by a tall, pretty woman whom Toby had only seen in photos. She was Danna. Parthenia and John Kendricks were there, and the beautiful Valentina was standing by Captain Caleb.

"We did it," Toby whispered. All she could think was that

they had another chance to save Tabby and Garrett. Stepping away from Graydon, she nearly ran to her mother and flung her arms around her. "I'm so very, very glad to see you!"

Lavinia Weber gave her daughter a cursory hug, then pushed her away, her face stern. "A woman in your condition needs to control herself."

"My condition?" Toby said as she put her hand on her stomach. It wasn't big but what curved out was very hard. It seemed that she was going to have a baby. She looked up in wonder at Graydon.

Smiling, his eyes warm, he took her hand in his. "Let's go home." He lowered his voice. "I have a piece of Japanese art I want to show you."

"I love skin art!" she said as she tried to keep up with his pace. They were in Kingsley House and it looked like they were again at a wedding. Since there was a ring on her finger and life growing inside her, it was a few months after the first wedding they'd attended—their wedding.

When Graydon flung open the front door, a blast of cold, wet Nantucket autumn hit them. He paused for only seconds as he removed his jacket and put it around her. He took her hand in his and they hurried down the lane.

When he opened the door to BEYOND TIME, they were greeted by the sight of a teenage girl trying to control five rambunctious young children. One boy, about seven, seemed to be determined to pull the logs out of the fireplace.

"Out!" Graydon bellowed in a tone Toby had never heard him use before. "Take the children and go to the party. Feed them."

"Captain Caleb said we are to stay here," the girl said, her face almost frightened.

"My brother does not own this house. Now go!" He squinted at the boy at the fireplace. "I take it you are Young Thomas. Leave that fire alone."

When the child looked up at Graydon/Garrett he seemed to be measuring how much he could get away with. He must have made a decision because he dropped the log and gave Garrett a defiant look. "Didn't want it anyway."

The children ran to the open front door, the two little girls taking the older girl's hands. "Thank you," she said to Garrett.

"Come on, Deborah!" Young Thomas yelled. "Let us go before the captain comes and paddles his little brother." He gave Garrett a look of daring, then, laughing, ran down the lane toward Kingsley House.

Graydon shut the front door. "Looks like I've been demoted to 'little brother.' If this is what my own younger brother has had to endure from me, I must apologize to him." When he looked back at Toby, his eyes changed from a man who was bellowing out orders to very warm to hot.

"Sir!" Toby said, her hand by her throat. "How dare you look at me like that! It's as though you're undressing me with your eyes." She fanned herself with her hand. "I do believe the heat of your gaze is making me feel faint. I find I must retire to my bedchamber." Demurely, she lifted her long skirt just inches, then started up the stairs. When she got a quarter of the way up, she turned and looked back at Graydon, who was still standing below.

"Oh, my," Toby said, "I do believe my undergarment is falling." Slowly, she began to pull her long, thin, nearly transparent skirt up until she revealed one slim, shapely leg encased in a white silk stocking that reached only to mid-thigh. It was tied with a very pretty blue garter.

As though she had all the time in the world, she retied the garter, then looked up at him with a small smile. "All done."

Graydon hadn't left the floor and the only sign he gave that he'd watched her were eyes so hot they looked to be on fire.

One second he was standing and the next he was running up the stairs. As he passed Toby, as a seeming afterthought, he wrapped his arm around her waist and kept going. "Oooooh" was all Toby could say as she held on to him as he carried her up the stairs and into the bedroom. Inside the room a fire was going, and even though this time there were no rose petals on the bed, she knew it was their room. All the decorations were things that she loved. From the upholstery to the pictures on the wall, to the little box on the pretty bedside table, it was all her taste. In the corner by the fireplace was a tall pair of boots that she knew belonged to Graydon. A heavy wool coat was slung across the back of a big wing chair.

Toby opened her mouth to say "I am home," but in one movement Graydon put her down and covered her mouth with his. The first time they'd been together she'd had to coax him to not be so gentle. But not this time.

He didn't bother with words or undressing. He slammed her against the bedroom wall and lifted her skirt. That's when he found out that, this time, she'd gone pure Regency. She wore nothing under her petticoat, just lots of warm skin.

Graydon unfastened his trousers with one hand and in seconds he set her down on him. Toby gasped at the sensation and clung to him, her legs easily going around his waist.

His thrusts were hard and fast and Toby felt them all through her body. Inside her, a growing urgency was released, building and building. Her head went back and Graydon buried his face in the soft skin of her neck. She could feel his whiskers, that very male mixture of rough and soft.

Faster, harder he moved and Toby went with him. She braced against the wall as her thighs tightened around his waist.

When she felt his body stiffen between her legs, she knew a release was coming within herself. She arched against him, her hips moving forward, just as his did.

They came together in a white-hot blaze of passion, his lips on hers. For a moment she didn't seem fully alive. It was as though part of her had escaped her body. Her eyes were closed and she thought that when she opened them, she would be back in her bedroom in Nantucket and this would all be a dream.

"Graydon!" she whispered, panic in her voice.

"I'm here, my love," he said, then carried her to the bed and stretched out beside her. He pulled her head onto his shoulder, his hand buried in her hair. His other hand went to her stomach, feeling the new contour through her dress. "Ours," he said.

She put her hand over his. "Yes, I'm sure of it. Oh, how I wish—"

His kiss didn't let her finish the sentence, but then he knew what she was going to say, that she wished they could stay where they were, that they could be married and raise their children together.

She snuggled against him and began kissing his neck.

"We have to return," he said softly.

"I know." Toby put her hands on the sides of his face. "Like last time, when we fall asleep, we'll leave here."

"No, I mean, we have to return to the wedding. There's a reason we came back here and I mean to find out what it is. If Garrett hired Dr. Hancock to attend his wife's lying in, there must have been a previous connection between them."

When she looked into his eyes, she saw deep anger there. "What are you going to do?"

"Take a sword to the man, cut him into pieces, and throw them into the sea to the sharks." His anger was so strong that he couldn't be still. He rolled off the bed and stood looking at the fireplace, his back to her.

"Graydon," Toby said as she lifted herself to her elbows, "you can't do that! Garrett will be the one punished for it."

He tossed a log onto the fire. "I know, but it's what I want to do." Looking back at her, he began to search his pockets. "I don't know—" He broke off with a smile as he pulled a piece of paper from his pocket.

"You brought something with you?"

"I thought—hoped—that re-creating our last time here would bring us back so, as an experiment, I filled my pockets."

"So you didn't do all that for me but for Tabitha?"

Graydon chuckled. "Yes. Did you not know how much in love with her I am? I especially like her little stripteases."

"Do you? But then, I hear she's deeply and passionately in love with Garrett, so they're even." She put a pillow behind her head and smiled at him invitingly.

Graydon looked as though he wanted to join her on the bed, but then he looked at the little desk in the corner of the room. "I put twenty-first-century coins in my pockets, a modern medical journal, some small tools, plus a timeline of history since 1806."

Her curiosity aroused, Toby sat up. "Is any of it there?"

"None of it," Graydon said, "except for a photocopy of Parthenia's letter to her mother."

"Oh!" Toby flopped back on the bed. "The infamous Dr. Hancock. Please tell me you aren't really planning to kill him, are you? Even in secret?"

"I thought of that, but no, I fear that Garrett will only hire another doctor. I need to do what I can to make sure no doctor gets near Tabby."

"How will you do that?"

Graydon picked up a quill pen. "I'm going to copy this letter and circulate it. I plan to say that it was written about someone I know in Boston. His wife was butchered by Dr. Hancock. Since Captain Caleb seems to rule the Kingsley family, I'll get him to swear that no doctor will touch my wife."

She got off the bed. "To make the letter believable, you'll have to remove the references to the island. Shall I help you?"

"Yes, please do."

When she went to the desk to stand beside him, he put his

arms around her waist and pulled her to him, his head against her growing belly.

"I love you," he whispered. "Here and now in this place and time of great freedom, I can bare my soul to you. Toby, I love you." When he looked up at her, his dark eyes were glistening with what looked to be tears.

She took his head in her hands and kissed his forehead. "I love you now, I love you then, and I will love you for all time."

For a moment he buried his face against her stomach, then abruptly he turned away and wiped his eyes. Without looking at her, he handed her the paper he'd brought.

Toby's hand shook as she took it. She'd only read it once before and she didn't relish doing it again. She took a breath. "Start it with 'My dear Garrett,'" she said, then reluctantly read the horrible letter again.

Garrett was so worried about his beloved Tabby that he hired a Dr. Hancock to come from Boston. He feared that the local midwife—of twenty years' experience— would not know what to do if aught went wrong. While Tabby's labor went on for hours, the doctor said he could not wait all night just for a baby to get born. He used forceps on her before her body was ready. Of course etiquette declared that he could not look at what he was doing so he used the steel monster blindly. He caught part of Tabby's womb with them, and when the baby was born, he pulled her insides out with it. He must have used too much strength as the baby died instantly, its little head crushed. While Tabby was screaming from pain, the doctor bled her profusely to make her calm down. As the odious man hurried off to catch the last ferry, he said that death was in the hands of God and that he'd certainly done all he could to save both of them. As Tabby faded away, we told her the baby was happily sleeping. She died with her silent infant in her arms, never knowing the truth.

No one has the heart to tell Garrett that the doctor killed his wife and son. With his temper he'd go after the man. I can tell you that no woman on this island cares what happens to the doctor, but we do not want to see Garrett hanged.

Chapter Twenty-four

$\mathcal{T}$oby wanted to go with Graydon when he went out to spread the word, but she was attacked with such a severe case of pregnancy sleepiness that she was swaying on her feet.

Seeing it, he smiled. "You and our baby need to sleep," he said as he led her to the bed.

"But I want to help." Toby could hardly keep her eyes open. "And what if I wake up at home and you're still here and—"

Graydon kissed her to silence. "Ssssh. I'm sure I'll be there soon afterward." He helped her to lie down on the bed. "Just rest."

Her eyes closed even though she tried to keep them open, but she held on to his hand. "What are you going to do?" she asked.

"First, I'm going to find the local potter."

Her eyes fluttered in alarm. "Promise me that you'll protect Garrett."

"I will," he whispered, then kissed her again and held her hand as long as he could as he went toward the door.

Toby heard the door close but she didn't look up. As her body was settling into sleep, images ran through her mind. Victoria in her green silk suit at Alix's wedding, Valentina in her low-cut dress at Parthenia's wedding. Dr. Huntley's face floated through her mind. What was it he said?

Toby didn't open her eyes but her mind became a bit more alert as she began to remember. "Both Valentina and Parthenia were there with her." That's what Caleb said.

Her eyes fluttered. "Tell the women." The words were in her head in . . . in Jilly's voice. "Tell the women." Graydon had said he was going to tell the head of the family, Caleb, but he was a man. And who knows what men would do? When Tabby went into labor he might be on a long fishing trip and return after it was all over.

As Toby pulled herself up to a sitting position, she kept trying to come out of her sleepiness. She put her hands on her hard, round belly. "I know you are very young but, kid, if you want to be born, you need to wake us up."

It took a few minutes, but Toby was finally able to open her eyes. She took a few deep breaths and began to feel herself becoming more alert. When she swung her legs off the bed she gasped because the baby kicked her.

For a moment she sat on the side of the bed, her hands on her stomach and smiling. "You're like your father, aren't you? You're ready to do battle to help people. All right, my dear child, let's go find the women."

She made it down the stairs to the empty ground floor and out the front door. Lightning was flashing in the sky but there was no rain yet. She hurried over to Kingsley House where the wedding was still going strong. She had yet to find out whose it was.

The first person she saw was Valentina sitting in a corner with Captain Caleb. Their heads were close together and they were whispering like lovers. Toby wished she knew more about their history so she could tell them about their futures. Didn't the captain go down on a ship? But that was when Garrett was with him. If Garrett didn't go, maybe the captain wouldn't either.

The baby kicked again, seeming to remind Toby to stay on the issue. Valentina wasn't the one to tell. She was too absorbed in the captain to pay attention to anything else.

Jilly—Parthenia—was sitting on a window seat cushion by herself, a cup of punch in her hand, and watching the dancers. "Tabby," she said, smiling. "I thought you went to bed."

"I did," Toby said, her mind racing to think of how to present the problem without talking about time travel, reincarnation, or other taboo subjects. "I had a very bad dream. A nightmare that was so very real." Toby then proceeded to tell everything she knew about that night in the birthing room. She told of the doctor being in such a hurry to get away to catch the last ferry, that he used the "steel monster."

Since everything had actually happened to poor Tabitha Weber Kingsley, Toby wasn't far into the story before she began to cry. Parthenia put her arm around Toby and gave her a handkerchief, but she didn't interrupt.

A few people came over to ask what was wrong, but Parthenia waved them away. When Toby finished her story, Parthenia led her out of the room, past the dancers, through the little service porch at the side of the house, then out into the cool, dark night. "No doctor will touch you," Parthenia said. "I swear it." She was leading Toby out toward the lane. "Now I want you to rest. It's not good for your baby to be so frightened. If you are scared, so is he."

"Or she," Toby said. Her legs were weak, as the emotion of the story had taken the energy out of her.

"No, it's a boy. I know these things."

Toby looked at her and nodded her head. Dr. Huntley had said as much about Jilly.

"I do not usually tell people what I see and feel, but I think you and I are kindred souls. And I believe your dream may have been real. I have worried about you since you married Garrett. I think that what you told me tonight was what I was seeing. You may trust me that no doctor will attend you. Valentina and I will make sure of that."

"Thank you," Toby said, and with the assurance, the overwhelming sleepiness began to return and she leaned heavily on Parthenia.

It was when they reached the lane that they heard the pounding of horse hooves on the cobblestones. The women halted and looked in the direction of the sound.

"Something is amiss," Parthenia said.

The horse came closer to them but didn't seem to be in danger of slowing down. When it was almost upon them, a flash of lightning cut through the night. Before them was a horse as black as the air around them. On top of it was Graydon, his snowy cravat clearly visible above his dark jacket. But above that was nothing. Where his head should have been was empty.

But in the crook of his left arm was Graydon's head, with its lifeless face, eyes closed, hair tied neatly back.

Toby looked up at the apparition on the horse, holding the head of the man she loved, turned to Parthenia, gave a little smile—then fainted.

Chapter Twenty-five

When Toby awoke, she didn't at first know where she was. There was such a deep silence around her that she felt as though she'd awakened in a vacuum. It took a moment for her eyes to clear and for her to realize that she was in her bed in Nantucket. Her cell phone was beside her bed, her iPad on the dresser, her laptop on her desk. Twenty-first century.

The room was dimly lit but she could see sunlight under the shades. Turning her head, she saw that there was no indentation in the pillow. Graydon hadn't slept beside her.

She put her hands on her stomach. Flat and empty. Instantly, tears came to her eyes. No baby, no husband, silent house.

"You're awake," Jilly said from the doorway, a tray of breakfast in her hands.

Toby pulled herself up and quickly brushed away the tears. "They're gone, aren't they?"

"Yes," Jilly said.

"Graydon was with them? He is well? Healthy?"

Jilly put the tray down. "Very healthy—if a man as truly miserable as he is can be called that. Why would you ask such a question?"

"I just wanted to know if he had his head on straight." She tried to smile at her joke, but couldn't.

Jilly took a big envelope from the tray. "Graydon asked me to give this to you."

When Toby opened it, out fell another envelope and a small book. As Jilly quietly left the room, Toby opened the smaller envelope.

My Dearest,

I could not bear to wake you, but my father called for his sons to appear together. I am his loyal subject and must return.

Please do not forget me. With all my love forever,

GM

Toby dropped the letter onto the coverlet. At the moment she didn't know how she felt about anything. It was all too soon and too raw for her to feel.

She picked up the little book and looked at it. It was old and raggedy, the cover torn and faded. *Forbidden Nantucket* was the title. "The stories the people of Nantucket don't want told," it read below the title.

She opened it to a marker and saw a drawing of a man in Regency dress atop a large, dark horse. The horse was rearing up on its back legs and in front of it was a middle-aged man holding a doctor's bag, his hand to his mouth as he suppressed a scream. He was terrified because the man on the horse had no head on his shoulders. The gruesome-looking head was tucked into the crook of his left arm and grinning maniacally.

The story with the gory picture was short. It said that in the early 1800s a local man had dressed up as a headless horseman and chased a Dr. Hancock, who was so frightened that he ran to the wharf and spent the night hiding inside a half-empty barrel of rum. In the morning he boarded the first ferry off the island and he never returned to Nantucket. The question the author asked was why was the good doctor chosen to be terrorized? He was merely visiting on that cold autumn night, a guest at a wedding, and had never before been to Nantucket. But it was said that the horseman chased him, and no one else, halfway around the island.

The book concluded by saying that when the author interviewed Nantucketers—this in 1963—no one wanted to tell him of the story. Most people said it had never happened. "Considering that Nantucketers have very, very long memories, this was unusual. Why was this Headless Horseman story hidden? And why was the horseman after the doctor from Boston?" the author asked. "No one would tell me."

Toby wondered if Graydon had stayed up all night trying to find a record of what he'd done that night while she slept. Had he searched the Kingsley House library to find the obscure book? At least now she knew why he'd wanted to visit the local potter. The face of the head had been made out of clay, a wig over the back of it. She knew he hadn't told her of his plan because she would have told him it was too dangerous. What if some local had taken a shot at him? But then, Garrett's family was as much a part of Nantucket as the sea was—and Nantucketers took care of their own.

When she looked at the picture she had to smile. He'd certainly scared the doctor away so he wouldn't ever return to the island.

All in all, it looked like there had been a reason, a purpose, to their getting together. Maybe she and Graydon were meant to go back in time and change what happened to Garrett and Tabitha.

And that was enough! Toby thought. To be able to do something like that was more than most people got to do with their lives.

As she began to eat the lovely breakfast Jilly had so kindly made for her, Toby thought the silence of the house was eerie. No clanging steel, no one laughing, no Lanconian being spoken. When she finished, she put her tray aside, fell back against the pillows, and looked up at the ceiling. She'd known this was coming so she shouldn't feel so bad. And she should not be angry at Graydon. Would it have been better if he'd stayed for a long, drawn-out goodbye? Clinging together, both of them in tears? Would that have been better?

The answer was that nothing on earth would make this hurt any less. She had done a very stupid thing. She had fallen in love with a man she couldn't have, so she deserved what she got!

As she lay there she thought about her choices now. She could go into a deep depression where she moped around for weeks, months even, or she could get on with life. Right now she had two jobs: to put in a garden for Jared's cousin's house and to pull off a huge wedding for Victoria. Between them, there would be plenty to fill her mind so that she didn't have time to think—or to remember.

As for what happened after the jobs were done, someday she'd meet a man, fall in love with him, and—

And what? she wondered. Spend her life comparing him to Graydon? What mortal man could live up to him? Graydon was a scholar, an athlete, an old-world gentleman. He could—

Toby closed her eyes hard. She couldn't allow herself to think like that, for that way lay madness. From the beginning, she'd always known what was going to happen. On the first day she'd met him, Graydon had told her about his coming engagement to the highborn Danna. He'd even described the ceremony in detail.

He'd always been honest with her.

She threw back the covers and stood up, and the saying "This is the first day of the rest of your life" came to her mind. Yes, this was a new beginning.

She put on a robe and her resolve lasted all the way down to the kitchen. Jilly was sitting at the table in the sunroom, reading a Cale Anderson novel, and didn't look up.

Toby's first thought was that Graydon had cleared that room out. From those windows she had watched him working out. That was the table where she and Graydon, Lorcan, and Daire had eaten many meals. She could almost taste the Lanconian cheeses, the griddle cakes. She could see Graydon and Daire drinking their beers and talking in the deep Lanconian language that had become so familiar to her.

I won't survive, she thought. Living alone in this house, which was filled with so many memories, was too much for her.

She went to Jilly, who looked up at her in question. "I can't do this," Toby whispered. "I can't—"

She broke off because Victoria—beautiful as always—came in through the door from the garden, and behind her was a tall, gray-haired woman Toby had never met before.

"Darling," Victoria said as she put her hands on Toby's shoulders and kissed her on both cheeks. "We thought you were going to sleep forever. Poor Graydon had to leave. We said we'd wake you but he wouldn't let us. He said you'd been through enough and that you needed your rest. Tell me, did you have another of your dreams?"

Toby thought Victoria looked ready to get out her pen and paper to record the whole episode. Pointedly, Toby looked behind her at the other woman.

Victoria stepped back. "This is a friend of mine, Millie Lawson, and she came to the island for a holiday, but she's going to help you with my wedding and that garden for Jared."

"Please forgive my friend," Millie said before Toby could speak. "All this is being piled on you rather quickly. I take it you had a recent breakup with your boyfriend?"

Toby thought it was a great deal more than that, but wasn't going to say so to this stranger. "Are you enjoying Nantucket?"

"Toby, dear," Victoria said, "I have also persuaded Millie to move in with you."

"What?" was all Toby could say, her face showing her shock.

Jilly stepped between Victoria and Toby. "Millie is a retired event organizer and she's worked for some big corporations, museums, even some embassies. She'd planned to stay on Nantucket until after Victoria's wedding, but . . ." Jilly trailed off.

"I find retirement to be deadeningly boring," Millie said, "and I've seen all the beaches and glorious sunsets I can abide. When Victoria said that her wedding planner might need help, I asked if I could volunteer my services. As for staying in your house, I'm sure you wouldn't want a stranger moving in with you."

Toby opened her mouth to agree that that wouldn't work when a movement in the garden caught her eye. Instantly, her heart leaped into her throat. It was Graydon, with Lorcan and Daire! But no, it was Jose Partida and his landscaping crew coming to work.

Toby's heart seemed to plummet to her feet and she knew that if she were alone she just might run upstairs and get back into bed—and maybe never get out again. She looked back at the woman. Her accent had a faint English tone to it and she certainly looked capable. "Yes," Toby said, "please help me with the wedding, and I have an empty"—the word almost made her choke—"bedroom upstairs. It will be easier to work if we are together."

"How wonderful!" Victoria said, then threw open the door and called out, "Jose, you darling man, I need help with some luggage."

When the two women went out the front door, Jilly put her arm around Toby's shoulders. "I know it doesn't seem so now, but you will survive this. Eventually, time will smooth things out."

Toby had heard that Jilly's first husband, the father of her two children, had been a horrible man. Jilly was a survivor of a great deal more than just a broken heart.

For a moment Toby hugged her, but then she pulled away. "Sometimes Victoria is heavy-handed and—"

"Imperious," Jilly said. "She's quite pushy, really."

"Yes. Very. But in this case I think it would be better for me not to live alone."

"So do I," Jilly said.

The sound of luggage being carried upstairs and Victoria giving the men orders took over. Within minutes, for the second time that summer, Toby had a stranger living in her house.

As Victoria left, she handed Toby a foot-tall stack of what looked to be letters. "Snail mail?" Toby asked as she took them.

"What can I say? I've invited writers, and that's what they do. See what they want and answer them. Have you decided on prizes for the best costumes yet?"

"Autographed copies of your books?" Toby suggested.

Victoria laughed. "How droll. You'd better have something engraved so their publicists can list it on Wikipedia. Let me know what you need, but I'll be in isolation while I write, so I may be difficult to reach." She lowered her voice. "Millie really is very good at her job, so trust her. And talk to her."

"How long have you known each other?"

Victoria waved her hand. "Isn't that a bit like asking a girl her age? Anyway, dearest, good luck." She left the house.

Jose came down the stairs. "That woman has a lot of luggage. You want us to clean up the greenhouse?"

"No," Toby said and thought how that had become Graydon's job. "I'll do it."

"You need to get outside," Jose said. "It's not good for you to stay in here so much." She knew he was right and she followed him into the garden.

Chapter Twenty-six

$\mathcal{T}$oby would have liked to spend some time getting to know Millie, but on the other hand, if she sat and talked, she might end up crying, then she'd—

She didn't want to think about what she'd do if she didn't have masses of work to keep her busy. As Toby went down the stairs on the first morning after Millie moved in, she smelled pancakes. They reminded her of Graydon's Lanconian griddle cakes and for a moment she almost ran back upstairs. But she took a few deep breaths, forced her mind to calm down, and went into the kitchen.

"I hope you don't mind that I made breakfast," Millie said.

"No, it was very kind of you, but you certainly don't have to wait on me."

"I enjoy cooking, but I no longer have anyone to cook for."

"Do you have a family?" Toby asked.

"Grown children who have no more need of me. What shall we tackle first today? Garden or wedding?"

"I think I'd better show you what's been done so far on both things. Lorcan was handling a lot of the details and I'm not sure where she left off."

"Lorcan? That's an unusual name. Who is she?"

"She's . . ." Toby's head filled with so much information that she couldn't speak of any of it.

"I apologize," Millie said. "I didn't mean to bring up bad memories. I take it Lorcan had something to do with the cad who walked out on you?"

Toby drew in her breath as anger ran through her. "No!" she managed to say. "Graydon did not 'walk out.' He is a loyal, honorable man who puts others before himself. He—" Breaking off, she sat down heavily on a chair at the breakfast table. "He did what he had to do," she whispered.

Millie sat down beside her and took Toby's hand in hers. "I'm very, very sorry for what I said. I don't know any of the facts. Victoria was rather vocal about how the man broke your heart. I think she'd like to boil him in oil, but I'm sure there's another side to all of it."

Toby looked up. The woman's face was very sympathetic. She was older, but she had utterly perfect skin, and Toby realized that at one time Millie had almost certainly been a beauty. Right now she looked as though she might cry in sympathy. "It wasn't like that. Victoria has it wrong. But still, I need time to heal from this and I don't want to talk about it. I'd just like to work and try to put the past behind me."

With a smile, Millie squeezed her hand. "I understand, but I also want you to know that I'm here if you do want to talk. I know some about men and tears."

"Thank you," Toby said, and realized that she did feel better. "How about if I show you the garden Jared wants me to put in?"

"And Jared is . . . ?"

"My landlord and friend," Toby said as Millie handed her a plate of pancakes. "What do you know about gardening?"

"That roses and lilies look good together."

"That's enough," Toby said and began to eat.

It didn't take long for Toby to realize that Millie had been modest about her knowledge of gardening and everything else. The woman was a powerhouse of information and efficiency.

After only a quick look at Jared's garden Millie said, "Keep it simple. Classic. Easy to maintain."

"My thoughts exactly," Toby said, and they began discussing what plants to put where, seating areas, and even a small gazebo at the back. By the time they'd walked back to Kingsley Lane, they were ready to make sketches using the measurements Toby and Lorcan had taken.

Jared had set up a complete design studio in Kingsley House, and with his permission, the two women began using his antique drafting table to draw the plans for the garden. And Millie set up a chart to keep track of what had been done and needed to be done for Victoria's wedding. By the third day, the two women were moving forward quickly.

Originally, the idea of the famous authors coming in costume had seemed to be an excellent one, but besides the letters, Toby had never received so many emails and text messages in her life. Some of them were so long they were almost scenes from a novel—and all the authors expected Toby to be an expert on Regency everything.

Victoria said, "Tell them you're not a copy editor and they can verify their own research." But the truth was that Toby could easily answer all their questions. After all, she had been there.

"How do you know so much about this time period?" Millie asked as they went over the flowers ordered for the wedding.

"I—" Toby began but stopped. What could she say? That she'd traveled through time? "I've read a lot of Regency novels," she said and looked back at the order forms.

During the weeks leading up to the wedding, Toby talked to Lexie a couple of times a week but things had changed between them. Toby got the idea that Lexie was concealing as much of the truth as she was.

"I'm fine," Toby told her friend. "Graydon has an entire country to run. He couldn't very well give that up just to stay with a commoner."

"Don't you read the news?" Lexie said angrily. "There's Prince William. And the future Queen of Sweden married her personal trainer."

"Oh, yes," Toby said. "That's in Lanconia's constitution. Physical trainers are okay but florists are out."

"Am I supposed to find that funny?" Lexie asked.

"So how are you and Roger getting along?"

"We're fine," Lexie replied, echoing what Toby had said. "I'm more concerned about you."

And that's how all their conversations went. Toby asked about Lexie; Lexie asked about Toby. But neither one told a lot of information.

As much as Toby tried to immerse herself in work, there were still times when she nearly lost it. A week after they left, Lorcan sent Toby a large package of cheeses and sausages, and some handmade lace. She'd had to use diplomatic channels to get the food through customs, but it had arrived safely.

Inside was a brief note from Lorcan.

We miss you every day and HE is very, very unhappy.

Lorcan

"Good!" Toby said, letting anger take over so she wouldn't give way to tears.

She shared the food with Millie, Ken, and Jilly. Millie bought wine and Jilly made a raspberry pie. The evening was good, and it was only when Jilly spoke of Lanconia that Toby put her hand up. She refused to listen to a word about the country.

But Ken said it anyway. "The engagement ceremony was postponed." He glanced at Millie, who kept her head down and didn't interfere or pry into the conversation.

Toby nodded. "That's because Rory still has his cast on. They can't let the wrong prince get engaged. It has to be Graydon who pledges himself to her."

"The official excuse was—"

Again Toby put her hand up, but this time Ken said nothing.

Besides refusing to read/hear/listen to anything about Lanconia, Toby made no effort to find out about Tabitha and Garrett. The last time she and Graydon had asked Dr. Huntley, Toby had spent days crying over what they were told. If their last visit hadn't saved those two, with Graydon gone, there would be no further chances to change what had happened. And this time there would be no one to hold her when she cried.

No, Toby told herself. It was better to stick to the present and the future. The past—and that included all things Lanconian—must stay where it was.

By the time the wedding day was close, Millie and Toby had become great coworkers. They were such an efficient team that they could act without words.

Millie was the one who designed the awards to be given for the best costumes—and they'd come up with so many categories that there would be few participants who didn't receive a Lucite plaque. Best hair, best headdress, best white gown, best shoes, et cetera. There was one for everything that she and Millie had come up with over a pitcher of margaritas. It had been a fun night.

The only bad moment had been when Toby said she wished she had some of the yellow cheese that Graydon didn't like.

"Who is this man Graydon I keep hearing of?" Millie asked as she refilled Toby's glass.

Toby was a bit tipsy but certainly not drunk. "A true prince of a man," she said as she raised her glass and took a sip.

"Is he the love of your life?"

"Absolutely not!" Toby said. "After Victoria's wedding I'm going to meet a man who will sweep me off my feet. He's going to be intelligent and educated and will make love to me all day long. No more virginity for me!" Toby drained her glass.

"You're a . . . ?" Millie asked, wide-eyed.

"Yes and no," Toby said as she put down her glass. "Tabitha had a great time but Toby got nothing. Honorable men are good on paper but in real life they're a pain in the neck."

"You have to tell me this story," Millie said.

"No," Toby answered. "Not now. Not ever. I'm going to bed. See you in the morning." She went up the stairs and fell into bed.

By the day before the wedding, both Toby and Millie were exhausted—but everything was in place. Victoria's dress—the white one, so Lorcan had won the bet—had arrived earlier that week from Martha Pullen and it was truly breathtaking. It was quite simple, low cut, high waisted, with three-quarter sleeves and a bit of a train that flowed behind the skirt. What made the dress extraordinary was the fineness of the Swiss cotton Martha and her ladies had used and their intricate white embroidery along the skirt and on the sleeves. Victoria, Millie, and Toby had gathered around it to admire the exquisite sewing, the precision and beauty of every stitch.

Millie knew some people in the costume department at the

Metropolitan Opera in New York and her dress had arrived packed in tissue paper. The gown was of pale peach satin covered with fine netting that was embellished with embroidery done in silver thread. Over the years, the thread had tarnished to a soft glow that enhanced the beauty of the dress. It was such a good reproduction that it looked like it had been hand sewn.

As for Jilly and Alix and their men, Dr. Huntley knew where clothing from the era was hidden away in boxes in the attic of Kingsley House. Ken dug them out, and he and Jared never stopped complaining about what they had to wear to the wedding.

Toby hung her own dress on her closet door and the sight of it brought back so many memories she could hardly stand up. She sat down on the side of the bed and stared at it, her mind flooding with images of her and Graydon together.

"Are you all right?" Millie asked from the open doorway. "Oh, my! Is that your gown? It is truly exquisite. Are you sure it fits?"

"I know it does," Toby said.

"Perhaps you should try it on to see."

Toby stood up. "I know it fits!" she said, her voice almost angry. "I've worn the dress often, even had it removed from my body. I've danced in it and laughed. I got married in it!" She put her hands over her face.

"I think I should leave you alone," Millie said softly.

"No, please," Toby said. "Don't go. Isn't there some work that needs doing?"

"We could check the chapel to see if the candles have been placed correctly."

"Good!" Toby said. "And we can light a few to make sure they don't drip. I don't want to have to scrape all that wax off again like I did the last time. If it hadn't been for Graydon—"

She took a breath.

Millie put her arm through Toby's. "It takes time, dear, but you will forget him."

"It seems that in the last few days my memories of him are even more intense. It almost feels as though he's calling me to him."

"Then perhaps you should go to him."

"Not possible," Toby said as she went down the stairs ahead of Millie and got her car keys.

It was the day before Victoria's wedding that Toby came apart. She awoke early and went downstairs to the kitchen. As she made herself a pot of strong, dark tea, she heard the TV on in the downstairs sitting room. Millie must be up already. She took her drink and went into the room.

Millie was on the couch watching a live CNN broadcast from Lanconia. She glanced up at Toby. "I keep hearing mention of this country and I saw that this was on. Do you know what it is?"

Toby's throat seemed to swell up as she looked at the television screen. There was a large room with a red rug, gold lighting fixtures, and what looked like blue silk brocade on the walls. In front were over a dozen tiny chairs with people in suits, the women with hats on, all of them with either pen and paper or a camera. At the back were TV cameras. "It's . . . I assume it's the engagement ceremony," Toby said.

Her common sense told her she should leave the room and not watch what was about to happen. But she couldn't make herself leave.

When Millie patted the seat beside her, Toby walked around the couch and sat down, her tea mug clutched in her hand.

The CNN broadcaster said that Prince Graydon of Lanconia was about to enter the palace room with Lady Danna Hexonbath, and he was going to make the announcement of their formal engagement.

"Graydon?" Millie said, looking at Toby. "This isn't your Graydon, is it?"

When Toby didn't answer, Millie took the mug from her and put it on the coffee table. Toby's heart was pounding, and like someone hypnotized, she stared at the screen.

After several long moments, out came the prince, as tall and handsome as she remembered. On his arm was Lady Danna, and she was as beautiful as Toby had always feared.

"They look very happy together," Millie said, sadness in her voice.

"Rory has always loved Danna," Toby whispered.

"Rory? Who is that?"

Toby came out of her trance and she stood up abruptly. "That is Rory, not Graydon."

She stepped away from the couch, her hands to the side of her head. "No no no no! He cannot do this to me."

"Do what? I don't understand."

"Graydon! He's going to make me have to be the villain."

"I'm sorry," Millie said, "but I don't understand what you're saying."

Toby pointed at the TV. "That is not Prince Graydon. That is his brother, Rory. Graydon is going to come here and say he's going to give up his throne for me!"

"Oh," Millie said. "Are you sure of that? That seems rather drastic. But if he does do that, what are you going to say to him?"

"That he can't do it, that's what," Toby said. She tried to calm down. "Maybe I'm wrong. Please watch that and see if they show someone they think is Prince Rory. If he's not there, then he's probably on his way here. I'm going upstairs to get dressed, then I'm going to the site."

She muttered, "Damn you, Graydon!" all the way up the stairs.

Chapter Twenty-seven

By the day of the wedding, Toby was telling herself that she'd been wrong about everything. The day before, she'd jumped at every sound, expecting Graydon to step out from behind every door.

But as the day wore on and he didn't appear, she began to settle down. She and Millie had wine with dinner and Toby went to bed early.

Today was the wedding, it was just six A.M., and she was already at the site. She wanted as much time as she could get to make sure everything went smoothly. Yesterday had been crazy, with many people arriving at the airport and expecting to be driven to their hotels. Toby had enlisted every cousin Jared had to drive people wherever they wanted to go.

As soon as Toby parked behind the chapel, she lifted the back door of her car so the waitstaff could get to the supplies she'd brought. Millie had a friend who was a calligrapher so the seating cards been hand lettered. In fact, Millie had added a lot of touches to the wedding that Toby had never thought of. They'd run everything past Victoria for approval, but she'd just waved her hand and agreed.

Victoria was so involved in the novel she was writing that she paid little attention to her own wedding. Toby had been concerned that Dr. Huntley would be hurt by her neglect but he was very protective. "She is writing Valentina's story and she feels it," he said. "Inside her, she knows the story. When she has it on paper, she will return to us."

This morning Toby saw an email that Victoria had sent late last night. The book was finished and she said she was going to sleep for about twelve hours. "My soul is at last freed," she wrote.

As Toby looked around the grounds, she searched for what still needed to be done. The tent was up, furniture stacked inside, and the chapel was packed with little chairs. "Opera chairs," Millie called them. "They're what they put in the boxes at the opera: hard, tiny, supremely uncomfortable. They don't want their patrons falling asleep."

Toby had smiled at the name. After this was over, she wanted to sit with Millie and ask about her life. But so far, she'd not had a chance to do that.

Some lights were hanging down from a tree and a ladder was leaning against the trunk. Toby was concerned that when the crews arrived, someone might walk into the wire. She pulled the ladder out, opened it, and climbed up to the top to fasten the strand of lights as high as she could reach.

"I knew I'd find you here," said a voice she thought she might never hear again.

Many emotions went through Toby at once: happiness, anger, longing, love. She tried to remain calm but when she took a step down, she missed the ladder and fell backward.

Graydon caught her in his arms.

All thoughts of being sensible left her as she looked into his dark eyes. As Lexie had once said, Graydon's eyes were smoldering.

Her arms went around his neck and her lips on his, their tongues meeting.

"I couldn't bear my life without you," Graydon said as he kissed her face, his arms holding her off the ground, so tight around her she could hardly breathe. "I missed you every moment."

Toby was kissing him back. She'd never thought to see him face-to-face again, certainly never to touch him. He was so warm, so familiar, so much a part of her.

She felt that he was walking but her mind was too full of his caresses, the pure joy of being near him again that she wasn't sure what was happening.

It was when he put her feet to the ground but never stopped kissing her that she began to come to her senses. He had moved them back into the trees, away from the chapel and the tents, and he was unbuttoning her shirt. Graydon was going to make love to her—to Toby, not Tabitha—here and now.

It took a strength she didn't know she had, but she pushed him away to arm's length. Graydon's eyes were like dark pools of desire, and he pulled her back to him.

"No," she whispered.

"You're right. We'll go home," he murmured, his face in her neck.

"Yours or mine?" she asked.

"Yours. I'm going to stay here. With you. Forever." His head was bent toward hers and he seemed to consider what he'd said as something that was already decided.

Again, she pushed away from him. "You can't do that!"

This time Graydon seemed to hear her, but he just smiled. "It will be all right," he said in a soothing voice. "You don't need to worry about anything. I've taken care of all of it."

"Have you?" Toby asked, her hands on his shoulders, arms extended.

"Yes." Graydon smiled sweetly. "Rory and I worked out a plan. Let's go somewhere private and I'll tell you everything."

"Private? Like my bedroom? We make love, then lie in each other's arms and you tell me what you and Rory have planned for my future?"

"Exactly!" Graydon said with a grin. "You and I always have agreed about everything."

Toby stepped away from him. "I want to make sure I fully understand this plan. I made a fool of myself when you were here by trying to get you to go to bed with me. But you refused."

"I had to return to my own country and I didn't want to take your maidenhood."

"But it's okay to do so now?"

Graydon smiled. "The plan includes that you and I get married. Today. I did some research and you and I can walk to the Nantucket courthouse, get a license, go upstairs, and a judge will marry us."

"We wouldn't have to bother with all this?" She waved her hand toward the tents and the chapel that could be seen through the trees.

At her tone, Graydon got his first inkling that Toby wasn't overjoyed with what he was saying. "We can have a huge wedding later," he said quickly. "At the palace."

"Oh? And what will be the name of the person I'll be marrying?"

"We need to talk about all that. I may have to continue being my brother."

Toby took a step toward him and there was anger in her

eyes. "I want to know about Danna. Does she know who she's marrying?"

Graydon stepped back. "Remember how you said I should ask Danna what she wants? That was brilliant! When I asked her, she had some rather strong opinions."

Toby took another step toward him. "What did Danna say?" She wasn't sure but she thought maybe Graydon's face was turning red.

"She, uh . . . It seems that she's always known who was me and who was Rory, and she said she had never really liked *me*. According to her I'm a 'sword stuck in its sheath.' It's a Lanconian saying and it means—"

"I can guess. Did she refuse to marry you?"

"Yes," Graydon said.

"So Danna dumped you and you came running to me. And now you're offering me a two-dollar wedding and a lifetime of living a lie and of hiding. If it's ever found out that you abandoned your kingdom for me, an entire country will hate me. Maybe the world will hate me. There will be books written about how I enticed you, a man who was groomed to be king, away from your destiny."

Graydon's face lost the soft, pleading look. His shoulders went back, his body rigid. He was The Prince. "I didn't understand. You want to be made queen."

"Oh, right. Then just your family will hate me. And if the truth of you and Rory is revealed, Danna's father will pull out of Lanconia and the country will be impoverished. And it will all be my fault." She lowered her voice and when she spoke, everything she felt was in her words. "What I want is for you to be king."

Instantly, Graydon lost his rigid stance and he went from being The Prince to the man she'd come to love. He put his hands in his pockets and leaned back against a tree. "You're right, of course."

When he looked at her, his eyes were so full of misery that Toby almost went to him.

But she didn't. "You shouldn't have come here," she said softly. "I was just beginning to think I could actually live without you." In spite of her good intentions, there were tears gathering in her eyes.

"Have you thought about me in these last weeks?" he asked. "At least some of the time?"

"Thought about you? No, I didn't. I lived and breathed you. I felt you in my heart, inside my soul. The air, the sun, the moon all reminded me of you. My body and my mind craved you, ached for you. I couldn't stand hearing your name or your country's. I couldn't even bear to search out Tabitha or Garrett. Every—" She looked at him.

Reaching out, Graydon pulled her to him, but this time it wasn't with passion. She folded her arms up inside his, her cheek on his chest and she could hear his heart pounding. It was as though she could feel his despair, his sense of helplessness—which exactly matched her own.

"Tabby and Garrett lived long and happy lives," he said softly. "I couldn't bear to search out their history either, but Lorcan and Daire did, with Aunt Jilly's help."

"Your Headless Horseman act saved them."

"No," he said, as he kissed the top of her head. "You did, in spite of me. You begged Valentina and Parthenia to allow no doctor near you. When Dr. Hancock wouldn't come to Nantucket, Garrett hired another one. Your friends locked him in a closet."

"Did they?" Toby asked, smiling against his chest. "And the baby?"

"Big fat boy followed by two more boys and a girl, who Valentina wrote was as beautiful as her mother."

"Did the children grow up to be happy?" she whispered. There were tears on her cheeks.

"Our descendents helped the world. A great-granddaughter campaigned to reform orphanages in New York. In World War II a great-great, et cetera, grandson saved an entire shipload of soldiers. Senators, governors, teachers, physicians, a famous female pilot, they're all there now, thanks to you. To us."

Toby nodded against him. "That was what we were meant to do and we did it."

"Yes," he murmured, his face buried in her hair, and she could feel the dampness from his tears. "In fact, we have a contemporary descendent, a young woman, who is in rather bad circumstances right now. Since she didn't exist until recently, I thought I might introduce her to a cousin of mine, Nicholas. It's said that he was conceived in 1564. They might understand each other."

She knew he was trying to cheer her up. "Graydon, I—"

"Sssssh," he said. "We won't talk of this anymore. Today, we'll be as we were. Tonight we will dance in the moonlight and drink champagne."

"One last time," Toby said.

"Yes," Graydon whispered. "The very last time."

Toby was in the big tent, the seating chart in her hand, and putting the place cards where they belonged. She and Millie had ordered used paperbacks of each author's work, then spent several evenings cutting and pasting pages. They made napkin rings and backs for the seating cards, and wrapped little boxes of chocolates in the author's own words. For the nonwriter guests, they'd used Victoria's books.

It was nearly four and it wouldn't be long before the guests started arriving in costume for the ceremony. Victoria's daughter, Alix, was going to oversee everything in the chapel, but Toby was to go home and dress before the guests showed up.

She dawdled over her tasks, straightening vases of baby roses, making sure the little nests made of shredded book pages contained enough seashells, checking the table that held the many awards to be given out, and talking to the caterers, who were beginning to set up. What she didn't want to do was go home where she wouldn't be surrounded by people.

She hadn't seen Graydon since the early morning. She didn't know where he was staying—or even if he was still on the island. Part of her wanted him to be there with her, but the larger part hoped she'd never again have to say goodbye to him. It hurt too, too much!

When her phone buzzed, she took it out of her pocket and saw a text message from Millie saying she needed to come home and get dressed. I'LL DO YOUR HAIR, she added.

The tears that were so close under the surface threatened to come out, but Toby blinked them away. Sometimes she felt that she'd spent her life searching for a real mother, someone to listen and care and—

"Grow up!" she said aloud as she put her phone back in her pocket. It wasn't as though she'd gone into this with Graydon without being warned. Lexie had told her not to. And—Toby told herself to stop thinking, then got into her car and drove back to Kingsley Lane. Millie met her at the door.

"If we don't hurry and get you ready, we'll miss the ceremony." Millie had on her magnificent dress with all its silver trim. Her hair was elegantly arranged, and sparkling out of it was a tiara that looked as though it were made of real diamonds.

"You look great," Toby said.

"And you look like your dog just died. What happened?"

Maybe it was the quiet or maybe it was the familiarity of home, but Toby's emotions took over. "He's here," she whispered.

Millie opened her arms and Toby fell into them, the tears

nearly choking her. Millie held her for a while, then half pulled Toby up the stairs to her bedroom.

"You talk while I get you ready," Millie said. "And start at the beginning. How in the world did you meet a royal prince?" Millie wouldn't let Toby sit down but pushed her toward the bathroom and told her to take a shower. "But don't get a drop of water on your hair. We don't have time to get it dry."

"Graydon loves my hair," Toby said.

Rolling her eyes, Millie pulled back the shower curtain. "Get in and wash the sweat off of you."

Toby obeyed and Millie stood outside and listened.

Once Toby began talking, she didn't seem able to stop or even slow down. She started at their meeting at Jared and Alix's wedding. "It was Rory who made Graydon swear to tell me he was a prince."

"And Rory is the brother?"

"Yes. Supposedly, they're identical twins, but Graydon is smarter, better looking, and just, well, more adult."

Millie hid her smile as she pulled the strings on Toby's corset. "So Graydon only planned to stay for a few days?"

"Yes, but then Rory broke his wrist and Graydon had to stay longer." She sat down on an ottoman while Millie unbraided her hair and brushed it out, and told of Lorcan and Daire arriving. "They didn't like me at first. I think both of them thought I was after Graydon because of who he was, but he set them straight." Toby told how they'd bowed before her.

"He sounds like a storybook prince. Surely there is something wrong with him."

"You mean the way he thinks he can do everything and that he needs no one else on earth? He bossed poor Rory around so much I sometimes felt sorry for him."

"He didn't do that to you?"

"I learned to tell him to stop it."

"What did you mean when you said you'd been married in

your dress?" She nodded toward the gown hanging on the closet door.

Toby might tell about her and Graydon, but there was no way she was going to reveal what had happened with Tabitha and Garrett. "It was just pretend," she said, then was silent as Millie worked with her hair.

"If I'm understanding you correctly, the brother is now engaged to the woman Prince Graydon was to marry. Doesn't that leave him free to marry you?"

Toby took a moment before answering. "If we did, his family would hate me. He has a mother who . . ." She took a breath. "I spoke to her once, or rather, listened to her. I felt sorry for Graydon. His childhood must have been very lonely with her for a mother. Ow!"

"Sorry," Millie said. "Your hair twisted around the comb. Couldn't you work out something so you two could marry?"

"That's what Graydon wants. He wanted us to go to the courthouse and get married today, but I said no. Can you imagine the two of us going to Lanconia and how he'd tell his ferocious mother that he'd married some American nobody? I'd spend my life being snubbed by her."

"Your comfort is more important than marrying the man you love?"

"No," Toby said. "The problem is that Graydon would be torn in half. How could he focus on helping his country if he were caught in a war between women? And if Lady Danna's father moves his business out of the country because of me, Lanconians would protest. Graydon couldn't do his best job under that kind of stress."

"How very noble of you," Millie said.

Whether it was the words or the way Millie said them, the tears began to come. Millie sat down on the ottoman beside Toby and put her arms around her.

"I'm not noble. I'd like to spit in the eye of all of them! I'd like to elope with Graydon then stand before that mother of his and dare her to say even one nasty thing to me. But I can't hurt Graydon. I love him too much to do that to him."

Millie held Toby away from her to look into her eyes. "All right! That's all the time we have for wallowing in self-pity. We need to get your face made up, put your dress on, and hurry to the chapel. Otherwise, we'll miss Victoria and Caleb's wedding."

"I don't think I can—"

Millie stood up, her shoulders back, and she looked down her nose at Toby. "You want the man you love to be a king, so you need to act like a queen. Queens do not allow others to see what they feel inside."

"Maybe in Lanconia they don't—"

"Carpathia!" Millie said in a tone that made Toby stand up.

"Okay, Your Majesty. My inner queen will now emerge."

Millie didn't smile, but put her hands on Toby's shoulders and looked her in the eyes.

"Your prince will probably be there tonight. He'll have on an eighteenth-century costume and look so handsome you'll swoon on your feet. If he again asks you to run away with him, will you?"

"Probably."

Millie glared at her.

"Okay. No to running away, no to a quickie marriage, but yes to a bedtime romp."

Millie frowned.

"That's the best you're gonna get."

"All right, then," Millie said. "Just let me know and I'll stay at Jilly and Ken's house tonight."

Toby grimaced. "With my luck with men, Graydon will have found another girlfriend by now."

"Not with all that blonde hair of yours. If he steps away, just lasso him with it and he'll come back."

Toby laughed. "How do you know about Graydon and my hair?"

"You told me, remember? Now let's see how fast we can get you made up."

Roger Plymouth's big, glass-fronted house was on the water at the south of the island. It was the kind of house that appeared in *Architectural Digest*. Inside, the furniture was all perfectly placed and everything was white and blue, the colors of the water and the clear air.

Lexie hated the look of the interior. People who lived on Nantucket wondered why the expensive off-island decorators could think of nothing except white furniture with blue pillows. The walls were artistically covered with cute reproductions of whales, with an anchor here and there. There wasn't a breath of creativity in the whole house.

Lexie had already told Roger that after they were married she wanted to redecorate the entire house. His reply was "Tear the place down and get your cousin Jared to build a new one if you want." Lexie's reply had been a lecture on useless extravagance. It had taken four hours in bed together to make up after that argument.

Right now Lexie was sitting on the white couch across from the identical white couch Graydon was sitting on. They were both in eighteenth-century costume and ready to go to the chapel for the wedding ceremony. She knew that he'd spent most of the day on the phone talking to people in Lanconia. It looked like it hadn't gone well because right now Graydon was slumped down, not sitting with his usual upright bearing. It was almost impossible to believe that he was descended from kings.

Last night Graydon had shown up late, one suitcase in his hand. When Roger opened the door to him, Graydon had asked

for a place to stay, and Roger had sleepily pointed him toward
a bedroom. When he got back into bed with Lexie he hadn't
bothered to tell her who was at the door. She'd assumed it was
one of his racing buddies and gone back to sleep.

Early the next morning she'd gone downstairs to see a mo-
rose Prince Graydon leaning over a bowl of cereal.

It took only moments of conversation to figure out that they
were both going to drop bombshells on Toby during the wedding. Not only had Lexie returned early, but she was going to
tell her friend that she was engaged to marry her boss. As for
Graydon, his unexpected presence was going to be more than
enough to shock Toby.

"Roger bought this for me in Paris," Lexie said of her pink
dress with the white embroidery overlay.

"It's very pretty. Nice ring too."

Lexie held up her left hand and looked at the five carat engagement ring Roger had given her. "I would have said I'd never
like a ring like this. It's too gaudy, too flashy, but . . ."

"But it's like Roger?"

"Yes," Lexie said. "I seem to be wearing him on my finger."
When she looked at Graydon, there was a small frown on her
face.

"Are you concerned about telling Toby of your engagement?" he asked.

"No, not really. I think she'll say she knew it was going to
happen."

"Probably," Graydon said. "She is a very perceptive person."

Lexie couldn't bear to see his misery and she had an idea of
how to help him. She had a feeling Roger could help. She stood
up. "I better go. You'll be all right here alone?"

"Perfectly," Graydon said, then reached out and took Lexie's hand in his and kissed the back of it. "Toby will be very
happy for you."

"I wish you two could—" She broke off, gave Graydon a smile, then left the big living room.

Upstairs, she told Roger that he needed to talk to Graydon. "Those two have serious problems."

"Not like us, you mean?" Roger asked, grinning. "It took a while but I grew on you."

"Like a fungus," Lexie said and moved away from his grasp. "Just be nice to him, that's all I'm asking."

"I'm very nice all the time."

"If I didn't think so, I wouldn't send you downstairs to help the guy."

"So what am I supposed to say to him?"

"I don't know. Boy things. But be gentle. The poor man is in pain."

Downstairs, Roger looked at Graydon. They were alone in the living room, both of them wearing tan breeches and short coats. Graydon had on slippers that his ancestor had worn while Roger had on tall boots. Roger offered Graydon a drink, but when it was refused, he couldn't help thinking how different the brothers were. Rory always had a laugh, but Graydon could depress a clown. So how did you talk to a future king?

"Oh, the hell with it," he said and sat down across from Graydon, drink in hand. "Lexie wants me to baby you but I can't take your gloom anymore. You can't give up. Do you hear me? You can't. Just look at what I did. I wore Lexie down. It took me years but I did it. This whole trip that she thinks just happened took a lot of work on my part. I got my little sister to lie for me so Lexie would go to France with her. Then she had to be so boring that Lexie was ready to jump off a building." Roger took a drink. "To get my sister to help, I had to promise the kid that Bobby Flay would cook at her next party. Anyway, I showed up in France wearing a cast when there was nothing wrong with my arm and I got Lex to go on a driving trip with me." He leaned forward to look hard at Graydon. "You know what I did? I let Lexie drive. You know it's True Love when you hear the grind of the gears of a V12 overhead cam engine and you don't say a word about it." He paused to let the horror of that image sink in. "If you give up just because a woman says she won't marry you, you lose the right to call yourself a man."

Graydon gave Roger a look of great patience. "In this instance, there are extenuating circumstances involved."

"Yeah, yeah, I know," Roger said. "You're going to be crowned king. So what? We all have handicaps. Mine is that girls think I'm useless. They think I'm pretty and rich but of no real value. Part of why I like Lexie is because she makes me do things. So what's this Toby girl do for you?"

"She keeps me from believing that I actually am a prince."

"And you're going to give that up because . . . ? Why are you giving her up?"

"For a country?" Graydon's voice was sarcastic.

Roger gave a scoffing laugh. "I don't know a lot about history but I think miserably unhappy men don't make good kings. You think about it. Are you a man first or a king first?" He drained his glass, set it down, and left the room.

Graydon got up and went outside to look at the water and think.

Chapter Twenty-eight

By the time Millie and Toby got to the chapel, it was already filling with guests. About half of them were in costume and as Victoria had predicted, they'd worked hard to outdo each other. Silks and satins, ribbons and gems adorned the women. One famous author said she was honoring Jane Austen, not Victoria.

"Glad that was cleared up," Millie said so sarcastically that Toby laughed.

It was evening and the two women were standing side by side at the open door of the chapel and handing out programs that announced the order of the ceremony: music (Verdi), a poem (read by Victoria's beloved editor), the vows (from the bride and groom). Jared's cousins were escorting people down the aisle.

"Now you know everything about me but I know nothing

about you," Toby said to Millie as she handed a brochure to a woman whose books rarely left the *New York Times* list. "Are you married?"

"Yes. To a lovely man. You might like to know that I wasn't born in this country and my marriage was arranged."

"You're kidding!" Toby almost didn't let go of the paper she was holding out, but a male true-crime writer pried it from her hand. "Oh! Sorry." She looked back at Millie.

"Not at all. It was put together by our parents, but what they didn't know was that my husband-to-be and I had a clandestine meeting before the marriage. He arranged it." Millie's eyes took on a faraway look. "It was at midnight and involved a horse and moonlight. I sneaked out a window and we rode bareback through a forest to where champagne and chocolate-covered strawberries were waiting for us." She paused to give out three more programs. "He and I stayed together until nearly sunrise, then we rode home." Millie seemed to come back to the present. "After that I would have followed him anywhere. He is the love of my life."

Toby sighed. "That's the most romantic story I've ever heard."

"No more than yours, dear. Didn't you have champagne and strawberries when you met your prince? Wasn't he so in love with you that he finagled a way to move in with you?"

"Yes to the move, but it wasn't because of love." She picked up another stack of programs.

"Then what was it? As far as I can see, the two of you were inseparable from the moment you met. You worked together, solved problems together. I just can't figure out how you left out the physical aspects of love. You've missed a lot by denying yourself some good ol' fashioned bed romping."

"We didn't," Toby said. "I mean, we did but we didn't. Graydon is a wonderful lover and I got pregnant on our wedding night, but—"

Millie was looking at her with wide eyes.

"I've said too much. I'd better go check on our seats to make sure no one has taken them."

Millie caught her arm. "It's none of my business, but sometimes problems can't be solved by logic or even common sense. Sometimes you just have to believe and to trust. If you give up love for fear of hatred, doesn't that make love the loser?"

"I don't know," Toby said. The music that began the ceremony started to play, and she pulled away from Millie to go to her seat. Ribbons had been strung across the two chairs that were reserved for both her and Millie. She untied the ribbons and sat down.

Minutes later, Caleb and Ken came through the side door to stand at the front. Toby knew that in the back Alix and Jilly were assisting Victoria as she awaited her moment to walk down the aisle on Jared's arm.

When she realized that Millie hadn't followed her and taken her seat, Toby looked back, but her new friend was nowhere to be seen. Instead, coming toward her was Graydon in his Regency-era suit—and Toby's heart seemed to leap into her throat.

When he sat down beside her, she knew she should tell him that was Millie's seat, but she didn't. Graydon took her hand, kissed the back of it, and tucked it into his arm. The little seats kept them pressed together.

The music changed, and Jilly, in pale pink with cream embroidery, came down the narrow aisle on the white carpet that was strewn with red rose petals. Alix was next, her dress the color of ripe apricots. Both women were carrying bouquets of white roses and tiny blue flowers.

As the wedding march began, everyone stood. Graydon whispered, "Where did the blue flowers come from?"

"New York. Millie got them," she whispered back.

"Who is Millie?"

"My assistant. You haven't met her."

Victoria, on the arm of Jared, who looked very handsome in his tan trousers and black coat, came last. In addition to Victoria's white dress, draped across her arms was a paisley shawl in hundreds of shades of green. Her emerald eyes picked up the colors and sparkled. In her hands was a small bouquet of white orchids surrounded by the little blue blossoms that Graydon had asked about.

Toby hadn't thought about it before but it was odd that she, who'd dealt with so many flowers in the last years, had never before seen those.

When everyone was at the front, the guests sat down and the ceremony began. There were the traditional words, but at the end, Caleb spoke. He said he would love Victoria "through the centuries, past turmoil and tears, past pain and joy, through loss and triumphs. I will love you forever."

By the time he finished, Graydon was holding Toby's hand so hard her fingers might break, but she wished he were clasping her entire body that tightly.

"Don't leave me to do everything alone," he said softly as the pastor pronounced Victoria and Caleb husband and wife. "Here or there, it no longer matters to me where I am. Just please be with me." When he looked at her, Toby saw the tears in his eyes.

She gave him one quick nod, then looked back at the kissing couple.

Graydon lifted her hand to kiss the back of it, then everyone started clapping and cheering and the bridal couple ran down the aisle.

"Now we can eat," said a man behind them and everyone laughed as they began to leave.

Toby looked up at Graydon. "I have things I have to do," she said.

"Can I help?" he asked.

She wanted to stay with him and talk, but she knew Millie couldn't handle the chaos of dinner by herself. "Yes," she said, walking backward from him. "Stack some of these opera chairs along the wall so there's room for people to sit in here. I'll send Wes in to help. Then please find Millie"—Toby was at the door—"and she'll tell you what else needs doing. I . . ." She hesitated.

"I know," Graydon said, smiling. "By the way, Lexie is here and she has a surprise for you."

"Let me guess. It's Roger. Are they married or engaged?"

Graydon laughed. "Engaged. She wants you to plan her wedding."

"Oh, Lord! How did I get this job?" With one last look at Graydon, she ran from the chapel to the tent, but she paused outside. She didn't know what she'd just agreed to or what was going to happen. All she knew for sure was that she was very glad Graydon was here. For the first time since he'd left the island, she didn't feel as though a big part of her was missing.

The first person she saw inside was Millie. "You missed the ceremony."

"No, I saw it." Millie's usually smiling face was stern. "I saw you and your prince and you two looked very serious. Where is he now?"

"I asked him to stack the opera chairs in the chapel."

"You called them that?" When Toby nodded, Millie said, "And you gave that job to a prince?"

Toby laughed. "Graydon can do anything! He can cook, clean, organize—"

"Run a country?"

"Yes, that too," Toby said, then lowered her voice. "I don't know for sure, but I may have just agreed to marry him."

"How do you not know for certain?" Millie asked but when

she saw that Toby was shaking, she led her out of the tent and helped her sit down in one of the chairs that had been placed outside.

"I'm scared," Toby said. "Really, really afraid. It's one thing for us to live here in my world, but . . ." She looked at Millie, the fear in her eyes. "He's a prince and someday he'll be king. He has a country to take care of. He has a mother."

Millie frowned. "I very much doubt that she's as bad as you think she is."

"She's worse. She'll hate me. By Lanconian standards I'm short and pale and—" She broke off to smile.

"What is it?"

"That's what I told Graydon he was."

Millie was watching her, seeming to be considering what she was saying. "I want you to stay here and calm yourself. Don't go anywhere while I go check on the guests." She turned away.

"Where did you get the blue flowers we used in the bouquets?" Toby asked.

"I told you. From New York."

"Graydon seemed to think they were unusual."

Millie had her back to Toby. "Did he? Did he ask about anything else?"

"No, just the flowers. Is something going on that I should know about?"

"What could there possibly be?" Millie said lightly and went inside. Once she was in the big tent, she turned toward the people, but at the last moment she went to the far side and stepped out into the surrounding woods. When she was hidden from everyone, she halted and waited. She put her shoulders back and her head up.

As she knew he would, Graydon stepped out of the trees. Instantly, he stopped in front of her and went down on one knee. He didn't have a sword with him but he held his arms out, palms down, and he bent his head so that his neck was exposed in complete surrender.

"You may rise," Millie said in Lanconian.

When Graydon stood up, his eyes were blazing. "What the hell are you doing here, Mother?"

Chapter Twenty-nine

"Nice dress," Graydon said. "Looks familiar." For the first time in his life he wasn't showing his mother the awed respect her office commanded. But then, he didn't think she deserved it given her trickery in showing up on Nantucket in disguise. She had on a gown her ancestress had worn in an official portrait. Had she come here to spy on Rory? "Can I assume that Father and . . . and my brother are all right?"

"If you're asking about Rory, he is perfectly well."

"Ah, so you know." Graydon did his best not to let his shock show. His mother had been spying on him.

"Know that my sons exchanged places? Of course I did."

"But you called and said horrible things about Rory to me. You—"

"You think I didn't know that was you on the phone and that you and your brother had changed places? I don't think

I've ever been so angry in my life! I'm still angry about it." Her voice was rising. "Wasn't it bad enough that you were planning to marry the woman your brother was in love with? That was cruel of you! If you'd taken him to the dungeon and tortured him you couldn't have hurt him more. He could heal from physical abuse, but he would *never* have recovered from what you were going to do to him!"

Graydon was looking at her in openmouthed astonishment. "But *you* chose Danna for me."

"What else could I have done? I had two sons thirty-one years of age and neither of you was showing any interest in finding a wife. And *you* were completely blasé when I said you were to marry Danna. And Rory said nothing! He was going to *let* you marry the woman he loved."

"Are you saying that you chose Danna because Rory was in love with her?"

"Yes, of course I did. I wanted to force your brother to speak up and declare for her. He needs to stop his life of running around the world from one dangerous sport to another."

Graydon's eyebrows were raised as high as they could go. "And what were your plans for me?"

"What I wanted was for you to fall in love with a young woman you could care for more than you love your country. I can assure you that that's what a royal marriage needs. But I gave up hope on your thirtieth birthday. When it comes to women, even Rory is easier to deal with than you."

Graydon had never been more astonished at anything he'd ever heard. All that he'd known about what was expected of him was being knocked out from under him. "Why?" he managed to whisper. "You sent Rory away when we were children. I don't understand."

The anger left Millie. "I know," she said softly. "But someday you'll have your own children and you will understand. I have had two jobs, one as your queen but another as your mother. I couldn't coddle you and kiss away your problems. I had to train you for the job you were going to take on."

She took a few steps into the woods, then turned back to him. "Trying to tame Rory was like trying to put boots on a fish. He would set a room on fire to get out of doing whatever he was told to do. But you, you thrived on discipline. You loved it. Your idea of misery was a day when you didn't accomplish something. You thought fun meant learning a new language, or you and Lord Daire would try to kill each other. You can't imagine the hours I've spent with your schoolmasters trying to find something that would make you laugh."

"Toby does," Graydon said. "I assume she is why you are here and not in the spa in Switzerland where I was told you were."

"I admit that I wanted to see what kind of female you were involved with. I was so curious! Was she someone who was in awe of you and encouraged your . . . your, ah, perfection? Or did she make you laugh? Did she refuse to call you 'Your Grace' and tell you to make yourself useful and stack the chairs?"

"Toby certainly does *that*." The anger was beginning to leave Graydon, but he couldn't release all of it. "It seems that you have been manipulating my entire life."

Millie's face showed her puzzlement. "Of course I have. That's the definition of my job."

"As queen to a loyal subject?"

"No!" she snapped. "As your mother, which, by the way, is my first job. The more important one."

"But I grew up so isolated. How did I need that?"

"Graydon, my dear son, you are a person who is loyal to the extreme. I wanted you to expand your friendships."

"Is that why you sent Rory away and later Daire?"

"Yes." She paused. "Who would have guessed that running off to be part of a wedding would do more than I had achieved in thirty-one years? I must thank your American cousin Jilly."

"So you came here to find out about Toby?"

"Yes. I was intrigued by what you and your brother were doing. Your father and I sat in his hospital room and laughed about it. Using the cell phone with the Russian was particularly ingenious. We were very proud of you both for pulling that one off."

Graydon was trying to absorb what he was being told. "Just out of curiosity, did you have anything to do with choosing Toby's dress?"

"Of course. Aria and I decided which one would be best. And before you ask, your grandfather J.T. knows nothing about anything. He is as upright and honorable as you are."

"Naive and trusting, you mean."

"What is it the Americans say? If the shoe fits, Cinderella."

For the first time, Graydon smiled. "I think you've been in this country too long."

"I am ready to go home to your father. The question is, what are you going to do now?"

"Can I take by your tone that you approve of Toby?"

"Yes," Millie said, smiling. "Nearly any girl could be trained to do the job, but what I wanted to know is if she loved you or the office."

"And?" Graydon had one eyebrow raised.

"She loves you so much that she will sacrifice her happiness for yours. She will make you an excellent wife and Lanconia will benefit from having her as its queen."

For a moment Graydon couldn't speak. It was difficult for him to truly understand that he was going to get to spend his life with the woman he loved. "Danna's father?"

"Don't worry about him," Millie said in a tone that was entirely aristocratic. "He hasn't made his fortune without stepping on some toes. He'll be content to be the father of a princess, not a queen, or I'll show him some Lanconian justice."

As Graydon ran his hand over his face, his mother was

watching him. "I have to tell Toby that she and I . . . That we can . . ." He looked around the area. "We started here near the chapel, with dinner and champagne. Maybe I can re-create that. I'll get a cloth and candles and—"

"Chocolate-covered strawberries," Millie said in a dreamy way that her son had never heard before. "Too bad you don't have a black stallion, but that costume you're wearing will have to suffice."

"Of course," Graydon said, blinking. He'd never before heard anything romantic from his mother.

"Go find her," Millie said. "Give me thirty minutes, then bring Toby to this spot. I will have everything prepared."

Graydon couldn't think of anything else to say. He gave a bow appropriate to his sovereign, then went back to the tent.

As soon as Toby saw Graydon, she knew something had happened. In fact, she'd never seen him as he was. He strode across the big tent, paying no attention to the many guests, his eyes only on Toby. She'd often seen him look like The Prince, but this man was The King.

"What happened?" she asked when he reached her.

"In thirty minutes I'm going to take you out of here, even if I have to ride through here on a black stallion."

Toby laughed. "You sound like Garrett—and like Millie's husband."

"What does that mean?"

As Toby handed out plates of wedding cake to a gang of children, she told him Millie's story of a moonlight picnic.

"Slipped out a window, did she?"

Toby was looking at him. "Graydon, earlier you asked me to not leave you alone and I nodded, but nothing has changed.

There are still insurmountable obstacles that we can't overcome. We—"

Bending, Graydon gave her a quick kiss and the kids around them started to giggle. "Twenty-five minutes," he said, then turned away and left the tent.

"Told you he was more than you could handle," Lexie said from behind her.

She'd shown up with Roger Plymouth on her arm and a fat diamond on her finger. She'd looked apologetic, as though Toby was going to be shocked.

After a flurry of squeals and hugs, Toby said, "Alix and I knew since Daffy Day that this was going to happen. The way that man looked at you was irresistible."

"I wish someone had told me," Lexie said.

"You wouldn't have listened. So tell me everything."

But at that moment one of the guests asked if it was time to give out the costume awards. She was one of the well-known writers Victoria had invited and she had on a divine dress of red silk trimmed in dark piping.

"Go!" Lexie said. "Take care of everything. We'll talk tomorrow. Where'd your prince go?"

"I don't know. I think Millie went after him. She said she wants to meet him." The crowd of guests were coming between the two young women, and Roger caught Lexie's arm and was leading her away.

"Tomorrow," Lexie called.

Nodding, Toby gave her attention to the prizes to be given out. Victoria, Millie, and Alix were supposed to help her, but Victoria had been dancing with her groom and they seemed oblivious to everyone else. As for Millie and Alix, they had disappeared. With a quick toss up of her hands in exasperation, Toby went to the awards table and began to decide who got what prize.

By the time Graydon returned to the tent, a lot of authors were carrying Lucite plaques and smiling. Toby didn't think she'd be able to leave, but Millie and Alix appeared and they practically pushed Toby out into the night. "You are no longer needed here," Millie said. "Not for the rest of the night. Go away."

"It's our turn now," Alix said. "And I'm going to drag Lexie away from Roger and make her help. I do hope her gorgeous fiancé puts up a fight and we wrestle."

"You better not let Jared hear you say that," Toby said, smiling and backing away. "But if you need any help with Roger, I won't be far away." She very much wanted to escape the noise and the lights and go to Graydon.

"Go!" Millie said and shut the door behind her.

Graydon was waiting for her just at the edge of the forest. She took his arm and walked with him. There on the ground was a setting out of a fairy tale: candles in candelabra set on a snowy white cloth, champagne, bread, pâté, cheeses, a silver dish full of chocolate-covered strawberries.

"How did you do all this?"

"I'm a prince and I have a genie in a bottle," he said solemnly.

There was a light in his eyes that she'd only seen on the night when they'd been married. But then he'd been Garrett and she had been Tabitha and they'd had their whole lives before them. "What has happened?" she asked again.

"Come and sit and eat," he said, "and we'll talk."

She sat down on the cloth across from him and while they ate he asked about what she'd been doing while he was away. He asked many questions about her new friend Millie, and Toby gushed. "I couldn't have done this without her. She really is the kindest, most helpful person I've ever met. She did my hair, helped me dress; she let me cry on her shoulder."

"I assume those tears were about me?"

"Of course," Toby said as she spread pâté on a cracker and put it into his mouth. "What else makes a woman cry besides a man?"

"Not what I wanted to hear. So how did you find this paragon of all virtues?"

"You sound jealous."

"I am envious of anyone who spends time with you."

"Graydon," Toby said, her voice serious, "nothing has changed. We can't—" He put a bit of cheese into her mouth.

After they finished eating, Toby leaned against a tree, and Graydon stretched out and put his head on her lap.

"What would you do if I were a normal man?" he asked. "Would you marry me?"

Toby didn't want to think about that. The champagne was going to her head and all she wanted was now, here and in this place. She stroked his forehead, her hand in his hair. "What would you do to earn a living?" she asked, teasing.

"I could be a chef. Or maybe a male stripper. I'll star in the next *Magic Mike* movie."

Toby wasn't fooled by his lightheartedness. "You cannot abdicate and become a stripper."

"This is a fantasy," he said. "If I were a regular sort of guy, like my cousins, and I grew up in Maine, graduated from Princeton—"

"And had a sweet, kind mother who didn't wear a crown," Toby said.

"Yes. How about a mother like your Millie?"

"That would be very nice," Toby said.

"Would you marry me then?"

"Yes. If you were Mr. Everyone I'd marry you in a second. I'd . . ." She paused. "If you weren't to be king, I'd jump on you right now and hold on so tight you'd not be able to breathe."

She saw Graydon's smile grow wider. "And I'd fight my mother for you, even if I had to use some of your Lanconian weapons. My father would be okay with it, but my mother—"

Graydon sat up. "What do you mean you'd fight your mother? What about me wouldn't she approve of?"

"Well, I know this is a fantasy, but if you weren't king what could you do for a living? You aren't exactly trained in a profession, are you? I can't see a want ad for a guy who can run a country. Maybe all the languages you speak could come in handy. You could—" She broke off because he kissed her.

"You do know how to take the royalty out of a man." He reached into the little watch pocket of his vest. "I have something for you."

He held out a ring that sparkled in the candlelight. It was an odd color and she knew it was a lavender diamond. She was unable to speak as he slipped it onto her finger. "I hope you don't mind that it's identical to the one Danna has, but then she's going to be your sister-in-law, so—"

"Stop it!" Toby stood up. "Graydon, this isn't funny. I was willing to play this game but this is too much." She tried to take off the ring but it stuck.

Graydon got up, pulled her to him, encircling her arms against his chest. He tried to kiss her but she turned her head away. "As far as I can tell," he said, "the only thing preventing our marriage is the lack of approval from outsiders. You don't seem to be repulsed by the idea of someday being the queen of a country. Please tell me you've at least thought of the idea."

"Not at all. Never."

"Did you know that when you lie, you blink a lot?"

Toby pushed away from him. "Okay, so I have thought about it. The idea of helping is an American curse. We're born do-gooders. We care. Someone's house burns down and we're there with blankets and food."

Graydon stepped toward her. "There's room for lots of reform in my country. There are some places up in the mountains where the children can't get to the public schools. I've thought of setting up some little one-room schools for them."

"America used to have those. They were very successful."

"It's just a thought of mine, but I'm too busy to oversee it. You saw what I had to do through Rory."

"Maybe Danna—"

"She likes animals. She wants to export our Lanconian sheep breeds. Toby, my love, the truth is that my country could use help in a lot of areas. If I can show that your presence would get approval from everyone, would you take on the job?"

She was frowning. "You know your fantasy isn't possible. Danna's father would withdraw and your mother—"

Graydon put his hands on her shoulders and looked into her eyes. "Do you love me?"

"Yes. You know I do. Like Caleb said, I've loved you throughout time."

"Will you marry me?"

"Not if—"

"Forget that. Do you want to spend the rest of your life beside me? Together? Could you bear my Lanconian ways, my Lanconian friends?"

"I've made it this far," Toby said. He was looking at her, waiting for her answer. "Yes, I'd marry you and stay by your side for always."

He lowered his head and kissed her. It was a kiss of promise, a kiss for the future. When he raised his head, there was a light in his eyes that said a decision had been made.

"But we can't—" Toby began.

Graydon put his fingertip on her lips, then, holding her hand, he walked around and put out the candles. When he looked back at her, she was smiling, her eyes dark with the thought of the coming passion. "Come on," he said, "I have someone I want you to meet."

"Oh, great!" Toby mumbled in sarcasm. He turned to look at her in question. "Yet again, I get a chance to lose this damned virginity of mine but you want to introduce me to somebody."

Graydon laughed. "I promise that I'll rid you of that burden very soon. In fact I just want to add some enthusiasm to it all. If I remember correctly, you like to be on top, and that takes energy derived from happiness." He began walking back to the wedding tent, still holding Toby's hand.

"What I remember is a blonde geisha on your back. You wouldn't consider getting a—"

"No, I would not," he said firmly.

They'd reached the edge of the woods and Toby saw Millie standing outside the tent, her back to them.

"Come on," Toby said as she pulled on Graydon's hand. "I want you to meet my friend."

When Millie turned around, Graydon abruptly halted and Toby looked at him in puzzlement. His shoulders went back, his head came up, then he gave a low bow. "Carpathia," he said in a tone that Toby recognized as coming from The Prince. "I would like to present my mother, Her Royal Highness, Millicent Eugenia Jura, Queen of Lanconia."

Toby looked from Graydon to Millie and back again, and began to hear answers to her questions. Graydon's mood change from depression to elation was caused by having talked to his mother, the queen. Images went through Toby's mind of the last weeks: laughter with Millie, girlfriend hugs, confessions, secrets revealed, bottles of wine and pizza shared. All of it hit her at once, whirling into a blur that seemed to take all the light away. "I think—" Toby whispered as she closed her eyes against the dizziness.

Graydon caught her before she hit the ground.

Holding her to him, he looked at his mother and gave a grin that showed his deep, soul-baring happiness. "She said yes."

Epilogue

As Toby entered her house, she wiped her sweaty forehead and pushed the hair that had escaped her braid out of her eyes. It was going to take her a while to adjust to the Lanconian ways. All morning she'd been in the garden working out with Graydon and his parents. She was now ready for a shower, then one last lunch with Lexie and Alix. This time tomorrow she'd be on her way to her new life. Millie kept telling her she would be great in all aspects, but Toby still worried. Only when she got there would she be sure that—

She halted because a young man she didn't know was sitting in her living room reading a newspaper. For a split second she thought of calling for one of the six guardsmen who were outside with the royal family. But then, it was Nantucket. The man could be yet another one of Jared's cousins.

She started to speak, but then he turned and looked her up

and down in a way that seemed to say she had failed some test. She had on her pink yoga top and her old gray sweatpants and some worn-out sneakers.

"Are you Lavidia's daughter?" he asked in a tone of disbelief.

"Yes, I am." Toby straightened her shoulders. She didn't like his attitude. "Who are you?"

"I am Steven Ostrand." His voice was full of pride. "I've been told you can cook. Is that true?"

"I don't know who you are, but I want you to leave my house this minute."

He gave a little motion of his eyebrows as though to say it was her loss, then stood up slowly. "Your mother said you have a temper and that I'd have to overlook it. I can see that she was right."

Toby started to reply to his arrogant statement when her mother burst into the room. Without so much as a greeting to her daughter, she hurried to the young man and clutched his arm in both her hands. "Steven! You aren't leaving, are you?" She glanced at Toby. "What did you say to him?"

"Mother, I don't know this man. I told him to leave my house."

"Oh," Lavidia said with a wave of her hand. "Is that all? You just need introductions. Steven, this is my daughter, who I told you so much about."

The young man peeled Lavidia's hands from his arm and stepped toward the front door. "Lavidia," he said firmly, "I think I should leave until this is sorted out." Again, he looked Toby up and down. "However, I'm not at all sure this can be arranged between us." With that, he went out the door.

"Mother!" Toby began but Lavidia didn't give her time to say any more.

"Look what you've done! Do you know how long it took me

to get that man to come here?! Your father and I met him on board the cruise ship. He owns a dozen supermarkets."

Toby was at last beginning to understand what this was about. "You tried to talk that man into marrying me?" She took a breath. "For your information I have met someone who—"

"One of those Kingsley men!" Lavidia half spat at her daughter. "I told your father when you ran off with that Jared that nothing good would come of it, but no one would listen to me. And now I hear that you're living in sin with one of them. What does he do for a living? Run a fishing boat? Really, Carpathia! Can't you have some pride in yourself?" Lavidia threw up her hands. "You'll just have to get rid of him, that's all there is to it."

"Toby," Graydon said from behind her.

She didn't turn but stepped back to be closer to him. She was having a strong sense of déjà vu. The night when she had been Tabitha and her mother had tried to force her to marry a young, grocery-owning man named Silas Osborne came rushing through her mind. Could this Steven Ostrand be Silas Osborne in another time?

When Lavidia looked at Graydon, her face went pale, as though from shock. Her eyes seemed to glaze over and her hand went to her heart. "I've seen you before. You want to take my daughter away but you . . . you can't take care of her. She will be in misery for all her short life." She said the words under her breath, as though she didn't hear herself.

Suddenly, Toby understood it all. For all the changes she and Graydon had made to the past, they hadn't taken away her mother's very deep fear of the future. Toby stepped away from Graydon, and for the first time in many years, she put her arm around her mother's shoulders.

"It's all right," Toby said softly. "He won't go to sea, and he won't leave us to fend for ourselves. Remember? Garrett stayed with us."

For the flash of a second, Lavidia's angry, worried face showed relief, then she frowned and stepped away from her daughter. "Whatever are you talking about? The sea? What does the ocean have to do with anything? Carpathia, I offered you a man who has an excellent future." She looked Graydon up and down. He had on a sweat-drenched T-shirt and ratty old sweatpants. "What can this man offer you?"

"A crown, a palace," Millie said from beside her son.

"Lavidia!" Toby's father said as he burst into the room, Steven Ostrand close behind him. "What on earth are you doing?" Turning, he looked at his daughter, the tall dark young man behind her, and the older woman beside them. His eyes nearly bugged out of his head. He was a man who kept up with world news and he recognized the people he saw. "By all that's holy, you are . . ." He couldn't finish his sentence.

In the next moment six tall young men wearing suits and earpieces entered the room. They were surrounding an equally tall older man who even in his workout clothes looked distinguished.

Toby's father was staring, eyes wide. He looked at his daughter. "Is he—? Are you and he going to—?" he managed to gasp out.

"Yes," Toby said. She and her father had always been able to understand each other.

"I don't like any of this," Lavidia said angrily. "Steven, would you please—?"

She cut off because her husband put his arm tightly around her shoulders. "They are the King and Queen of Lanconia, and this young man is the prince. He's going to marry our daughter and Toby is going to be a princess."

It took Lavidia a full minute to understand what her husband had said to her. Her lifelong job had been to make sure her only child would be taken care of and now she was seeing that it was going to be done. Decades of worry were released from her in one giant gush.

She looked at her husband. "I—" She didn't finish, as she fainted in his arms. With laughter in his eyes, Toby's father looked up. "I think she's very happy."

Acknowledgments

As always, I'd like to thank my readers on Facebook, where I post about the daily process of writing. The ups and downs, the good and bad, it's all there. The very kind comments and answers to my many questions encourage me to keep going. Thank you.

Find true love with

Jude Deveraux's

Nantucket Brides...

The beloved Montgomery-Taggerts are back.

Sparks are flying and chemistry is sizzling.

But the past — and legend — is a powerful thing.

Prepare to be enchanted.

headline
ETERNAL